'It's all very interesting, ...
think it's a completely crazy idea, and the answer
is no, of course it is. You didn't seriously expect
me to even think of it for a moment, did you?'

'Stranger things have happened,' said Georgie.
'Who knows how you'll feel after a few more
days of Mr Popplewell dogging your feet?' She
got up. 'Give me a ring when you've realized that
it's the best thing you can do. Lovely England,
lovely Alwyn Aumbry, how can you give it all
up?'

She handed Gina a card and vanished. Gina sat
and looked at the curiously old-fashioned card
with its engraved copperplate. GEORGIANA
HARTWELL, it read. That gave Gina a jolt. Oh
well, she thought, I should have guessed Georgie
has to be short for something, and why not
Georgiana? She probably loathes the name as
much as I do.

Gally Marchmont lives and works in the West Country.

Wild Grapes

GALLY MARCHMONT

PHŒNIX

A PHOENIX PAPERBACK

First published in Great Britain by Orion in 1996
This paperback edition published in 1997 by Phoenix,
a division of Orion Books Ltd,
Orion House, 5 Upper St Martin's Lane,
London WC2H 9EA

A CIP catalogue record for this book
is available from the British Library.

ISBN: 1 85799 981 9

Printed and bound in Great Britain by
The Guernsey Press Co. Ltd,
Guernsey, Channel Islands

For
Sue, Johnny, Oliver and
Oh Be Joyful Marshall

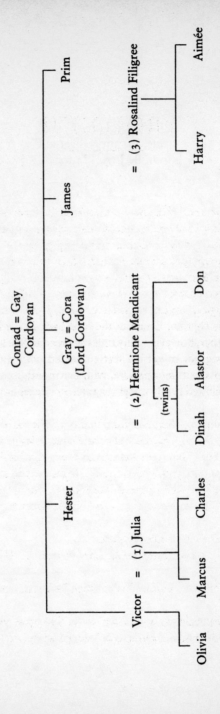

PROLOGUE

Children not obligatory. 12.40 from Oxford. You'll be met.
Gina read the postcard once more, and flipped it over again. An improbable smiling pig leered at her from within a heart-shaped frame. Beneath it, in flowing letters, it read, HARTWELL HAMS ARE THE HEART OF A MEAL.

She looked out of the window at the scenery rolling by. The train flashed through a station, rattled over some points and settled back into its steady rhythm. Gina put the card back in her bag. It wasn't going to help her, however many times she read it. She leant back into her seat, trying not to get her feet entangled with those of the tall ungainly woman sitting opposite, with her mouth in a firm line and her big feet planted firmly under the table in size eight brown leather sandals.

A don, thought Gina. Unquestionably a don. Is that what will happen to me? Will I become taller and even thinner and develop a wart on my cheek, and wear straight grey hair in a bun?

A man went past, brushing aggressively and heedlessly against the table, catching the pile of papers at the corner. Not noticing, he went on his way; Gina rose to her feet to help the woman gather up the pages.

She received a tight smile in thanks.

'The pages aren't numbered,' she ventured. 'Won't it be a problem?'

'I never number them until I've finished,' the woman said. 'I know how they go.'

She saw the puzzled look on Gina's face. 'I wrote it, you see. It's my manuscript. Of course, I number it before I send it to the publisher.

They wouldn't know what to do with it otherwise, they're all half-witted, those copy editors.'

'You're an author, then,' Gina said weakly.

'Yes,' said tight-lips, returning to her manuscript.

Gina gazed out of the window. A don, possibly, but in that case an unusual don. A don who wrote erotic novels in her spare time, judging by the few paragraphs which had caught her eye as she picked up the pages.

The train began to slow down. People stood up, pulling their bags down from the luggage rack, looking round for a bin in which to deposit sandwich wrappings and plastic cups.

Nothing is what it seems, thought Gina, as the train slid into the station. She gazed idly out of the window, and took in the station name just as the guard called out, 'Heartley Junction. Change here for all stations to Heartsfield.'

Gina hastily crammed the card into her shoulder bag, dragged down her other bag from the rack and hurled herself through the compartment. Doors were already slamming shut as she jumped down on to the platform.

A whistle blew, the train began to move. Gina stood on the platform, a bag in each hand, watching the windows flick by. As the train accelerated, she saw the woman who had been opposite her, her hand raised in salute, a distinctly wicked smile on her face.

How very peculiar.

The other passengers were making their way to the 'Way Out' sign. Gina looked about, wondering where the train to Heartsease left from. A man in uniform came up to her.

'Heartsfield train?'

'Yes.'

'Platform three, across the bridge. Due in fifteen minutes.'

Gina heaved her bag on to her shoulder and walked down to the end of the platform where a latticed bridge crossed the two main lines. She looked down on to the gleaming rails and then down on the other side. The line there ran parallel to the main lines for about a hundred yards and then curved off into the distance.

There was nobody else on the platform. In fact, there didn't seem to be anybody else on the station. The man who had given her directions had vanished; presumably he was up above in the old signal box which was now labelled 'Ticket Office', with a large arrow pointing up the narrow steps.

It was hot, with the intense, powerful heat that can overwhelm the English countryside on a still June day. Gina felt sticky in her long linen skirt. It was, she knew, crumpled and probably sagging behind as well. She sat down on the only bench, her bags beside her. Beyond, fields shimmered in the sun. Gina brushed a trickle of sweat from her eyes with the back of her hand, and, from force of habit, scanned the station once more, just to make sure that Mr Popplewell wasn't lurking behind the litter bin.

Two weeks ago, I didn't know Mr Popplewell even existed, Gina thought gloomily. Now I jump when I hear footsteps in case his lanky frame is suddenly going to appear, or the phone rings and it's his high-pitched, lisping voice on the other end.

CHAPTER 1

'Americans in Oxford are lost souls come home to roost,' said a very English voice.

'Hi,' said Gina, as the lights changed, and the stream of traffic surged forward. She pulled herself back into the saddle and joined the wavering line of bicycles heading for the city centre. The other cyclist had been quicker off the mark and she could see his boyish figure some yards in front, before he peeled off to the left with a cheery wave of his hand.

Gina sniffed the fume-laden air uncomplainingly; there was still, just, a breath of freshness in it, wafted from the river and Christchurch meadows in the hustle and bustle of the morning city. Am I a lost soul? she thought. Could be, it's true that Americans get a little crazy when they come here. Either that or they get cynical and leave as fast as they can. Maybe I'd be a lost soul wherever I was. New York has more lost souls than Oxford, I'll bet.

Gina slid to a halt outside the post office and hauled her bike on to the pavement. She looped the chain round a handy drainpipe where another bicycle was already propped. A familiar and unlocked bike.

Zoë was inside, queuing patiently and reading a book.

'What are you doing here?' said Gina, joining in at the end of the line. 'You were still in bed when I left the house.'

'Yes, but you took the scenic route; I came straight here.'

'You've forgotten to lock your bike again.'

Zoë was about to deny this strongly, then found her lock tucked into her jacket pocket. 'Keep my place,' she said, thrusting her book into Gina's hands and darting out.

'Still there,' she said when she came back two minutes later. 'I can't

5

afford to lose another bike, it's so tiresome having to walk everywhere.'

'It's habit, locking them up.'

'And they get taken just the same.'

'True,' said Gina.

'And there's no point wishing one could afford a car, because it's just as likely to get stolen, and moreover, you'd be completely stationary most of the time. Time to get out of the city, I think, we should live in the country.' Zoë gave a dramatic sigh.

'I've come for a passport form,' said Gina as the queue shuffled forward. 'For Alwyn. Do you think I need to stand in line, or would they have them out somewhere?'

'They have shelves of passport forms over there,' said the woman behind them. 'Never the one that you want, mind you.'

'I'll have a look,' said Gina. She was back in a minute, empty-handed.

'No luck?'

'No. New passports only; Alwyn wants a renewal. So I'll have to wait. Why is it so busy in here this morning?'

'Pension day,' said the woman behind them. 'Worst day of the week. Don't go to Marks, either. Out of here, straight off there, cluttering up the aisles looking for a nice piece of cake. They're a menace.'

'Are you in early tonight?' Gina asked Zoë as they reached the counter.

'No,' said Zoë, tucking her stamps into her purse. 'Cinema, with Tim.'

'See you much later, then,' said Gina as the clerk with a stiff little moustache and a suspicious expression reluctantly handed over the form for Alwyn.

Gina didn't care to think about passports. It reminded her that although her passport was in good order, her visa wasn't.

Illegal alien, she told herself as she folded the form carefully away in her bag. Like from Mars. Only nobody's noticed, and luckily you don't turn green or grow antennae when you're one of the illegals. Just keep your head down, and nobody will notice.

She pushed thoughts of passports and visas to the back of her mind and went on her way; pick up something for lunch at the market, call in at the dry cleaners for Alwyn's suit, then off to Jude's to begin the day's work.

Gina loved all the Oxford colleges, but Jude's was where she had done her postgraduate work, and where she now worked for Dr Aumbry, fellow of the college and a highly regarded historian. It was covered with scaffolding just at present, which rendered it rather unappealing from an aesthetic point of view, but Gina knew and loved all the gargoyles presently undergoing cosmetic surgery under the flapping plastic. Rumour had it that they were caricatures of past fellows of the college, and that whenever they were restored, the masons added a new set of features in honour of the existing incumbents.

'Hideous lot they were in that case,' Fergus had remarked flippantly one day. 'Mind you, the present ones are just as bad. Mouldering away in an Oxford college does nothing for your looks.'

The men working high above her head sent down some appreciative whistles and comments as she turned into the arched entrance. A female student, scurrying past, informed Gina that she was going to bring it up at the next meeting; it was outrageous that the college didn't insist on workmen who had been obliged to conform to the NWNH code as set out by the women's inter-collegiate group.

'NWNH?' said Gina wonderingly to herself as she wheeled her bike round to the sheds.

'No whistles, no hassles,' explained a tall girl who was likewise stowing her bike away. 'Verbal rape, don't you see?'

Zoë and Fergus thought that funny, too, when she told them about it later that evening. They were sitting companionably around the table, eating hot buttered toast; they usually wound up in the kitchen to discuss the day's news while having a last morsel before bed.

'Anything else happen today?' said Zoë, carefully scraping the last of the chocolate and hazelnut spread out of the jar with her knife. 'I have nothing at all to report; I had my usual totally tedious day at work, and then Tim took me to a film which was so dull I fell asleep almost at once.'

'I did a long day's work on my equally tedious doctorate,' said Fergus, yawning from behind a lurid tabloid as he reached out for the last piece of toast. He paused, looked at Gina, and offered it to her. 'Your need is greater than mine,' he said, smothering a yawn. 'You're far too thin.'

'That's okay,' said Gina. 'You go ahead.'

'What about you?' Zoë asked. 'How are the Tudors?'

'Just fine,' said Gina, wiping the crumbs from the table and taking Zoë's plate and knife over to the sink to wash. 'I wish I'd lived then, I'm sure people were much more vibrant and lively in those days.'

'Risky times,' said Fergus. 'Any day might be your last, it must have given an extra buzz to life. Still, I know what you mean, I'm sure we all live smaller, meaner lives these days.'

'Think of the smells,' said Zoë, licking the chocolatey spoon before Gina removed it from her grasp. 'And talking of smells, is Jessica going to be in there for ever? I don't know where she got that shower gel from, but my word, it's strong.'

For reasons best known to the builder of the house, the bathroom had originally been part of the kitchen. In fact, when Fergus's father had bought the house for him at the start of his time at Oxford, the bath itself had been in the kitchen, with a slab arrangement on top acting as an extra work surface.

'That won't do,' Fergus's father had said.

Fergus had rather thought it would; the idea of a bath in the kitchen amused him. 'Have a bath and fry your eggs at the same time.'

Fergus's father took no notice, but summoned a builder recommended by a neighbour.

'Didn't know any of these houses still had a bath in the kitchen. 'Course, in the old days they all did. Heat the water on the stove on a Saturday night, and the whole family would take a bath. Pretty filthy water by the time you got down to the nippers. No trouble about this, sir. I can extend that area at the back where the basin and the necessary is, if you take my meaning, and we can fit a bath in there.'

'With a shower?' asked Fergus hopefully.

'Why, we can manage a shower if that's what you want. And if your dad's prepared to pay for it,' he added, shooting Fergus's father a quick glance from under his bushy eyebrows.

Much to Fergus's surprise, his father had been prepared to pay for it. A man of substantial means, he was nonetheless not one to throw his money about. A Scottish wife of frugal habits didn't encourage him to spend, but, as he told Fergus, when a job's to be done, you may as well get it done properly. 'You'll need to have everything shipshape here, you'll want to be sharing with other men from your college. And even girls, and they won't want to live in a dump.'

'Girls?'

'All you students share with girls, nothing to it, no particular friendships. It'll be strange, after an all-boys school, and it wouldn't have done in my day, but times change. Good idea if you ask me, if it's just you and your chums, the place will be a pigsty.'

'You mean we get girls in to clean up for us?'

'You do not,' said his father amicably. 'You get girls in and they'll make you clean up. No point in living like a bunch of slobs.'

Gina banged on the door, and got a sudsy comment in reply. 'I think she's dyeing her hair,' she said.

'What colour this time?' said Fergus, interested. 'I liked that purple shade.'

'Oh, no,' said Zoë. 'I'm dying to go to the loo, and I want to go to bed. Being bored is so exhausting. Honestly, I do wish something exciting would happen, to make all our lives change.'

'Don't wish that for me,' said Gina, wiping up the last of the dishes and stacking them away. 'I love what I'm doing, I love being in Oxford, I want to live in England for ever, and I want my life to go on just as it is. And it's going to.'

'Famous last words,' said Fergus, folding up his paper and easing his long frame up from his chair. 'Goodnight, everyone.'

'Goodnight,' said Zoë, yawning. 'I'm sure you're right, though, Gina; everything will just go on exactly as it is, day after day after day. What a ghastly thought.'

'Someone enquiring for you, miss,' the Jude's porter said cheerfully as she picked up Alwyn's post early the next morning.

'For me? What kind of a someone?' she asked cautiously. It was unusual for people to leave messages for her at the college.

'A young man,' the porter said. 'Not one of ours, I don't think. He looked official. He's over there.'

And over there he was, all thin, nasty, six-foot-two of him. He stooped over her as he held out a lifeless hand.

'Miss Heartwell? I'm from the Home Office.'

Zoë didn't believe her when she told them.

'The Home Office writes, they don't send officious young men to track you down.'

'Well, they did. Oh, he had a letter as well, but he said they had had considerable difficulty tracing me, and it was part of his job to make quite sure that I understood that I was now in the country illegally and must depart within twenty-four hours.'

'Twenty-four hours! Gina, that's impossible. What are you going to do?'

Gina shrugged, fighting tears, putting on a calm face. This is a panic-free zone, she told herself.

'Does Alwyn know?'

'I went straight to him and told him. He wasn't very pleased, deep in something as usual. And I suppose I was a bit incoherent. Anyway, he loped out, and had a word with Mr Popplewell, who was hanging about, talking to the swans I suppose. Then he came back and started making all kinds of phone calls.'

'Any use?'

Gina shook her head. 'Not really. Two weeks instead of twenty-four hours. But out. I can reapply when I'm back in the States, but apparently because my visa expired and I stayed on illegally, they won't be very keen to let me back in.'

'Alwyn will miss you. He's never had a research assistant as good as you, he said so to Miss Crowe; she told me when I met her in the High this morning.'

At any other time, that would have pleased Gina hugely. Now it just seemed one more bitter rub.

'I don't want to go back to America,' she said.

'Why not? You've got family there, haven't you?'

'Only my father. I hardly ever see him, and I don't think he'd put out the flags if I showed up at his studio.'

'Your parents are divorced, aren't they.'

It wasn't a question. Gina's housemates knew little about her family, since Gina rarely spoke about her private life, but Zoë knew that her parents had separated when she was little. Friends of Fergus's had split up some months before, and Gina had shown a rare anger, abusing them for going their separate ways. 'They've got kids. Don't they know what divorce does to kids?'

Everyone else had wondered at her vehemence. 'Come on, Gina, everybody gets divorced. It's better for the children than having your parents rowing all over the place.'

'No, it isn't,' Gina had insisted. 'What's better for the kids is having both their parents right there at home with them. That's what they need.'

Fergus's friend had shrugged. 'Adults have their needs, too.'

'Then they shouldn't have kids,' was Gina's reply. 'I grew up with divorced parents, and take it from me, it's a stinky way to start your life.' Then she had clammed up, angry with herself for her revealing outburst.

'Yes,' said Gina.

'What does your dad do?'

'He's an artist. A painter.'

'A good one?'

'He's supposed to be,' said Gina without much interest. 'Pictures in the Met, big exhibitions and so on.'

'He'll be pleased to see you.'

'Maybe,' said Gina. 'Now that I'm grown up and not likely to be a drag on his career.'

'Is that what he thought you were?' Zoë was shocked. 'I don't believe it.'

'That's what he said. Once I came along, Mom didn't want to camp out in a studio, eat at any old time, carry on the way they'd done before. She wanted me to go to a decent school, have a normal home, friends. And she wanted that for herself, too, a normal life. He said they weren't compatible. What he meant was, he wasn't going to live any differently, and if she didn't like it, too bad.'

Gina looked out of the window with distant eyes. 'He used to throw me up in the air, and Mom would shout at him that he had paint on his hands, he'd get paint on my clothes, and he'd say, "I'll never leave you, kid, I love you to bits."'

'He must have loved you,' said Zoë. 'Fathers do.'

'Love you and leave you, just like all men.'

'Did he keep in touch with you?'

'Through my mom. I didn't want to see him again, not once I was older, and I saw what he'd done to Mom's life. She had a hard time for quite a while.'

'Where is your mother? Can't you go to her?'

'In Italy. Living with a member of the Mafia.'

'The Mafia? Not seriously?'

Gina sighed. 'Well, he's a dapper little businessman with an awful lot of money from uncertain sources. Besides, how can I go to Italy? I need a visa for that.'

'If your mother's there, they have to let you in.' Zoë tried to keep the doubt out of her voice.

'I'm not a minor,' pointed out Gina. 'I'm twenty-four. I expect they'd let me in if I had my papers in order, but I'd have to go back to the States first in any case.'

The front door banged, and Fergus came into the kitchen, a friendly greeting on his lips which died unspoken as he saw Gina's face.

'What's up?'

'You tell him,' said Gina to Zoë. 'I'm going to make some phone calls.'

Fergus made to follow her, but Zoë put out a restraining hand.

'Leave her, she's upset.'

Fergus listened to Zoë's account of the Popplewell incident in silence, his face darkening. 'What a nerve,' he said finally. 'Is Aumbry helping?'

'A little,' said Zoë fairly.

'Not enough,' said Fergus crossly. 'He uses Gina, I don't know why she can't see it. She's besotted with him; what a waste of time.'

Gina came back into the kitchen, her big dark eyes shadowed with worry.

'Have you got the money for the fare?' That was Fergus, always practical.

'No,' said Gina. 'I won't have a cent once I've settled my rent and paid my bills. But Alwyn says he'll advance the fare if it turns out I really do have to leave.'

'Does he think you might not?'

'He says a lot can happen in a fortnight. He's going to get on to contacts in the Home Office, talk to some MPs he knows . . . I don't think it'll do any good. This Mr Popplewell looks very determined in his limp way.'

'He probably gets a bonus for everyone he throws out.'

Fergus handed Gina a cup of coffee. 'Drink this. I put a slug of brandy in it, good for shock.'

'Going to Sam's party tonight?' asked Zoë.

They're changing the subject, thought Gina. Trying to make me feel better.

'I'm sorry,' she said. 'It's going to be difficult for you to find anyone to take my room, so close to the end of term.'

'Don't worry. We're not going to think about it until it happens. As Alwyn says, a lot can happen in two weeks. Now, you finish your coffee and go and get changed. I'll take you out for a meal before we go on to Sam's.'

'Fergus, I can't afford a meal out.'

'I said I'll take you out. You never listen, Gina, that's your trouble.'

'And how come you've got the money to go out?'

'Cheque from my parents,' said Fergus triumphantly. 'I had a birthday last week, in case you've forgotten.'

'You were going to use that money to settle your account at Blackwells.'

'Blackwells can wait,' said Fergus grandly.

CHAPTER 2

G ina emerged damply from her shower to find herself face to face with Alwyn, who was sitting at the kitchen table. Fergus was pouring him a drink.

'Oh,' said Gina, startled. Alwyn had never been to the house; although invited to their not infrequent parties of one sort or another, he kept a careful professional length from his students, and in the case of Gina, from his research assistant. 'Just as well,' one of his friends remarked caustically as he came into the SCR. 'They all buzz round him as it is. Must drive Angela mad, and I can't see why they do it.'

'Charm,' said Miss Crowe, sitting like an evil bat in a huge and battered leather chair. 'Just wait till the telly people get hold of him. It won't be a few moony undergraduates then, it'll be millions of housewives.'

The friend made a moue of distaste and sat down, with a world-weary sigh, to the task of marking the near-illiterate paper handed in by one of his more sporty students.

Charm Alwyn certainly had. Gina had succumbed to it two years ago, when she first started working with him. She would have worked for Satan if he had been researching the particular area of Tudor politics which she found so fascinating. Instead of Lucifer, however, she got Alwyn.

Blast him, she thought, trying to smooth back her tangled wet hair into some semblance of order. As compelling as Old Nick and, if she was honest with herself, almost the main reason why she was so desperate to stay in England.

Alwyn approached the whole matter in his scholar's way, nailing down the facts.

'Your visa has in fact expired?' he enquired. 'You have checked it?'

Gina nodded.

'When, exactly, did it expire?'

'Um, about five months ago.'

'Five months! I see why the Home Office is getting restive.'

'I had a friend whose visa expired and they didn't notice until he left the country two years later.'

'Why didn't you apply to have it renewed?'

'I knew they wouldn't. I've been here too long, you see. They're afraid I'm establishing rights of residence or whatever they call it.'

'You were at university in London, if I remember correctly. Then last year here in Oxford, doing your M. Litt. Before that?'

'I was at school here, sixth form. I used to go back to the States in the vacations, so I guess that didn't really count. And now I'm not a student any more. I need a work permit.'

'I see. Yes, I can understand why the Home Office might be getting tetchy. Why the disinclination to go back home?'

How could he ask such a thing? 'I'm kind of stuck into the work here.'

'I could recommend you to Professor Thriblinck at Columbia. He is doing some fine work on this period. He's a scholar for whom I have the greatest respect.'

Thriblinck indeed. What was a Thriblinck to her, when she was here working with an Alwyn Aumbry?

'It's difficult in the States. Working on the Tudors, I mean. Since they didn't have any,' she added unnecessarily.

A smile flitted across Fergus's face, and Alwyn frowned at Gina. 'You have a point,' he said. 'Although with computer access, these days . . .'

'It isn't the same,' said Gina firmly.

'Perhaps not. Well, I shall see what I can do, but I don't hold out any great hopes. They're tightening up on these visas, I gather.'

He finished his drink, thanked Fergus in his courteous way, told Gina he would expect her at the usual time the next morning, and made his way out.

'Wow,' said Zoë, who had bumped into Alwyn on the doorstep. 'The great man himself coming to call. Gesture of solidarity?'

Fergus frowned. 'Doesn't like the thought of losing such a good and cheap research assistant if you ask me.'

Gina made a sound of protest from under the towel with which she was vigorously drying her hair.

'It's true, love,' said Fergus. 'You put in an enormous number of hours for him, you know. Way beyond the call of paid duty, in my opinion.'

'It's a fascinating subject,' said Gina defensively.

'And a fascinating historian,' said Fergus under his breath.

Zoë turned her mind to practical matters. 'Gina, are you planning to wear those clothes on the bed?'

'Yes,' said Gina. 'Why?'

Zoë shook her head. 'Won't do. Sam's feeling grand. It's a Jessica tonight.'

Fergus groaned. 'Shit, you're right. Has anybody seen a clean shirt?'

A Jessica was a dressy occasion. Although Jessica officially lived in the house, she spent very little time there. She was rich, and the cupboard in the room she shared with Zoë was stuffed with her very good clothes. Luckily, these were in a variety of sizes; Jessica's weight and shape yo-yoed and changed as binge followed weeks of self-denying work-outs in the gym. Zoë and Gina could always find something to fit them, and they invariably borrowed her dresses for smart dos. Jessica was presently going through a stage of shabby black, and was quite happy to lend her clothes out.

'Not that we ever ask her, these days,' said Zoë, holding out a dashing red number for Gina to inspect. 'This will fit you; it must be about size zero from when Jessica was into ballet.'

'Brand new,' said Gina. 'Look, the label's still on it. I can't wear this.'

'Of course you can,' said Zoë, swirling in front of the mirror with a thirties beaded slinky held against her. 'What about this for me?'

'No,' said Gina. 'Too sophisticated. It'll worry Tim.'

'Mustn't worry Tim,' said Zoë with a sigh, putting the beaded dress back and pulling out something much milder from Jessica's Laura Ashley period. 'You'd better hurry, if you're going out to dinner with Fergus first. Lucky you, you're off to the Jupiter Inn.'

Fergus had been in a prophetic mood that evening, thought Gina, as she leant back against the hot metalwork of the station bench. A highly coloured butterfly flitted down on to the flowering bush in the neat bed beside the bench. In the distance a sheep baaed, others baaed in answer. Moaning about how hot they are, Gina thought idly.

It hadn't been hot that evening at the Jupiter; it had been distinctly chilly outside while she and Fergus waited for their food, and Fergus had remarked, so casually, that you never knew what was going to turn up.

'You could meet someone this evening at Sam's, your whole life could change.'

'You mean a *coup de foudre?*' said Gina, interested despite herself.

'I was thinking rather of meeting someone who has a brother or a friend high up in immigration, something like that, actually.'

'Always so practical,' said Gina, rubbing his arm affectionately.

'Of course,' said Fergus, looking into the middle distance, 'you could get married. That would solve your problems – providing you married a British citizen, of course.'

'No British citizen wants to marry me,' said Gina lightly.

'There's always me.'

Gina was touched. 'Fergus, you are so kind. Whatever would Charlotte say?'

'I suppose she wouldn't care for it,' said Fergus.

'My life wouldn't be safe,' said Gina. 'You know how ruthless she can be.'

'Yes,' said Fergus. 'Well, it's an offer.'

'I couldn't, you know,' said Gina.

'Couldn't what? Marry me?'

'Marry anyone who didn't really want to marry me. I don't actually believe in marriage, you know. If my parents hadn't got married, then they wouldn't have had that messy divorce. I could never trust anyone enough to marry them, I don't think.'

She lapsed into a pensive silence.

'Penny for them,' said Fergus presently.

Gina came back to earth with a start. She had been thinking how settled she felt in England, how little she wanted to go back to the States and the fretful, fast-paced life her father led, how blissful it would be to be able to live, as of right, in this wonderful, ancient country, for ever and ever.

'Nothing in particular,' she said.

'Thirty-two,' called the man standing at the door of the inn.

'What number are we?' Gina asked.

'That's us,' said Fergus, glancing at his slip of paper and getting to his feet.

Gina hadn't thought she would have any appetite, but Fergus had chosen the right place to bring her to. The Jupiter seated its guests at long refectory tables, and served oval platefuls piled with food at a modest price. Game was a speciality in season, great roasts of meat in the winter, and on this chilly evening the golden, honey-covered wild duck which was slapped down in front of Gina seemed extraordinarily inviting.

'I expect you haven't eaten all day,' observed Fergus, passing Gina the heavy china salt and pepper pots.

'No, I haven't,' said Gina, her mouth full of delicious duck.

They were both right. She did meet someone at the party who changed her life – at least for the time being, thought Gina with some bitterness. And no, it wasn't a *coup de foudre*. It was a tallish girl with dark curls, an olive complexion and a frank stare.

'Hello,' she said. 'Have we met?'

'I don't think so,' said Gina.

'I'm Georgie Hartwell.'

Gina was surprised. 'I'm a Heartwell, too. How are you spelling it?'

'Not quite the same as yours, Hart without the E.'

'How do you know how I spell mine?'

'Because I asked,' said Georgie. 'Come and sit down over here, I want to talk.'

She elbowed aside the crowd who stood between her and a wide sofa to one side of the big room. Three people were already sitting on it, but Georgie was having none of that. 'Would you excuse us, please?' she said, with an enchanting smile. 'We have something important to discuss.'

Now, if I tried that, thought Gina, they would have glared at me and told me to bugger off. Instead, obediently, apologizing for being there, they took themselves off.

'Sit,' said Georgie, patting the sofa. 'I hear you've got visa trouble.'

'Who told you that?' Gina wasn't sure she liked too many people knowing what was happening.

'One hears, you know,' Georgie said airily. 'Now, listen, I may just be able to help.'

Gina was sceptical; scepticism grew to open astonishment, as Georgie blithely set out her wild and impossible plan.

Absurd, Gina thought, now as then. It had seemed so preposterous in that Oxford room, and it seemed just as preposterous now, but here she was, waiting for the train that would take her to Heartsease. Heartsease!

'Look,' Georgie had said. 'This guy, Harry Cordovan, he's some kind of cousin, don't let that worry you, he wants to get married, okay. It's to do with wills and so on, the older generation not convinced that he's the right sort, rather irregular in his lifestyle. You know the kind of thing. From what I know about his family, it's a bit rich, considering the way they carry on themselves, but there you are. So!'

Gina waited. 'So?'

'So, you marry him, of course,' said Georgie impatiently. 'Problem solved. My family stop hounding me to marry him because it's a good match, you get your English passport, Harry moves up the codicil list.'

Gina stared at Georgie. Was she mad? A practical joker?

'Neither,' said Georgie. 'If it worries you, marrying a stranger, don't let it bother you. He's terrific. Oh, and gay, of course, so no need to worry on that score. That's what bothers the family, you see. A bit of the queer stuff on the side, no problem. Out and out gay, bad news.'

'There is no way,' said Gina, 'absolutely no way that I would even think for one moment of marrying a total stranger.'

'Don't be absurd,' said Georgie. 'You're out of touch. People do it all the time. Usually, it'd cost you, but I'm giving you the chance of it all for free. There's nothing to it. Off to the registrar's office, kiss kiss, buckets of fizz, lovely hol abroad, then home to separate rooms, a good allowance. Live here, live in London, wherever. In due course, a divorce. Not compatible, shame, such a nice couple. Then you're home and dry.'

'Why do you pick on me for this utterly bizarre plan? Why not a friend of yours?'

'Ah, that's the point. The family might be fussy about who young Harry marries. If they think you're me, it'll all be fine.'

'What?'

'Well, being a cousin and so on.'

'They'll know I'm not a cousin.'

'There's the beauty of the scheme. They won't. Harry knows me, because we've met recently. None of the others have seen me since I was little. And we look alike, you must admit.'

Gina looked at Georgie. Yes, there was a similarity, but it was a similarity of colouring and physique, not of personality or style. Side by side they looked very different. Georgie gleamed with good health, she had plentiful curves and an air of opulence. Gina looked like a heroine from a black-and-white French film, with her emphatic bones, vulnerable smile and dark, bruised eyes.

'That doesn't matter,' said Georgie cheerfully. 'Infants don't have personality and style, at least not so that fairly distant relations would remember. And don't worry about my family tipping up for the wedding and spilling the beans. I'm an orphan, no brothers, no sisters, just one set of grandparents who live on an island off the coast of Scotland, and who never, ever, leave it. We might have to fudge a few photos if the need arises.'

'Wouldn't you mind your grandparents thinking you were married when you aren't?'

'No,' said Georgie. 'I plan to live abroad, you see.'

'It's all very interesting,' said Gina politely, 'but I think it's a completely crazy idea, and the answer is no, of course it is. You didn't seriously expect me to even think of it for a moment, did you?'

'Stranger things have happened,' said Georgie. 'Who knows how you'll feel after a few more days of Mr Popplewell dogging your feet?' She got up. 'Give me a ring when you've realized that it's the best thing you can do. Lovely England, lovely Alwyn Aumbry, how can you give it all up?'

She handed Gina a card and vanished. Gina sat and looked at the curiously old-fashioned card with its engraved copperplate. GEORGIANA HARTWELL, it read. That gave Gina a jolt. Oh well, she thought, I should have guessed Georgie has to be short for something, and why not Georgiana? She probably loathes the name as much as I do.

She didn't tell anyone about the conversation when she got back to the house in the early hours of the morning. In fact, when she looked back on it as she lay sleepless in bed, it had a surreal quality; she hardly believed it had ever taken place.

Just as surreal was Mr Popplewell. Gina assumed that he would have gone back to London. Surely Home Office officials lived and worked in London? This one was apparently in no hurry to get back to London.

'On out-of-office expenses, I should think,' said Fergus as they fled from a favourite pub where they had found Mr Popplewell grinning mirthlessly at them over a glass of non-alcoholic beer. He had appeared in Bodley; fortunately the Librarian had woken up for once and ejected him as forcefully as his sixty-three years and mild disposition would allow. Gina had spotted his over-tall figure walking across Magdalen Bridge, and darting behind the heaped-up fruit and vegetables in the covered market.

Just as unsettling were the notes and messages from Georgie which appeared on the doormat or in a book she had left on the library table or were handed to her by the college porter.

'Billets-doux,' he said with a leer. 'Ever so many notes, of course I shouldn't take them in, it's not my job, you aren't a member of this college, are you, my duck? But I was young once, had my assignations . . .'

And that I don't believe, Gina said to herself crossly, as she walked round the cloisters to Alwyn's staircase. Another note from Georgie, this time proposing a meeting. 'I'll call round at your place tonight, hot news!'

Gina at once decided to be elsewhere, but she was no match for Georgie who turned up at tea-time, complete with a letter from Harry Cordovan, full of enthusiasm for Georgie's plan.

'Send the wench down with all possible dispatch,' he had written in a careless scrawl. 'Does she drive, or do you need train times?'

'Please leave me alone,' said Gina furiously. 'My life is difficult as it is, without you nagging away at me.'

'But I can resolve all your difficulties,' said Georgie coaxingly.

Fergus came into the kitchen carrying a pile of books under his arm. He looked thoughtfully at Georgie, who smiled delightfully back at him. 'I'm so concerned about Gina, she looks as though she's been abandoned at the orphanage. We must help her sort out these problems with the Immigration people, don't you agree?'

'All her friends are doing what they can,' said Fergus repressively. Gina was pleased, in some dim recess of her mind, that he didn't seem impressed with Georgie's charms.

'Gina, I'm going to put in a few hours at the library. Can you leave a key out under the boot scraper? I can't find mine.'

Georgie left soon after Fergus, in a whirl of people she had to see, things to do. 'I'll leave Harry's letter. I know you'll come round, it really is the only sensible thing to do.'

Gina was too worried and harassed to wonder why Georgie had been so persistent. No one could want to help a cousin as much as she seemed to. Besides, people who knew Georgie had warned Gina how self-centred her new acquaintance was.

'There must be something in it for her,' one friend said with foreboding. 'Something, moreover, that is present and tangible. I never heard of Georgie Hartwell lifting a finger to help anyone else unless there was some advantage to her.'

CHAPTER 3

'Four more days,' said Zoë, in gloomy tones.

'Yes, and two of those are the weekend,' said Gina.

'Doesn't look too good,' said Fergus, who was thoughtfully eating a large piece of toast generously spread with Cooper's best.

Gina picked up her cup of coffee. Bitter, she thought. I don't want it, I don't feel like eating or drinking anything.

Zoë was having none of that. 'What good will starving do you? If you don't eat, you'll end up depressed. And you're not going to wake up feeling pleased with life because you've lost a few pounds; you've none to spare. Besides, you need to eat properly; to eat lots, in fact, then you'd look less haunted. And you'd look better in Jessica's dresses.'

'I won't need to look better in Jessica's dresses; I won't be wearing them.'

'Nothing in the post?'

'No, nothing in the post,' said Gina. 'And I won't be able to eat Cooper's marmalade when I go back to America,' she said, almost in tears.

Fergus put his arm round her and gave her a squeeze. 'We're not beaten yet,' he said in his kindly way. 'My father is still doing what he can, and hasn't Alwyn come up with anything?'

'A return ticket,' said Gina, reaching for a tissue. 'He says he can't raise anyone who could help, they're all away on House of Commons jollies, or, in the case of officials, not answering calls. Things are tense at the moment, apparently, government likely to fall, everybody watching their backs.'

'You should understand all about that,' said Zoë. 'Just like Tudor politics.'

'Not half so interesting or subtle, actually,' said Gina. 'The upshot is, nothing doing. Hence the air ticket.'

'When for?'

'It's open, but I'll have to book a flight for Monday. Popplewell will be on the doorstep by then, ready for the kill.'

'He was in the garden yesterday,' said Zoë casually, as she helped herself to toast.

'What, in our garden?' said Fergus, reddening as generations of landowners rose in him. 'You should have rung the police, got him for trespass.'

'He was peering in a downstairs window, so I threw one of Jessica's old skates at him.'

'Did you hit him?'

'Unfortunately not, but he scarpered pretty quickly.'

'It's a nuisance for you, all this,' said Gina apologetically. 'It's gotten beyond a joke. You'll be glad when I've left.'

They didn't bother to answer that one, but simply looked at her in silence.

'Okay, okay,' she said, lifting her hand in defeat. 'Thanks, anyway.'

She got up from the table. 'I'll be back sometime this afternoon. To pack.'

'I'll give you a hand,' said Zoë. 'I can take the afternoon off.'

'Won't the University Chest crumble without you?' Fergus always teased Zoë about her work.

Zoë had what was, for Oxford, a fairly demanding administrative job with the body which handled the University's financial affairs, but she didn't kid herself. 'We aren't what Gina would call a hot-shot outfit, as you very well know,' she said. 'And friends are friends.'

Gina set off down the High, keeping a wary eye out for Mr Popplewell. Not wary enough; he cornered her in Blackwells.

'I understand you have bought your ticket,' he said. 'We would like you to make a reservation, a ticket isn't quite enough to convince us that you mean to depart.'

'I'm going to go, isn't that enough for you?' hissed Gina.

Mr Popplewell didn't lower his voice, but since it was in any case a soft voice, further rendered unintelligible by his lisp, he didn't attract the attention of other customers. Much to Gina's relief; she didn't want the whole world to know she was being deported.

'You're harassing me,' she spat at him.

'No, Miss Heartwell, I'm simply doing my duty. If everyone abused our rules of entry and residence in the way you have, then where would we all be?'

I know where I wish you were, thought Gina. Bulgaria, or some unpleasant commune in China. Someplace where all the inhabitants were Popplewells, bureaucratic, relentless, humourless.

'I'm going, okay? Now, for God's sake, leave me alone.' He made no move. 'If you don't go, I'll summon the manager and tell him you're molesting me.'

He moved. Not far, because Gina could see him lurking outside on the pavement. No problem. Gina turned into the Eng. Lit. section and dived through the staff door, glad that one of her many friends had once worked in the shop and had showed her all the back ways in and out.

Free of the Popplewell, she made her way towards an Italian restaurant in North Oxford, there to meet an informant.

'I'm broke,' Hugh had cheerfully told her. 'But if you buy me lunch, I'll tell you what I know about Georgie Hartwell, and I know quite a lot.'

Gina was broke, too, but she had borrowed the money from Alwyn, promising she'd send him repayment from the States.

He waved her suggestion aside. 'No hurry, you can pay me back in the autumn.'

'I won't be here,' said Gina.

'Yes, you will,' said Alwyn. 'You've got a return ticket. Go straight to the Embassy or Consulate when you get back to America, and apply for a work permit. I'll do what's necessary here; given time, there are a lot of strings I can pull. I'm not letting you go, it would interrupt my work greatly, and it's far too important for that.'

'I'd like to come back, of course.'

'No question,' he said, slightly impatient now. 'It would be a serious setback to begin with another research assistant at this point. You're used to my way of working, I haven't got time to start again with someone else. No, no, you have a nice holiday, come back for

October. I'm going off for a few weeks myself, in any case,' he added in a throwaway manner. 'With Angela.'

Bloody Angela, thought Gina.

'I'm going to have an enormous pizza,' said Hugh. 'How rich are you feeling? Can I order lots of extras on top?'

Gina laughed. 'I've borrowed some money, so go ahead. I don't mind what you order, as long as you give me the low-down on Georgie.'

'Great. In that case we'll have a bottle of wine.'

Gina absent-mindedly ordered an American Hot. Then she waited while the waitress dumped a jug of iced water down in front of them.

'Well?' she said.

Hugh poured himself a glass of water and looked furtively round the restaurant. It was early, and they were the only people eating there. 'That's why I chose this place,' he explained. 'A bit off the beaten track, you see. Georgie would never come here, and I can't see any of her snouts trudging out this far.'

'Snouts?'

'Georgie's a journalist,' Hugh reminded her. 'At least, that's her buzz of the moment. It might not last, things usually don't, not with Georgie. Still this phase has gone on a lot longer than usual, so you never know.'

'Start at the beginning,' said Gina. 'How do you know Georgie?'

'My sister and she were at school together,' said Hugh. 'She came up to Oxford the same year as me, I got to know her a bit, parties and so on. Then she moved into a flat with one of my college friends, so I got to know her a bit better. About that time she got very heavily into student politics. The hard stuff, demos, chucking bottles at policemen, that kind of thing. It finally became too much for her college, and she was flung out. No degree, but that doesn't matter too much when you're going to inherit the Hartwell millions.'

'Hartwell millions? What millions?'

'Don't you know anything about her? Her family started and still own Hartwell's Hams. Come on, you must have heard of them. Of course, it isn't just hams any more. Her great-grandfather was a butcher with ideas. Next generation, chains of shops, then all kinds of food processing, factories, exports, speciality lines. The family didn't go from clogs to clogs in three generations, either. They made a packet, held on to it, and went out to make some more. Georgie's parents died when she was quite small; I believe a canning plant in Argentina blew up when they were visiting it – anyway, the long and the short of it is that when granny and grandpa pop off, she rakes it all in. And she gets quite a handy payout in any case when she's twenty-five; a lot of family trusts mature.'

'How do you know all this?' said Gina, astonished. She didn't know half so much about most of her friends.

'I made it my business to find out. I always fancied marrying an heiress,' said Hugh disarmingly. 'Giant pizzas every day of one's life, do you see?'

'Possibly,' said Gina. 'Is it easy to acquire an heiress?'

'It's not necessarily difficult,' said Hugh. 'And Georgie rather fancies me. However, one has to draw the line somewhere, and I'm afraid my line stops this side of Georgie. She's poison, you take it from me.'

'Oh,' was all Gina could say.

'Why do you want to know, in any case?' asked Hugh.

I'd have asked that right at the beginning, thought Gina. 'She's come up with a . . . Well, a kind of business proposition.'

'Don't touch it,' said Hugh instantly. He leant back as the waitress plonked a huge pizza in front of him, and another one in front of Gina. 'Any business proposition will be one hundred per cent to Georgie's advantage and zilch to you, you take it from me.' He twisted in his chair, an elegant affair, not designed for the long, loose limbs which Hugh had wound round them. 'Where's that wine?' he said.

'Careful with that chair, young man,' said the waitress as she banged the bottle down triumphantly on the table. 'We'll charge you if you break it.'

'Fascist,' said Hugh, glaring at her departing back. 'Now, where were we?'

Gina was thinking hard as she retrieved the key from its place under the boot scraper and let herself into an empty house. Fergus was obviously spending a full day in the library, and no Zoë, either; she couldn't have left work as early as she had planned.

27

Gina felt the need of company as she climbed on a chair to haul down her big suitcase from on top of the vast Victorian wardrobe which dominated her room. She put it on the bed, opened it half-heartedly and blew at a wandering spider. Indignant at being disturbed, it zoomed behind the bedstead. Wish I could just scuttle away and hide, thought Gina.

She was trying to make herself believe that this was it, that she was actually packing to go. And to go where? Home? She didn't have a home in the States any more. But then, she told herself, lots of people her age didn't have homes. Why should she, a well-educated, capable, single woman be so reluctant to return to her own country? She'd have to get a job, well, of course she'd have to earn her own living. What did she expect? The trouble is, she told herself as she pulled an armful of clothes out of a drawer, that I will admit to being well-educated and single, but no way do I feel capable.

How ironic, she thought, that she could work anywhere in the States as of right, but would have great difficulty, whatever Alwyn said, in prising a work permit out of the Brits. Whereas Georgie could live and work anywhere in England – or Europe, if it came to that, but couldn't even get an entry visa to the States, let alone be able to work there.

'She can't believe it,' Hugh told her. 'With her money and contacts, she's rarely thwarted. Now she's got this chance of a job on a New York mag – a friend has offered it to her, of course – and the Yanks, sorry, I was forgetting, the Americans, will have none of her.'

'Why not?'

'Student record,' said Hugh. 'In her salad days she flew out to America and joined in a few of your home-grown rumbles, as if the ones here weren't enough. A police record here, on FBI files over there ... No, it won't wash. She can be Hartwell's Hams fifty times over, they still aren't keen to have her.'

And they wouldn't want me if they knew how I feel about going there right now, thought Gina, discarding a pile of undies which had seen better days.

'Hey,' said Zoë, bursting into the room, a bottle of champagne in one hand and two glasses in the other. 'If you're chucking out that slip, I'll have it. It's much better than my long one, which is in pieces.'

Gina shrugged. 'I shan't need it,' she said. 'Help yourself. The rest of them are a bit tatty, though.'

'Mmm,' said Zoë. 'Nothing wrong with this at all. Are you sure you don't want it?'

'I'm not going to be wearing long dresses, not any more. No more parties, no more dances.'

Zoë cleared a space on the chest of drawers and put the bottle and glasses down. She looked at her friend, distressed by the sadness in her face. 'You've got shadows under your eyes,' she said finally. 'You aren't sleeping properly.'

'No,' said Gina. 'Anyway, I always have shadows under my eyes. Same as my mother. My father used to tease her about them, but he loved her eyes. So he said.'

'Forget about all that,' Zoë suggested. 'It isn't your father betraying you now, you know.'

'No, of course not,' said Gina in a flat voice.

Zoë returned to safer ground. 'In any case, why no more parties? Why no dances, no balls? You love them.'

'Yes, well, one has to grow up sometime. We're all a bit superannuated in this house, you know. Not Jessica, she's still an undergraduate, but the rest of us. We're carrying on as though we were still students, and we aren't.'

'Fergus is doing a Ph.D.,' said Zoë, tugging at the champagne cork.

'He shouldn't be. He should be getting stuck in somewhere, earning a living.'

'I suppose so, but he'll earn a better one with a Ph.D. under his belt. Besides, he likes it here.'

'So do we all, but it's cloud-cuckoo-land, pal. This isn't the real world.'

'I'll take Wonderland, or Through the Looking-Glass, against reality any day of the week,' said Zoë, sitting down with a bump on the bed and making the springs rattle. 'Goodness, how I hate my work; it's lovely to have the afternoon off – or it would be, if it weren't such a doleful occasion. Here you are, drink up.'

Gina took the proffered glass and held it close to her ear to listen to the bubbles. 'What are we celebrating?'

'Nothing, I suppose,' said Zoë. 'There's nothing to celebrate. I just thought it would cheer us up. Grim business, packing.'

'Specially when you haven't a clue where you're going,' said Gina.

'Ring your dad,' said Zoë practically. 'Never mind what he said or didn't say to your mum in the year dot. He's still your father. If he's there, then you're okay while you find your feet. If he isn't, then you can think again. Fergus must have friends in New York.'

'Fergus has friends everywhere,' agreed Gina.

Gina's desk was an old-fashioned, roll-top one. It didn't fit into any of the other rooms, so Gina, much to her delight, had acquired it together with the shabby rose-patterned carpet and the big, ugly wardrobe when she moved into the house. Now Gina looked at it unenthusiastically; it was going to take hours to sort all the papers out. Where had she put her address book? Not her everyday, Oxford one, a looseleaf notebook which she carried everywhere; that was in her bag. She needed the address book from her Other Life, a smart Liberty one, given to her endless birthdays ago by a mother trying to encourage order in her life.

She pulled open one of the small flat drawers inside the top of the desk. A few old bills, and a clutch of invitations pinned together. Dances, drinks parties, please speak at a debating society, a Pooh party, a garden party with croquet . . . Pinned together to be brought out and laughed or sighed over, in years now far in the future.

Centre drawer; no, it won't be in here, thought Gina, that's where she'd put her passport and ticket. There had been no address book in it.

'What is it?' said Zoë, alarmed, as Gina froze, gazing into the little drawer she had just opened. 'Is there a beetle in the drawer? Or what?'

Gina jerked the drawer fully out and snatched at the passport which lay there. She brandished it in Zoë's face. 'Look,' she said. 'Look!'

'Calm down,' said Zoë. 'Yes, it's a passport. What's so amazing about that?'

'Don't you notice anything about it?'

Zoë lifted her shoulders. 'No. It looks exactly like mine . . . Oh! Is it mine? How did it get in your drawer?'

'It isn't yours,' said Gina definitely. 'It's a British passport, No. 0294768, belonging to one Georgiana Hartwell.'

'But you're Georgiana . . . Oh, oh, I see! A *British* passport. Yours is an American passport, of course. Gina, just what is going on?'

Gina slumped on to the bed, her head in her hands. 'Someone,' she said finally, lifting her head and dragging her hands crossly through her hair, 'someone has taken my passport. And also,' she jumped to her feet and rushed to the drawer, 'yes, and also my air ticket.'

'What? Let me see.'

They ransacked the desk. Every envelope was opened, every piece of paper shaken. There was no doubt about it, Gina's passport and tickets were gone.

Zoë investigated the British passport. 'Georgiana Hartwell,' she said. 'She's the one who made such a noise when she worked on *Cherwell*. Now she works for another Oxford mag, doesn't she? A town one, not university. Do you know her?'

Gina nodded. 'Slightly.'

'It's up-to-date, this passport. Funny, she looks quite like you. From her passport photo, anyway; of course, people never look like their mug-shots when you meet them. But why is it here? And where's your passport – and the ticket? Do you suppose Popplewell broke in? Perhaps he's flipped and decided to play pass the passport.'

'Broke in!' Gina and Zoë stared at each other, and then made a simultaneous dash for the door. Gina went upstairs to Jessica's attic room, Zoë flew into her own room. Together they investigated Fergus's room.

'They look just as they usually do.'

'Nothing of mine seems to have been touched, but we'll have to get Fergus and Jessica to check nothing of theirs is missing.'

The sitting room looked as it always did. Untidy, but not at all as though a thief had been searching for anything. Besides, there was the TV set, untouched; Fergus's music and all his expensive black boxes and speakers were sitting where they always did.

'No ordinary thief.'

'No ordinary thief would take one passport and leave another,' agreed Gina.

'No,' said Zoë briskly. 'Upstairs, Gina, fetch the bottle and our glasses, then down here. I want to know what you've been up to, and more about how G. Hartwell crossed your path. She sounds like very bad news to me.'

So Gina told her. She's not going to believe this, thought Gina, as she filled Zoë in on the bare bones of her encounters with Georgie. And what she had discovered at lunchtime.

'I know Hugh Kirkoswald,' said Zoë unexpectedly. 'He's an ass, but mostly truthful. He wouldn't make up any wild stories; not enough imagination, for a start. Anyway, it's all perfectly clear now. She's taken your passport and ticket, reckoning that with the similarity of names she can use it to fly to New York and become you. I wonder how she got in. No windows broken, or locks wrenched, are there?'

'I know exactly how she got in,' said Gina. 'She was here, she knew I'd be putting the key under the boot scraper. She just helped herself.'

'Let herself in, nicked your papers and, as a gesture, left you her passport. Not a bad swap, really,' pointed out Zoë.

Gina looked at her friend in amazement. 'Zoë, you aren't seriously suggesting that I just hang on to this passport and pretend I'm her?'

'Why not? You'll have to leave Oxford, at least for the time being, because it's no good Comrade Popplewell seeing your name on that flight list if he spots you strolling up and down the Broad. No, if you aren't here, and the flight records show someone of your name and with your passport number has left for New York, then he'll take himself off. No one else will wonder about it; when you come back to Oxford, you can just say you've got a permit. Don't tell me Alwyn will ask to see it.'

'No, it would never cross his mind,' said Gina. 'I'm just the researcher. Useful, if there; not given a thought if I'm not.'

Zoë gave Gina a quick look. 'Might do you good to get away from Oxford for a while. Why don't you go and suss out this Harry?'

'Zoë!'

'I'm not suggesting you marry him. Just go and stay. Harry Cordovan is Georgie's cousin, did you say? Then his people live in a fantastic house, I've seen pictures of it. Go and be a house guest for a while.'

'You're crazy. This Harry guy will just throw me out, especially when I say nothing doing on the marriage front.'

Zoë considered the matter. 'I don't think he will,' she said at last.

'He won't want his family to know that he was prepared to marry a complete stranger in order to get his hands on whatever it is. So all you have to do is threaten to spill the beans. He'll have to let you stay.'

Gina's mind was off on another tack. 'You know, I don't see what use a wife would be to him without children and so on. If it's a matter of inheritance. I asked Georgie that, just out of interest, you understand, and she said lots of married couples don't get round to having kids for ages.'

'Got an answer for everything, Georgie has,' said Zoë.

Gina laughed; the first real laugh that Zoë had heard from her for days. 'She said she'd check it out for me. Hey, that woman really has got a nerve, do you know that?'

Zoë's mind was on practicalities. 'You won't need that big suitcase. I'll lend you my bag, the squidgy one.' She thought for a moment. 'We won't tell the others about this.'

'Not Fergus?' said Gina, worried.

'No, not Fergus. He's too upright and scrupulous, he'll try to dissuade you, get you to report the missing passport to the police.'

'Popplewell would never believe it if I said someone had just come in and taken my passport. "Oh, and by the way, they left this one in its place".'

'No, he'd probably get you put behind bars. So, if you value your freedom, then don't say anything to Fergus. And not Jessica, either, might as well announce it on Radio Oxford.'

'If you really think there's any point . . .' began Gina, still doubtful.

'You tell me what else you can do,' said Zoë. 'You've got no money, no right to be in this country and you're in possession of someone else's passport. You're in trouble. What you need is sanctuary, and in a place where no one knows you, where you've never been, and where not even the most zealous Popplewell could possibly find you.'

CHAPTER 4

Gina heard the train coming long before she saw it. It gave a final, cheerful whistle as it rattled round the curve of the line and pulled into the station.

The man in the uniform reappeared, chanting, 'Heartley Junction, change here for London, Platform 1, Reading, Oxford and Birmingham, cross the line by the footbridge to Platform 2. Mind the step now, mind the step. This train will now call at Long Ease, Little Ease, Corda Episcopi, Heartsease, Upper Heartsfield and Heartsbury.'

Gina clambered up on to the train, which was much higher than the platform. Another passenger stretched out her hand to take Gina's big bag. 'Terrible these trains, there's ever such a to-do when there's old people or someone in a wheelchair. Special steps and ramps, holds the train up every time. Don't know why they don't raise the platforms on this line, I don't really.'

Gina thanked her helper and sank into a corner seat. The train gave a loud shriek and a series of wild lurches, and then started to trundle back the way it had come.

Gina stood up and pulled the window down. 'We're going the wrong way.'

'No, no, don't worry,' the helper said good-humouredly. ''Tis only shunting yards up that way. We go back on to the other line and then down under the bridge.'

Gina stayed hanging out of the window as the train performed its ritual shuffle. It reversed on to the curved line, waited for the points to change with a satisfying clang, and then chugged forward in a straight line. The signal clunked up into its STOP position and the train began to gather speed as it rumbled under the dark bridge.

They emerged into a green world. The train was running through a cutting, and the banks were like green walls on either side. Further up the slopes, trees and shrubs grew, making a canopy of branchy green.

'Heaven,' said Gina.

''Tis pretty,' the helper agreed. 'All the visitors, they do like this line.'

She showed her own appreciation of the natural beauty all around by settling her ample form into a comfortable position for a good snooze.

'Watch out for the Heart Gorge,' she said before closing her eyes. 'They all ooh and aah over that, and take pictures. Not to worry if you haven't brought your camera, you can buy a postcard.'

Postcard, thought Gina. Her life had been reduced to a few words on a postcard. She'd had enough of postcards. Good thing Fergus hadn't got to the post first, and found her instructions from Georgie. He'd have been suspicious at once, but fortunately Zoë had been up first, the postman had come early, and so she had escaped interrogation.

The train was pulling up a steady incline, still enclosed by banks and trees. Then it levelled off and burst triumphantly out of the green tunnel, and Gina looked out over a far-reaching greeny-grey landscape, with hills undulating into the distance. Far below, a river gleamed in the sunlight.

This is beautiful, thought Gina. Why did no one tell me it was so beautiful? Why have I never come here before? Scotland and Wales and the Lake District had been awe-inspiring, damp and striking in turn . . . but this! This was magical.

Little stations came and went, little stations with such strange names. Gina looked at her map. Heartsease was the next station, and there, clearly marked on the map, was the house itself, Heartsease Hall. Had it given its name to the village and therefore to the station? Or had the house taken its name from a village already there when it was built?

It must be some two miles from the station, thought Gina. Who would come and meet her? If no one did, would there be a taxi? How could she arrive at the house and announce herself; what if Georgie in a callous mood had played another practical joke on her?

*

The kitchen at Heartsease Hall would have gladdened the heart of any National Trust official. Huge, stone-flagged, and inconvenient, it looked much the same as it would have done three hundred years before. True, the cavernous fireplace was empty now, with no spits and toiling dogs or cooks. A modern range and a series of hobs and ovens had taken over the role of the fire, but a long oak table, black with age, still ran down the centre of the room. Outside, numerous sculleries and offices led off a cobbled yard, and hummed with freezers and large American fridges. A commercial dishwasher had long since taken over from a bevy of scullery maids and their deep sinks, and, in the laundry beyond, German hi-tech white goods were much in evidence.

Guy was in the pantry, shaking the last drops of water off a pile of lettuce leaves before depositing them in a plastic bag in the fridge. He looked round as Hester appeared at the door.

'Guy, Harry wanted us to pick up Cousin Georgiana at the station. I would have asked Jarvis, but he's nowhere to be found. Are you busy? Can you go?'

Guy shut the fridge door and followed Hester into the main kitchen, untying his immaculate white apron as he went. He didn't need to say yes; of course he would go. Everyone who worked in the kitchen always did what Hester asked them. So did most of the family, although anyone could see that Victor sometimes fretted and chafed under his sister's kind authority in all household matters. 'You run your business, Victor,' she would say in that quiet, peaceful voice, 'and I'll run the house.'

Whatever Gina had expected, it wasn't this lovely youth, who moved so gracefully and had such a warm smile on his perfect features. 'Are you Georgiana?' he said.

She stared at him for several seconds before she came to her senses and mumbled that, yes, she was Georgiana. She was about to ask if he was Harry when he introduced himself.

'I'm Guy,' he said. 'I work for the Cordovan family. Harry was so sorry he couldn't collect you himself, but he was called away to London, and won't be back until later.'

His voice was that of an actor; in fact, thought Gina, trailing after him, feeling more crumpled than ever, he looked as though he had just wandered out of a performance of *A Midsummer Night's Dream*.

He helped her up into the passenger seat of the high-wheelbase car. Delicate, thought Gina, when a good shove from behind is what he should have done, for I feel exactly like a hot animal being transported by its farmer. 'A pig, perhaps,' she said out loud without thinking.

Guy's face lit up with a beautiful smile as he settled into the driver's seat and started the engine. 'Did you say pig? Do you like pigs? Do you know about them? Of course, I suppose you would, Hartwell Hams and all that. I adore pigs, and we have some wonderful pigs here. Gloucester Old Spots in the orchards, and a herd of Berkshires. Of course, Berkshires are a problem, they're so reluctant to breed.'

'I'm afraid I don't know much about pigs,' said Gina quickly. It would be bad enough pretending to be the Ham heiress from the Highlands without having to appear knowledgeable about pigs. 'I just felt rather like a pig. Hot and bothered and being heaved in and out of transport.'

'Naturally, I can understand that,' said Guy, vowels impeccable. 'And the pigs your family business would deal with, well, they must be rather common pigs.'

'Very common,' agreed Gina.

That settled, Guy became the perfect escort, pointing out features as they went past, warning Gina when a jolting was coming. 'We've come the back way, across the estate. It's much quicker, although you do miss the approach and the famous view of the house. But of course, you've been here before.'

'Not since I was little,' said Gina firmly. 'I'm afraid I don't remember anything about it.'

'Then you have a treat to come,' said Guy enthusiastically. 'Heartsease Hall is the most fabulous house. It's a privilege just to be allowed to work here.'

Gina didn't think it would be appropriate to ask if the family were as fabulous as the house. Zoë had dug out some fat book of landed families and had recited names to her. 'You must know at least the names of some of your cousins and other close family. Now, you think that Harry's grandmother and Georgie's grandmother were sisters?'

'So Georgie said.'

37

'That makes it very easy. Harry is the son of Victor Cordovan, and there are lines and lines about him and family. Listen.'

'But so many of them,' Gina had said, dismayed, as she listened to the names. 'Dozens. They can't all live at the house, can they?'

'A lot of them seem to,' said Zoë, consulting her tome again. 'You'll soon get the hang of who everybody is, once you meet them.'

'Are you always called Georgiana?' Guy asked politely. 'I believe I've heard them call you Georgie.'

'Yes, Georgiana is rather a mouthful, isn't it?' said Gina. 'I used to be called Georgie when I was younger, but now I prefer Gina.'

'Oh, much prettier,' said Guy approvingly. 'Georgie's a bit Famous Five, isn't it? Not that I didn't adore the Famous Five, but when you're grown up . . .'

Gina hoped that her refusal to be a Georgie wasn't going to raise suspicions, but, really, she was not going to take on that creature's nickname on top of everything else. And people would notice if they said 'Georgie,' and she didn't respond.

Any room arranged for a visitor by Hester was perfect, and the Yellow Room was no exception. Gina felt more of a cheat than ever as Hester swept open drawers – all lined with yellow striped paper – opened wardrobe doors, and took Gina into the opulent bathroom. Then she left her. 'You'll want to change after that journey,' she said.

I must look awful, and sweaty, too, thought Gina. But no one could suspect Hester of hints or cattiness; all she had was an instinctive feeling for other people's comfort.

'I hope you'll be happy in here, my dear,' she said, with a last look round. 'Make yourself at home; we all hope you're going to make this a good long stay, after so many years.'

The door shut quietly behind her, and Gina went at once to the window, drawn by the view, down over lawns and woody places with streams to a distant river. And then, away on the horizon, a thin silvery line of sea. She could hear the unearthly cry of a peacock, subdued voices, the chug of a tractor. Leaning out of the window she watched Guy, apron on, walking neatly along the gravel with bunches of herbs laid out in exquisite order in a shallow basket which he held on his arm.

This, Gina said to herself, is another world. Get a grip on yourself, she went on; have a shower, get changed, and then you'll feel more in control. She opened her bag and looked doubtfully at the few summer clothes she had brought with her. Something told her that she might need much more than this; perhaps, she thought wildly, they even change for dinner.

Gina hesitated outside the heavy oak door into the Great Hall, a watching stranger. She could see a blonde woman, not young, but possessed of flawless bones which gave her a memorable beauty. She sat near a window, balancing a delicate china cup and saucer in one hand while she flipped the pages of the gardening magazine with the other. Classy, yes, but hardly dressy, thought Gina, blinking at the faded T-shirt, filthy khaki trousers and strange thick-soled plimsolls which the woman was wearing. Not my type of person at all, Gina said to herself. Hester, presiding over the tea-cups and cucumber sandwiches, seemed a friendly and more approachable figure, although even she had an air of confidence and certainty which made Gina feel uncomfortable.

At that moment Hester looked over to the door and saw Gina. 'Come in, have some tea. Prim, this is Gina.'

The blonde woman gave Gina a piercing look. 'You don't take after your mother,' she said. 'Hester, put some of those sandwiches aside and I'll take them with me. I can't be long over my tea, not with the weather like this.'

'Haymaking,' explained Hester, handing Gina a cup of tea.

Gina had just managed to control her hands enough to stop the teacup rattling audibly in its saucer when the door at the other end of the hall flew open. A tall, bearded man came in; Gina would afterwards swear that all the curtains swayed and the teacups rattled, just for the sheer energy of him.

Radiating authority, he bore down on Gina with a pleased look on his face. 'Little Georgiana,' he said, sweeping her into a powerful hug. 'How delightful.'

Gina felt quite dizzy, not just from having the breath half crushed out of her, but because of the enormous masculinity of him, which was almost tangible.

'Hello,' she said weakly.

'Georgiana prefers to be called Gina,' said Hester. 'Have a cup of tea, Victor, and there are cucumber sandwiches. Gina, this is your cousin Victor.'

'The head of the household at Heartsease seems to be this Victor Cordovan,' Zoë had informed her. 'Now, I've heard of him. Magic touch with failing businesses. Takes them over, stirs them up, sells them on. He was originally in fireworks, then he sold out to a defence firm, well, one loud gunpowdery noise is much like another in that world, I suppose. Made quite a pile, could have sat at home and minded the family acres, but he got bored; which is why he started on these other companies.'

He doesn't look in the least bit like a businessman, thought Gina. Far too big and magnificent for one thing, and far too amiable for another. His deep voice and ready, rich laugh filled the hall as he questioned Gina about her family and the family business. Fortunately, he answered all the questions himself. Gina rather wished that Zoë had been able to give her more than the bare bones about the Hartwell empire; still, from what she'd seen of Georgie, she hadn't looked as though she would be at all interested about how her Hartwell Ham money was actually made.

Prim saw Gina's expression and laughed. 'Don't mind Victor,' she said. 'He always booms at people.' She rose and perched herself on the arm of the large sofa where Gina was sitting. 'Go away, Victor,' she said commandingly. 'I want to reassure Gina that we aren't all like you.'

Victor, not at all offended, went back to the table to demolish a few more cucumber sandwiches. Prim turned to Gina, her mind on growing things. 'Are you interested in the land; farming, horticulture, gardening?' she asked.

'Um,' said Gina. 'I don't know very much about it.'

Prim was surprised. 'You have such excellent conditions on Uish. I'd always understood that the gardens there were exceptional, that you can grow remarkable plants because of the Gulf Stream. Tropical plants.'

Hell, thought Gina, thoroughly rattled. Gulf Stream? What was that? And tropical plants in Scotland? Her experience of Scotland made her think of warm underwear, not palm trees and frangipani. 'I never took much interest in the gardens,' she said.

Prim was shocked. 'I must visit Uish one day. But while you're here, we'll see if we can't get you keen on it; after all, you'll inherit it one day, and then you'll need to know all about it.'

No, I won't, thank goodness, thought Gina. And I bet Georgie sells it as soon as she gets her clutches on it, can't see her residing on a Scottish island, however tropical the vegetation.

Prim was, Gina realized, a woman with a one-track mind. 'You must meet Don, do you remember him at all?'

Don? Gina couldn't remember a Don from Zoë's briefing. It sounded as though he must be family, but who?

Prim didn't wait for an answer; just as well, thought Gina.

'He's building up the vineyard here, people are always interested in vines, it would be a good place to start.'

'I'd like that,' said Gina, her interest caught. 'I didn't know there were vineyards in this part of the world.'

Boobed again. Prim looked at her with eyebrows arched in surprise. 'You must do! Heartset is famous for its wine, there were vineyards here in Roman times, and over the last twenty or thirty years a lot of wineries have started up.'

Gina could hardly answer, yes, but we Americans, especially ones who've lived in California in the Napa Valley, don't think of anywhere in England in terms of vineyards.

'Of course, I had forgotten,' she said.

At this rate they were all going to write her down as several cents short of a dollar. She bit nervously into a tiny egg and cress sandwich, wishing that she had found out more about this family; wishing that she had never come, wishing that she was sitting peacefully among her books and papers in Oxford.

What with one thing and another, Gina was feeling very ill-disposed towards Harry when she retreated to her room after tea. Okay, she hadn't been stranded at the station, but that was all the help she'd had. Harry must have known she'd have to run the gauntlet of several members of his family without having a clue who they were; after all, he couldn't guess that Zoë had looked the wretched family up. And that had only given her the bare bones.

No, this wasn't going to work, Gina thought as she lay on her extremely comfortable bed with her hands folded behind her head. It was only a matter of time before a serious slip showed her up for what she was: a fake, an impostor, a fraud.

CHAPTER 5

The calm peace of a serene evening was broken by an ear-splitting roar. Gina flew to the window, just in time to catch sight of a black figure on a motorbike hurtling round the side of the house.

Immediately a door on the ground floor opened, and Victor's powerful voice roared out.

'How many times do I have to tell you NOT to ride that damn bike of yours over the gravel?'

His voice faded into an indistinct growl as he went in pursuit of the motorcyclist. Gina returned to her thoughts.

Not for long. Two minutes later, the black-clad motorcyclist flung himself into her room. Without knocking.

'Hi,' he said, taking off his helmet. 'You must be Gina. I'm Harry.' He shut the door. 'Pa won't think of looking in here for me, at least not for a while. He's rampaging over the other side of the house at the moment.'

What incredible eyes was Gina's first, startled reaction. Almost black, and with a wicked gleam to them. Taken with the slanting eyebrows, and tremendous coiled-up energy, Harry wasn't her idea of a pushover. Curse Georgie, how could this man be described as a real sweetie? She stood up and held out her hand. 'Hello, Harry,' she said in a deliberately neutral voice.

'You sound pissed off with me,' said Harry cheerfully. 'I'm sorry I wasn't here to meet you, but it was crisis-time at the London end, so I had to nip up and sort everyone out. Good journey back, a hundred and seven minutes, near my best time.'

He kicked off his heavy black boots which had, Gina noticed, silver and red wings painted on them. Then he divested himself of his leather jacket and trousers.

'You don't mind, do you?' he asked, peeling down to a skin-tight pair of jeans and a black T-shirt. 'Incredibly hot in this lot, but of course, you have to wear them on the road. Have you got a glass in your bathroom? Silly question, with Hester in charge. I'm dead thirsty, gasping.'

'Feel free,' murmured Gina, but of course he was already there, gulping the water down without taking a breath.

'That's better,' he said. 'I hope you managed okay, no *faux-pas*, no monocles shooting off in the drawing-room? Good, excellent. I'll risk the lion's rage and nip up to my room for a quick shower and change. Then we'll whiz out to a pub for a few moments' chat before dinner. Fill you in on things, it can get a bit complicated here. Wait for me in the stableyard, ten minutes, okay?'

He was gone, taking his gear with him. Gina wanted to shout, 'No, not okay,' down the passage after him, but he wouldn't hear, and if he did, he would probably take no notice. In any case, unless she was going to own up and depart at once, she'd have to get through dinner, and it would be a lot easier if she could pump Harry first.

'No eavesdroppers here,' said Harry, putting their glasses down with a flourish. Gina, suspecting she would need a clear head, was having a tonic water. Harry was sampling something that looked as though it was made of bat's blood.

'Eavesdroppers?'

'Yes, family, people who work on the estate, friends, the landlord . . . you know. Our local's the Bunch of Grapes in Heartsbane, excellent inn, I'll take you there for dinner one evening. But of course, every word you say gets reported straight back.'

'Straight back?' said Gina, bewildered. 'Who to?'

Harry pursed his lips. 'Could be Pa. More likely Julia.'

'Julia. Victor's wife. Well, was.'

Gina tried to remember. Victor, married one, Julia Cordovan; two, Hermione Mendicant; three, Rosalind Filigree. Obviously goes in for wives, Zoë had observed.

'Not your mother, then?'

'No. Let me explain.' Harry settled himself more comfortably on

44

his bench. He was, in his own way, just as graceful as Guy, but his looks were far more masculine. Presumably he got his energy from Victor, although he was of a lighter build. Plenty of muscles, though, as Gina had already noticed. She didn't like wispy little men, nor pudgy large ones. Not that it mattered, she reminded herself. These Cordovan men were strictly look-but-don't-touch as far as she was concerned.

Harry pressed his fingertips together in an echo of a bygone lawyer. 'Pa married Julia about a million years ago, when they were both young and presumably knew no better. Then Julia got a lot of fancy ideas of her own, and went off to read medicine. Naturally, Pa wasn't putting up with that, so he divorced her. Nasty affair, so one hears, although of course it all happened before I was born. She's his cousin, so there was quite a family row about it all, one is told. Then Pa got hitched to the divine Hermione, who'd had the hots for him for years. Oh, Pa and Julia did have two sons along the way; fairly bad news, both of them, but, fortunately, rarely at Heartsease.'

'Hermione wasn't your mother?'

'No, no. Herm popped twins, a girl and a boy, and then followed it up with Don. He's really Dennis, can you beat it? Shows you what Hermione was like. Anyway, Victor got fed up with her and set up house with Rosalind. She's my ma. Presently in Africa as far as one knows, she does get about a lot. She had me, and then Aimée.'

'I haven't met Aimée yet.'

'No, you'd still be reeling if you had. Fairly memorable, Aimée.'

'That's it, is it?' said Gina, feeling dazed by the size and complexity of her newly-acquired family.

'Except for Olivia. Brilliant woman, philosopher, lives in Cambridge. Another half-sister of mine; nobody's too sure who her mother is. An encyclopaedia, probably. She's one of Pa's little efforts on the side, you see, but definitely one of the family. I get on okay with Olivia, actually.'

'So your father's married to Rosalind, but she's away?'

'No, no. They parted quite a while ago. Then Julia, by this time a high-powered gynaecologist, floated back into Pa's orbit, and he decided he rather liked the look of her after all. She is fairly stunning, I have to admit, but oh boy, is she one jealous lady! She moved back in with Pa because, in her book, marriage is for good, and mere

45

details like the law of the land and two subsequent wives don't worry her a jot. You'll meet her tonight, you won't have seen her at tea because it's clinic day.'

'Clinic?'

'Yeah, pregnant ladies. Well, girls, mostly, and hardly a husband between them. Julia lectures them all, and they eat out of her hand, strange things hormones do to you, I wouldn't put up with it for a moment.'

Gina drank her tonic water in silence.

Harry was thinking, his dark eyes narrowing with concentration. 'Who else is there that you might come across?'

'I met Prim,' said Gina.

'Yes, she's Pa's sister. So's Hester. He has brothers as well, don't worry about them.'

'What happens if someone mentions them; shouldn't I know who they are?'

'Just smile, no danger of a difficult silence in this family, everyone's always got plenty to say. Keep your mouth shut and then you won't put your foot in it, and no one will rumble that you aren't Georgie Hartwell of hammy fame.'

'I've said I prefer to be called Gina.'

Harry sucked in his breath with a dramatic whistling sound. 'Unwise, definitely unwise.'

'Now look here, Harry,' began Gina.

'Time to go,' said Harry, rising swiftly from his bench. 'Dinner at half past, don't want a black mark on your first evening, do you?'

'I was just trying to say,' went on Gina as Harry's very fast car throbbed into life.

'I never listen to conversations that start with "Now, look here",' said Harry. 'Matter of principle. Settle down, enjoy the ride, enjoy the dinner tonight, enjoy Hester's overpowering hospitality, just relax. I'll bring you out for another ride tomorrow, and we can talk some more, in a pleasant way, I do trust. We're safe on this side, this is out of Cordovan territory. The villages of Heartsease and to the west are family strongholds.'

'Where was the pub we've just been to?'

'Griddle,' said Harry. 'We're just going through Haggle, then we hit Snitch, then we're back in Victor and Julia's domain. So mouths buttoned, thoughts controlled and mind your Ps and Qs. Julia's a stickler for good form.'

In the kitchen, Guy was delicately frying little squares of bread for the gazpacho. Victor was very fond of spicy and piquant food, and Maria, who had cooked for the family for the last twenty years, considered that it was hot enough for an iced soup this evening, even by her southern European standards.

'Just a little bit more crisp, these croûtons,' she said to Guy, inspecting the pan as she went past.

'Ready in two minutes,' said Guy. He pulled out a length of greaseproof paper and tore it off with a quick flick of his wrist. 'They can drain while I chop the cucumber, and then it's ready.'

'Where's that girl?' said Maria. 'Never around when you want her.'

'I can hear her in the outer scullery,' said Guy. 'Listen.'

'Yes,' said Maria, brandishing a large wooden spoon and heading for the distant corner where Esme was yodelling and carolling among the suds.

'*Ahora*, take those earphones off!' shrieked Maria.

Esme was oblivious. Strains of the Italian opera blasting through her earphones were audible even to Maria. Mingled with Esme's own singalong noises, the overall effect was, Maria considered, horrible. She advanced and snatched the earphones from Esme's head.

'*Ave Maria purissima*, you are not even listening to a good Spanish tenor, a Carreras, or Placido. No, you listen to that fat Italian.'

'Pavarotti is the goods,' said Esme, not at all put out by losing her earphones. 'What's the fuss, Maria?'

'Fuss? Dinner is ready, everyone is there, waiting, picking quarrels with each other because their blood sugar is so low.'

'They don't need low blood sugar to pick a quarrel,' said Esme, drying her hands. 'You want me to go tell them grub's up, I suppose.'

'Do it with grace and courtesy for once,' pleaded Guy as Esme, six foot in her flip-flops, made her way through the kitchen.

'Grace and courtesy?' said Maria contemptuously. 'That one? Never! The sooner she goes back to Australia the better, that's what I say.'

'I couldn't agree with you more,' said Guy, deftly tipping the gazpacho from its chilled bowl into an ornate soup tureen with feet and a curly top. 'But she and Mona from the village are getting very, very friendly, I have to tell you.'

'*Ayi!*' said Maria, casting her eyes up to heaven.

Esme came back into the kitchen, slap, slap on the stone floor. 'Right-o,' she said. 'that's them all sitting down ready for their din-dins. Except for the new girl, she isn't down yet. Who is she? I passed her in the hall this afternoon; she doesn't look very happy.'

'She's a cousin,' said Guy repressively. 'She's staying for a while. Now, I'll take the soup in, and you follow with the tray of garnishes.'

'That soup's cold!' said Esme in disbelief.

'It's a chilled soup, stupid one,' hissed Maria. 'A speciality of Andalucia, where I come from.'

Esme was intrigued. 'I thought you were Spanish.'

'Give me strength,' said Guy.

'Where have they put this cousin?' said Esme, falling into place behind Guy.

'In the yellow room,' said Maria.

'You helped Hester get it ready this morning,' Guy pointed out.

'Yeah, well, I thought she was just being fussy, doing out the room. Hope the owls won't disturb the cousin.'

'Never mind the owls,' said Maria. 'You take that soup in right now, this instant, because otherwise my fish will be spoilt and then I will kill you.'

'You're the boss,' said Esme, padding after Guy. 'But don't expect me to eat any of that cold soup for my tea. Ugh!'

The small dining-room where the family was assembled was dark, even on a summer evening, since the stone mullioned windows let in the minimum of light. Candles flared on the sideboard and on the deeply polished table.

Victor crushed a roll and flattened his white napkin across his knees. He looked across at the empty place. 'Where's Gina?' he demanded. 'Harry, you should be looking after her.'

'She's coming,' said Harry. 'Went back to get her watch.'

'Nervy-looking,' said Victor. 'Needs feeding up; what's she been doing to make her look like that?'

'I remember her as a very bouncy, robust child,' said Hester. 'She does have a troubled look to her; never mind, a quiet spell in the country with us will soon bring the colour back into her cheeks.'

Harry tilted his chair back and flashed an amused glance at his aunt. 'Quiet spell?' he said mockingly. 'Here?'

Gina slid into the room, awkward because of being late. Then she took in the full glory of the dining-room, and let out a surprised 'Oh!' as she saw the intricately plastered ceiling and the exquisite tapestries on the wall. The seventeenth-century hangings were in faded shades of green and grey and cream, although they must once have buzzed with colour. They depicted scenes from classical mythology; across from where Gina was standing a languishing nymph was being approached by a vigorous-looking satyr. Further along, Persephone wandered in the fields, and there was Venus in the foam.

Gina gave a sigh as she came back to the present day to find that Victor was standing beside her, introducing her to the big, golden woman with a watchful face who sat at one end of the table.

Julia gave her a cool nod. 'Good evening, Gina. Hester was right, you look worried and unrested. Drink plenty of water, my dear, it does wonders for the complexion, you shouldn't have those dark shadows under your eyes at your age.'

Victor sat Gina on his right, next to Harry. 'A cosy family party,' he said jovially as he sat down again.

Prim, who had changed into another pair of less faded trousers and a clean shirt, sent him a single malevolent glance before turning her attention back to Hester. They were discussing vine weevils in some considerable detail. At the other end of the table, Julia was holding forth about an interesting patient she had seen that day.

'One look and you could tell it wasn't a urinary tract infection. Well, of course the smell of the discharge is an immediate giveaway.'

Revolting though this conversation was, Gina felt that it was a lot better than her own interrogation by Julia which followed. Unlike the others, Julia had little time for polite enquiries to make about the Hartwell family. Just a few remarks about what an admirable couple Gina's supposed grandparents were.

'They never got on, of course, quite incompatible; in fact I believe they loathed each other. But they stayed together through thick and thin, their marriage vows meant something to them.'

Victor wasn't having any of that. 'Nonsense,' he said. 'The only

49

thing that's held them together is money. He made some, she provided some more; excellent dowry she had. There was no way they could split up, no way at all.' He nodded at Gina. 'Not much of the other trouble these days, well, there wouldn't be, not at your grandmother's age. No one would look at her now, I dare say.'

Even if she had known what they were talking about, and these people being so ruthlessly dissected were her own family, Gina wouldn't have known how to reply. Luckily, Julia, having got the social niceties out of the way, changed the subject.

'Tell us about yourself, Georgiana.'

Harry was lolling back in his chair, obviously much amused. 'She likes to be called Gina, Mother.'

'Gina, very well. Have you any boyfriends? How old are you now? Must be what, twenty-four? High time you were married, nothing like marriage to keep a young girl out of mischief. Best place for all those urges is the marriage bed, and none of these unmarried mothers running round on social security will persuade me otherwise. If you choose right, some man who is good in bed, then there's no need for promiscuity. Keep him happy, plenty of good food, regular rest, then he'll perform well when you want him to, and you'll have a good marriage.'

Gina didn't know what to say. Harry winked at her. 'Pay no attention,' he said. 'It's Julia's hobby-horse, marriage.'

Julia gave Harry a frosty look. 'Not a hobby-horse, Harry; don't be impertinent. I know what I'm talking about, which is more than you do.' She wiped her mouth with a napkin and waved an imperious hand at Esme. 'Over here, Esme, some more of this soup.'

Gina watched, fascinated, to see how skilfully Julia manoeuvred the soup over her magnificent bosom. She wasn't a young woman, nor was she slim or trim or any of the things which are modern necessaries for fashionable attractiveness. She was, however, magnetic and overpowering and very sexy, and Victor, whom Gina suspected of having a roving eye, was clearly feeling uxorious this evening; judging by his bedroom eyes when he looked at Julia.

Hester in her kind way now began a stream of gentle questions about Gina's well-being, whether she liked tea or coffee in the morning, were the spa salts in her bathroom to her taste, or did she prefer a shower gel, there was an ultra-light quilt in the wardrobe if she found it too hot at night, did she care for a hot or cold drink when she went to bed?

Gina had to concentrate hard to give sensible answers. They must think I'm very stupid, she said to herself as she um-ed and er-ed her replies. Then, horror, Hester began on her family. Had she seen Jack recently? Was it her Aunt Sophie's girl who had got married in the spring? How was George's back, she'd heard he'd had to go into hospital . . .

Hester came to her rescue as the fish remains were carried out. 'Gina doesn't spend much time at home these days, do you, Gina? Too busy organizing this and that at Oxford, from what Harry has told us.'

'Yes, of course, that was where Harry ran into you, wasn't it?' said Victor.

'Tell us about your writing work,' said Hester.

By the time an elderflower ice had come and gone, and the cheese had been passed round, Gina felt as though a steamroller had been over her.

'I'll take my coffee to my office,' Victor told Esme.

'Right-o,' said Esme. 'Is there a good game on tonight? Who's playing?'

Victor looked like a naughty boy caught out in a misdeed. 'I'm going to do some work,' he said with dignity.

Esme gave a snort of laughter and clashed a few plates together.

Guy, who had come in on silent feet, cast Esme a withering look and took the tray from her.

'Coffee in the library for everyone else?'

'Not for me, thanks,' said Prim. 'Time for a bit of weeding in the veggie patch before it gets dark.'

'We'll have it in the drawing-room tonight, I think, Guy,' said Julia. 'And, Victor!'

Victor paused at the door.

'Don't be late to bed tonight.'

Gina slunk away to her room, pleading tiredness, as soon as she could. She waited for twenty minutes or so, to make sure that Hester wasn't going to come tapping on the door to enquire about her well-being, or offer her again the nightcap she had refused earlier. Then she opened the door and, wincing every time a floorboard creaked, made her way down the back stairs, hoping to be able to slip out unobserved.

'Hello, Gina,' came an antipodean yell, as she reached the bottom. 'Do you need something?'

'No, I'm all right, thank you,' Gina shouted back. She had to shout; Esme had a radio going full blast with Act 3 of *I Puritani*. 'I just came down the wrong stairs. I only wanted a breath of fresh air.'

'Can't say I blame you,' said Esme. 'Sweat pours off you, night like this. Here.'

She obligingly held the back door open for her, and Gina found herself in the stableyard. She could hear voices over on the other side, and paused. Esme was behind her. 'Don't worry about them, it's only Guy flirting with Harry. Harry's tuning his motorbike. Harry's always tuning his motorbike, should get himself a new one if you ask me.'

Gina made an agonized sshing noise, but Harry was too intent on his revs and Guy too intent on Harry for either of them to notice her.

'Best place to go is on the terraces,' said Esme kindly. 'The mozzies don't bite nearly so much there.'

'Thank you,' hissed Gina, who knew exactly where she was going.

Once free of the house and its ubiquitous inhabitants, she set off along the drive. She had come this way with Harry, and had noticed a red phone box on the triangle of green outside the village pub. Armed with 10p coins, because something told her the phone wouldn't take a card, she made her way out of the gates and along the darkening lane to Heartsease.

Mercifully, the light in the telephone box had long since ceased to function, otherwise Gina would have been spotlit and visible to all the houses grouped round the small green. As it was, she felt that eyes were on her as she peered at the dial, anxious to get the numbers right. The phone rang at the other end.

Let Zoë be in, Gina prayed. And let her answer the phone, not Fergus.

'Oxford 429817.'

Zoë.

Relief.

'Zoë,' said Gina. 'It's me, Gina.'

'Who, oh, Gina! Great. Speak up, this is a terrible line. Or can't you, are you in a hall?'

'No, I'm in a phone box,' said Gina in her normal voice.

'That's better. Is someone with you?'

'No, no, that's why I've come out to the village. I just feel that people are listening.'

'I know the feeling,' said Zoë. 'I grew up in a village like that, and do you know what? There always was someone listening. Look, give me your number, and I'll ring you back.'

'Can't,' said Gina. 'Blank space on the dial, I think it must have faded.'

'Probably removed in the war to fool the Germans,' said Zoë. 'Quick, then, before you run out of money. Your news first, and then I'll bring you up to date at this end.'

'It's no good, Zoë, I'm coming back to Oxford. I can't go through with this.'

'Marrying Harry? I thought you said from the start there's no question of that. Is he being difficult?'

'No, no, he's rather kind, actually, and we haven't even discussed . . . well, what you're talking about. No, it's just that I can't possibly go on pretending to be Georgie. They ask me impossible questions which I can't answer, and besides, Zoë, this isn't an ordinary family!'

'Very upper class?' said Zoë. 'Bit stiff and dim and unfriendly?'

'Oh, not at all. They're just, oh, different. I suspect they're all wildly clever, and I'm sure they know I'm up to something. This is premier league, here, Zoë, I'm playing in the wrong game.'

'No, no, you're imagining it,' said Zoë. 'Now, listen, you can't come back. Popplewell's still sniffing round.'

'Popplewell? He can't be,' wailed Gina. 'He knows I've left the country.'

'He's not too sure. He turned up on the doorstep and started asking all kinds of nosy questions. Fergus soon sent him packing, but he does suspect something. You'll have to stay where you are.'

'No, I won't,' said Gina firmly. 'I'll come back to Oxford and tell the truth . . .'

'And be had up for deception or a misdemeanour or disturbing the peace and then they'll deport you, and put squiggles all over your passport and you won't have a hope in hell of ever coming back.'

'Oh, bugger,' said Gina.

'You mustn't blow it now,' urged Zoë. 'I know you can carry it off. Don't let them frighten you. Look, I have to go, I can hear Fergus, you know how nosy he is, he'll want to know who I'm talking to.'

Gina heard a rustle at the other end, and then Zoë's voice, very clear and precise. 'It's my Aunt Alice, Fergus.' Then, in a whisper, 'These English families aren't so bad when you get to know them. Really. Bye.'

Click.

No, thought Gina gloomily, as she pushed open the door of the kiosk with her shoulder. They're much, much worse.

CHAPTER 6

Rattle. Crash. Bang.

Esme banged a cup of tea down beside Gina's bed and slopped over to the window. 'Great day,' she said enthusiastically, drawing the curtains back. 'Hope the owls weren't too noisy. I hate owls.'

Gina, who had passed a sticky and restless night, pursued by winged motorcyclists, Popplewells in drag and a raging white bull, mumbled her thanks. Esme shut the door behind her with a loud thud, and then immediately opened it again.

'Forgot to say, breakfast in half an hour.'

Although only half past eight, the sun streaming in at the window already carried the promise of almost tropical heat. Owls? thought Gina, sliding out of bed and heading for the bathroom. Yes, she remembered hearing owls last night. Several different sorts of owl, judging by the varied hoots which had interwoven her dreams.

She didn't look in the mirror; she knew all too well what she would look like. Grim.

A powerful shower refreshed her somewhat, but the air was still hot and heavy. Shorts, she decided. Usually she kept those for walking; the sights that hot weather brought out in city streets were enough to put anyone off shorts. But this was the country, she was in a sense on holiday – better to think of it like that than to admit she was in hiding.

Gina had very good legs, but she realized the shorts were a mistake as soon as she came into the breakfast room. Guy, who was hovering round with plates, greeted her with a 'Love your shorts,' but Victor's glance was altogether of a different kind, and Julia didn't look at all pleased. Hester, who probably never noticed what anyone was wearing, at once offered tea, coffee, fruit juice, and led Gina through an assortment of cereals, eggs, fish and various rolls and kinds of toast. 'What do you normally have for breakfast, my dear?' she asked.

Gina didn't like to tell her that it was a slice of toast and an instant coffee if she had time. Except for Sundays, of course. Lovely Sundays, when Fergus cooked what he called a proper breakfast at about eleven o'clock in the morning, and they sat in a room strewn with Sunday papers, eating platefuls of food which lasted them until a late supper. Gina wondered if she'd ever enjoy another one of those leisurely Oxford days; somehow at the moment it didn't seem very likely.

'No point looking back all the time,' said Harry in bracing tones.

'What?' said Gina.

'I can tell, you were feeling mournful about something in the past. The food reminded you, I expect. You know what smells and tastes are like. Ex-pats getting a whiff of cut grass and going all moody at the thought of England, forgetting the wet, the dirt and the general nastiness of life. Or, contrariwise, poor exiled Mediterraneans like Maria getting a scent of cypress or orange blossom. You can tell those days with Maria, because her crème caramels don't set and she gets into a very Spanish temper.'

'I wasn't looking back,' said Gina, crossly. Nobody likes to be told they're backward-looking.

'Yes, you were. Dreaming of happier days. No point, always best to assume the best days are ahead of you. Who knows what the day may bring?'

Who knows, indeed? thought Gina, trying to cover her knees with a large linen napkin and wishing that Victor would concentrate on his paper. The day might bring discovery, her unmasking as an impostor. Or it could, terrible thought, bring Popplewell or one of his colleagues; maybe his office was filled with Popplewell clones, all going about the country doing their duty. Gina took another unenthusiastic mouthful of muesli.

'Don't know how anyone can eat that rabbit's food,' said Victor, crunching into a piece of toast with his excellent teeth. 'Not enough to keep body and soul together. Makes you fart, too.'

'Victor, that's enough,' said Hester. 'Gina, what would you like to do today?'

Harry answered for her. 'Can you be a sweetie and show Gina around the house and so on this morning, Aunt Hester? I'm going to be a bit tied up until lunch. This afternoon I might take her over to the vineyard. You'll enjoy that, Gina. Then we could have a swim.'

There was nothing Gina could say. She couldn't claim she had work to do or letters to write; in fact, it was very strange, having nothing to do.

'You'll want to drop a line to your grandparents, I expect,' said Hester. 'Leave the letter on the hall table and I'll see it goes with the rest of the post.'

Another trap. Gina shot Harry a look of mute appeal, which was wasted; Harry was sliding out of the room, giving Guy's shoulder a quick caress as he went past.

'I don't know if Aimée's in her room,' said Hester, giving a tap on the door. 'You haven't met her yet, have you?'

A soft, low voice called for them to come in, and Hester opened the door into a room that could only be described as a bower. Light, silvery green muslins and gauzes fluttering gently at the windows and around a huge four-poster bed. The walls, Gina saw with astonishment, were decorated with more exquisite tapestries. The artist had once more chosen classical themes, all to do with love in this room, and Gina blinked as she took in what the nymphs, satyrs and assorted Grecians were up to.

'Shocking, isn't it?'

Aimée was reclining on her bed, her dark hair tumbling over very white shoulders, while a filmy wrap did little to conceal her beautiful breasts.

'Cousin Georgiana, isn't it?' Aimée said with an inviting smile. 'Come and sit here,' and she patted the bed, 'and tell me about yourself. Are you in love? I can see you are. It isn't Harry, is it? Of course we all long for Harry to fall in love, but women aren't entirely his thing. Not at present, anyhow.'

'Aimée,' said Hester, quite sharply for her. 'It's time you were up. Mrs Slubs will want to do your room; you know she wasn't able to get in until the afternoon yesterday.'

Aimée stretched her arms gracefully and yawned. 'Yesterday was wonderful, Aunt Hester. Do you know, last night . . .'

Hester cut her off at once. 'I don't think we want to hear about last night, thank you. Gina can't stay, I'm just showing her around the house.'

Aimée's almond-shaped eyes danced. 'Dear Aunt Hester, weren't you ever young and in love?'

'No, I wasn't, as you well know, and thank goodness for it.'

'But don't take Gina away,' Aimée pleaded. 'I can see, she's in love with a man who doesn't love her, and then there must be someone in love with her; you couldn't be so pretty and not have a lover, could she, now Hester, admit! I want to hear all about it.'

Hester made a disapproving clucking noise as she put a hand on Gina's arm. Gina left the scented room reluctantly, her senses spinning. Just looking at Aimée and being in that room was enough to make one feel that any passing man would hardly be safe; pull yourself together, Gina said to herself, trying to get a grip on her feelings.

'I expect Aimée's changed a lot since you last saw her,' said Hester. 'She would only have been a baby then, although even then she was a most attractive and charming child; everyone adored her.'

I bet they did, thought Gina, coming to a more normal frame of mind and body as Hester led her along the passage.

'It's Aimée's twenty-first birthday on the twenty-third of June,' Hester went on.

'Midsummer Eve. The Feast of St John,' said Gina without thinking.

Hester shot her a surprisingly astute glance. 'Very appropriate, one might say. We're giving a ball for Aimée on that evening. You'll still be here, of course, you'll enjoy that.'

'No way,' Gina was about to say, but she stopped herself in time. 'I hadn't expected a ball.'

'No, I noticed you hadn't brought any cocktail or long frocks; I was surprised. There are a lot of parties at this time of year, even in the country, surely you entertain on Uish?'

'No, no,' said Gina hastily. 'My grandparents are old, and . . .'

Hester looked puzzled. 'How strange you should say that. I'm sure that when Cousin Jack last wrote, he mentioned quite a number of festivities.'

Curse Cousin Jack and his busy pen, thought Gina. 'I'm working now, in Oxford, you see, so I don't get to so many parties.'

Hester laughed confidently. 'Now, I know that's not true. You must send for some more clothes, or if you want a shopping spree, Bath has some excellent shops and I'm sure Harry will take you over there. He goes quite often, on business.'

And what do I use to buy clothes with? thought Gina. I've hardly got any money left. And I must find out, quickly, what Harry's business is before I put my foot in it. Georgie had been maddeningly vague when she'd asked about Harry. 'Oh, he's in messages,' she had said. Gina could hardly ask Hester what Harry did; never mind, she would have some time with him this afternoon and find out more about him.

Now I understand how people can fall in love with a house, thought Gina, as she succumbed to the enchantment of Heartsease Hall. It's a work of art, not a place to live.

'I have never, ever seen such a beautiful, magical house,' she cried, as Hester led her through one superb room after another. The Chapel, with its high-beamed ceiling, the Great Hall, the Little Hall, the courtyards, which led to the Jacobean Tower, the kitchens, the Dance Room. The wide, polished wooden stairs in the oldest part of the house, the room King Charles II slept in, the Red Room, the Library, the Sun Room, so-called because of the great sun painted on the ceiling. Tapestries everywhere, treated in those happier days like wallpaper, cut round doors, curved round cupboards and corners.

'All this is the old part of the house,' said Hester. 'It was started in about 1370, and the Great Hall was built after the Battle of Bosworth, in 1485. The family did very well under the Tudor kings; they had a knack of being on the right side at the right time. They rose in the world, and in the seventeenth century took off to build a huge mansion on the other side of the county. That's why so little of this part was changed. Tenants and minor members of the family lived here, and it wasn't until the end of the eighteenth century that one of the countesses came to live here. I believe she and her husband agreed to live apart, for various reasons which it's best not to go into.'

Hester led Gina through the kitchen, and out into the gardens. 'The countess decided she needed more room, but by that time, of course, Gothic was fashionable, so instead of pulling down the old house, she built alongside it, in the Gothicke style. That's why when you look at the house from where the front is now, it all looks so harmonious.'

Gina wandered in a happy daze through the formal gardens at the rear of the house, and then round to the orchard, where large spotted pigs grazed happily under the trees.

Another Eden, she thought. I can't leave this, go back to America, where a house a hundred years old is considered ancient.

Hester was pleased to find Gina so appreciative. 'Of course, it will all be new to you; you were so small when you were last here. Your parents loved it here, you know.'

Lucky Georgie, thought Gina. To have even a slight connection with all this, the right to come and be part of it; not as a visitor, but as one who belonged here.

Gina wandered idly through the gardens, supposedly helping Hester to pick flowers for the house, but mostly just looking and marvelling as each turn brought a new prospect of the house, or a new and wonderful view. It was late on in the morning by the time Hester looked at her watch and said they had better be getting back; Harry would be waiting for Gina.

He wasn't. True to form, there was a message instead. 'Held up, postpone vineyard, meet you downstairs at five for swim.'

Gina didn't mind having an afternoon to herself. She assured a concerned Hester that she would be quite happy on her own.

'Aimée's vanished, of course,' said Hester with a worried frown. 'You could spend the afternoon with Prim, but I'm afraid you'd find you'd have to work very hard, she always makes people help. And you look a little frayed, if you don't mind my mentioning it.'

Lunch, fortunately, was an informal cold meal laid out in the smaller dining-room, and Gina found herself eating alone with Hester. Victor had driven to Bristol, it was Julia's day at the hospital, and Prim had taken a picnic into the fields.

Hester apologized for the lack of company at lunch; Gina could hardly say that she was much relieved to be spared the full force of the family for a few hours. She was to be spared further; Guy, who kept the social calendar, reminded Hester that Victor and Julia were dining out at Heartsbury. 'Prim says she'll eat at the cottage, Aimée's got a hot date as usual, so I expect it will be one of Maria's experimental nights.'

'Nothing sinister,' Hester assured Gina. 'It's just that when there are only one or two of the family here, and particularly when Victor isn't here, Maria tries out new dishes. It has to be perfect for Victor, you see.'

'Is he very fussy about his food?' asked Gina, surprised. He seemed to her to be a man of large appetites in every sense; she wouldn't have put him down as a gourmet.

'No, Victor loves his food and will eat almost anything. But Maria feels that he's the head of the house and needs to be treated with special respect.'

'Quite right, too,' said Guy. 'Victor's marvellous; it's no wonder people want to please him.'

'Hmm,' said Hester.

Gina felt she'd escaped from prison as, wheeling a bike which Esme had cheerfully found for her, she headed for the gates.

'There are lots of bikes around,' Esme had said. 'Lots of everything with this family, I tell you that for nothing. Here's one, hold on, I'll pump up the tyres for you.'

Gina protested; she could perfectly well pump up the tyres for herself.

Esme waved her away. 'No, no, you look bushed. I like doing anything physical. And I don't blame you, wanting to get away from this place. I mean, I know they're your family and all that, but cripes, they aren't half a bunch of weirdos. There!' She gave the back tyre a good squeeze to make sure it was firm – Gina was surprised it didn't burst on the spot – and then said she was off to have a couple of sets of tennis with Jarvis. 'He does the gardens, when Prim lets him, but it's his afternoon off. See you later.'

At least there's one uncomplicated being in the house, thought Gina as she reached the bottom of the steep drive and mounted the bike.

Gina was used to cycling; she went everywhere by bike in Oxford. As she pedalled along the leafy lanes, her spirits rose. It was surprising, but she had to admit that some of her panic had subsided. It must have something to do with the feeling of remoteness here; Popplewell seemed a world away. This was an ancient place, people had roots here, this was the kind of countryside she had dreamed about when she first came to England. Settled, belonging to a large clan, rich; the Cordovans were the family she had never had. It must be so different, not being an only child, Gina thought, as she toiled hotly up a small hill and then whooshed down the other side. Imagine having all those brothers and sisters, as well as numerous uncles and aunts, and cousins and in-laws . . . Lucky Harry.

She had brought her map with her, but wasn't heading anywhere in particular. When she reached a crossroads, she took the direction with the most appealing name. Oath's Sluice turned out merely to be a cottage and a water mill; Utter Oath had several very pretty thatched cottages and a village shop. Gina bought a can of Coke and a postcard of the village, although there's no one I can send it to, she reminded herself as she got back on her bike.

After several miles more of meandering about the countryside, being passed by the very occasional car, and herself passing several lumbering tractors, she stopped and consulted her map. She had actually travelled in a large circle, and was back in what she suspected was Heartsease territory. She looked up at the signpost. That way were Long Ease and Little Ease. The road opposite was signposted to Heartsease and Heartsbane. She'd come from Corda Episcopi, so it would have to be the fourth way. It was only a pretence; the minute she saw 'Heartwell, 1' on the arm, she knew that was where she was going.

Heartwell was charming. Like Heartsease, it had a central green, but this was much bigger than Heartsease's tiny triangle. This was large enough to boast a duckpond, complete with ducks, a maypole, and an uncomfortable-looking iron bench with a plaque on the back saying it had been put there in memory of the Rev. Gartsop, Vicar of Heartwell 1921–7.

Gina stopped and leant her bicycle up against a handy tree. Across the green was a small Norman church, and next to it was the St Ogwell's Junior C of E school. Nearer to her she could see a village shop cum post office, a bakery and a gift shop which also offered teas.

Gina was tempted by tea; she loved a good tea, but then she had had lunch, far more than her usual quick snack. The church, then, she thought.

She wandered round the church and into the graveyard beyond it. The gravestones were old, and most of them tilted slightly drunkenly forwards or to one side. The same names occurred again and again: Heartwell, Gartsop, Slubs. Gina was intrigued; ancestors of hers must lie under the springy turf. Bees hummed and buzzed about the honeysuckle which tumbled over the church wall. How peaceful, thought Gina, relishing an elusive scent of cut grass. How English.

She pushed open the heavy door and stepped into blissful coolness. She could hear the murmur of voices further up the nave, but she paused at the entrance to absorb the musty smell and look at the crusader's tomb which lay at her feet. More peaceful in the graveyard was her next thought, as she heard voices raised in argument. She moved up the nave, and found herself in a hive of industry. There were several women entangled with wire above the altar, and two more swarming up a stepladder which was propped up beside a broad Norman pillar.

'Flower Festival,' said a voice in Gina's ear. 'An annual event, and one we pride ourselves on. Can I help, or have you just popped in to view our beautiful church?'

It was the vicar. Gina could and did praise the church, although she couldn't bring herself to praise the ghastly banners and slogans which drooped about the interior, obscuring what was probably fine stonework. She was just cycling through Heartwell, she explained, and had been struck by the beauty of the church. The vicar made pleased vicar noises, and was about to move away, when Gina, on an impulse, asked if she might look at the parish registers.

The vicar looked at her in surprise. 'Of course,' he said. 'They are open to all, only unfortunately, in these sad times, we have to keep them locked away. I will just tell Mrs Bodkin where I am, and then I will be at your disposal.'

The vicar was obviously quivering with curiosity as to why she wanted to look at the register. Gina felt a version of the truth would be best. 'One of my family came from these parts, quite a while back,' she explained. 'My own name is Hartwell, only without the E. But I

63

have a friend whose family were here more recently. I said if I was here, I'd look her family up. She's abroad, you see. Her name is Heartwell, too, spelt like the village here.'

'How very interesting,' the vicar said. 'Very interesting indeed. Of course, the Heartwells were squires here, although sadly, few are left, and none of them live at Heartwell House; well, it was sold many years ago. Although the present occupants, albeit recent arrivals, are most um, pleasant people. So this is very interesting. Let me see . . .'

The bygone Heartwells were fascinating. The names ran through the centuries, reflecting the fashions of the times. Marys and Elizabeths and several Thomases gave way to Charlottes and Jameses, to be followed in due course by Fredericks, Augustuses and Louises. There was even one Algernon Adolphus, Gina noticed with delight, and she was rather taken with an early Puritan ancestor called Pure-of-Heart Heartwell.

'You seem to know your way about old records,' remarked the vicar.

'I'm an historian,' said Gina, her impostorship forgotten.

The vicar was so fascinated by the family ramifications that he didn't notice that Gina seemed far more interested in her 'friend's' relatives than in her own remote ones.

To her surprise, her mother's wedding was recorded there. She was about to exclaim that she never knew she had been married in England, but bit her tongue just in time.

'Is that your friend's mother?' asked the vicar, seeing her interest. 'She didn't marry anyone from these parts, Serge Zandermann, a foreigner, I feel sure.' And he laughed heartily.

Gina was moved, thinking of her parents going through a wedding ceremony here in this small English church, so far in every sense from their subsequent lives. It had been a June wedding; was it a hot day like this? she thought, coming out of the church into the stifling hot air. She was sure the weather had turned even more sultry since she had been in the church. She'd get herself an ice at the shop, and then cycle back to Heartsease. At a leisurely pace; the day seemed even warmer than before.

As Gina was taking her leave of the vicar, a woman with streaky blonde hair, wearing a dress and shoes classified by *Vogue* as being suitable for the country, came up to them and interrupted her without any attempt at an apology.

No manners, whoever she is, thought Gina, edging away.

'It's the altar *flowers*, Geoff,' the rude woman said. 'I've brought some hibiscus, glorious *colours*, quite beautiful. Molly Gartsop isn't very keen, but I do think they would look particularly *good* there.'

A hunted look came into the vicar's face.

'Um,' he said. 'Well, the altar flowers do present a problem.'

'Of course, I understand that Molly usually does them, and that her father was *vicar* here in the year dot, but really, if you want to attract *visitors* to the church, you do need to have a more contemporary *approach* to the arrangements, if you don't mind my saying so.'

The vicar clutched at the nearest straw. 'Don't go,' he said to Gina in a desperate voice. 'Lori, this is Gina Hartwell. Her family come from here. Gina, Lori Mowbray. She lives at Heartwell House.'

Lori's eyes swept over Gina, taking in her shorts and polo shirt and her sandals; not a designer item to be seen. 'Hi,' she said, with no great enthusiasm.

'Hello,' said Gina. And then, to the vicar, 'Thank you again.'

'How long are you staying at Heartsease?' asked the vicar.

'I'm not sure,' said Gina.

'If you have time, come again. I'll gladly get the parish records out for you.'

'That's very kind.'

'Heartsease?' Lori said sharply. 'Are you staying in the village?'

'Miss Hartwell is staying at the Hall.'

'What, with the Cordovans?' Lori was clearly incredulous. 'Are they *friends* of yours?'

'Miss Hartwell is a relation,' said the vicar, who was enjoying himself.

Charm flowed out of Lori, and a wide professional smile sprang on to her face.

'*Hartwell*. Goodness, how slow I am. Your family might once have lived in my house. Did they? Have you ever been there? No, well, you absolutely have to come and see it. Of course it was in the most shocking *state* when we bought it, primitive, quite primitive, but it's amazing how people with taste can *transform* a house. No, I insist, you can spare a quarter of an hour, of course you can. I'll ring up

Heartsease Hall and explain where you *are*. In fact, I can run you back, we have a four-wheel drive, it takes bikes, everything. No, it's *absolutely* no trouble.'

Gina's protests were words on the wind as she was shepherded away from the church porch.

'Don't worry about those altar flowers, Geoff,' Lori flung over her shoulder at the vicar. 'I'll be along later to finish them.'

CHAPTER 7

Harry thought it was terribly funny when he heard where Gina had been. She arrived back at Heartsease, red-faced and breathless, at ten past five.

'You needn't have hurried,' he said. 'Five o'clock was only an indication, we aren't talking appointments here.'

'I hurried to get away from that dreadful woman,' said Gina. 'She wouldn't let me go, I had to see all round the house, well, it is a lovely house, I will admit, but even so! And the questions! She obviously thinks the whole family at Heartsease are appalling.'

'She doesn't know us,' said Harry. 'At least, we don't know her.'

'That's what annoys her,' said Gina.

'Don't you find it very *difficult* at the Hall?' asked Lori, throwing open the door to her artfully cosy kitchen, which had an Aga at one end and a fat sofa at the other. Dog baskets, gingham cushions, and darkened beams with kitchen tools and bunches of herbs and dried flowers hanging on black hooks completed the look.

'Difficult?'

'Such strange people. Impossible to talk to, they don't seem to live in the real world. Of course, we don't really *know* them, but since we moved down here we've naturally become very involved in everything, I do think one has to be *part* of the village, don't you agree? Just because we live in the big house, it doesn't mean we don't want to be *involved* in ordinary village life. But anyhow, those people at the Hall, I'm sorry, they're family, I know, but they don't have any sense of community. I do believe in contributing to social life around you, but you never see any of them *doing* anything.'

'I think they all work,' said Gina cautiously.

'Work! Well, they hardly need to, from what I *hear*. And what kind of work? I mean, I know what work is. Although we've moved out of London, and now with the girls – I have two daughters – I don't work full time, I still *freelance*. And of course Gareth works all the hours there are, *desperately* long hours, he gives everything to his work, he *slaves*.'

Gina was starting to feel very defensive about the Cordovans, although I can't think why, she said to herself, they're no family of mine. 'Victor works, he runs several businesses,' she said. 'And farms. Prim farms, too, and there's the vineyard.'

Lori had gone quite pale. 'Farming!' she said. 'I know all about that. Victor Cordovan's prize cattle come marching through the village here, *mud* everywhere. Nobody seemed to want to do anything about it, I suppose they're all overawed by the thought of the Cordovans and let them get *away* with anything. It's going to change, there are one or two other families who have moved *recently*, and they are appalled, appalled by the *way* those cows are allowed to stampede along and tear up the road edges.'

'Country usually means cows and mud, doesn't it?'

Lori had got the bit between her teeth. 'And then the *tractors*. Early in the morning, the most terrible racket.'

'I expect people here are used to it,' said Gina, trying to calm her down.

'Well, it's time they *stopped* being used to it, and made a fuss,' said Lori. 'It won't do, *spoiling* an attractive village like this because the local landowners choose to treat the roads as though they *belonged* to them.'

'Which they do, of course,' said Harry, still highly amused.

'What, all the way over there?'

'Oh, yes. What then?'

'This is all gossip,' said Gina.

'I love gossip,' said Harry. 'Come on, spit it out.'

'If you really want to know,' said Gina, laughing, 'she thinks the whole family is amoral, with attitudes and behaviour that have no place whatsoever in today's world.'

'I like it,' said Harry. 'Almost, I think I want to know this Lori person.'

Gina shook her head. 'Take it from me, you don't.'

'Next thing, of course, she'll be round, claiming you as a friend. Do you think she'd be Victor's type?' Harry added lightly.

'If she comes round, I will be elsewhere,' said Gina. 'And what is Victor's type? I would have thought Julia was enough for anyone.'

'Heifer-eyed Julia,' said Harry thoughtfully.

'That's hardly polite.'

'No, Julia's all right, but she does have a knack of knowing where the weak spots are and going for them.'

'You sound sore.'

'I am. Marriage, that whole business, Julia pushes it very hard, and she wants me to get married as quick as poss; give up the boys, settle down to normality. Oh well, if you marry me, then we'll find out what it's all about.'

Gina was just about to say, not to worry, she had no intention of marrying him when Zoë's warning about the Popplewell came back to her.

'We hardly know each other yet,' said Gina.

'No,' said Harry with a sigh. 'But it's hardly a *coup de foudre*, is it?'

'Do *coups de foudre* ever really happen?'

'I'm sure they do,' said Harry, looking out over the terrace to the distant sea. 'That's what I long for, to be overwhelmed by love for someone. On first meeting, to see someone and just know, this is it, this is a hand out to eternity.'

'Hmm,' said Gina, slightly put out by this, and startled by Harry's unexpected romanticism.

'Come on,' he said abruptly. 'It's too hot to worry about silly neighbours or married life. Let's go for a swim. We can drive to the sea, there's a cove where we can bathe; but I warn you, the sea will be distinctly chilly. Or we can use the pool here.'

'This one?' said Gina, looking at the round pool with a statue of Neptune on an island in the centre.

Harry laughed. 'No, this is strictly ornamental, and fish, for the use of. There's a swimming pool, I thought Hester showed you round the house.'

'She did, but no pool.'

'It's in one of the conservatories. This is Prim's territory, full of growing things, you see, so Hester doesn't take much notice. Get your swimming costume, unless you're going to bathe in the nude, and I'll meet you by the kitchen door. And don't look so prudish, Victor never wears a costume in the pool, nor do Julia and Prim. Noble, nude and antique, that generation.'

'Oh, my!' said Gina.

'Do you know you do sound pure American sometimes,' said Harry. 'Of course, it's hardly surprising.'

'No, it isn't,' said Gina, trying to make herself sound entirely English. 'This is just amazing.'

The conservatories had been built beyond the stable block some time in the last century, when a Victorian Cordovan had been struck by his visit to the Great Exhibition. The guidebook didn't like them at all.

These Victorian glass buildings are quite out of keeping with the fine, unspoiled mediaeval appearance of the Hall. Unfortunately, past and present owners of the house have preferred to let them remain, and now the planning laws would prevent their being demolished.

Harry led the way through the small entrance house, which took them into the central part of the glass houses. 'This is the Great House,' he told her.

Gina looked up in awe at the glass which arched elegantly over ornate metal supports and struts.

'All of thirty feet,' said Harry, looking up as well. He patted a thick palm trunk. 'This is a banana tree. No monkeys, unfortunately, but several kinds of tropical birds.'

Gina could hear them, and see flashes of exotic plumage. 'Heaven,' she said.

'Yes, a positive garden of Eden,' said Harry. 'It's all very clever, actually. Victorian ingenuity at its best. There's a spray system which comes on about every forty minutes, that's why it's so tropical in here. The water is drawn from a stream higher up, it's all terribly energy-efficient. The heating is underground; not necessary in the summer of course.'

Gina put out a hand to brush against the thick, shiny leaves. 'Wonderful smells.'

'Plants from all over the place, here. One or two so rare that Kew came to take cuttings. Another ancestor spent most of his life up and down distant swampy rivers, sending back specimens. Wouldn't be allowed these days, and in the end he was eaten by a crocodile.'

They wandered through the paths set in the foliage, emerging at a set of double doors. 'The Small House,' said Harry, standing aside to let Gina through. 'This is the pool.'

'Oh!' was all Gina could say.

Harry looked sideways at her rapt face, and smiled. 'Nice, isn't it? I've always liked the classical touch.'

Gina gazed at the elegant columns ranged round the pool, which did indeed give a classical effect. The pool was rounded at one end, and above it water poured out of a dolphin's mouth into a huge shell, running over the edge to splash down into the pool.

'That is neat,' she said.

'It was originally an ornamental pool,' said Harry. 'Pa had it made into a swimming pool years ago, when Charles was little.'

'Charles?'

'My half-brother. Julia's son. He's lame, from an accident when he was a baby, and swimming was supposed to help his leg. I don't think it did, he's still very lame; however, we all have the benefit. Changing rooms over there, ladies to the right, gents to the left. Shower and so on are self-explanatory. Lots of towels, robes and so forth about – help yourself.'

Gina floated on her back. A faint breeze from the line of doors and windows at the far end which opened out on to the gardens ruffled the surface of the pool. She could just hear the birds in the adjoining house; otherwise it was completely tranquil.

Only I don't feel tranquil, she thought. This place assaults the senses, not just at first, but all the time. Tranquil was not the right word for it; there was none of the peace promised by the lush surrounding countryside, none of the peace she'd felt in Heartwell churchyard. This house dazzled and captivated you, with its perfect setting and countryside, with the lush leaves and flowers of the gardens and the luxuriant tropical growth in the glass-houses, but it didn't make you feel safe, Gina decided. As a home should. At least in her book it should. On the other hand, homes were rarely exciting, and Heartsease House undoubtedly had an atmosphere of life and excitement about it.

Perhaps it was the remarkable people who lived in the house and had a larger-than-life quality to them. Lori saw them as old-fashioned and arrogant. Georgie saw them as rich cousins. The villagers saw them as a family rooted in the place in the same way as the church or the hills. She, Gina, found them – well, what did she find them?

Disturbing. That's what they were.

Harry dived into the pool and swam up beside her. Then he turned and floated on his back too.

Gina gave a snort of disbelief, and plunged her head under the surface. Harry pulled her up and trod water beside her, his eyes mocking.

'Seen something?' he enquired guilelessly.

'You're swimming naked.'

'Yes, well, I always do. When I'm among friends.'

'We aren't that friendly,' said Gina firmly.

'I'll swim entirely on my front, so as not to offend,' said Harry, spurting off. 'Then you can admire my behind. My best friends tell me I have a wonderful bum.'

Gina swam decorously to the end of the pool, retreating under the shell so that the water came down in front of her like a curtain.

'Go and put a costume on,' she shouted through the cascade.

Harry pulled a mournful face, and then slowly pulled himself out of the water and on to the side.

'Don't you find water and the tropical ambience terribly sexy?' he asked. 'I do.'

One look showed Gina that this was so. 'Off,' she yelled fiercely. 'This minute. And have a cold shower while you're in there,' she added to his back, as he strolled at an easy pace towards the changing room.

'Prude,' he countered. 'Besides, I'm basically not that interested in women.'

I don't think I'd take a bet on that, Gina said to herself as she ventured out from her shell. And I am not a prude.

*

'If you are in a temper, Guy,' said Maria, 'then please go away. Temper will spoil my parfait, no one can cook in a temper.'

'Aw, that's not right,' said Esme, who was passing through the kitchen looking huge in a tennis skirt and shirt. 'You're always in a temper.'

Maria banged her wooden spoon on the table. 'Impertinence I will not have.'

'Okay, okay, keep your hair on,' said Esme, continuing on her way to the tennis court. She stopped at the door. 'Oh, Harry says he's going to take Gina out, so we'll be two less for dinner.'

Guy put the mixing bowl back on to the Hobart and snapped it into place with a loud thunk. 'It's too bad,' he said. 'Harry took her out last night, they've been swimming together, and now he's taking her out again.'

'Ha,' said Maria. 'Harry learns what it is to be a man, which is, I think, a very good thing.'

'Harry is extremely masculine,' said Guy indignantly.

'Yes, but with men; this doesn't count, being unnatural and against all principles. Now, it is time for Harry to grow up and forget about beautiful boys and friends from school and all these English vices and become a proper man, learn how to please a woman. This cousin is very pretty, very lively, a good sense of humour. She will be good for him.'

She gave the table another thump with the spoon, and sent Guy off to get the ice cubes. He muttered disconsolately into the chilly depths; that was all the thanks you got for putting yourself out the way he had.

Maria was having none of that. 'Making big eyes at Harry and Mr Victor is not putting yourself out. And all this is to your benefit, all experience for when you open this grand country house hotel you dream about. So you be quiet, and watch to see how you put this mixture in to make the parfait exactly as it should be.'

This time Harry headed towards the coast. 'There's a good restaurant down near the cove,' he said. 'Only don't tell Maria, she takes it as a personal affront if we eat French food.'

'Maria is a very good cook,' said Gina, enjoying the air rushing past her face from the open window.

'Maria is a genius,' said Harry. 'On the other hand, you're never alone when you eat Maria's food, because some member of the family is always there.'

'Here, too,' said Gina, enjoying Harry's momentary discomfiture as they went into the beamed dining-room to find Aimée ensconced at a small table with a much older man. And a very dashing one, too, thought Gina.

The man was so busy gazing at Aimée, who was looking extraordinarily lush in a red and white silk dress, that he didn't notice her brother waving from the other side of the room. Aimée smiled a devastating smile at Gina, gave a tiny wave, and returned her attention to the matter in hand. Literally in hand, as the man was now kissing the inside of her wrist.

Harry frowned. 'Aimée's going to get into serious trouble one of these days,' he grumbled in the manner of brothers down the generations.

'I expect she can look after herself,' said Gina. How could you criticize someone who was as entrancing as Aimée?

'Easily,' said Harry. 'All she ever thinks about is sex. No, I wrong her,' he added in fairness. 'Love is what Aimée's about. Overwhelming, passionate, all-absorbing love. Plenty of action, too, but it's never simple lust, she'd think that very crude. No, she enslaves men, makes them fall desperately in love with her. Then it's off to someone new.' He crumbled a little roll from the basket of bread which the waiter had thoughtfully placed on the table. 'Trouble is, it's catching. Spend ten minutes with Aimée and you'll find yourself thinking about nothing else but the delights of love.'

'She's lovely,' said Gina.

'There you are, another one succumbing to her wiles. Watch it, or you'll find yourself wrapped round one of her cast-offs before you know where you are. When she's finished with them, she finds them new soulmates; she's always matchmaking. She goes to weddings every weekend.'

'Thank you,' Gina said to the waiter who handed them a small hand-written menu.

'Also today we have monkfish, fresh, very delicious. And, when it

74

comes to dessert, I will recommend the clafoutis with mixed fruit; very special, for today.'

Harry looked appreciative. 'Good. We'll have that. You'll like that, Gina.'

Gina opened her mouth to protest that she would rather choose her own meal, admitted to herself that it was what she would have chosen in any case, and shut it again.

They had coffee in the tiny garden outside, which overlooked the dark, restless sea. Little ripples of surf caught the light, then tumbled back into the waves. The restaurant was down a narrow track, which led nowhere else, so the only sounds were the clink of diners still eating in the dining-room, murmurs of staff in the kitchens and the slow suck and gentle slap of the sea. The air was salty and warm, with drifts of honeysuckle and jasmine from the plants in tubs round the patch of green where they sat.

Gina had wanted to find out more about Harry and what he did, but he was like quicksilver, darting and sliding away from all her artful questions. He laughed at her. 'No, I'm not going to tell you anything more about me, you'll just have to find out as you go along.'

'Why so secretive?'

'I like secrets. Besides, you know quite a lot about me.'

'Esme told me that you own and run a courier service in London, and that you have a company based in Bath to do with optics – the communicative kind, not prisms. I also know that you're the youngest of the family. And that you say you're gay, but you want to get married. That's about it.'

'That's all there is.'

'No,' said Gina, stretching her legs out lazily, enjoying the light wind on her bare flesh. 'That's half a portrait. Tell me more. What about particular friends? What kind of person do you fall in love with?'

Harry moved his chair round, so that he was looking out to sea. 'That's exactly it. I've never been in love.'

'With a woman, you mean?'

'No, not with a man or a woman. Sex, yes. I like sex better with women, it's more intriguing. But I like men better for their company, I understand how their minds and hearts work, I can get closer to them. I've had crushes on men, ever since I was at school, and I've had what you would call extremely close friendships. But, as far as I know, I've never been in love.'

'Perhaps you have, only you don't realize it.'

Harry was certain on that one. 'No. Whatever it is that happens with Aimée, the way men feel about her, I've never felt that. And what's so infuriating is that once they've fallen in love with her, it's as though they've been touched, they know how to do it, and bugger me, they go off and fall in love with other women. It's a whole new world, and I want to be part of it.'

'What's this to do with getting married?'

'Getting married is practical. I'll explain it to you, because I don't suppose Georgie did, or if she did, she'll have got it wrong. My pa, Victor, doesn't own Heartsease.'

Gina sat straight up in her chair with surprise. 'He doesn't? Then who does?'

'My grandfather.'

'Victor's father?'

'Yes. Conrad Cordovan. A younger son of a younger son, as it happens. Connected to the Hart-Cordovans, who are our grander cousins. The main branch of the family lived at Heartsease until the seventeenth century. They'd done very well for themselves, places at court, all that. So they moved out, built themselves a big new pile on the other side of the county.'

'Yes, Hester told me.'

'After the Second World War, the house wasn't used much, and it was an expensive second house to look after. A drain even on my rich cousins' resources. And after the last war, it was finally put up for sale. The main family must have been a bit strapped for cash, or just didn't want to be bothered with it. You could hardly give away old houses then, and the land wasn't worth much.'

'And your grandfather bought it.'

'Indeed he did. The week before the news filtered through that his distant cousins were looking for a buyer – all very discreet in those days, no glossy ads in the posh mags – well, just before then, my grandpa had been in Ireland and had bought a ticket on the Irish Sweepstake.'

'And he won?'

'Yes.'

'Heaps?'

'Not heaps, no, but enough, so he bought Heartsease and the land with it, and moved in.'

'What a lovely story,' said Gina.

'With a sting in the tail. The old man didn't bother with looking after the house or the land. He'd bought it from some atavistic whim; it was the family home. All he wanted to do was hunt and shoot and fish. Anything else was a boring waste of time.'

'And so?'

'And so, Victor started to grow up and he saw everything going to rack and ruin. He realized that if something didn't happen, he wouldn't ever inherit Heartsease.'

'How old was he when this dawned on him?'

'Knowing Pa, about nine, I should think. He waited until he was seventeen, and then, with the help of his brothers and sisters, all of whom also wanted the Hall to stay in the family, he booted Grandpa – and Grandma – out. Ultimatum time. I'm not sure what means he used, but I don't suppose he was very scrupulous about it. He took over, banished them to a perfectly nice house in the north where Grandpa could carry on killing things, and took up business to re-store the family fortunes. And to buy more land.'

'But he never owned the house?'

'No, that was part of the deal.'

'But he will when his father dies?'

'Not necessarily. It might not be wise, taxes and so on. No, the plan is to leave it to one of us.'

'You're the youngest.'

'True. But look at the others. Victor doesn't want either of his and Julia's sons to take over, because he can't stand them. He thinks Marcus is extremely dangerous, which he is, and that Charles is a fool, which he isn't. If either of them had some delightful grandchildren pattering about, it might be different, but they don't.

'The next son is Alastor. One of Hermione's twins. He's into the arts in a big way, which means he needs to live in London. He's also hopelessly in love with a woman who has no time for him. He won't look at anyone else, let alone marry them. He likes Heartsease, but he's not going to let it dictate what he does with his life. His words, not mine.'

'What about your other brother?' Gina was so fascinated that she had forgotten to drink her coffee. She took a sip.

'Must be cold,' said Harry. 'I'll order some more.' He made a movement to get up, but Gina wasn't having that.

'No, no, go on. You were saying about Don.'

'Yes, you haven't met Don. He's a good guy. Pa's been trying to marry him off for ages, but the trouble is, he's always having affairs with married women. He also has a wild side, and from time to time lets rip with some fairly uninhibited young women. A good time is had by all, I understand, but it doesn't add to his desirability as a husband.'

'Your sisters?'

'Olivia isn't interested in Heartsease. Not abstract or abstruse enough. Anyway, although she's Victor's daughter all right, there is this slight cloud of mystery about her mother. She turned up in the nurseries here as a baby, and that's all anyone knows. Except for Victor, and he's not telling.

'Then there's Aimée, need I say more? Can you see her managing the estate? What a joke. And Dinah, that's Alastor's twin sister, well, Dinah could run anything. The trouble is, she won't ever marry. She loathes men.'

'How old is she? Is she afraid of men? Won't she get over her dislike of them?'

'No way. She's twenty-nine, currently shacked up with a bint from Scotland, and she isn't remotely interested in men. She's very attractive, so men are drawn to her, but she swats them away like flies. No hopes for a dynasty there.'

'You're gay, too. Victor's got a problem.'

'I'm not so committed that I won't consider getting married.'

'For the sake of the house and land.'

'Precisely.'

'Very cold-blooded.'

'No, it isn't. I see it as a business arrangement, because that's what's left to me. If I fell in love, then I wouldn't be doing this, but I reckon I lack some vital chemical or gene in my make-up. Passion, yes. Sex, yes. Love, in its most romantic sense, no. That's why I jumped at it when Georgie told me about you. You need to get married in the same way as I need to get married – for practical reasons. And Heartsease is worth it, don't you agree?'

'This is absurd,' said Gina.

'Have you ever been in love?'

'Of course I have.'

'Are you in love with anyone now?'

Gina was silent. It was her turn to look out to sea. Gina didn't like personal questions, especially about her emotional life. She had thought she was in love with Alwyn. But she hadn't thought about him since she had arrived at Heartsease. Hardly surprising, considering everything else she'd had to think about.

Crush, she said to herself bitterly. That's what she'd felt for Alwyn. Entirely unreciprocated, he had clearly never given her a thought of an amorous kind, and he hadn't even turned out to be a good friend. Yes, he was sorry to lose a research assistant, but it was obvious that he regarded her departure as a nuisance, not in any way a personal loss. More fool her to trust him, just because he was an older man whose mind and work she admired. He'd taken great care to keep her at arm's length, now she came to think about it; he knew how I felt, Gina realized, flushing at the thought. How humiliating. Perhaps he laughed about it with Angela . . .

'No,' she said, making her voice sound cool and controlled. 'No, I'm not in love with anyone right now.'

'Watch those Americanisms,' said Harry lightly. 'We don't want to give the show away.'

'Couldn't you have married Georgie?'

A look of revulsion came over Harry's face. 'Georgie's vulgar,' he said shortly. 'Vulgar mind, vulgar ways. And she has a streak of malice in her which doesn't appeal to me at all. I'm grateful to her for suggesting you; I just hope the idea sprang from her love of interfering with other people's lives and getting them organized, as she put it, and not from any evil plan that we don't know about.'

Harry leant back in his chair and raised his arm to summon the waiter.

'So have we got a deal?'

I won't be cornered like this, thought Gina. 'Not yet,' she said. 'I need more time to sort everything out in my head.'

'Be my guest,' said Harry courteously. 'But then you are, aren't you.'

Touché, thought Gina, with a last glance at the sea.

CHAPTER 8

Zoë knew it was going to be a bad day before she even opened her eyes. She had a headache, for a start. One of the headaches she got on heavy Oxford days when there was thunder in the air.

The milk was off. This she discovered after she had poured some into her coffee.

The post brought an outrageous tax bill, an ecstatic postcard from a friend staying with her current lover in his villa on a private island off Sicily: 'Heaven on Earth!', a reminder from the dentist and a letter from her brother asking if she'd like to look after his three small children for a week while he and Fiona went away. 'Since we know you aren't planning to have a holiday this year, we thought it would be a nice change for you.'

In a fit of pique, Zoë deposited the post in the bin, poured the solidified cup of coffee down the sink, and set off for the station.

At least, she told herself, trying to look on the bright side, at least she had taken the day off work. Work was becoming increasingly irksome. She didn't find her colleagues interesting, she loathed her new boss, and she knew perfectly well that it was a job which was taking her nowhere. However, work wasn't so easy to find, particularly in Oxford, with hordes of keen young graduates jostling for positions. Work paid the bills. Work meant security and a pension.

Security, Zoë said to herself in disgust, as she got on to the train. Pension! What was the matter with her? She should make an effort, get another job. Perhaps move to the country, but what job could she do there? She was fed up with living in towns, though.

True, she liked Oxford, but not as much as she had done once. Oxford belonged to the incredibly young-looking undergraduates, not people like her, who had finished at the University three years ago. When she was older, she might like to come back, but now, she felt a has-been.

But such an effort to change jobs, and for what? Another office, another set of people talking about mortgages and holidays and the car. Interesting for a few months, with new work and getting to know new people, and then the same stale round.

The journey to Bath only took about an hour, but it seemed endless to Zoë. She changed at Didcot, in her mind adding giant toadstool caps to the cooling towers of the power station as the train pulled out of the station. Then into Bath, the station seething as the London train came in, delivering arty and musical types for the festival. I hate festivals, thought Zoë.

She was meeting Gina at midday.

'At Waterstones, by interesting travel books,' Gina had hissed down the line before ringing off abruptly.

There's another person whose life is a muddle, thought Zoë as she walked up Pierrepont Street. Hankering after that rather tiresome Alwyn, getting into a fix with her visa. Why isn't life simple? Why did I find Tim so boring that I had to give the only man around at present the heave-ho just at the time of year when one most needs an escort?

Zoë turned several heads on her melancholy progress through the centre of town. She didn't care for her type of looks, longing to be dark and exotic, but there were plenty who found her wide blue gaze and oval face very fetching. She was tall, too, which made it easy for Mr Popplewell to follow her; he just had to look out for her shoulder-length silver-blonde hair.

Zoë reached the bottom of Milsom Street, and balanced on the edge of the kerb, waiting to nip over the road and dive into Waterstones. She watched for a gap in the traffic and then, among the crowds waiting to cross further down, she spotted Popplewell. Being so tall and thin, with squarish specs, he was as noticeable as Zoë in his own way.

Zoë shot across the road, narrowly avoiding the screeching and hooting cars and ran into Jolly's, praying that Gina was safely inside

Waterstones. Once inside the store, she resisted her first instinct to fly, and instead slowed down to saunter through the lingerie department. That will embarrass him, she thought.

Not so. Nothing embarrassed a Popplewell in pursuit of his prey. He skulked behind the carousel of lacy bras and matching panties, looking absurd, in Zoë's view; from his own viewpoint, he was simply a man doing his duty.

Deliberately not looking in his direction, Zoë headed for the stairs. She went through the kitchen department and into the café, took a tray, carefully inspected the cakes and pastries, took two, asked for a large coffee, and threaded her way to a table on the other side. Next to the other exit.

She put everything on to a table, and then went back to the till to get a spoon, sending Popplewell hurtling back behind a wall of kitchen gadgets. Then, having sat down, she got up once again; back to the till, this time to get a napkin.

Popplewell was thrown off his stride by this to-ing and fro-ing, so he retreated a little further away, still keeping a close eye on Zoë. She was obviously settling down for a while; she had opened a book and was slowly nibbling round the edges of her first pastry.

Greed, thought Popplewell disapprovingly. Popplewell ate a wholesome diet, based on nuts and organic vegetables.

Inevitably, a shop assistant approached him, inviting him to attend the demonstration of a new grater. Momentarily, his attention was caught.

' . . . thus preserving all the vitamins and minerals in raw vegetables such as the carrot and turnip,' the assistant was saying.

Fatal lapse. He could have sworn it was only half a minute that his eye had been off Zoë. Leaving the indignant assistant in mid-sentence, he galloped through the restaurant and through the swing doors which Zoë had been sitting beside.

Zoë stepped out from a corner by the till, listened with satisfaction to the sound of clattering feet on stone stairs fading into the distance, and headed for the other stairs.

Gina was browsing among the travel books, wondering who could want to buy a guide to holiday breaks in Düsseldorf, when Zoë arrived breathless beside her.

'Quick,' she said. 'Popplewell!'

Gina stood rooted to the spot. 'Popplewell?' she repeated. 'What are you talking about?'

'He's here,' Zoë said urgently. 'In Bath. He must have followed me, horrible man. On the train, how dare he!'

'Where? In this shop?'

'No, he went whizzing out of Jolly's because he thought I had gone that way, oh, there's no time to explain. He'll probably come in here, he was always following you into bookshops, wasn't he? In Oxford?'

'He mind-reads,' said Gina crossly. 'He simply seemed to turn up wherever I was.'

'Sinister,' said Zoë, peering out of Waterstones. 'I can't see him; come on, we'll make a dash for it.'

'You look tired,' said Harry as he opened the car door for Gina. 'Did you meet your friend? Did you have a good day?'

'No,' said Gina shortly.

Harry slid the car into gear, wondering what had happened to make Gina look so tense.

'There was a tedious man hanging about, so we went to Bradford-on-Avon on a bus.'

'Very pretty, I hear, Bradford-on-Avon.'

'Maybe, if you happen to want to be there.'

'Who was this tedious guy? An admirer?'

Gina was about to explain about the awfulness of Popplewell, but then restrained herself. Better if Harry didn't know how desperate her case was. 'He follows my friend about,' she said.

'Is your friend worth following about?' asked Harry idly, increasing speed as the traffic thinned out.

'Yes,' said Gina, and, sitting back, closed her eyes.

'I see,' said Harry, switching on the radio. 'A little Bach, to soothe your fretful spirits?'

'I am not fretful,' said Gina.

'My mistake,' said Harry.

Zoë, just as fed up as Gina, tore into the station as the Oxford train was announced. She had left her book somewhere on the day's irritating roundaboutations; no way was she sitting on the train all the way to Oxford without anything to read. So she flew to the bookstall and only just made it on to the train, ending up in a crowded, hot and stuffy carriage, squashed tightly against all too many end-of-day, needing-a-shower commuters.

All I need, she thought, wrenching open the copy of *The Lady*. An article about Victorian maidservants. Who cared? Recipes for greengage jam. Greengages! Where were these people living? She flicked through several pages of neat clothes, which she dismissed out of hand as dowdy, and read the ads for school matrons, care wardens; nanny wanted for adorable four-year-old. Bet he's a baby Popplewell, thought Zoë viciously, as she ended up in the Houses-to-let section.

'Heartset,' she read. *'Cottage in peaceful village near famous Heart Gorge, 6 miles from sea. 2 beds, 2 recep, available until September. Reasonable terms. 01888 039 6007.'*

I never knew a family so keen on afternoon tea, thought Gina in an exhausted way as Harry drove at top speed towards Heartsease. 'We'll just be in time,' he said confidently, swearing at a pair on a tandem and blowing his horn furiously at a man driving a tractor.

'You're very rude,' observed Gina.

Harry gave a snort of laughter. 'That's Jack Lychen, he does it deliberately, loves to hold cars up. Needs a kick up his backside from time to time, teach him to share the road with the rest of us.'

Ruthless, thought Gina. I hate ruthless men. Popplewell, Victor, Harry. My father. Oh, hell. And she shut her eyes, trying to blot out an unsatisfactory day.

'This will revive you, Gina,' said Hester, passing her tea and a slice of cake. 'You look quite worn out. Was Bath very hot and tiring? It always gives me a headache on hot summer days, so close and heavy.'

Gina sank back into her chair and let the soothing words flow over her. The clink of fine china, the faint chocolatey smell from a delicious cake, birdsong outside the windows . . . She relaxed. Maybe life wasn't quite so unsatisfactory after all.

'Here's Nicky coming across the lawn,' said Hester. 'How hot she looks.'

Gina turned her head to see a woman with an aureole of red hair come flying into the room. 'My dears,' she said dramatically. 'The heat! I'm prostrate with exhaustion. Guy, as you love me, pour me some tea.'

'You shouldn't be in the sun at all in this weather,' said Guy earnestly, pouring her a cup of weak tea and adding a slice of lemon. 'With your complexion the sun is so dangerous.'

'I walked up from the quay,' said Nicky. 'What a mistake on a day like this.'

'You can go back along the top,' said Harry without much sympathy.

'Jarvis will drive you,' said Hester. 'I'm glad you're here, Nicky, because there are one or two points which have come up.'

Harry wandered over to the window, and Gina pulled herself upright.

'Who's that?' she said, *sotto voce*. 'More family? Should I know her?'

'Nicky? No, she isn't family, she's a neighbour. Organizes things. Helps Don with the vineyard, on the admin side. Worships him, which is very yawn-making. At the moment she's organizing this ball for Aimée.'

'Is it going to be a very big affair?'

'Yes,' said Harry. 'Everything to do with Aimée is larger than life. I expect Hester and Nicky will rope you in if you give them half a chance.'

'I'd like that,' said Gina. 'If I can be of any use.'

Harry was amused. 'I thought you were a scholar, sorting dates and poring over Tudor household accounts. A ball is hardly in your line, is it?'

'As it happens,' said Gina with dignity, 'I was on the committee for my college ball when I was doing my M.Litt., so I know a little about it.'

'I'll tell Hester,' said Harry. He glanced at Gina. 'Good time to announce a marriage, at a ball.'

'An engagement, perhaps.'

'Ah, but your circumstances won't allow all the formal doings, will they? It's going to have to be hotfoot to the registrar, everything signed and sealed.'

Yes, thought Gina gloomily, and Popplewell under the bed to make sure the marriage is consummated.

'Don't nag,' she said irritably.

Harry raised a sardonic eyebrow. 'Was I? I didn't mean to. Just reminding you that time is not on your side.'

Time never is, thought Gina.

Tea over, Gina felt that half an hour stretched out on the terrace would be a good idea.

No such luck. She had no sooner chosen a chair than there was the scrunching of feet on the gravel and Prim's voice rang out. 'Gina,' she said. 'Find a bicycle. I'm off to the vineyard; you can come too.'

It was more an order than a request; Prim had an inbuilt air of authority. Even so, as she headed for the stableyard, Gina wondered why she didn't just say no. The Cordovans have a way of taking it for granted that people will fall in with their plans, that's why, she told herself, as she wheeled the bicycle out of the stable.

She mounted and wobbled dangerously across the cobbled court and through the archway. Prim was waiting for her, resting on her bike. She led the way along one of the lower terraces and then plunged precipitously into the wood, bumping down a path made uneven by the roots of the many trees which towered above them.

'Beech,' shouted Prim. 'And larch and spruce. And holly, and oak.'

Wonderful trees, acknowledged Gina, as she fought her twisting bike; it was a relief when they turned through a gate and continued along a dusty track.

Prim braked abruptly, the tyres throwing up a jet of bone-dry earth. 'Better walk from here. Too rutted; you might fall off, Gina.'

Gina sensed that if Prim had been by herself, she would have ridden on quite happily. She didn't argue; but walked on, dabbing at her sweat-filled eyes with the corner of her T-shirt and wishing she was anywhere except in this baking heat.

'Sorry, am I going too fast?' said Prim considerately, slowing her pace.

Hate you, thought Gina. 'I'm all right,' she said untruthfully.

'Nearly there,' said Prim in bracing tones as they passed through a tall and well-worn stone archway into the central courtyard of what looked like an old church.

'This was a mediaeval priory,' Prim explained, as she balanced her bike against a sign with NO BIKES printed on it in large white letters. 'It has all the original monkish cells which Don uses for storing his wine. The monks used to make wine here, you know, a few centuries back.' She waved at one side of the building. 'Offices there, and a half-hearted shop.'

'Shop?'

'Don mostly sells to wholesalers and restaurants, but quite a lot of people these days like to buy direct. Nicky was going to run it, but she got into such a state over Don that he had to shelve the idea.'

'Nicky,' said Gina. 'The redhead.'

'Tiresome woman,' said Prim. 'It's ridiculous to get het up about a man like that. Any man, doesn't matter who it is; he won't be worth it. I've never got into a state over any man, I'm thankful to say. Enjoy them while you're with them, then leave well alone.'

Gina was intrigued by this glimpse into Prim's private life, and would like to have heard more, but Prim was on the move again. 'We'll go and see the vines,' she said, heading off to a wooden door in one corner of the courtyard. 'Do you know anything about wine, Gina?'

'I used to . . . I've stayed with some friends who owned a vineyard in California,' said Gina.

Prim turned her head and looked at her with interest. 'A brief visit?' she asked.

I don't think living there for ten years counts as brief, thought Gina. 'I went most summers for a while,' she said.

'Excellent,' said Prim. 'You'll have a good idea what's going on here. Can you see Don?'

'I don't know what he looks like,' said Gina.

'Don't you remember him? No, I don't suppose you would; both children last time you saw each other.' Prim shaded her eyes and looked down over the terraced vines which stretched right across the hill and down nearly to the river. 'He'll be down here somewhere,' she said confidently.

He wasn't. At that moment, Don was in the shop, or what passed for a shop, serving a pair of customers who had bought a bottle of the best sparkling wine, and then discovered they had no money to pay for it.

The wife knew instantly who was to blame. 'Idiot,' she spat at her husband. 'To come all this way, in the heat, and then discover you have left the cheque-book and your wallet at home.'

'I thought you had the cheque-book, in your bag,' he said.

Unwise.

'And where is this bag? You drag me out on this impossible day, saying we must choose this special wine together, and expect me to carry a huge, heavy bag?'

'It isn't huge,' protested the man.

His wife was just beginning to enjoy herself. 'And in any case, I don't want to have this nasty English wine, made from turnips or nettles, and done up in fancy bottles. Why not champagne, and bought from a proper shop, not this shed with no proper facilities? You make such a song and dance about our wedding anniversary, but do you care so very much? Not enough to buy good wine in a good shop!'

The man, thin, dark and worried, with a clever face, looked appalled.

'Nadia, this is proper wine, the best. I wanted us to have this tonight to celebrate being here in Heartset and because it's our anniversary.'

'That for so-called English wine,' said Nadia with a snap of her fingers.

Don was enjoying the scene. Nadia, with her black hair, high cheek-bones and dark eyes sparkling with temper was well worth looking at.

'The wine is good,' he assured her.

'It doesn't matter if it's good or not, we have nothing to pay for it with. And I tell you, my husband has no money to pay for luxuries such as good wine even when he remembers his wallet, because he is one useless man, in every way useless. And I don't believe you in any case, you work here, of course you say the wine is good. Otherwise you'd lose your job.'

'Madam, I own the vineyard,' Don said gravely.

'Then I feel sorry for you,' she came back instantly. 'To pretend to make good wine; to grow grapes here in England is stupid.'

She folded her arms and swung round to turn her back on them.

Don's mouth twitched. 'Are you staying near here?' he asked.

The man sighed. 'Not staying, exactly. We've just moved here; we've bought Oracle Cottage.'

Don came out from behind the rudimentary counter and held out his hand. 'Don Cordovan,' he said.

'Wintersett,' the dark man said. 'Byron Wintersett.'

Don raised an eyebrow.

'Yes, unfortunate, but true,' said the man. 'He was an ancestor, you see, and my mother's favourite poet.'

'You could always call yourself Ronnie, I suppose,' said Don.

'Yes, I could, couldn't I?'

Don laughed. 'My real name is Dennis,' he said. 'More unfortunate than Byron, in my opinion. Look, take the bottle, drop in and settle up at any time.'

Nadia spun round. 'Ha, now you start living on tick.'

'Hardly tick,' Byron protested mildly.

'Tick. I don't want to drink wine that hasn't been paid for.'

'In that case,' said Don, 'please accept the bottle as a house-warming present from me. If Oracle Cottage is still the way I remember it, you're going to need some cheering up.'

Gina stood uncertainly at the threshold of the shop, wondering at the wild words hurling past her as Nadia worked herself up for a full-blown tantrum. A dark man was looking helplessly at her, and another, shorter man, youngish, with a good-humoured face had retreated behind the counter.

Which is Don? thought Gina. The tall dark one, or the other one with the delightful twinkle and the big nose and the early signs of baldness? Neither looked at all like the other Cordovans; perhaps Don was elsewhere.

Prim came briskly into the shop and answered her unspoken question. She took one look around the shop, and pounced on her nephew. 'Don,' she said. 'What is going on? Why are you cowering there?'

'I'm not cowering, Prim,' said Don, recovering his dignity.

Not at all like the others, thought Gina, but what a nice man! She felt surprisingly drawn to him; given what the Cordovans she had

90

met so far were like, Don was definitely a surprise on the right side of the ledger.

'And who is this shrieking foreigner?' went on Prim, looking at Nadia with such disapproval that Gina wanted to laugh.

'A new neighbour,' began Don, but he was interrupted by a new torrent from Nadia.

'I am not a foreigner. I am English, I have a passport to prove it, there is no question of it, here is my husband, English to the tip of his . . .'

'That's enough,' said Prim in quelling tones. 'Of course you're not English, English people don't behave like this. What are you, Russian? Polish?'

'Now she calls me Polish.'

'Bother you, Prim,' said Don. 'You've set her off again.'

'Nonsense,' said Prim. 'That's enough, wherever you come from. I can't believe that any nation would put up with scenes like that, quite unnecessary.'

Nadia, momentarily silenced, stared resentfully at Prim.

'Neighbours, did Don say?' Prim addressed Byron, ignoring Nadia's flashing eyes. 'Where do you live?'

'We've just bought Oracle Cottage,' said Byron.

'It's a wreck,' said Prim matter-of-factly.

Byron smiled for the first time, a slightly crooked smile that lit up his dark face in a most attractive way, thought Gina.

'A wreck indeed,' he said. 'We're more or less camping out there at the moment, but I hope to restore it quite quickly. I'm an architect, you see.'

'Ha,' said Nadia. 'An unemployed architect, tell them that,' she said.

'Stop breathing so hard and heaving like that,' said Prim. 'You'll hyperventilate, it's very bad for the system. An architect? New houses or old?'

'I mostly do restoration and conservation work,' said Byron. 'Nadia's right, though, the firm I worked for in London has just gone under; there isn't a lot of work around at the moment.'

'You'll have plenty to do with Oracle Cottage,' said Prim. 'What does your wife do?'

Gina thought that it must be very annoying to have someone ask your husband what you did instead of applying directly to you, but on the other hand, it didn't seem likely that Nadia would answer sensibly at present.

'She's a linguist,' said Byron, with some pride.

'Not much call for linguists in this part of the world,' said Prim. 'Better find yourself something else to do, help your husband through a difficult time.'

Nadia curled her lip scornfully at Prim. 'I can tell you what I wouldn't do, and that's have a crummy shop like this. You say this wine is good, which I certainly don't believe, and nor would anyone else, if they came here to buy it. It isn't old-fashioned or rustic or charming in here, just shabby and depressing-looking. And, if you sell fine wine, then where are other fine things to go with it? Delicacies, for instance. Hopeless!'

Don gave Nadia a warm smile. 'I dare say you're right, Mrs Wintersett, but I'm busy on the growing and production side, and I don't have time for a shop.'

'Then find someone who does.'

'I did, and she . . . um, found she couldn't manage it.'

'Give me that wine,' said Nadia, snatching the bottle out of Don's hand. 'Also some of that, what do you say it is? Chardonnay? We shall see. And we'll take a bottle of that, too.'

Byron was looking uncomfortable. 'Nadia, you're forgetting that we left our money behind. And besides . . .'

' . . . And besides, we can't afford bottles of wine. I know. But we are buying this; yes,' she said as she whirled round at Don, 'we will buy it with our hard-earned cash, not being a plutocrat like you. I will bring the money tomorrow. Then I will see if it's any good, and if it is, then I will come and make a shop here for you, full of such things that people will come for miles around to buy wine and food here.'

She swept up the wine and her husband, and sailed out of the shop, giving Prim a look of loathing as she went.

'Foreigners,' said Prim.

CHAPTER 9

'What are you doing?' said Fergus.

Zoë looked up from a pile of papers. 'Sums,' she said succinctly, returning to the pile.

'Overdrawn again?'

'Not at all,' said Zoë with dignity. 'I'm twenty-three pounds in credit.'

'And only three weeks until you get paid.'

'I shall economize.'

'Starve, more like.'

Zoë pushed her chair back from the kitchen table and ran her fingers through her hair. 'Hell,' she said, without rancour.

'Why hell at this particular moment?' said Fergus, picking up another kitchen chair and planting himself down on it. 'What's different from last month, or any other month? You usually manage.'

'I don't want to manage,' said Zoë crossly. 'I want to go on holiday. In fact,' she said, her eyes narrowing in concentrated thought, 'I want to give up my job.'

'Ah,' said Fergus.

'Ah, nothing. I hate my job, I find it utterly boring and unrewarding. And I don't want to do it any more.'

'Then a holiday is a necessity,' said Fergus calmly. 'Two or three weeks on the Mediterranean or the hills of Italy, and everything will look quite different when you come back.'

'Yes, worse.'

'You'll feel refreshed, and the job will seem much more tolerable.'

'Not unless there's a coup in my absence, and all the people working there change, and the work transforms itself into something entirely different.'

'Have you spoken to your boss about how you feel?'

'Does one converse with a python?'

'Zoë,' said Fergus, laughing at her tragic expression. 'Come on, it isn't that bad. Do you want to earn more money, is that it?'

'No. I mean, yes, of course I want to earn more money. Who doesn't? And, all right, you don't need to say it, it's folly to even think of throwing up a job when all around are people who've been made redundant and can't get another job, or people who've never even got to first base jobwise.'

'It wouldn't be very sensible. Have a holiday, get into a better frame of mind, stick with your present job for the time being and look around for something else meanwhile.'

Zoë rounded on Fergus. 'Easy for you to be sensible and practical! You've never had a job; oh, I know you've worked in the morgue in your vacs and all the usual things, but not a day-in, day-out office job. With a pension. You just go on being a student, you have no idea what it's like for the rest of us.'

Fergus had to admit that Zoë was right. 'This is a treat in store for me. But honestly, Zoë, you can't afford to give up your job. Twenty-three pounds isn't going to last you long.'

'No, I suppose not,' said Zoë. 'Make some coffee, Fergus, out of kindness; I must clear my fuddled head.'

Fergus busied himself with beans; he loved using the grinder.

'You haven't heard from Gina, have you?' he said casually, tipping the ground coffee into the glass jug.

'Heard from Gina?' said Zoë, her mind moving reluctantly into gear. Sharpen your wits, she told herself. 'No, why should I?'

'She hasn't phoned or anything?'

'I would have told you if there'd been a call from America.'

'I just hope she found somewhere to stay. I'm worried about her.'

'Don't be; I'm quite sure she's got somewhere to stay. Somewhere really nice.'

'Look, I just think she might have had problems finding a place, if her father wasn't there when she got to New York. You don't seem very concerned,' he added crossly.

'Problems?' said Zoë. 'Oh, no, I don't think so. Not in New York.'

Fergus wondered at Zoë's slightly disconnected answers. 'You sound as though you need that coffee. Here you are.' He put her coffee down in front of her. 'Black, to wake you up. I'm surprised that Gina hasn't been in touch, that's all. She could have written to you, and you'd forgotten to mention it.'

'If she'd written, I would have told you,' said Zoë, picking her words carefully.

'Lord,' said Fergus. 'Talking of letters, I nearly forgot. There's one for you; it came this morning after you'd left. Looks like a bill.'

Zoë took it, made a face, and put it on the table unopened.

'Open it up,' said Fergus. 'That twenty-three pounds may not be enough.'

'You open it if you're so keen,' said Zoë, wandering over to the sink to rinse out some mugs. 'And when you've read it, you can put it in the bin. That's where all my post goes these days; it's far too depressing to keep.'

'Wow,' said Fergus, investigating the contents of the envelope. 'I'll put it in the bin if you like, Zoë, but it seems a shame.'

'How much?' said Zoë in gloomy tones.

'Two and a half thou,' said Fergus.

Zoë shrieked and dropped a mug, which broke neatly in half as it hit the floor.

'That's my Spot mug,' said Fergus in aggrieved tones.

Zoë snatched the paper from Fergus. 'Oh, my God, you're right. How can I owe that much, what's it for?'

'Zoë,' said Fergus patiently, 'calm down. You don't owe them, they're paying you. There's a cheque in the envelope, look.'

Zoë stood in utter disbelief, gazing at the cheque.

Fergus bent down to pick up the broken pieces of mug. 'What are you going to spend it on, apart from a new mug for me, of course?'

'Where did it come from?' said Zoë, still bemused.

'The letter tells you,' said Fergus. 'It's a prize draw. Did you go in for a prize draw?'

'I must have done,' said Zoë doubtfully. 'I can't say I remember entering anything.'

'It doesn't matter,' said Fergus. 'Let me see the letter again. Look, you must have bought a ticket at that show we went to in the spring.'

Zoë was sitting at the table again, scuffling through her bills, making a kind of chanting noise. A thought struck her. 'Fergus, do I have to pay tax on this?'

'No, I don't think so,' said Fergus. 'If I were you, I'd put half of it in the bank, and blue the other half on a holiday.'

'Don't be so depressing,' said Zoë. 'First, I'm going to take you out for dinner. Then I'm going to give in my notice and go on a shopping spree for some new clothes, what bliss. And then I'm going to take a cottage in a particularly pleasant part of the countryside for at least four weeks.'

'Most unwise,' said Fergus, shaking his head.

'I've got the rest of my life to be wise,' said Zoë.

Gina found Nicky installed in the Little Library, a perfect oval room which was lined with curved bookshelves. Nicky was sitting at a table in the centre of the room, stacked trays of papers neatly in front of her and a telephone at her side.

'Hi,' said Gina. 'Can I help?'

Nicky looked at her doubtfully. 'Help?'

'With the arrangements for the ball. Harry said you might like some help.'

'Harry said? When did any Cordovan think about helping anyone but themselves? And you're one of them, aren't you?'

'Not exactly, no,' said Gina, perching on the table. 'Is there a lot to do?'

'Yes,' said Nicky with no very great enthusiasm. 'It's my job, so I can't complain.'

'It's interesting, though, isn't it? Organizing parties and so on for other people.'

'I don't mind the food,' said Nicky. 'The rest of it is fairly tedious. Everyone wants a new theme, each one has to be smarter and bolder than the neighbours'. By the end of the season you're racking your brains to come up with anything different.'

'Does Aimée want something different?'

'Oh, the Cordovans don't give a bugger what their neighbours have had, they couldn't care less about being smarter or grander. They just take it for granted that what they want is automatically fine. Don't you loathe them?'

'Um,' said Gina. 'I don't know them very well. I can't say I do loathe them, no.'

'Harry's probably the best of them, he seems to be taking good care of you. He'll have an ulterior purpose, though, don't let your guard down for a moment.'

Gina was intrigued by Nicky's dark comments. 'I met a woman who lives in Heartwell House,' she said. 'She doesn't like the family much, either.'

'Her,' said Nicky, dismissively. 'Her! She's just beside herself because the Cordovans aren't remotely interested in being what she would call good neighbours, meaning asking her and her ghastly husband to dinner, helping with the fête and generally joining with her in patronizing everyone in sight.'

'I thought you said the Cordovans were patronizing.'

Nicky stared at her. 'I said no such thing. The Cordovans are arrogant, ruthless, oblivious of anybody else's well-being and generally all-round wicked, but patronizing, no. It wouldn't even occur to them. The world divides itself into people they know and like and the rest, who have no existence as far as they are concerned. Victor met that woman in a memorable encounter over his prize cattle, and knew at once that she wasn't going on his list of people he knows and likes. She made no effort to attract him, so he's unlikely to want to take her to bed; they haven't a hope of getting in here, however hard they try.'

'Perhaps Lori isn't Victor's type.'

Nicky gave her a penetrating look. 'He hasn't got a type,' she said directly. 'And I hope you haven't succumbed to Victor's charms, because although he's rarely averse to a quick swive while Julia's attention is elsewhere, he's at the moment in hot pursuit of a Swiss girl. She's got amazing tits; he loves big breasts.'

'Where does she live?' said Gina, intrigued.

'Where do you think? Switzerland, of course.'

'Then he doesn't see much of her.'

'Nonsense, he flies over every week. He's there today, as a matter of fact. Didn't you notice he wasn't there at breakfast?'

'I was a bit late down,' admitted Gina.

Nicky turned her attention back to the list in her hand. 'If you really want to help, you can find me a pavilion.'

'Pavilion?'

'Yes, you know, the kind of tent affair they had at mediaeval jousts – or so Hollywood would have us believe. Swagged and colourful.'

'Is there a firm which does such things?'

'Yes, but there are none available for that date. We should have booked months ago. You see, the message was, no marquees. They all hate marquees here; quite right, too. And they don't need a marquee, not with the Great Hall and all the other good-sized rooms.'

'So why the pavilion?'

'A last-minute whim of Aimée's. For the disco. On the lawn beyond the terrace. Pretty idea, and quite feasible, but it has to be this particular kind of pavilion. Done up inside in an oriental style to boot; I think she's been watching old Rudolf Valentino films. That's my big headache of the moment, so if you can solve that, I'll be your best friend. I suppose you don't actually work for a living, do you? Aren't you porky treats?'

'I'm also an historian,' said Gina, forgetting herself for a moment.

'Well, tracking down a mediaeval pavilion should be right up your street,' said Nicky, not sounding very hopeful.

'Give me the number of the people who do these tents, and tell me where there's a phone I can use, and I'll see what I can do.'

'I told you, sweetie, booked solid, nothing to be got out of them,' said Nicky, handing her a card.

'No, but they may give me a lead,' said Gina.

Nicky shrugged. 'I shan't blame you if you don't get anywhere, I'll just shout and curse in my normal way. Phone and a table through there, in the library proper, be my guest.'

Byron was feeling extremely hungry. He had breakfasted on a bar of chocolate, having been ejected from their diminutive temporary kitchen by Nadia in one of her most forceful moods.

'I have no time for you at all today, no, and probably not tomorrow either. You'll have to feed yourself, eat dandelions, I don't care; just leave me to get on with this.'

'I'll get myself a sandwich for lunch.'

'Do that.'

He looked at the wrapped pies and pasties in the village shop and sighed. He didn't feel quite so hungry any more. He bought a paper, murmured his thanks, and wandered out of the shop. The Bunch of Grapes beckoned invitingly from the other side of the little square. 'Beer Garden,' the sign read. 'Freshly made sandwiches and bar food.'

I can't afford pub lunches, Byron told himself sternly. Poof, said his unruly self. Drop in the ocean; what difference will a sandwich and a pint of beer make? Think of the size of your overdraft and the fact that after the end of this month you won't have a penny coming in.

'Good afternoon,' said a friendly voice behind him. 'Coming for a jar?'

It was Don Cordovan.

'Hello,' said Byron.

Good. It would be bad manners not to accompany him.

'I often pop in here for a quick lunch,' said Don, greeting the bosomy blonde woman behind the bar with a cheerful wave as he headed for what was clearly his usual table. 'I like it here,' he told Byron. 'Fresh air from the garden, but not too many buzzing things flopping into one's beer. I find the outdoor life greatly overrated, especially during a hot English summer. And then, indoors, you get Madge's astonishing bosom to gaze upon.'

'There is that,' said Byron.

'Look, but don't touch,' said Don. 'Madge's husband is a big man with a quick temper.'

'You must spend a lot of time out of doors,' said Byron, looking at Don's smooth tan.

'Ah, work, that's different. Now, what will you have? Here's the delectable Madge come to take our order. If that's fish pie I can smell, Madge, I'll have some. I can recommend it, Byron, they make it with swordfish and mussels and prawns and plenty of cream.'

'I was going to have a sandwich,' said Byron doubtfully.

'Fish pie for two,' said Don. 'And I'm buying the drinks, this is my home ground.'

Byron took several grateful gulps of the cold beer.

'How's Oracle Cottage?' asked Don.

'Not too good,' said Byron. 'Worse than I'd expected. It's going to take a lot of time.'

'Get a firm in,' advised Don.

'Can't afford it,' said Byron. 'Not until I can find some work.'

'Lot of old houses around here.'

'Yes, but probably not needing my services. Or able to afford them. Householders aren't exactly splashing out these days.'

'A lot of you architects in the same boat, I understand,' said Don with sympathy.

'Yes, too many of us around.'

Madge brought two plates of fragrant fish pie. Byron's hunger had returned with force; I hate sandwiches, he reminded himself as he plunged his fork in.

Don applied himself to a mussel. 'What's your wife up to?'

'Nadia? God knows. I expect you'll find out in due course.'

'Good cook, is she?'

'Very, when she wants to be. She doesn't often cook for me, unfortunately, but I know when we've had friends and so on she produces the goods.'

'What is she, Russian?'

'Yes.'

'Met her over there, did you?'

The fish pie didn't taste quite so delicious any more.

'Yes,' said Byron.

'Fell in love, got married, new freedoms with the fall of the Berlin Wall?'

'No, it was ten years ago,' said Byron. 'And yes, I fell in love with her, and married her.'

'Ten years. No children?'

'Nadia doesn't want children,' said Byron shortly. 'She wanted, and got, a British passport, life in the West, a professional husband. Not, I fear, as successful a husband as she would have liked, but there you are.'

'She's still with you after ten years,' pointed out Don.

'Yes, and I often wonder why,' said Byron. 'Perhaps after a week or two in Oracle Cottage, she won't still be with me. We've had the odd sticky patch, but nothing like this before.'

'Women are very surprising,' said Don.

'Are you married?' asked Byron.

'No, no,' said Don.

'A particular friend?'

'Oh, several.'

Byron sighed. He wasn't envious of Don, he was just thinking how appalling it would be to have not one Nadia to cope with, but a clutch of them.

'Hard work,' he said. 'Several, I mean.'

'But rewarding,' said Don, wiping his mouth with the napkin.

It was fish on the menu elsewhere that lunchtime. Guy was loud in his praise of Maria's paella as he deftly heaped it on to a huge oval dish. 'Not that it isn't always good, but this is perfect.'

'A pity then that people are late for lunch!'

Gina had been very apologetic when Guy had finally tracked her down to the library.

'I ring a bell,' he said.

'I was on the phone,' said Gina.

Guy's expression clearly said that good guests were not on the phone at lunchtime.

'Phoning Uish?' said Harry slyly.

'Actually,' said Gina, sliding into her seat, 'I was ringing up about a pavilion for Aimée's ball.'

Aimée pushed her glossy dark hair back from her face and gave Gina a ravishing smile. 'Nicky says you've found just what we need,' she said. 'From a film company.'

'Neat work, that,' said Harry. 'Julia, we ought to buy one of those pavilion things, I was looking at the pic. Just right for the garden here. Rig it up as an outside dining-room.'

Julia looked disapproving. 'Very uncomfortable, when we have a perfectly good dining-room in the house.'

'Where's the romance in that?' said Harry. 'Think of it. Long summer evenings, late sunlight dappling the canvas, little pennants fluttering in the breeze.'

Aimée's eyes shone. 'A bower of bliss,' she said happily. 'With silken cushions and Persian rugs.'

'And several packets of Kleenex for afterwards,' said Harry sourly.

'Don't be crude,' said Julia. 'Aimée, you must try not to dwell quite so much on the erotic side of life.'

'It's the only side of life that interests me,' said Aimée simply, forking a mouthful of paella into her mouth. She gave her shoulders a languorous shrug. 'Some people have a talent for mundane matters, such as accounts or gardening or diseases. I have a talent for love. Lucky me.'

Julia gave up. 'I shall want to eat early tonight, Guy. Please tell Maria.'

'Off on a toot while Victor's away?' enquired Harry.

Julia's look would have quelled anyone but Harry. 'I am attending a meeting in Heartsbury. On teaching safe sex in schools.'

Aimée looked up. 'How boring,' she said in her soft voice. 'Safety and sex, ugh!'

Harry laughed. 'A contradiction in terms, don't you think, Julia?'

'I have no time for it,' said Julia. 'If schools spent more time teaching proper academic subjects, and less time on how to be a Lesbian and introducing sadomasochism, these poor young people would all be much better off.'

'We had condoms on bananas at school,' said Aimée, thoughtfully selecting a peach from the well-filled fruit bowl. 'It was disgusting, and quite unnecessary.'

'Liberals,' said Julia scornfully. 'All quaint ideas and no sense. Guy, I shall be in the study this afternoon. I'll have tea in there at four-thirty. And please bring it yourself; Esme broke a cup last time.'

Guy nodded. 'Coffee now?'

'No, thank you,' said Julia. 'Harry, you're spending too much time at home. Your business will suffer.'

'My business is fine, Julia.'

'It won't be if you neglect it.'

CHAPTER 10

'Hi, Pa,' Harry called down from an upstairs window.

Victor stopped, looked up, glared, and went on his way into the house.

'No luck,' said Harry, startling Gina as he landed beside her.

'I thought you were upstairs,' she said.

'I was, in my room, but I slid down the banisters. Thus puzzling you with my speedy arrival,' he explained.

'Who's had no luck?' asked Gina.

'Pa. With his Swiss bint.'

'How do you know?'

'I can always tell,' said Harry. 'If all had gone well, meaning that he'd got her into bed at last, there would be a happy curl to the mouth, a lightness of step, a general air of being well-pleased with himself. These characteristics are, you can see for yourself, all absent.'

'How absurd,' said Gina, laughing.

'Don't mock,' said Harry. 'It's true. He's walking firmly, he isn't smiling, there's a look of pent-up energy, so clearly the chase is still on.'

'What about Julia?'

'Julia will do all right, he'll pounce tonight. Of course Julia knows exactly what he's up to, so she'll give him a hard time.'

'You're very disrespectful about your parents. Apart from speculating on their private moments together.'

'One, they aren't my parents,' said Harry, counting off on his fingers. 'Okay, Victor is, but not Julia. Two, it isn't disrespectful, just honest. Three, these moments aren't so private. Julia hurls abuse at him, the whole house resonates. Just you wait. It reaches a crescendo, and then . . . Silence. And you don't need to have any imagination to complete the scenario. Besides,' he continued, taking Gina by the arm and leading her out of the door and towards the orchard, 'I hate Julia; why should I be respectful?'

'You hate her? Why?'

'She nags,' said Harry.

'Nonsense,' said Gina bracingly. She was thinking about Victor. 'Does your father often have these, oh, fancies?'

'All the time,' said Harry cheerfully.

'No wonder Julia gets narked. I wouldn't put up with it.'

'She'd be jealous even if he didn't give her any grounds, it's in her nature. So he might as well go ahead and enjoy himself.'

'What happens if he really falls for one of these other women? Wants to divorce Julia?'

'I told you, he's already done that. They didn't marry again, as far as I know. I suppose my ma divorced him; I hope so, since she's acquired a new husband.'

'So Victor could just arrive back at Heartsease with a new wife?'

'He's too canny for that. Can you imagine the scenes? And another thing, Hester wouldn't like it. Victor relies very heavily on Hester for all his creature comforts. Besides, he always comes back to base; these others are just flings. It's not altogether surprising; I have to admit, Julia's got what it takes. If you like that type, which I don't; all cow's eyes and creamy flesh. Of course, what's really funny is when some other man starts making up to Julia. Wow!'

'Not allowed?'

'Definitely on the no-no list as far as Victor's concerned.'

Gina's mind was in the Alps. 'If this Swiss girl isn't interested, why does he bother?'

'He loves the chase,' said Harry simply. 'He can plot and plan and work out strategies. I have to say, he's usually successful in the end. After all, he's got a lot going for him, even if he isn't young. Still plenty of action there, one supposes.'

'Are you going to be the same?' asked Gina, leaning against a gnarled apple tree and looking thoughtfully at Harry.

'Me? Good Lord, no. Wonderful in bed, of course, please try me; but I'm much more the faithful type than Pa. When I find my heart's delight, that's it. Or even if I don't, I still won't emulate Victor.'

'What is your type?' Gina asked.

Harry wasn't going to be caught out like that. 'Dark, with sparkling if wounded eyes, abandoned curls, tallish, slim . . .'

'Not like your father, then.'

'His tastes are exaggerated,' said Harry primly.

'I don't believe a word of it,' said Gina. 'I expect voluptuous silver blondes are what you go for.' She plucked a green fruit from the tree. 'Have a sour apple.'

'Thank you,' said Harry courteously.

Guy knocked loudly on Esme's door. 'Esme? Where are you? What are you doing? You're needed in the kitchen, it's a full house tonight.'

He was answered by a soft wailing sound. He paused for a moment, and then opened the door. Esme was lying, face down on the bed, stark naked.

Guy averted his eyes. 'Esme, why are you making that peculiar noise? Are you in pain?'

Esme twisted her head round to look at him. 'I should say so; agony is what I'm in.'

'Have you eaten something?'

'No, I've been out in the sun and I've burned my bum.'

Guy took a quick look at that portion of Esme's anatomy. Her large and handsome bottom was indeed very red.

'I can't move,' said Esme.

'And what were you doing in the sun with a bare backside, as if I couldn't guess?' said Guy severely.

'None of your business. But I can't work tonight.'

'Indeed you can,' said Guy. 'Victor's back, the whole family will be in for dinner, we can't do without you. Wait there.'

'Listen, I'm not going anywhere, mate. Just don't you think you're going to get me up,' she yelled after him as he slipped quietly out of the room.

He was back in a few minutes, with aspirin and a tub of homeopathic belladonna tablets in one hand and a tube of painkilling sunburn lotion in the other.

'Take these two by mouth,' he said, 'and apply this externally to the other end.'

'I can't,' moaned Esme. 'You'll have to do it.'

'Oh, really,' said Guy.

'It's nothing to you, a woman's bum. Get on with it.'

'I never thought the day would come when I'd have to do this,' said Guy with distaste, smearing the lotion liberally over the affected parts.

'Shut your eyes, you might get to enjoy it,' said Esme.

'I hardly think so,' said Guy with dignity. 'There. Now, get up, get dressed and get yourself into the kitchen. You've got five minutes.'

'Fascist,' muttered Esme, as Guy shut the door behind him.

Gina was alone with her thoughts, and she wasn't finding them good company. Hester had gone shopping, and Gina was regretting that she hadn't gone with her, for there was nothing particular to do at the Hall. Harry was in Bath for the afternoon, Nicky was in London, the kitchen was abuzz with some special effort of Maria's.

It was too hot to cycle, too hot for any but the most minimal effort. She would walk down through the woods to the river and wander along the bank. Gina didn't feel in the mood for Cordovans at the moment, and there was little chance of meeting any of them down by the river.

She set off across the terraces. The Cordovans were a very hard-working lot, she had to admit. She had always imagined that to be rich was to have limitless leisure and few worries. A state so far removed from her own experience that she had never seriously contemplated how the rich filled their days. No need to strive to pay the rent or to find the wherewithal to buy a new car or to save for a holiday; a recipe for idleness. Yet the Cordovans all seemed to be busy from dawn to dusk.

Aimée? She was the exception. There was a life spent in the pursuit of pleasure, to be sure. Although, presumably, you didn't have to be rich in order to spend your days like that. All you'd need to do would be to pick your lovers judiciously and funds would doubtless be there for whatever you wanted.

Musing on the turbulent lives of her hosts, Gina walked and slipped and slithered down the steep paths which zig-zagged their way down to the banks of the River Heart. She rejected the broad, grassy tracks, which led gently downwards; feeling reckless, she took short-cuts, plunging off the path and down steep and narrow tracks.

Hardly wide enough for a bunny, Gina said to herself as she hurtled down an extra slippery patch. Good thing she was wearing trousers, otherwise her legs would be a mass of scratches. As it was, she was glad to get to the bottom and on to a more orderly path, which wound its way along beside the meandering river.

Gina had borrowed a map from Hester. Was there anything a visitor might need that she couldn't at once provide? Gina wondered as she unfolded the sheet. Bend in the river . . . she looked up. Check, yes, bend in the river. On the other hand, there were several bends in the river; you could in fact say the river was all bends. So you couldn't be sure which one this was.

Gina looked for other landmarks. Dovecote, the map said. Yes, she'd passed a dovecote on her way down. A large, pretty building with a domed roof and much fluttering of white wings as she'd approached. But had she gone on down this path, or that one there?

Gina gave up, and tucked the map away. She could walk along the river either way. She felt in her pocket for a 10p piece she'd noticed there. 'Heads right, tails left,' she said, flipping the coin. Tails, so to the left.

Gina walked slowly along, ducking now and again under the long green branches which hung over the path and dipped down into the water. She felt hot, jungly hot, so kept in the shade as much as she could, relishing the whisper of a breeze which now and then stirred the leaves for a moment, and sent little ripples across the surface of the water.

She paused to admire a heron, fishing among the thick rushes at the water's edge. Far away, in another great bend of the river, she could make out the figures of two men in a boat. They were doing something with nets as they worked their way up against the current.

I can hear peacocks, too, she thought; they would be up at the hall, trailing their feathers across the terrace.

She smiled as a kingfisher zoomed past in a flash of colour. I feel happy, Gina thought suddenly. Perfectly happy, with a happiness like that of a summer childhood, with no yesterday and no tomorrow. No fears, no worries, just a warm and delightful and fascinating world.

Happy?

Gina's adult self wasn't having any of that. Think of all you've got to worry about.

You're an impostor who could be unmasked at any moment.

You need to make a decision about Harry.

Victor has been eyeing you, and you have to admit it, you find him pretty attractive.

You have no money.

And that lot's just for starters. These hours of pastoral idyll are pure illusion. Stop trying to dream the hours away, there's no way to escape reality.

Reality? Gina had no time for reality this afternoon. It was too hot, too pleasant for reality. Reality could wait.

She passed two small boys fishing with their father. He touched his tweed hat – tweed hat? in this weather? – as she went past; one of the boys gave a pleased wiggle as he felt a bite on his line.

The grassy path became more pebbly, more purposeful. A sign said, To the Quay.

I don't want the quay, thought Gina. Quay suggested activity and people. I'll take the other fork, she decided.

And about a quarter of a mile further on, the dusty lane became altogether more serious, with tarmac and trimmed grassy sides. She had come to a village. Heartsbane, said this sign. Underneath, in scrawly letters, a wit had written: 'Twinned with Coeur de Lyons'.

Heartsbane didn't have a green. It had a single road, lined with houses, opening out into a small square with a horse trough set against one wall and a trickle of water pouring into it from a spout above. That was the only sound or movement. The inn sign with its gaudy purple grapes hung straight and still in the heavy air.

Just as Gina was thinking how peaceful it was, a series of shrieks and a stream of foreign words ruptured the tranquil spell. Gina didn't exactly understand them, although one or two seemed vaguely familiar. However, a curse is a curse the world over.

The sounds were coming from a tumbledown cottage set slightly back from the road on the other side of the square. Gina, always curious, headed for the noise. She tracked its source to an open window at the side of the cottage, and, opening the gate which hung on a single hinge, went to investigate.

'Huh, come to pry and poke your English nose into what doesn't concern you!'

Gina drew back. Then she recognized the speaker. 'Hello,' she said. 'You were in the shop at the vineyard. Is something wrong? Can I help?'

It was an unnecessary question, and Gina was already on her way in through the kitchen door. She leant over the sink and heaved the sash window up, holding it while Nadia removed her arm. She lightened her hold and the window crashed down vindictively.

Nadia was clutching her arm with her other hand; her imprecations were louder and sounded much more threatening.

'Run it under cold water,' said Gina practically. 'That will help the bruising.'

'This bruising needs no help,' said Nadia dramatically. 'It will leave me black and blue without any help from cold water.'

'No, I mean the cold water will *reduce* the bruising,' said Gina, turning the tap full on. It belched, banged and finally spat out a few brown blotches.

'Oh.'

'You see?' yelled Nadia. 'You see what I have to put up with? The window attacks me. The imbecile has turned the water off, so that all I get is brown bits. How can I cook in these conditions?'

Looking around, it seemed a miracle to Gina that Nadia could even think of cooking in the tiny kitchen. So cramped, and so hot; what a pointless way to spend an afternoon.

'Do you need to cook?' said Gina doubtfully. 'On such a hot day? Wouldn't a salad be easier?'

'Of course, we live on salad, I will cook nothing for us in this horrible place. But I cook for that Cordovan man who grows wine, to show him what he should be doing in that nasty little place he calls a shop.'

'Don,' said Gina.

'Yes, Don he calls himself, although I don't know what kind of name that is for a serious man of property.'

'What are you making?'

'I have made it. Complete, finished. I was leaning over to open the window to give me some fresh air while I cleared up, and whoosh, down it comes, cutting my hand off.'

'So what is it?'

'What you're looking at there is wild boar pâté.'

'Wild boar?' Gina stared at Nadia in amazement. 'Where did you get wild boar?'

'The forests here are full of wild boar,' said Nadia with satisfaction.

'Are you sure?'

'It's farmed,' said a man's voice just behind Gina. 'The boars are kept in a fenced area of wood up near Corda Episcopi.' He noticed Nadia's immobile arm. 'Nadia, have you hurt yourself?'

Nadia's eyes flashed. 'Yes, because you cannot be bothered to fix the window when I ask you to.'

Byron was very apologetic. 'I was going to do it, Nadia, it's on my list.' He wiped a dusty arm across his hot face. 'There's so much to do, that's the trouble. Listen, is that arm okay? Did the window come down on it very heavily? Should we get a doctor to look at it?'

'This person here . . .'

'Gina,' she said helpfully.

'This Gina here tried to run cold water on to it. But, no, there is no water because you have turned it off.'

'Lord, of course. Darling, I'm so sorry, I'll go and put it back on straight away.'

He dived round to the front of the cottage; the tap gave a final shudder and murky water shot out with great force.

'Nothing wrong with your water pressure at any rate,' said Don, appearing at the cottage gate. 'Is this a party? Does one have to be invited?'

'You,' spat Nadia. 'It's to show *you* how things should be done that I take all this trouble.'

Don smiled at her. 'Thank you,' he said.

'I make you pâté from wild boar and also some special sausages and wine sorbet, and there are many, many other things you could have to sell there at your vineyard.'

'I'm looking forward to sampling them,' said Don politely. 'Byron was singing your praises, saying what an excellent cook you are.'

'Ha, I have other skills as well, but those he doesn't praise.'

Don and Gina both started to speak.

'You first,' said Don.

'No, it was nothing,' said Gina. 'Nadia, what about that arm?'

'Let me see,' said Don. He looked at Nadia's reddening arm. 'I tell you what, I'll run you up to the Hall and my aunt can have a look at it. I'm on my way there in any case, for dinner.' Another thought struck him. 'Actually, I've got an idea. Byron, go and tidy yourself up a bit. Nadia, put on a frock. You can join us for dinner.'

Nadia was outraged. 'What manners! Here is this Gina, and you invite us and ignore her.'

Don laughed. 'Sorry, of course you don't know who Gina is. She's staying at the Hall, a cousin of ours.'

Nadia stared at Gina, a long, hard, appraising look. 'A cousin? Of yours? Of this oh-so English family? This is surprising.'

Gina felt herself go red. 'I'm a distant cousin,' she said.

'A distant cousin with Russian blood,' said Nadia shrewdly.

'Nadia, you're embarrassing Gina,' said Byron. 'I think Gina and Don probably know if they're cousins or not. Don, it's extremely thoughtful of you, but we can't possibly intrude on your family for dinner.'

'Of course you can,' said Don. 'It's an excellent idea, because our family gatherings always end in a quarrel. I don't get involved; I'm not a quarrelsome person, but everyone else does. Best to have visitors, makes them think twice before they start shouting at each other.'

He saw the doubt lingering on Byron's face. 'Are you on the phone yet?'

Byron nodded. 'The telephone people came this morning.'

'Then I'll give Hester a ring and tell her to expect us.'

'Two extra for dinner,' Guy sang out as he came into the kitchen.

'Two more? Who more? Why? How can I be expected to feed two more just like that?' Maria's voice was loud with indignation.

'Aw, give over, Maria,' said Esme, plonking a jar of Vegemite down on the kitchen table. 'You know you always cook more than enough. What's two more? Pass the bread, Guy.'

'I don't know how you can eat that stuff,' said Guy, wrinkling his nose as he cut Esme a neat chunk of bread.

'It's good for me,' said Esme, spreading Vegemite liberally on her bread. 'Keeps me in good health.'

'Well, you certainly look healthy,' said Guy with no particular enthusiasm.

'Come on, then, sick it up,' said Esme. 'Who's coming tonight? Anyone worth knowing?'

'The new couple from Heartsbane. An architect and his wife. She's foreign, they say,' he added. Guy had his own impeccable sources and knew all about Byron and Nadia.

Maria glanced across at Esme. 'Sit, when you eat. You are a savage.'

'No can do,' said Esme amicably. 'My bum is giving me real gyp.'

'Your bum is what?' Maria was horrified. 'You have piles in my kitchen? This is intolerable!'

Guy didn't like low talk. 'Esme has a sore behind, Maria, that's all,' he said. 'She got sunburnt this afternoon. She can't sit down.'

Maria's horror turned to outrage. 'And why is your behind exposed to the sun? I never heard of such a thing. It is like the monkeys in the zoo.'

'Very like the monkeys in the zoo, if you ask me,' said Guy under his breath.

'I want to hear no more of this,' said Maria, brandishing a spoon. 'Esme, you have eaten enough. Back to work; all those pots must be washed and cleaned until they shine.'

CHAPTER 11

I magine living here for the rest of your life.

Gina felt a shiver down her spine as she looked at the ravishing view spread out before her.

She leant further out of the bedroom window, breathing in the summer air and its scents, the quintessence of an English summer. Imagine being part of this family, this English tradition. Having your home here, among the narrow lanes and green fields with a silver river winding between them. It must be beautiful in winter, too; think of it glittering with hoar frost on a December morning.

And I *am* becoming fond of Harry, Gina thought. Not madly in love with him, not in love at all, but so? He was prepared to settle for second best. And how many wild, overwhelming romances survived more than a very few years?

Georgie had misled her; Georgie would, of course. Harry wasn't looking for a quick hitch in the register office and then separate lives. Do I want to be married to an English bisexual? Gina asked herself.

Lots of women were.

According to her friends, all too many Englishmen who had suffered the rigours of the very English, very peculiar, all-boys public schools spent the rest of their lives in some degree of ambivalence as far as sex was concerned. Could you bear having Guy and others like him making sheep's eyes at your husband? Was a husband like Victor any better?

Better not to think about Victor; that was a thought which quickened your senses. Better not to think at all; thinking was too much of a strain on a summer's evening. Live in the present; count your blessings, as Fergus was always saying. She was free of the fear of the Popplewell, she was staying in this astonishing house, she was getting used to the family, even beginning to like them. Life was calm; life was, all things considered, good.

Beware the happy mood, an ancient philosopher might have said. On the table downstairs in the hall were magazines, newly arrived, not yet passed on to various members of the family and staff. Idly, Gina picked up Nicky's copy of *Gossip!*

She froze. There, right across the centre spread, was a picture of a hot party in New York, with Georgie in a vestigial black dress, winking at the camera. 'Georgie takes the town by storm,' read the caption. And in the block of text underneath, all in large letters for those subscribers who read with their tongues sticking out, was an account of the meteoric rise of young English journalist Georgie Heartwell.

In a flash, Gina whipped the magazine away. Footsteps sounded; in desperation, she stuffed it under the cushion of the sofa which was placed between two doors.

'Drinks on the terrace,' said Guy. He had a tray of glasses in his hand and was obviously waiting for Gina to go ahead of him. She went, wondering when she would have an opportunity to retrieve the magazine and shred it. You couldn't trust an expert housekeeper like Hester not to make sure that the sofa cushions were regularly taken up and shaken. She might even do it every night.

Dinner began badly, with Victor holding forth on the Home Office and the dregs of society they saw fit to let into the country while keeping out such useful souls as musicians, Hong Kong businessmen and, for some obscure reason, irrigation experts.

Harry enlightened Gina in a whisper. 'Pa has a big deal going in water, but they won't let him employ the engineer he wants. He's an American; the Home Office insist he can find a Brit who has the same qualifications.'

'And foreigners who marry English men and women they don't like – or in some cases, they don't even know – simply to be able to live and work here. And arranged marriages. Mediaeval, no place for it in a modern society.'

'It's the custom in their countries.'

'Then let them stay in their countries and have their customs there. I never heard it was part of our culture.'

'We have no culture now, Pa,' said Harry, stoking the flames. 'It's a multicultural world we live in now.'

This brought a minor explosion. 'You may live where you choose, Harry. I'm not going to live in a cultural hodge-podge, with a bit of sitar music here, a bongo drum there, have a look at Chinese history, learn strange languages at school when you can't even speak English. It's an ignorant assumption that if something comes from a hotter part of the world, it must be wonderful, and we all have to treat it with reverence.'

'Calm down, Victor,' said Prim. 'Harry is just being annoying.'

Victor glowered across the table at his youngest son and then turned to the subject of foreigners from the erstwhile Iron Curtain countries. 'Sensible move for a woman to trap a westerner, can't blame them for wanting to get out from that system,' he said illogically. 'Fool men not to realize what all those exotic-eyed women were up to; still, they learned the hard way, waking up to find themselves married to a temperamental Pole or a fiendish-tempered Russian.'

'Pa,' said Don firmly. 'That is enough.'

Gina cast a quick look at Byron, who had a fixed expression on his face, and Nadia, who was muttering into her asparagus.

'And now I've got this Popplewell buzzing around me,' complained Victor, tearing a roll with his strong fingers.

Popplewell?

Gina went cold.

'Who's Popplewell?' asked Harry.

'Some freak from the Home Office, sniffing round one or two of my companies, making a fuss about work permits. I employ people who can do the work, I don't care where they come from. If I say on the application that the work can't be done by a national, then that's the situation. I don't need reptiles like this Popplewell lecturing me. And I won't put up with it. Popplewell had better watch his step.'

Gina swallowed hard. 'Can your father take on the Home Office?' she asked Harry in a whisper.

'No problem,' said Harry. 'Squash 'em like flies once his blood is up. Not a man to cross, Pa.'

'I can believe you,' said Gina.

Victor had realized his *faux pas* on the subject of Russian wives, and was busy making matters much worse.

'My apologies,' he was saying sincerely to Nadia. 'Wouldn't have said a word if I'd realized you were one of these escapees from communism. Well done, and your husband didn't do too badly, did he; women like you don't grow on trees. Think of all the dull, grey Englishwomen he might have married. Worked out all right, has it? You must have been here a while, perfect English, and of course that whole business there is finished now. You're still married, aren't you? And I dare say you still sleep together, lots of sex, that's what keeps a marriage going.'

'I think you've embarrassed our guests quite enough,' said Julia calmly. 'I don't consider the secrets of the marriage bed are a suitable topic for discussion at the dinner table.'

'When you think what she talks about . . . ' whispered Harry.

'Have some more asparagus, Mrs Wintersett,' said Hester. 'Grown in our own vegetable garden. Now, tell me what your plans are for Oracle Cottage.'

Esme was clanking away at the sideboard, humming happily as she dished out a basil sorbet. Julia watched her with growing disapproval.

'Esme, are your pants the wrong size? Why are you squirming like that?'

Esme plonked a plate in front of Gina. 'Made of leaves,' she informed her. 'Seems strange to me, but Maria swears it's okay.' She raised her voice. 'No, Mrs C, I'm not wearing pants. In fact, I don't usually wear a skirt, this is the only one I've got.'

Victor eyed the large white canvas skirt and thought that it was just as well.

'Then control yourself,' said Julia.

'It's just sunburn,' said Esme as she went the rounds with more plates. 'On my bum, it's very painful. Guy rubbed some cream in, but I don't think it's altogether worked.'

'Come over here and I'll look at it for you,' said Julia, laying down her napkin and getting up from the table.

'No,' said Victor at once. 'I do not want to see Esme's bottom displayed while I'm trying to eat my dinner. This is not the zoo.'

'You shouldn't want to see my bottom at any time,' said Esme severely. 'Not that I'd show it to any man anyway, but at your age, your mind should be on other things.'

'At my age?' Victor was furious.

'What about Guy, then?' Harry asked.

'Aw, he doesn't count as a man,' said Esme scornfully. 'He isn't anything.' She gathered up the empty bowl and hobbled out of the room. Julia resumed her seat, Victor dug his spoon into the sorbet.

'Staff,' he said ominously.

To turn his mind to other matters, Don asked his father how things had gone in Switzerland. This was a mistake. Victor told him in morose tones that things had not gone at all well. Victor's mind was on Cucki's exquisite breasts; Don was thinking about dairy products from cloven-hoofed creatures.

'Oh, that,' said Victor, switching his mind from Swiss delights to money. 'No, we'll sort it out all right. That reminds me. Hester!' he bellowed down the table.

'I'm talking, Victor,' said Hester.

'Never mind that, if I don't tell you now, I'll be bound to forget it. I've asked a chap I met in Switzerland to stay. He's going to be in England for a few days, so he's coming at the weekend.'

'Who is this man?' Julia asked suspiciously.

'A painter. American. Well-thought-of, good work, I might buy a picture, although I gather they come expensive. Called Zandermann. Serge Zandermann.'

The Cordovans never lingered *en famille* after dinner. Tonight, as usual, they dispersed as soon as the last mouthful of cheese had been eaten. Guy offered coffee in the drawing-room, but there were no takers. Victor and Julia were off for a heavy session in the bedroom. Prim had watering in mind and Aimée, as always, had an assignation.

'I'm going to wander along to the Bunch of Grapes with Byron and Nadia,' announced Don. 'They're looking a trifle shell-shocked. Coming, Gina? Harry?'

Byron protested that they should be getting home, but Don took no notice. Harry announced that he and Gina were going to have a swim, and might join them later.

'I'm not sure if I want to swim,' said Gina. 'Not after a meal, and besides, my wits are befuddled, I've had too much wine. And I, too, am suffering from shock.'

'Tell me about it,' said Harry soothingly.

They were by now in the hall, and Gina felt under the cushions on the sofa. Still there, thank goodness.

'What's that?' asked Harry. 'Oh, Nicky's rag. I adore that one, I read it on the loo when she's finished with it. What's it doing hidden under the cushions?'

'Does everyone else read it?' Gina asked anxiously.

'Don't think so,' said Harry. 'Plenty going on in their own lives, they've no need to read the salacious details of publicity-hungry nobodies.'

'Look,' said Gina dramatically.

'Ah,' said Harry. 'Now, that is unfortunate.' He pursed his lips as he read the text.

'Anybody who looks at that is going to be suspicious,' said Gina. 'Don't tell me she doesn't look more the Georgie your family knew than I do.'

'What? Oh, I see what you mean. I feel you worry unnecessarily, you know. This isn't a very good picture. A good thing it's not properly labelled, they've spelt her name as though she were you, not herself. I tell you something, if Victor knew this number in the come-on dress was his coz, he'd be furious. Vulgar, our Georgie, as I told you.'

'It's not just that someone here might see it,' said Gina. 'It's Popplewell.'

'Popplewell? Oh, the officious bureaucrat who's got up Pa's nose. What's Popplewell to you?'

'He's the one who found out my visa was overdue, and hounded me.'

'I see.'

'He's suspicious anyhow. I didn't tell you, but he was the man following my friend in Bath the other day. He must have thought she would lead him to me.'

'Got it,' said Harry. 'Should he be a *Gossip!* reader, he'll click on at once to the fact that this trollop in the piccie isn't you.'

'That's not all,' said Gina. 'You haven't heard the worst.'

'Worse than this Popplewell guy?' said Harry, amused by her increasingly doleful expression.

'Much,' she said tragically. 'This painter who's coming, Serge Zandermann . . .'

'Yes?'

'He's my father.'

This final revelation was too much for Harry, who burst out laughing.

Gina was affronted. 'You don't understand! And this afternoon I was feeling so happy – and so safe. Oh, do stop laughing. It isn't funny.'

'It's extremely funny,' said Harry, making noble efforts to restrain his laughter. 'What a tangled web, you have to agree.'

'That's all very well, but what do I do?'

'I will have to work out a plan,' said Harry. 'Meanwhile, here we are, a blissful evening, you can see the stars, bright as they are, through the glass roof. Put on your very fetching costume, and have a refreshing swim. No Popplewells or wandering fathers are lurking here, you're perfectly safe.'

From them, yes, but what about you, thought Gina; she wasn't at all sure about the look in Harry's eye.

'What are you thinking about?' she asked as she swam decorously past him.

'Etchings,' he said blandly.

Etchings? Gina didn't like the sound of that. On the other hand, it was very warm, and she had had a lot of wine, and she did feel in need of comforting . . .

Harry dried her in a most beguiling fashion before propelling her upstairs. 'I live in the solar,' he said, guiding her towards a huge and historic-looking four-poster bed.

'Why aren't your parents in this room?'

'It's a long time since it was the principal bedroom. They have a big room, complete with bathroom, in the tower. Over there,' he said, gesturing to one corner of the room, 'is a tiny chamber, with two squints. When we are not otherwise occupied, I'll show them to you.'

'Uh,' said Gina.

Harry kissed her, politely, but, thought Gina, quite interestingly.

'One looks down into the Great Hall, the other into the adjoining Chapel.'

Gina's mind wasn't on squints or Great Halls or chapels, but rather on what Harry was busy about.

'Harry,' she managed to say, pushing him away by a few inches. 'I don't think this is a good idea.'

'I do,' said Harry, who was definitely enjoying himself. 'Of course, being a perfect gent, I'll stop if you tell me to, but I think it would be a pity. I feel that a good time is going to be had by all.'

'What are you doing?' shrieked Gina.

'Sssh,' said Harry. 'They'll hear you in the Hall.'

'Who will hear me?' asked Gina, giving up the unequal struggle and doing a little exploratory work of her own.

'Ghosts,' said Harry. 'Mmm, blissful flesh. Not much of it, mind you, but what there is is definitely all right. Now, be quiet, you'll have to get used to this, if we're going to get married.'

But I don't want to marry you, a small uninvolved part of Gina's brain was saying quietly. And this is comforting, not to say exciting, but is it helping? Sex isn't about helping; on the other hand, it can complicate matters. And then, was it right to make love to the son while you were wondering enviously what the father might be doing elsewhere?'

It all gets murkier and murkier, thought Gina.

'Champagne,' said Don cheerfully. 'You need it, sudden exposure to Victor in full flood is very startling to the system. No, no, no quibbling. I sometimes drink beer, never touch horrors like whisky and vodka, but, needless to say, I'm a great wine man. Wilf always keeps a bottle or two of decent fizz on ice for when I pop in. Nothing like it for a summer drink.'

Wilf passed a bottle of Krug across the counter, glistening with chilly droplets. He plucked three tulip-shaped goblets down from a rack, drew out a tray from beneath the counter, and handed the whole lot over with a flourish.

Don steered them through the pub and into the garden. It overlooked some of Don's vines; from it you could take a narrow path down to another terrace at the bottom of the hill, on the river bank.

'We'll stay up here,' said Don. 'Too hot to climb back.'

'Besides, there's a breeze up here.'

Don gave a charming smile as he saw Nicky perched on the wall. 'Come and join us,' he invited. 'I'll get another glass.'

'Let me,' said Byron, jumping up.

'I thought you were ignoring me,' said Nicky, flashing her green and golden eyes at him.

'No, no,' said Don. 'I was surprised to see you here, though. Since you weren't at dinner at the Hall, I had supposed you were away.'

'The prospect of the whole Cordovan family was too much tonight.'

Byron came back with the glass.

'This is Nicky,' said Don. 'And these are Nadia and Byron. Nicky is working for the family at the moment,' he explained. 'So she usually dines with us at the Hall. My sister has her twenty-first birthday coming up, and Victor is giving a ball. First for several years; the Heartsease balls used to be quite a tradition.'

Nadia sipped her champagne appreciatively. 'You're the one who tried to do a shop for Don, only failed.'

'I don't think we'll go into that,' said Don hastily.

'Why?' said Nadia.

'Personal reasons,' said Nicky. She gave Don a smouldering look. 'I was going through a bad patch around then. Family-wise. It was all rather too much.'

'And family-wise, all's well now?'

'Don't be nosy, Nadia,' said Byron uncomfortably.

'I'm not nosy,' said Nadia. 'I like to know.'

'Anyone will tell you,' said Nicky. 'No secrets around here. I split up with my husband. We have two small children. It's all a little difficult.'

'Did your husband get up to hanky-panky with another woman? Or another man, this being England?'

'No,' said Nicky, beginning to squirm under the relentless interrogation. 'Not exactly. We just found we didn't get on.'

'When there are small children, it's your duty to get on,' said Nadia severely.

'Nadia!' Byron tried again.

Don was savouring his champagne, and watching the two women

with an amused look on his face. 'It's interesting to hear a young woman talk about duty,' he observed. 'What about Nicky's personal fulfilment?'

'Nicky's fulfilment should wait,' said Nadia firmly.

Don raised an eyebrow at Nicky. 'You see, my dear. A novel viewpoint.'

Nicky blew into the bubbles in her glass, and said nothing.

As Gina came out of Harry's room, she bumped into Aimée, who was wafting past in a cloud of silk negligee. A look of displeasure crossed her lovely face.

'You've been in there with Harry. You reek of sex. It's appalling.'

'I what?' said Gina, completely taken aback. How could she reek of anything, bathed and splashed as she was with one of the dozen delightful essences in Harry's bathroom?

'You've been making love with Harry. No, not making love, having sex.'

'I hardly think . . . ' began Gina.

'What a mistake, what a risk,' said Aimée dramatically.

What was she on about? wondered Gina. Risk? Harry had used a condom, these were dangerous times. Mistake?

'You should learn about love, not have sex in passing like a person who hasn't any feelings, any emotions, like a whore in the streets. Only in your case for comfort, not for money.'

Gina was furious. If ever there was a *grande horizontale*, it was Aimée. How dare she lecture her on sexual morality?

'I dare because I've no time for idle sex and instant lust,' said Aimée scornfully. 'My affairs are of the heart, they are amours. Not casual encounters, scratching an itch.'

'It's absolutely none of your business what I do with my body,' said Gina, flabbergasted at this attack.

Aimée took no notice. 'You should discover what love is. First, there's the attraction, dalliance, flirting. Heartache and despair,' she added in languorous tones. 'Elation and wild happiness and becoming one person with your lover. What does this have to do with rolling around on an old bed with Harry?'

'How do you know I don't love Harry?' enquired Gina.

'That's a stupid question,' said Aimée. 'Just think about what you've done, and you would do again at the beckoning of a finger with who? My father? Another of my brothers? Leave it alone. Wait until love comes creeping up and taps you on the shoulder. Then you'll know what I'm talking about.'

She was gone, leaving a livid Gina on the landing.

I hate this family, Gina said to herself, heading for the stairs and the safety of her own room. I hate all of them. And she burst into tears; tears of fury and rage and sadness for the difference between what she had just done with Harry and what Aimée had been talking about.

'Bugger them all,' she shouted as she banged her bedroom door behind her.

CHAPTER 12

'All fixed,' said Harry.

Perhaps, Gina had thought as she wandered the terraces in the light mists of dawn, perhaps, when I see Harry again, I'll find I am in love with him. And so all my problems will be solved.

She wasn't, and they weren't.

'Fixed?' she said doubtfully.

'Your weekend. I've found somewhere for you to go today until Sunday.'

'Where?' said Gina, thinking of places where Popplewell might roam.

'Just round the corner. Next village, actually. Don't worry, your pa won't find you there, visitors to the Hall never wander into the villages on their first stay; too much comfort and space at home. Sometimes they leap into powerful cars and drive hither and thither to the races or rowing or a ghastly golf do, if sportily inclined. But they tend to give Heartsbane a miss.'

'I can't imagine Dad roaring around the countryside in a powerful car,' said Gina, thinking of her bohemian father. 'And I don't think races are his thing.'

'No, I can understand that. Even so, I think we can guarantee to keep him away from Heartsbane.'

'He may want to go to Heartwell,' said Gina, remembering.

'Why should he?'

'He and my mother were married there.'

Harry was surprised enough to show it. 'Were they, now? A romantic, your father? The sentimental type? Likely to revisit the scene of his nuptials? Blissful marriage, was it? And by the way, we have spoken only of your father. Where does your mother come into all this? And why, if I'm not prying, is your pa called Zandermann while you are Heartwell?'

'My mother's name is Heartwell. When she and Dad split up, she went back to using her own name. I stayed with her, so I had her name as well.'

'And she came from these parts?'

'I guess so. The name, and being married here . . . She never talked that much about her upbringing in England. But she and Dad got married here in Heartwell, it must have meant something.'

'She never lived in Heartwell?'

Gina shrugged. 'Not that I know of. Mom's not one to look back. She lives in the present.'

'Where is the present at the moment?'

'What? Oh, I see what you mean. In Italy.'

'Does she work there?'

'No, she lives with some creepy guy who's rich; she doesn't need to work.'

'And your dad lives in America.'

'New York.'

'Serge? Zandermann?'

'Father Russian, mother Lithuanian, if you really want to know. Emigrés. In the thirties.'

'So they met in America.'

'No, in London. Dad was over here for an exhibition. They met on the tube.'

'Ah.'

'Dad picked Mom up on the Piccadilly Line.'

'Did he?'

'Literally. She had slipped on the escalator and was in danger of being squashed by the rush-hour crowds. Dad's a big man, and he rescued her. They got married two weeks later, and divorced five years after that. End of story.'

'So why did they get married at Heartwell?'

'Don't ask me, I wasn't there. Her family came from here; I suppose she felt it was better than Chelsea register office or some anonymous church.'

'Have you any grandparents alive?'

'Both my mother's parents died at the end of the war. I've got a Russian grandma, but she's anti my mother and anti me. She wasn't very keen on me to start with, wanted a grandson. So when my mom upped and offed, we lost touch.'

'Sad, really,' said Harry.

'No different from any number of other people.'

'But you haven't got any real family.'

'No.'

'Unlike me. I have family in abundance.'

'Yes, lucky you,' said Gina lightly.

Harry snapped out of his questioning mode and moved into gear. 'Okay, this is the plan. I'm taking you to Sybil Longthorpe. She has a cottage in Heartsbane, lives alone, except for her grandchildren who come on visits. They're due, but not yet, so she has room.'

'Is she a friend, or family?'

'So much of a friend that she's almost part of the family. She was a classics teacher; brilliant, used to coach us all in the hols – apart from Aimée, of course, who's impervious to education except for love poetry. She started my sister Olivia off on her very distinguished academic career.'

'She sounds a bit formidable.'

'No, tough-minded, but a good egg. She's retired from teaching; she writes books now. Very successfully.'

'I don't know the name.'

'She uses various pseudonyms,' said Harry.

'Won't Hester and Julia – and everyone – think it odd if I disappear for a weekend?'

'Not at all. We shall say you are an ex-pupil of Sybil's and wanted to see something of her while you're in these parts. I doubt if anyone will make any closer enquiries.'

'If you're sure . . .'

'Best I can do. Pack whatever you need, and I'll take you over, introduce you. Jarvis is going to pick up your pa at about half past twelve, so we need to get a move on.'

I feel like a refugee, thought Gina, as she trailed upstairs to her room. I don't want to stay with a strange classics teacher, I bet she's ghastly. And whatever will I find to do in the evenings?

*

'You're the woman from the train!' exclaimed Gina.

Sybil Longthorpe was, indeed, tight-lips on the twelve-forty from Oxford. However, she didn't seem at all tight-lipped standing in the garden of her cottage, with her long stripy skirt billowing around her and a welcoming smile as she saw Harry.

Harry gave her a boisterous hug. 'Do I take it that you and Gina have met?'

'Not met, but we sat in a train together.'

'I got off at Heartley Junction, but you went on.'

'Yes, I was going down to the coast to see my daughter. Normally, of course, I would have changed at the Junction, as you did, to come on the branch line to Heartsease.'

Porny books, Gina was thinking, as she remembered the manuscript she had helped to pick up. That's what she writes; hardly surprising that she uses a pen name.

'Come in,' said Sybil. 'Now, Harry, why all this secrecy? Why do I have to pretend Gina was a pupil of mine?'

'Only so that she has a reason for nipping off for the weekend. We've a guest coming that Gina knows. For various reasons, she doesn't want to meet him at present.'

'Fine. No, I prefer not to hear any more. It sounds distinctly murky, and I don't want to be involved. I'm very happy for you to stay here, my dear. You can help me put up the swimming pool I've just bought.'

Swimming pool? Gina wondered if years among the Greeks and Romans addled your wits.

'They call it a splashpool. A giant paddling pool. It's for my grandchildren. My study overlooks the garden at the back. They can play in the pool; I can work; we're all happy.'

'Excellent notion', said Harry. 'I'll leave you to it. See you anon, Gina.' He gave her a quick kiss on the cheek, and another enthusiastic hug to Sybil.

'How like Harry,' said Sybil thoughtfully, as he disappeared round the corner.

'In what way?' said Gina.

'Vanishing at the first sign of work.'

'I thought he worked quite hard.'

'Oh, yes, but to his own benefit. Not for others.'

'He's been very kind to me.'

'I'm sure he has.' Sybil became brisk. 'I'll show you your room. Let me warn you, it's tiny. A shock after the Hall, but the bed is comfortable, and I dare say you'll find it peaceful without the owls.'

'There do seem to be a lot of owls about at the Hall.'

'Yes, well, there would be, wouldn't there?' said Sybil cryptically, as she led the way indoors.

'Sitting room to your left, my study to your right, kitchen through there. Watch your head as we go upstairs, there's a beam . . . oh, yes, well, you know about the beam now. Bathroom, my room, your room, box-room. Coffee?'

'Thank you,' said Gina, putting her bag down on the little trestle table at the foot of the bed. She looked around the enchanting room, white muslin fluttering at the windows, old roses on the wallpaper and counterpane, and a faded rose carpet on the floor.

'If you hang out of the window, you can see the sea,' said Sybil. 'However, you'll probably land on your head in the garden first, so I wouldn't advise it. Come down when you're ready.'

The little white van drew up outside the cottage with a squeaking of brakes.

'Wilf,' said Sybil, not looking up from the instruction manual.

Wilf came round the side of the house, carrying a large white cardboard box which was obviously heavy.

'Two doz of the usual, Sybil,' he said. 'Got a visitor, have you?'

Sybil straightened up. 'I expect you've met Gina, who's at the Hall. An old pupil of mine.'

Wilf's face lost its foxy, enquiring look. 'Ah, that's it, is it? Another of they learned ladies, is it?'

'That's right,' said Sybil. 'Lovely to have her here, and she's going to help me put up a pool in the garden.'

'I'd heard you'd been buying an item in a big box,' said Wilf. 'Terrible time you'll have with that. I bought one once, when the kids were small. Easy to put up, they said.'

'And wasn't it?'

'Easier to build a house,' said Wilf with relish. 'You'll be at it all weekend, a-swearing and a-cursing. Well, when her's done, come along to the Bunch of Grapes and have one on the house to celebrate.

You'll have earned it, to be sure.'

'Just let me get my purse,' said Sybil. 'Two dozen, you said? Here you are.'

'And thank you,' said Wilf. He took a last look at the box containing the pool, and gave another disconcerting whoop of laughter. 'I'm glad 'tis you and not I that's got to struggle all weekend with she,' he said ominously, and climbed back into his van.

'Beer,' said Sybil as she opened one of the boxes Wilf had brought. 'Czech beer. A particular brand which I acquired a taste for when I was out there for a while. You can't buy it at the off-licence, but Wilf gets it for me. Put somehbottles in the fridge; we may need it if Wilf's not exaggerating.'

'This looks quite straightforward,' said Gina, frowning at an exploded diagram of a pump. 'Apart from the drawings, that is. The first thing we hkve to do is level the site.'

'That,' said Sybil, looking at the bumpy patch of grass where she proposed to put the pool, 'could vresent a problem.'

After several hours' work, it became clear to Sybil and Gina that neither of them were at all practical.

'I can keal with electricity,' said Sybil. 'I can clear a drain, even heave a tile back on the roof. I can garden. But this is beyond me.'

'The trouble is,' said Gina, 'that although they say "level the site", they don't tell you how.'

'Do you think it matters how level it is?'

'It says in the instructions, later on, when you've actually got the sides up, that if when the water is in, it isn't level to within an inch, then you have to take everything down and start again.'

'I don't like the sound of this,' said Sybil darkly.

'Did they give you any advice where you bought it?'

'They said two people could put it up in about three or four hours.'

'But no mention of this levelling business?'

'Not a word. I would never have bought it if they'd come clean and explained about having to do all this shovelling work before you even get the pool out of its box.'

'A lot of folks back in the States have these,' said Gina. 'But they put them on concrete, or in their front yards, which are level anyway.'

'Back in the States? Are you American? I thought I detected a very slight accent.'

Gina could have kicked herself. 'I am American originally,' she said. 'I've been over here for years. At the moment, I'm, well, nobody here knows I'm American.'

That earned her a very sharp look from Sybil.

'They won't know about it from me,' she said. 'So don't worry about it.'

'Thank you,' said Gina. Perhaps she owed it to her hostess to explain things a little more.

'Definitely not,' said Sybil quickly and firmly. 'From what you and Harry have said, it's clearly a complicated business, and I want no part in it. I presume whatever it is you're up to has no spiteful intent? You aren't a journalist, sniffing out some scandal about people here? Not out to get the Cordovans? They're old friends, as you know.'

'No,' said Gina. 'It's a personal matter, it won't harm anyone.'

Was that true? If she were to get married, to Harry, would that count as harming him or his family? If they expected a piggy fortune, and there wasn't one?

'Oh, to hell with it all,' she said, sending Sybil's expressive eyebrows flying up. 'Let's get back to this levelling business.'

Sybil sighed as she looked at the round patch of ground they had measured out, using a piece of string held by a skewer in the centre. 'What we need,' she announced, 'is an expert.'

Gina sat back on her heels, dusting the soil off her knees. 'An architect,' she said. 'Architects must know about level ground.'

Sybil wasn't convinced. 'I think they don't begin until someone else has done the levelling.'

'No, no,' said Gina. 'They must know how it should be done, even if they've never scrabbled about at ground level.'

'In any case,' said Sybil, 'there is no architect at hand.'

'Oh, yes, there is,' said Gina, getting to her feet and stretching her cramped legs. 'He lives at Oracle Cottage.'

'Of course,' said Sybil. 'The new people. I hardly know them.'

'Then here's your chance.'

Byron was alone at Oracle Cottage. He peered down at them from his perch on the exposed loft beams. Nadia was over at the vineyard, he explained. 'Probably yelling and screaming at poor Don,' he said rather hopelessly.

'Do Don good to have someone telling him what,' said Sybil in forthright tones. 'What's your wife screaming about?'

'She feels he ought to do something about the shop there.'

'And so he should,' said Sybil. 'I've been telling him that for years. His wine's doing well and he likes his work, but he's far too lazy. Thinks it's too much effort to put himself out for commercial gain; he doesn't realize how good it would be for the village. We don't want to be inundated with tourists, but a few more passing through would be good for trade all round. And if he got the shop going, it would provide work for one or two women in the village. They need it.'

Byron eyed Sybil with new respect. 'There is that,' he said. 'Well, Nadia's very forceful once she's made her mind up that something needs to be done, so we shall see.'

A few bits of plaster detached themselves from the remains of the ceiling and landed beside Sybil. 'Come down from there,' she said. 'I'm getting a crick in my neck talking to you, and we need your expert advice.'

He climbed down the ladder and landed beside them, shaking plaster out of his hair. 'Sorry,' he said, as some powdery flakes flew over Gina.

'Nasty things, old ceilings,' said Sybil.

Gina was looking up at the cavity in the ceiling with awe. 'Whatever is that made of?'

'The laths are wood. The plaster is a right old hodge-podge. Animal hair to bind it together, reeds, old bits of shell from the lime they used . . . ' He sneezed. 'All incredibly dusty.'

'Are you bringing the whole ceiling down?' asked Sybil.

'I hope not,' said Byron. 'I hadn't intended to bring any of it down, but Nadia went through a woodwormy board upstairs last night. She ended up with one foot dangling through the ceiling here.'

'I bet she was furious,' said Gina, thinking of Nadia's temper.

'She wasn't very pleased,' said Byron, trying not to think about it.

'How can you possibly live here?' asked Sybil, looking about at the derelict surroundings.

'It's a matter of camping in the one or two sound rooms while we do it up.'

'We?'

'Me, mostly. Nadia's very good at decorating, though,' he added defensively.

'No doubt, but it's going to be some time before you get to the paintwork.'

'Oh, I don't know,' said Byron optimistically. 'Can I offer you some tea? Or a cold drink? There should be something in the kitchen.'

'No,' said Sybil. 'Thank you very much, but what we need is your help. If you would be so kind as to step over to my cottage and give us some advice, I will give you some excellent foreign beer. Cold beer.'

'Let me just wash my hands and I'll be with you,' Byron said with alacrity.

'I admire your cottage every time I go by,' said Byron. 'Who lives in the one next door? The pink one?'

'No one,' said Sybil, pausing briefly to quell a small weed which had poked its nose up next to her convulvulus. 'It's rented out, holiday and short-term lets. Usually it's full for the whole summer, but the people who were coming had to cancel. There'll be some other people coming tomorrow; I put an ad in, and it was let very quickly.'

'Is it yours, then?' asked Gina.

'Yes. I bought the two of them together, years ago, when my husband was alive. We were going to knock them together, make a bigger house. But he died first, and I didn't need the room. It's a very useful extra income.'

'I'm sorry about your husband,' said Byron. 'Dying, I mean.'

'Oh, it was a long time ago,' said Sybil cheerfully. 'Into the back garden, the path goes round there.'

Byron gazed in a puzzled way at the round brown patch. 'What exactly are you trying to do?' he asked at last.

'Put up one of those above-ground pools,' said Sybil. 'Level the ground, it says in the instructions. But how?'

Byron's face cleared. 'Oh, I thought perhaps you were planning a tower or a small observatory or something. A mistake, possibly, just here.'

'Yes, well, I'm not. The problem is, how do you get ground level?'

'That's easy,' said Byron. 'You need a peg, string, a piece of four-by-two and a long spirit level.'

'There's a skewer there, with a length of string,' Gina pointed out.

'That won't do,' said Byron, eyeing the lopsided arrangement. 'I'll nip back home and get what you'll need. It has to be level, otherwise when you bolt the outside wall together, the holes don't match up. Also, you can get wave trouble. Although,' he went on, looking doubtfully at Sybil, 'I don't suppose you're planning on making waves.'

'Good gracious, I'm not going in there,' said Sybil. 'It's for my grandchildren.'

'Oh, I am sorry. Well, in that case, unless they are unusually subdued, it's best to have it level.'

'You sound as though you speak from experience.'

'I do indeed. My brother has one of these pools for his youngsters. The really tricky bit is getting the liner in.'

'That's good to know,' said Gina glumly. The thick blue plastic sheet in the box had a look of bad news about it.

'Don't worry,' said Byron. 'It's not so difficult when you know what you're doing. I'll be around to give you a hand when it gets tough.'

'You go and get the spirit level, and I'll open the beer,' said Sybil.

Don helped himself to another chunk of the pâté. 'Delicious,' he said. 'Quite delicious. What else have you got here?'

Nadia had brought a cloth with her, to clean the wobbly counter before spreading a damask cloth on it and laying out her goodies.

'Mmm. What's this?'

'Wine cake.'

'Excellent.'

'Here's a list,' said Nadia, slapping it on to the tablecloth. 'A list of all the food I can make, all with local produce and your wine. You see?'

Don ran his eye down the list. 'Nadia, where did you learn to make all this?'

'From my mother. We had a dacha in Russia. My father hunted, my uncle brought wine from near by, from a friend, and we made this food.'

'Could you make enough to sell?' asked Don, looking round at his shabby surroundings. 'And where would you sell things? It's all a bit basic here.'

'You've room for a kitchen here,' said Nadia. 'Then this part, you should do it up slightly old-fashioned. Polished wood. Dark, not pine. Shelves. Refrigeration, of course. Wine along here, food here. A freezer for ices and sorbets.'

'And you want a job here?'

'No. I'll make the food and sell it to you. You sell it for more, at a profit. I'll mind the shop when it's slack time. For the rest, there'll be local people who want work.'

'It'll have to be for next summer,' said Don.

'Nonsense,' said Nadia. 'This summer. Byron can come and do the shop for you. Only you have to pay him a proper rate.'

'He's an architect, not a joiner,' Don objected.

'He does the design, a joiner makes it. He knows all about joiners. You use MDF, then it costs not much and looks good.'

'And if I say no,' said Don, getting up and wiping his mouth on a large handkerchief.

Nadia looked at him with her forceful, brooding eyes. 'Then I spit on you, and curse you for being so complacent and for being satisfied with what is third-rate.' She cast a scornful eye around the shop. 'No, fourth-rate. And anyone who comes here to buy wine, they'll think your wine is fourth-rate, too.'

Don would take no criticism of his wine. 'No, no,' he said. 'I sell very few single bottles. Buyers come down to the cellars, they buy in dozens.'

'Maybe people will come to the shop and buy a bottle and some pâté or sausages or ices, and then they come back to buy a case.'

'Maybe,' said Don.

Nadia glared at him.

Don smoothed his head and looked at Nadia. 'You'd have to do it all,' he said. 'If you can't manage the financial side, book-keeping and so on, you'll have to find someone who can. My accountant will keep a close eye on the figures. If they look good by the end of September, then we'll keep going.'

'They will,' said Nadia, with supreme confidence.

'Then we'll drink to it,' said Don, going out to the old fridge at the back.

'Cheers,' said Nadia, drinking the cool wine with enthusiasm.

'*Na zdorovya*,' said Don.

'I go now and tell Byron,' said Nadia.

'Get estimates,' said Don. 'But Byron will know all about that.'

'Of course he will,' said Nadia with pride. 'Byron knows about everything.'

'By the way,' said Don, as Nadia reached the door, 'we usually do a good trade on the wine side at Christmas. Have you got any ideas for that? I don't suppose you kept Christmas in Russia.'

'You're crazy,' said Nadia, but this time without rancour. 'My family have always been Christian. And I know what English people like at Christmas, to give as presents and to eat themselves.'

'Just as long as it isn't pickled herrings,' said Don into his glass of wine.

CHAPTER 13

For some time Lori and her husband Gareth, when he could spare the time from his TV production company, had been eyeing three cottages in the centre of Heartwell. They formed a little terrace of their own, they had immense period charm, and no one seemed to live in them.

'Curtains in the windows,' pointed out Lori, as she went to buy the few items she got each week to show she supported the village shop.

'They aren't up for sale, as far as one can tell,' said Gareth, unwrapping the dog's lead which had wound itself round his legs. 'Any more information from the people in the village?'

'They're hopelessly *vague*,' said Lori with a frown. 'They must *know* who owns them, but they aren't letting on.'

'Why are you so keen on them?' asked Gareth's sister, down for the weekend. She peered shamelessly in through one of the windows. 'Nasty little hovels inside; the way some types live in the country is revolting.'

Tara lived in Muswell Hill, and wrote wordy stories about Urban Life, which won prizes and were much reviewed if little read. 'I'm going to the country this weekend,' she had announced to her latest lover.

'Why?' he had asked.

'To remind myself how unpleasant it is. The rural dream is a rebarbative dereliction of the modernization of culture.'

Her lover rolled over in bed and went back to sleep, thinking drowsily that it would be a treat for him to have a monosyllabic weekend for a change.

In fact, Tara found the country very soothing. The house was comfortable and stylish; she could patronize her sister-in-law on no particular grounds except that she was out of touch with London life, and, in the family circle, she could talk quite normally. Long, complicated sentences and unusual Latinate words dug up out of the thesaurus are quite tiring to the brain. Of course, if she met any strangers while in Heartwell, then she immediately became polysyllabic once more. Tara had her public to think of.

Gareth explained about buying village property – he called it taking a stake in the community – and renting it out to holidaymakers. 'The punters pay incredible prices,' he said.

'Oh, well, if you're only thinking of money,' said Tara superciliously.

Lori rushed to acquit Gareth of anything so sordid. 'It's the *best* thing for villages like this,' she explained. 'It improves the housing stock, otherwise these houses are just left to *rot* away.'

Tara looked at the houses through narrowed eyes. 'You might interest a decaying artist in them.'

'A what?' said Lori, thinking she must have misheard.

'Decaying artist; darling, you are out of touch, aren't you? The only interesting art form at the moment deals with objects decaying and rotting away. It represents the eternal entropy of our lives to a state of degradation and dissolution.'

'Cottages would be a change from some of the works I've seen,' said Gareth. 'They smell.'

'Art should involve all our senses.'

Lori was always excited at the prospect of Tara coming to stay, and always wondered why, within an hour of her arrival, she wished her sister-in-law had stayed in London. Gareth, who spent his working life with people like Tara, seemed to take her in his stride. 'It's the artistic temperament,' he said with some pride.

Deep inside Lori, a little voice said that it was no such thing, and that Tara was selfish, self-absorbed and spoiled.

Tara was also greedy. This was something she couldn't be in London, because to enjoy hearty food would be considered uncool beyond bearing. Here, in the country, she could eat what she liked, and lots of it.

'I'll cook dinner for you tonight,' she said.

Lori protested. She had it all arranged, food bought . . .

Yes, thought Tara, smart food, to show that she hasn't succumbed to country ways. 'No, no, I don't want you to go to all that trouble. I'll cook tonight, put whatever you've got in the freezer.'

'Sea bass,' said Lori a little sadly, for she had gone to a lot of trouble to acquire a fashionable fish.

Wild boar, Tara was thinking. I remember there's somewhere around here where they sell wild boar. If it's been hung properly, ready to cook . . . Her mind drifted off to visions of succulent meat, potatoes cooked in olive oil and rosemary. And wine; red wine. Lori would offer sparkling mineral water and a white wine so dry it would rip the back of your throat off.

Tara gave a self-satisfied smile, and came back to earth. 'No, Lori, if you cook the sea bass I shan't eat it. We could go out, but there isn't anywhere decent around here, so I'll cook.'

Heartsbane had a pub and no shop, Heartwell a shop but no pub. Since the villages were barely a quarter of a mile apart, the residents of each village regarded themselves as honorary residents of the other village, and thus benefited from both establishments.

Sybil and Gina walked to Heartwell quite early in the morning. Sybil liked to get her shopping done and out of the way; Gina knew there was no chance of bumping into her father at that time of day, even supposing he were to want to visit Heartwell. He was not a morning man.

They had an amicable squabble about who was to pay in the shop, reaching a compromise by Gina insisting that she would pay for the chicken which was to be picked up at the farm on the way home.

'I'm very well-off, you know,' observed Sybil as they went into the shop. 'My books make a lot of money.'

Phil the shopkeeper had served them in his grumbling way, telling Sybil about Godfrey Cowans at Raven Cottage.

'Sitting out there in the sun, just like a Christian who has nothing to be ashamed of.'

'Eve's taken little Irene back to her parents, I hear,' said Sybil.

'Yes, and now he be trying for custody, but they won't take no nonsense from him, not knowing what they knows.'

'I'm glad that's sorted out,' said Sybil. 'Have you got another packet of the dark brown sugar? Thank you, and two boxes of matches, please.'

They dumped the shopping on the kitchen table and Sybil headed for the kettle.

'Pool?' said Gina, who could see the large box through the window. She didn't sound very enthusiastic.

'We'll have to have a go at it,' said Sybil, also without enthusiasm. 'Still, it should be easier now we've got on to the assembly. Bless Byron for doing that levelling for us.'

'Surprisingly practical for a professional man,' said Gina.

'Coffee, first,' said Sybil. 'Then, if you like, you can give me a hand getting things ready next door. Arriving at about three, she said.'

'Sure I'll help,' said Gina. 'Does it need cleaning, or what?'

'No, Mrs Slubs does the cleaning, but I need to make up the beds, check the fridge, make it look welcoming.'

'I'm not sure how many are coming,' said Sybil, as she took an armful of sheets and towels from the linen cupboard in Kingfisher Cottage, as the next-door cottage was called.

'Why does it have a name and yours not?' asked Gina, as she followed Sybil up the stairs with a biscuit box and clean muslin curtains.

'I can't be doing with all that for myself,' said Sybil. 'The cottages didn't have names when we bought them, and I don't need a name for mine. 1, The Cottages is a perfectly adequate address. But you need a pretty, countrified name to attract people when you're letting out. There are a lot of kingfishers about if you know where to look for them, so it's Kingfisher Cottage.'

'I saw a kingfisher by the river a day or so ago.'

'Beautiful birds,' said Sybil, as she led the way into a bedroom. 'I think the best thing to do is to make up the three beds. That's one double and the two singles in the other room.'

The beds were made, towels hung on racks and the newly washed curtains up at the windows in no time. Sybil and Gina retreated downstairs to arrange flowers from Sybil's garden in various pots and vases.

'Pretty nice for them,' said Gina, standing back to admire her arrangement. 'Flowers everywhere, and a tray laid for tea; milk and eggs in the fridge. Even cookies, I mean biscuits, by the beds.'

'That's that,' said Sybil, having a last look round before shutting the door behind them. 'Now for that dratted pool.'

Prim was looking after the wine sales that morning, while Don walked the vines, checking progress, recording comments of work needed, making sure that the rabbits hadn't chomped their way through the plastic tubes which protected the bases of young vines.

Gareth and Lori were put out that Don wasn't available. Tara was amused at the thought of anyone wasting their time on English wine; she looked at the selection of bottles with an expression on her face as of one humouring children.

'I did want to have a word with Don,' said Gareth, slightly huffy. He was a dark, rather jowly man given to wearing pink shirts. His hair was slightly too long, his ties too vigorous, his teeth white and gleaming. Beauty and the beast, thought Lori for one disloyal moment as she looked at Prim's golden hair and skin and her deep blue eyes.

'I can ask him to ring you,' said Prim. 'Meanwhile, did you want some wine?'

'Yes, a case of Special Reserve, please.'

Prim pushed open the big sliding door and called out into the courtyard. 'Esme! A case of the Special Reserve, please, in the shop.'

She made out a bill, and stood, still, graceful and completely at ease as Gareth wrote a cheque. She was wearing cotton trousers and a polo shirt and made Lori feel uncomfortable.

Tara didn't like the look of this local hick at all; in some strange way, she made her, Tara, seem provincial and unfinished. Tara wasn't one to keep her uneasiness to herself, so she hit back with rudeness as Esme came in, carrying the box of wine as though it weighed nothing.

'Gareth, you aren't seriously expecting me to drink English sparkling wine, are you?' She gave a tinkly laugh. 'Supporting local crafts is one thing, but you might as well expect me to drink Australian.'

Esme put the box down with a thump. She towered over Tara, and gave her a look full of contempt. 'You don't want it, you don't have to drink it. You're the loser, mate, because this is good stuff.'

'Are you an expert?' said Tara with an insincere smile.

'On wine, yes. My dad owns vineyards back home – that's Australia, in case you want to know – and some in France, too. I know one hell of a lot about it, a lot more than you do, I'd bet. And I don't ever say a wine's no good until I've tried it. Same as everything else in life.'

Lori tried to smooth everyone down. 'Esme, isn't it? I thought you worked up at the Hall.'

'Yeah, but I come and give a hand here when I can. Makes me feel at home to be among the vines, and I keep fit moving a few boxes around.' She flexed her biceps, cast a final look of scorn at Tara and went back to her heaving.

Prim, completely unmoved, handed Gareth his receipt. 'Can you manage that?' she asked. 'I can take it to the car for you.'

His masculinity challenged, Gareth staggered out to the Discovery, and heaved the box into the back.

They drove silently back to Heartwell House.

'Peasants,' said Tara, as they got out of the car.

'I don't know who that lovely woman was, but she didn't look like a peasant to me,' said Gareth warmly.

Lori gave him a look. 'That's Prim, Victor's sister. She's worth millions, in her own right.'

'Oh,' said Gareth.

They went inside.

'Have you got any brothers?' Sybil asked.

'No,' said Gina, fuming as she tried to push one aluminium curved piece into another. 'Why?'

'Because I was thinking how much this reminds me of building electric train layouts. My son had a lot of track and not much patience.'

'Hell,' said Gina, as the pieces finally slid together, leaving her with an inside piece about eight inches shorter than it should be.

'There's the doorbell,' said Sybil. 'It'll be the people for Kingfisher Cottage. I'll just give them the key and show them where things are, and then I'll be back.'

'Fine,' said Gina, not looking up from her next pair of curved bits.

She'd got the hang of it, finally, and the pieces slotted together on the ground in an approximation of a circle.

Strange, thought Gina, as she moved slowly round on her hands and knees to adjust the joins. Three weeks ago, if I'd looked ahead to now, I'd have thought I might just be in Oxford. More likely, I would be in New York. I could never have imagined that I would be in a cottage garden in Heartsbane, staying with a pornographic novelist, putting up a swimming pool. It just goes to show, she told herself, that you can't even begin to think about what twists and turns your life might take.

Gina came back to the matter in hand, and looked at the instructions again. *Support the metal wall once erected with stout wooden pegs.* Stout wooden pegs indeed! Where were these people living? Where could you get pegs like that these days? It didn't look as though they were important, you took them away as soon as the wall was up and the liner filled with water. It wasn't as though there was any danger of wind, either. The only wind they'd had for days was this tiny, fretful breeze which hardly stirred the leaves.

Upstairs in Kingfisher Cottage, Zoë tested the mattress on the double bed. Perfect. She looked at her suitcase and sundry bags and decided unpacking could wait until later.

Fergus stood at the bottom of the stairs, huge against the low ceilings and beams of the downstairs room. 'I've made tea,' he announced.

'I didn't bring any milk,' said Zoë. 'And where did you find tea?'

'All laid on,' said Fergus.

'That's kind of them,' said Zoë, coming carefully down the steep stairs. 'Fergus, I'm going to love it here. Glorious countryside, and you can smell it's not far to the sea. Wonderful. Wish you could stay.'

'I've got work to do,' said Fergus. 'And Charlotte mightn't like it.'

'Charlotte doesn't like anything,' Zoë said under her breath. 'No, I didn't say anything, Fergus. Are those biscuits? I'm famished. We'll have to find out where the nearest supermarket is – do you suppose we have to go all the way to Heartsbury?'

'I do not,' said Fergus. 'Don't worry for tonight. There'll be a local shop for necessities, and we passed a farm selling meat and vegetables.'

'What an effort,' said Zoë, very much a Chicken Kiev from Waitrose woman.

'I shall cook it,' said Fergus grandly. 'Your landlady, whose face looks somehow familiar, will tell us when the farm shop closes. Have some more tea, and then you can get your bearings in the village.'

'No hurry,' said Zoë, opening the door from the kitchen into the garden at the rear. 'I've got weeks to explore.'

Fergus joined her outside. 'Apples,' he said knowledgeably, looking at the trees. 'And pears.'

Zoë's attention was caught by strange thumps and bangs from the next door garden.

'I hope I'm not going to have noisy neighbours,' she said. 'Fergus, can you see what's going on?'

Fergus wandered along to a place where the hedge was lower and looked over into Sybil's garden. 'No need to worry,' he reported. 'They seem to be erecting a pool. I daresay your landlady has grandchildren.'

'I don't mind children,' said Zoë, who had found a swinging sofa and had settled herself in. 'They can't be worse than my brother's brats. Pull up that seat, Fergus, and relax.'

Crash!

Gina sat up in bed, her heart thumping, as the sound of tin roofs collapsing filled her bedroom. Thunder?

She flew to the window and looked out. The slight breeze of earlier had blown itself into a gale. Trees rustled and branches whipped dramatically backwards and forwards.

Then that noise again. Dustbins blowing about? A shed roof come off?

Her door opened and Sybil stood in the doorway, clad in a pair of nifty silk pyjamas and a handsome man's brocade dressing-gown in dazzling colours. 'It's that bloody pool,' she said dispassionately. 'That metal wall is bowling about the garden as though it were a piece of paper.'

Gina pulled on a pair of jeans, found her deckshoes and followed Sybil at speed down the stairs.

The wall of the pool, so carefully placed into its base that afternoon, had lifted clean away. They had done a good job bolting the two ends together, so there was this circle of metal, forty-seven feet round and three feet high, swirling round the garden like a hoop, crashing and rattling as it went.

'What on earth can we do about it?' yelled Gina into the wind. As though it had heard her, it came hurtling towards her and she hastily jumped out of the way.

'We've got to get hold of it, pin it down,' shouted Sybil.

In a momentary lull, they could hear a voice in the next-door garden.

'Of course, woken them up, wonderful start to a holiday,' said Sybil crossly.

It was a powerful voice. 'Can I help?'

'Yes,' screamed Sybil as the wind rose again. 'There's a gate at the bottom of your garden.'

'If he's awake, he might as well come and help,' Sybil bellowed at her. 'He's big.'

'Good,' cried Gina.

Then, two minutes later, a tall, familiar figure came up the path, clearly visible in the light from the shed lamp.

Fergus, thought Gina. Oh, no, it couldn't be Fergus. How could he be here? Why? Was she dreaming?

It was Fergus. No mistaking him at all, as he gave a powerful tug at the wall, subduing it into a mere grumbling, thumping piece of metal.

'Zoë, go round that side,' he called.

Zoë? She had to be dreaming. Why would Fergus and Zoë be staying in the cottage next door? And from what Sybil had said, the people renting were planning a stay of several weeks. Why hadn't Zoë said anything about coming here?

Gina's only instinct was to get away from the cottage, where Sybil would undoubtedly drag her down to meet the new neighbours. Without thinking, she fled through the gate and started to run down the road.

She had to acquit Zoë of secretiveness. Zoë had no way of getting in touch with her; she had forbidden her to write or to ring the Hall. 'Popplewell probably has agents in the post office, scrutinizing your mail,' she had told her.

Gina was by now thoroughly scared. Not by the imaginary footsteps coming after her, because there were none, but simply by being out in the open in the full force of what felt like a hurricane. A branch gave a dramatic crack and crashed down on to the road beside her.

Gina increased her pace, running past the sign that said 'Heartwell', determined to find shelter away from this terrifying, elemental wind. She had to slow down as she came in sight of the row of cottages, her sides heaving. I'm not very fit, she told herself.

A dark figure emerged from the shadows at the side of the road, giving Gina a nasty shock. As the figure loped off, she shrank into the hedge and watched whoever it was pause by the shop to be joined by someone else.

Intrigued now, Gina moved slowly after them, keeping to the shadows, hoping that any noise she made would be drowned by the rackety wind and rain. She was soaked to the skin, and water trickled down her face from her wet hair. Since I can't get any wetter, she thought, there's no point in trying to shelter.

The two figures reached the three terraced cottages and slipped inside the end one. Not so interesting, thought Gina, and then her ears caught the sound of a vehicle coming from the other direction.

A truck drew up outside the cottages and gave a quick toot on its horn. The windscreen wipers lashed backwards and forwards with an audible squeak, then subsided into silence as the driver turned his engine off and swung himself down on to the road. He went round to the rear of the truck and rolled up the back with a loud rattle.

The door of the end cottage opened and light spilled out for a second before it was switched off. Gina could see the feeble light of a half-powered torch wavering about. The men – or women, how could you tell in the darkness and rain? – had a whispered conversation, and then two of them disappeared round the back of the truck. They staggered back with a large box each, which was taken smartly into the cottage.

This was repeated for several loads, and then the driver got back into his truck, started the engine and drove off into the darkness. The other two locked the cottage door, and left, one heading across the green and the other back towards where Gina was lurking.

Phil the shopkeeper, Gina said to herself as she recognized the burly figure. He hadn't noticed her skulking in the shadows as, whistling through his teeth, he opened the shop door. Gina heard the ping of the shop bell and heaved a sigh of relief. Not that Phil had struck her as the dangerous type, but she had a feeling that, whatever Phil and his friends had been up to at such an unlikely hour of the night, they wouldn't appreciate an audience.

The shopkeeper shut the door behind him; there was a clunk as a bolt was pushed to. Gina was alone once more in the dark, wet, windy summer's night.

Smugglers, she said to herself. That's what they were.

So much for the peaceful rural scene.

CHAPTER 14

The journey back, undertaken at a more seemly pace, took Gina longer than when she had come. Especially since she had to scramble over the huge fallen branch which had blown down and now lay across the road. The lashing rain beat against her face as she headed into the gale. By the time Gina pressed Sybil's doorbell she was drenched, exhausted and longing to be out of the wild weather. Sybil opened the door, making pleased noises, and Gina fell into the cottage.

'Why did you hare off like that?' asked Zoë, balancing the tray as she pushed the door shut with her foot.

'Because of Fergus, of course. Walking up the path, large as life; what a shock. It's a bit much, Zoë, your turning up here, no warning, and bringing Fergus.'

Zoë put the tray down on Gina's bedside table, and flopped on to the bed. 'Poof, it's hot up here.'

'That's why I'm sitting here by the window, trying to get some air,' said Gina peevishly. 'You'd think that the storm last night would have cooled things down, but it's hotter than ever. Pass me that glass of water, I'm parched.' She took a long drink. 'I suppose Fergus is still downstairs?'

'Mmm,' said Zoë, flicking idly through the books on the shelf by the bed. 'Talking about last night's storm. Apparently, a big tree came down in the village in the early hours, on the green. Didn't squash anyone, but none the less, great local excitement, I gather.' She pulled out a book. 'Actually, what Fergus is doing is flirting like mad with your Sybil.'

'Flirting? With Sybil?' Gina was incredulous.

'Flirting. Mutual admiration society. One look at Fergus's manly legs – he's wearing shorts, you see – and a bit of the McEttrick charm, and you could see she was quite won over. He, on the other hand, thinks she's funny and interesting and clever; I feel like the fourth leg of a stool down there.'

'Shorts,' said Gina in disgust. 'He obviously feels he's on holiday.'

'It's only for the weekend,' said Zoë. 'Then he'll have to get his beaky Wellington nose back to the grindstone. I'm sorry, Gina, I had it all planned, village near Heartsease, but not so near that I'd be obtrusive, on hand when you needed a break from your adopted family, no hassle.'

'Huh,' said Gina. 'Whose idea was it that Fergus should come along for the ride?'

'His,' said Zoë after a moment's thought. 'Yes, he suggested it.'

'How long is he going to be here today, in Sybil's cottage?'

'Lunch now, and then he's going to finish the pool for her, and I shouldn't be at all surprised if they weren't making plans for this evening.'

'Oh, it's too bad,' said Gina. 'I don't want to be cooped up in this little room for hours and hours.'

'With shingles,' added Zoë.

'Shingles? I haven't got shingles.'

'Yes, you have. We had to have some excuse for your being up here; it's a funny guest who doesn't ever join the party. Shingles sounds nice and infectious. Fergus offered to bring the tray up, but I told him how painful shingles is. That'll keep him away, you know how Fergus frets and worries when he's ill.'

'Why not plague, and a cross on the door and be done with it?' said Gina resentfully.

'Now, no bitterness, I'm only trying to help. I say, this is a very saucy book. Is it yours?'

Gina glanced at the paperback Zoë was holding up. It had a lascivious scene depicted in shades of grey and rust on the cover, with the title blazoned across the top in heavy silver lettering: *Antics at Antioch*.

'Certainly not,' said Gina.

'It looks good,' said Zoë, skipping through a few pages. Her eyebrows rose. 'Wow! Do you think your Sybil reads this sort of thing? Bit racy for someone of her age.'

'No, she doesn't read them, she writes them,' said Gina.

'Writes them!' Zoë was impressed. 'Well, hats off to her.' She looked at the spine of the book. 'The Madam Press. I've heard of them. They sell thousands and thousands of these.'

'Hence the signs of comfort all around you,' said Gina.

'Tell you what, I think I'd better go down and keep an eye on Fergus. This biddy knows a thing or two, I can tell that much. Dear Fergus would be shocked to pieces if he saw this; it's like putting your hand out to stroke a kitten and discovering you've got a panther sitting there.'

Zoë paused at the door. 'I don't know why you don't just come clean with Fergus, Gina. Much simpler.'

'He'll disapprove terribly, you know how law-abiding he is. Probably straight on the phone to Popplewell and then I'll be for it.'

'I don't think Fergus has got much time for young Popplewell,' said Zoë. 'And I know he's worried about you, he's been fretting because we haven't had a card or a phone call.'

'Tough,' said Gina.

Harry's office was humming with activity as he walked through the outer area to his room. As he divested himself of helmet, boots and the rest of his biking gear, Sally came in.

Harry had no time for flashy young secretaries; he wanted someone with poise, experience, a sense of humour, no family problems, no boyfriend crises and who could spell. Sally, a grandmother of fifty-two with tremendous style and a degree in French, was the answer. Harry was the envy of all his colleagues and friends.

'Letter to sign,' she said, putting the folder on his desk. 'I've done the rest. Tickets for the exhibition in Paris next week; are you still going?'

Harry shrugged on a jacket over his polo-necked shirt. 'No,' he said briefly. 'Can't get away just at the moment, things a bit tense back at Heartsease. Jaspar can go. Any news?'

Harry hadn't been into the office for a few days, and he loved to catch up on the gossip.

'Janos is engaged; he's going to marry that girl he's been going out with. He's over the moon.'

Harry raised his eyebrows. 'What, the astonishingly exotic girl from an atoll? Does she realize what she's letting herself in for, marrying a Hungarian?'

'They'll have beautiful children.'

Harry pulled a face. 'Children!'

'Janos is already designing the nursery.'

'Oh, great,' said Harry, flipping through his mail in a dissatisfied way.

'Your friend William rang, can you meet him for lunch.'

'Too much work,' said Harry. 'I hate William, boring on about his wife and how happy they are. I don't believe a word of it, I think it's armed warfare in that household. I daresay she keeps him in one of those smart units in the kitchen that she's so proud of.'

'I hear she's expecting a baby,' observed Sally.

'Oh, terrific,' said Harry. 'Then I'm definitely not having lunch with him, he'll be drooling on about Vicky and baby names. And look,' said Harry, tossing a thick cream envelope down on to his gleaming black desk. 'A wedding invitation. Another one. All I do is go to weddings, my morning coat is wearing out. Mr and Mrs Nestor . . . their daughter Penelope . . . Good God, she's marrying Esmond. Esmond! I can't believe that Esmond is getting married.'

Sally silently left the room and came back with a cup of coffee.

'Don't do that, Sally,' said Harry, who was still gazing at the invitation. 'I can get my own coffee.'

'Just for once,' said Sally. 'You need reviving, all this matrimonial and paternal news is clearly disturbing you.'

'I should think so,' said Harry, flinging himself into his exceedingly comfortable black leather seat. He gave it a few discontented swivels. 'If it goes on at this rate, I won't have an unmarried friend left.'

'It catches you in the end,' said Sally. 'Unless you're going to be a "bachelor, forty-three", and we all know what that means.'

'What?' demanded Harry. 'What does it mean?'

'Calm down,' said Sally. 'A man who isn't married or living more or less permanently with a girlfriend by the time he's forty isn't going to get married. Or if he does, it'll be hard going.'

'Boyfriends, that's what you mean,' said Harry, now in the sulks.

'Possibly,' said Sally. 'But you've plenty of time yet.'

'Little do you know,' said Harry.

Nerina put her spiky green head round the door. 'Hawwy,' she lisped. 'Dan's off, toothache. We're a wider short.'

Harry hurled himself from his chair. 'See to all this, Sally,' he said. 'I'll call back tonight and take the papers home with me. Nerina, pass me my helmet.'

'Gareth, what does "jejune" mean?' Lori asked as he came into the kitchen on a coffee hunt after a late lie-in.

'Sterile, isn't it? Something like that. Look it up in the dictionary. Silly sounding word, why did that pop into your head?'

Gareth was in a pair of boxer shorts and a cotton dressing-gown, and his tanned stomach curved gently over his waist elastic as he bent down to find the coffee cream in the fridge.

Lori poured him out some coffee. 'Tara.'

'Oh, Tara.'

'She said it about the *guest* room. She said all those rich colours and swags were jejune.'

'Tara doesn't know the meaning of half the words she uses,' said Gareth, deep in his Sunday paper.

'She wasn't being *complimentary*, though, was she?'

'Probably not,' said Gareth. Vestiges of nursery loyalty kept him from saying that Tara thought making complimentary remarks was a waste of good breath. 'You like the way you've done it up, presumably?'

'Yes. Well, I *thought* I did.'

'Then I wouldn't worry what Tara thinks about it. If she doesn't like her room here, then she can stay in London.'

Gareth was feeling a little sour about his sister; her behaviour last night at dinner had, he felt, bordered on the offensive. Since Gareth had one of the thickest skins in the business, this would have astounded his friends and colleagues.

The wild boar had been roasted to a turn, the sauce was exactly right, the potatoes quite delicious. All was going well, and Tara was too busy eating to say much, when the family circle was disturbed by a peal on the period doorbell.

'Who's that?' said Gareth with a frown.

'I'll get it,' said Lori, reappearing a few minutes later with Don behind her.

'Sorry to break in on your meal,' he said, with an amiable and unapologetic smile. 'Prim told me that you wanted a word, Gareth. I was passing, so I thought I'd drop in. Knew you wouldn't mind, Mrs Slubs told me you were only family for dinner.'

'No, no, delighted to see you,' said Gareth. 'Let me pour you a glass of wine.'

Don stretched out his hand and picked up the bottle. 'Not a bad wine,' he said.

'Tara chose it,' said Lori.

'What have you been eating?'

'Wild boar,' said Tara.

'Good choice then,' said Don, replacing the bottle on the table. 'Yes, I'll have a glass of that, Gareth.'

'Are you having more wine, Gareth?' said Tara sweetly.

'I am,' said Gareth.

'Gareth's company have just done a programme on drinking,' said Tara to Don. 'About how many units you should drink a week, and how much it costs the health service to cope with disorders caused by alcoholism.'

'I don't think a glass of wine constitutes alcoholism,' said Gareth crossly.

'And there was the series on obesity, wasn't there?'

'Thank you, Tara.'

'Units,' said Don thoughtfully. 'Strange that one of the great pleasures of civilized man has come down to being units.'

Tara was there, a sweet smile still on her lips. 'Civilized?' she said. 'I don't think anyone talks about civilization these days. If you're talking about Western post-industrialized society, no sociologist would allow you to use that term. It implies that other socio-ethnic groups not part of the Western cultural imposition are not civilized.'

Don gave Tara an amused glance as he held his glass up to the light. 'Excellent,' he said.

'I don't think we need to go into that at the moment, Tara,' said Gareth.

'It's a subject that needs to be logomachized,' said Tara. 'Without a methodological apprehension, your inferential grounds are meaningless.'

'Meaningless,' repeated Don. 'Yes, indeed.'

That had been bad enough. But bloody Tara had gone through his work over the last eighteen months, suggesting, all the time, that his concern for black Northern Irish transvestites, urban gays in the north of England and for the problems of depressed teenage muggers was superficial and cynical in its approach.

And all this in front of Don, who clearly found it very funny.

'Isn't it?' said Lori with a moment of unkindness. 'Superficial and cynical, I mean. Don't you do it because it's what the programmers want?'

'I suppose so,' said Gareth. 'I'm bloody sure the viewers don't want it, but it gives the powers-that-be a pleasant feeling of somehow caring more deeply about mournful issues than anyone else.'

'Besides, upbeat stories aren't newsworthy.'

'Very true, my love,' said Gareth, feeling mildly comforted and turning his eyes to the astonishing goings-on in Tooting. SECRET ORGIES IN CHURCH HALL, screamed the headlines.

How peaceful life in Heartwell is, by comparison, thought Gareth. No excitement here beyond an argument over the church flowers. Give me London any day, that's where Life is.

'You do *realize* Tara's got her eye on Don?' said Lori, as she loaded the last of the dishes into the dishwasher and shut the door with a bang.

'Tara's got a boyfriend,' said Gareth absently, still deep in Tooting.

'I'll make a *bet* with you; she'll be down here much more often.'

'Not on the weekends when the children are home from school,' said Gareth. He had laughed when Lori noticed that, despite Tara's solicitous enquiries about their daughters and professed enthusiasm for their company, she never came at the weekends when they were at home.

It was deliberate, of course. Tara always removed the term's dates from the cork noticeboard in the kitchen and stowed the paper away in her bag. You couldn't leave things like that to chance.

*

Zoë knocked on the door and looked in as Gina answered with a wary, 'Who is it?'

'Bored?' asked Zoë.

Gina just looked at her.

'Good news, you can come out for a bit. Fergus and Sybil and I are going off to a garden.'

'A garden?'

'Yes, to look at some special plants. Fergus is very knowledgeable, which is quite unexpected, and Sybil's a real enthusiast, so off we go. Stay within sound of the phone, I'll ring to let you know when we're starting back. You should have at least three hours of freedom.'

'And then no doubt Fergus and you are coming to eat here?'

''Fraid so. I asked Sybil over to our cottage, but they vetoed that. I can hear the car revving up; natives are getting restless. So it's supper on a tray for you, I hope you've got lots you want to read. Bye!'

Gina bounded out of her room as the sound of the car died away. She was feeling decidedly displeased, and her displeasure was aimed mostly, and quite unfairly, at Fergus.

Stupid man, she said as she wandered out into the garden. What did he want to come here for? Why couldn't he have stayed in Oxford? And why did he have to get all budsy-wudsy with Sybil, instead of minding his own business?

Three hours, Zoë had said. What should she do?

Vineyard, she decided. She'd buy a bottle of something fizzy as a thank-you to Sybil. There would be plenty of time to do that and be back for Zoë's warning call.

Tomorrow she'd be going back to the Hall, what a relief. At least she had settled in there in her impostor's guise. Having to skulk and pretend here in Heartwell on top of that was just too much, she told herself as she crossed the road. She set off down the footpath which would take her across two fields and then join up with the track which led to the vineyard.

The scars of last night were still with her; she'd never felt nervous walking alone in open countryside, but now she did. She walked briskly, jumping over the stile between the two fields and almost running the last hundred, wooded yards to the track.

That was better, and she slowed down to a gentle stroll more suitable for the hot, heavy weather. Through the archway, into the courtyard. There was the shop, and on the door was a large sign. CLOSED.

Gina cursed under her breath, and was turning to go back when the door flew open. Nadia was standing there, attired in a rather grubby blue and white striped apron. She was glaring.

'What do you want?' she demanded.

'Some wine,' said Gina, going back to the shop door.

'It says closed. Can't you read?'

'I know it says closed,' said Gina, irritated. 'That's why I was going away.'

'Without any wine?'

'This is a pointless conversation,' said Gina. 'If you're closed, then I'll go.'

'Where will you go?'

'I'll go to the pub when it opens, and ask them to sell me some wine. Or the village shop will be open later, and I can buy it there.'

'Oh, no, you won't. You can buy it here, from me. Come in, come in.'

Gina shrugged at this perversity, hesitated for a moment and then went through the door. Inside she stood still in surprise, looking round at the chaos about her.

'Whatever's happened?' she asked. 'Did burglars get in?'

'Burglars? What burglars? I did this, by myself. My husband should have helped, but he has to work in our house today, because he wasted time already helping some woman in the village to build her swimming pool.'

'That was Sybil and me,' said Gina. 'I'm sorry if we took your husband away from important work. He was very helpful, and he did offer to come.'

'Of course he offers to come, when a pretty woman asks him. He says it was to help the old woman, but then he thinks I'm stupid. So, you like the look of my husband, huh?'

'I like Byron, yes,' said Gina.

'Take him,' said Nadia dramatically. 'Take him! He would be pleased to get away from me, I'm just his Russian wife who married him to get a passport.'

Any English person would have been acutely embarrassed by this, would have hastily bought whatever bottle was nearest, and then would have fled from the shop, apologizing.

But Gina wasn't English. She was an American, and half-Russian herself, and, without ever having behaved like that herself, she understood Nadia's temper. Besides she was very interested in this mention of marrying someone to get a passport.

'Calm down,' she said. 'I'm not after your husband. I can tell you, my life's quite complicated enough as it is without adding Byron to the mixture. No, don't start up again. Listen, *did* you marry Byron for a passport?'

Nadia's eyes darkened tragically. She became a broken woman, an exile from Siberia, a dying swan.

Gina went on looking steadily at her. 'Well?'

'Okay, I tell you the story. Do you like stories? This story is a good one, with a kink in its tail, like all the best stories.'

CHAPTER 15

'My great-grandmother left Russia in 1917, in a hurry. Everything then was at sixes and sevens, you know that?' Sixes and sevens was a good way to describe the Russian Revolution, thought Gina. 'Yes, it was,' she agreed.

'Her family weren't aristocrats, but her husband, my great-grandfather, who was much older than she was, was a merchant, he did a lot of business in America. He could see the way things were going. So she left her baby with her older sister, and went to the States. The sister and baby were supposed to follow, only they never did.'

'How dreadful.'

'They didn't get killed, it wasn't dreadful at all.'

'No, I mean being separated from her baby.'

'I don't think she minded so much. She was only seventeen, and was having a good time, and then she had more children.'

'Oh!'

'Her sister brought up the baby, my grandmother, with her own children. They did okay, which means they survived the thirties and the war and so on. Despite the difficulties, Babushka, which is what we all called her, managed to keep in touch with the family. She used to write to my mother, and then, from when I was about ten, she wrote to me. In English and French, because she said it was good for me to practise foreign languages.'

'French?'

'Didn't I say? She went to live in France, after the war. She loved Paris, and of course there were a lot of Russians there. My parents are both engineers, but I studied foreign languages. I always thought, one day, I will go to Paris and meet my great-grandmother. If you are good at languages, you can get sent abroad, with trade delegations and so on, as interpreter.'

'Did you?'

'They never sent young ones, they didn't trust them. They always sent Oleg or Olga, in their fifties, big boots, warts on their chins. No romance or escaping for them.'

'But you met Byron.'

'Yes, and this is what is so terrible. There he was, very good-looking, charming, English, rather shy . . . I wasn't interpreter to his party, but I arranged it so I swapped with the girl who was. She was married to a doctor, and had a small son, she didn't need to meet any young westerners. For this, I gave her three oranges.'

'And you fell in love with Byron?'

'I wanted to go to Paris, to see my great-grandmother. She was so old, I knew it must be soon. It was terribly important for me, to see her. You wouldn't understand, it was an obsession. I had all her letters, from when I was a girl, I felt closer to her than I did to my own mother. And I told her things that I never told my own mother. And I promised, "Babushka, I will come and see you in Paris."'

Gina didn't find any of this surprising. She had heard endless stories about separated families; Russians who were more interested in the lives of their distant relations than they were in what was happening around them every day. And for a lonely child, growing up in hard times, her contact with her great-grandmother in France would be like a window on to another world.

'So I decided to marry him. I had a boyfriend of my own, a Russian, and we were in love, genuinely in love. But I went after Byron, and fascinated him, and made him fall in love with me. Cold-blooded, huh?'

'I expect I would have done the same,' said Gina in neutral tones. She could see that Nadia was quite ready to launch into a temper at any hint of criticism.

'It's so easy, with an Englishman. These boys who have been to good schools, they know nothing, nothing at all, where women are concerned. It's like stealing from a baby. So, a lot of fuss and problems, but finally, we were married, and I could leave Russia, and we went to Paris for the honeymoon.'

'So you got to meet your great-grandmother at last.'

Gina could see tears gleaming in Nadia's angry eyes.

'No. She died, the week before we came. I was too late even for the funeral.'

'Uh, uh,' said Gina. Poor Nadia, she thought. And then, poor Byron.

'Poor Byron, indeed,' said Nadia, with a dramatic sigh.

'Did he ever find out why you'd married him?'

'Yes.'

'How?'

'I told him. There, by my Babushka's grave.'

'Ah.'

'He has ridiculous ideas of honour, he wouldn't leave me. He said I was his wife, and he wasn't going to leave me to cope in a strange country on my own. England, he meant.'

'You seem to have coped very well. Couldn't you leave him?'

'That's probably what he would like. That's what he hopes for.'

'Then why on earth are you still together?'

'Because, after we were married and we had come back to England, I realized I was in love with him. Gregor, my fiancé in Russia, pooh, I knew I felt nothing for him any more. It was only Byron.'

'So what's the problem? I suppose he isn't in love with you any more?'

'He is, he is! Or he says he is,' she added darkly. 'Only, now, he doesn't believe that I love him. Whatever I say, he thinks I just stay with him out of convenience, or because I feel sorry for him.'

'What a muddle,' said Gina, trying not to laugh.

'It is not at all funny,' said Nadia. 'It is very bad for our sex life, which is now practically non-existent, because he thinks if I want to make love I'm being kind, and then, flop, nothing!'

'It's a difficult situation,' said Gina.

'Impossible,' said Nadia. 'Impossible. Now, which wine, sparkling did you say? You will take two bottles, and I give you a special price.'

'I only want one, for a present.'

'Then you take two, one to drink yourself, or with a lover. Harry perhaps? That's eighteen pounds, I've given you a good discount.'

Gina knew when she was beaten, and handed over the money. 'It's going to be heavy to carry back,' she said.

'Why? Where's your car?'

'I came along the footpath.'

'It's not so far,' said Nadia. 'I walk everywhere, carrying much heavier things than that. We can't afford to use the car. Walking is good for you, and carrying, too. Makes you strong, eh?'

They were only a mile from the cottage when Zoë, wedged in the back between a palm and something with dark leaves and aggressive prickles, suddenly remembered that she should have given Gina a warning call. Peering round the palm, she tried to attract Sybil's attention.

Sybil, deep in conversation with Fergus, who was sitting in the front on account of his long legs, took no notice.

Zoë abandoned discretion. 'Sybil,' she said. 'Please could we go via Heartwell and the village shop. I need something.'

Sybil and Fergus, both politely thinking of items of feminine hygiene, made no objection.

'Gina?' said Zoë. 'At last! Where were you, I thought you were never going to answer.'

'Harry's here. He says that my father's left, so I can go back to the Hall. How long are you going to be?'

'About five minutes.'

'Oh, Zoë, you aren't serious! You said you'd ring when you started back. Where are you?'

'The phone box at Heartwell.'

'Where are Sybil and Fergus?'

'In the car. They think I've gone into the shop; they're so busy yakking they haven't noticed I'm here instead.'

'Take as long as you can,' said Gina. 'Give me time to collect my belongings.'

'You can always come back for them later,' said Zoë. 'Draw the curtains up in your room, and we'll pretend you're still there, asleep.'

'When's Fergus going back to Oxford?'

'Tomorrow.'

'Thank goodness.'

*

Harry found the whole business very funny, as Gina flew about the cottage collecting various bits and pieces.

'It'd be very lively being married to you,' he observed, as Gina thrust an armful of clothes into his arms. 'You'd never know what you were going to do next. Can't these go in your bag?'

'No room, I've just stuffed everything else in there. Now, let's go, quickly.'

They passed Sybil's car at the corner, Gina hastily ducking her head down as though she was rummaging in the glove compartment.

'Perfect timing,' said Harry. 'And we'll be back in time for tea. I could just do with a cucumber sandwich.'

Back at the cottage, Zoë was suffering from shock.

'Wasn't that Harry in that car we passed?' Fergus said to Sybil as he retrieved the palm and pulled Zoë out of the back. 'Harry Cordovan?'

'Yes,' said Sybil, surprised. 'Do you know him?'

'Known him all my life,' said Fergus breezily. 'I meant to drop in at the Hall while I was here, but I haven't got round to it. I'll call in tomorrow before I go. Are you all right, Zoë? Hiccups?'

Zoë rushed inside, followed at a more sedate pace by Sybil, who was looking very amused, and by Fergus, whose mind had returned to the serious engineering works out in the garden, namely the pool.

'We should have it ready by this evening,' he told Sybil. 'It can fill overnight, and I'll get the pump fixed up for you first thing in the morning.'

'I can do the pump,' said Sybil.

'No, no, I know you want to get on with your book. I'll see to that, and get the chemicals in for you. Then it's all set up and ready for when your grandchildren come.'

'Thank you,' said Sybil, with a warm smile.

'Creep,' thought Zoë, listening from the kitchen. A bottle of fizz on the kitchen table caught her eye.

She read the label round its neck: 'Sybil, Thank you very much, love, Gina.' That's right, leave it out for everyone to see, she thought, whisking it into the cupboard under the sink as Fergus came in.

Plan, she said to herself. I need a plan. How am I going to find Gina and warn her about Fergus before he tips up to say hello, and runs smack into her?

Gina was surprised to find how much it felt like coming home to be back at the Hall. Tea was being served on the terrace under the shade of three enormous canvas umbrellas. Aimée was reclining on a ship's chair under the shade of a huge oak, with an elegant swain in attendance. A game of croquet was in progress, with Victor, immaculate in a linen suit and panama, stroking his hand thoughtfully over his trim beard as he planned a shot to crack his opponent out of the game.

'Never take on Pa at croquet,' warned Harry, as he dropped into a deckchair. 'He's a killer, and if you should chance to beat him, he'll take weeks to forgive you.'

'He looks as though he's enjoying himself,' said Gina, shading her eyes with her hand.

'At his most jovial,' said Harry. 'Wait until someone knocks his ball away; thunderous isn't the word.'

'I always thought croquet was kind of a genteel game.'

'No way,' said Harry.

'China or Indian?' said Guy, materializing over her shoulder. 'I hope you had a good weekend with Sybil, Gina.'

'Thank you, yes,' said Gina, thinking how wonderfully restful it was here, and what an exhausting weekend it had been.

'Seven o'clock, Guy?' said Harry, without opening his eyes.

'I'll be ready,' said Guy, gathering up plates and cups.

'Where are you going with Guy?' asked Gina.

'Gay club,' said Harry, now apparently almost asleep.

'*Where?*'

'In Heartsbury.'

'I mean, did you really say a gay club?'

'I did. Do I detect a note of disapproval in your voice?'

'Why should I disapprove?'

Because I do, Gina thought. One minute in bed with me, the next down at the gay club. That's sordid. Yes, I know I felt I could put up with a bisexual husband, but he should keep his other amours private. No place is less private than a gay club, of all places.

'You can do what you like,' she said coldly.

'I shall,' said Harry imperturbably.

'I can't imagine what a gay club in a cathedral city must be like.'

'Great place,' said Harry. 'And don't angle to come too, because I'd lose all my cred if I turned up with you. Besides, I don't want to take you.'

'Fine by me,' said Gina. 'I don't want to go.'

'Touch of homophobia?'

'Not at all. I'd just rather go to a club where there are straight guys.'

'You do get some there, trying to pick up the women who've gone so that they can have a good night out without being pestered by the blokes.'

'It all sounds very complicated,' said Gina stiffly, putting her cup down and struggling out of her deckchair.

'In a huff?' said Harry.

'I couldn't be bothered to be that,' said Gina. 'I have some letters to write.'

'If you're writing to Georgie, give her my love,' said Harry, settling back into his snooze.

Men, Gina said to herself as she went through the arch into the orchard. I hate men.

A nearby pig gave a friendly grunt.

'Exactly,' said Gina.

'I'm not sitting on that terrible little train for hours, and then more hours waiting at wherever it is for a connection to London,' said Tara.

Lori was talking on the phone to her elder daughter. 'Just a minute, darling, Tara's saying something.' She put her hand over the mouthpiece. 'You can't expect Gareth to *drive* you all the way to Heartsbury, Tara. There's nothing wrong with the train. Sorry, yes, new gym shorts? Yes, you can ask matron to get them at the shop, but be sure to get ones that fit properly. You *know* how matron allows for growing room. No, darling, the last ones had to go back, they were down to your *knees*.'

Tara fell into a sulk, and, as Gareth came into the room, began to complain about the appalling journey she was faced with because Lori felt he, Gareth, couldn't drive her to Heartsbury. 'It's hardly far, only twenty-five miles. Nothing; when you live in the country you expect to drive that all the time.'

Gareth ignored the flapping signals from Lori, and thought for a moment or two. 'Lori's right,' he said finally. 'Nothing wrong with the train from Heartsease. However . . .'

'And how often do you take it?' said Tara, much put out.

'That's different. Anyhow, I'll take you to Heartsbury this time, because there's a chap I want to see there about a programme.'

Lori finished her phone conversation with a promise to send more pocket money, and frowned at Gareth. 'Does that mean you won't be here at *all* this evening?'

Gareth shifted under his wife's gaze. 'No, well, I suppose not.'

'And then off to London tomorrow for the *week*, and I won't see you until late on Friday, if I'm *lucky*. Wonderful.'

'Shut up,' said Gareth without rancour. 'I thought I'd stay down here tomorrow, and buzz up on Tuesday morning. I may even come back down on Tuesday evening, or on Wednesday; I've got work I can do here.'

Lori's face lightened. 'Good. Don't forget it's sports day on Saturday.'

Gareth adored his children, and loved going to school dos. He showed off terribly, and embarrassed the girls to the nth degree, but Sports Day was one of the highlights of his year. 'Terrific,' he said. 'And I hope that bloody PE teacher has put Melissa in a decent heat for the hundred metres, no idiots with two left feet careering about the track like there were last year.'

Lori made soothing noises, and Tara went off to the kitchen to pack up a substantial food parcel for herself, some to eat on the train, some to have when she got home and some for the freezer. Every little bit helps, she told herself.

Zoë felt very strongly that there were better ways to spend a hot June afternoon than trapped inside a circular swimming pool, ironing out wrinkles.

'This water in here is cold,' she informed Fergus. 'And why am I on my hands and knees in here while you're out on dry land?'

'It's important work, checking the railing at the top,' said Fergus. 'And it's essential that we get all the wrinkles out.'

'We,' said Zoë indignantly. 'The choice of pronoun is interesting.'

'I'm reading the instructions and finding out what has to be done.'

'And I'm doing it.'

'You need the exercise.'

'This isn't exercise, it's torture.'

'It's to help Sybil. Besides, if you weren't doing this, what would you be doing? Lying on that swinging sofa affair and reading a book.'

'Blissful thought,' said Zoë angrily, as she bludgeoned a particularly unruly wrinkle into flatness.

Fergus turned to bribery. 'If we get this finished, I'll stand you a drink at the Bunch of Grapes.'

'You'll stand me more than one, Fergus McEttrick,' said Zoë darkly.

Wilf welcomed the two of them like old friends. 'Caught the sun, I see,' he said to Zoë. 'Been sunbathing?'

'Not exactly, no,' said Zoë.

Fergus took Zoë away into the garden before she could complain about her afternoon, and calmed her down with a cool drink.

'Pity Gina can't join us,' said Zoë unthinkingly.

'Difficult, when she's in America.'

'What?' said Zoë. 'Oh, yes, of course. I meant, it would be nice if Gina hadn't had to go back to America and could be here with us. In Heartset, I mean. In England. Instead of America. Where she is.'

'Have some nuts,' said Fergus. 'You've obviously got a rush of alcohol to the brain on an empty stomach; it isn't good for you.' He chewed a cashew reflectively. 'I'm worried about Gina.'

Zoë gave a start and slopped some of her drink on to her leg. 'Clumsy of me,' she said, dabbing at it. 'Why are you worried?'

'I'd like to know where she is; she should have got in touch by now. It isn't like her, I would have expected her to let us know her address. And how can we help with permits and visas if we don't know where she is? She could be anywhere, for God's sake. New York, California, Mexico . . . Don't you care? I mean, I thought she was your friend. She could even be back in England, for all we know.'

Zoë took a deep breath; calm, she told herself, keep calm. 'Back in England? Now, that's one place she can't be. How would she get back into England without a visa?'

'No, okay, I know, she's in America. I know she can't be in this country. It's just that I could have sworn I saw her in that car being driven by Harry Cordovan.'

Zoë thought fast and furiously. 'That's because you've seen Harry with Matilda.'

'Matilda?'

'Matilda Fotheringay,' said Zoë, with increasing confidence. 'Sybil was telling me about her. Dark, olive skin, Spanish ancestors. Very like Gina, I should think. Curly hair. You know.'

'Have you met this Matilda?'

'Not met exactly, no, but she's around. Makes you think about Gina, though, doesn't it? And how nice it would be to have her back again. Never mind, I'm sure she's having a great time, making lots of new friends, rediscovering America. Out on dates every night.'

'Hmm,' said Fergus, without enthusiasm.

Don was spending his Sunday evening in the way he liked best; relaxed, good wine at hand, and female company. Only one today, a minor drawback, since Don preferred a crowd, but he wasn't complaining. He was lounging on the verandah of his house; he was naked, slightly pink and curvy, and very happy.

Nicky was pleased too, but filled with all the doubts and guilts which Don was a stranger to.

'Love me?' she asked hopefully, trickling cold wine over Don's tummy.

'Mmm,' said Don, never one to commit himself.

'I've bought a stunning dress for the ball,' ventured Nicky, lying back against Don.

He took a grape from the bunches lying beside him on a silver dish and dropped one into her mouth.

'Aimée's party, yes, of course. I'd forgotten that.'

Nicky twisted round to look at him. 'Don, you've got four people staying overnight. Have you forgotten?'

'I expect so,' said Don. 'Nice people, I do trust.'

'I expect so,' said Nicky.

'Luscious young friends of Aimée's?' asked Don hopefully.

'You'd like that, would you?'

'Always,' said Don.

'What are you thinking about?' said Nicky presently.

'Vines.'

'How unusual,' said Nicky with a sigh.

'They need rain. I'll have a word with Prim, find out how she sees the summer shaping up.'

Another pleasurable pause. Nicky was just beginning to feel at ease, when Don passed his hand over the top of his head in a thoughtful way, and shattered her calm.

'I'll ask that Tara whatshername, the one staying at Heartwell House, to the ball. You'd better send her a card. Or put her down on mine.'

Nicky couldn't believe it. Her eyes stung with tears as she got up violently and abruptly, sending her glass of wine flying.

'What a waste,' said Don.

'You are a bastard,' said Nicky, her red hair flaming out like an aureole as the sun fell on it.

'She amuses me,' said Don, quite unconcerned.

'Don't I?'

'Constantly. But I know you so well, and novelty counts. And you'll be busy at the ball with this and that; one needs a partner on one's arm at these affairs, don't you agree? If you feel you want a partner for yourself, you could ask Roger.'

'Roger? My husband?'

'I should think he'd love it. Of course, just to complicate matters, he might like to come but to bring a partner of his own. I do hear rumours about a delectable girl from Corda Episcopi.'

Nicky picked up Don's glass and flung the contents in his face. He moved his head gently to one side, and only a few drops touched him.

'Temper, temper,' he said. 'Do you know, life is full of amusement? I never fail to marvel at the rich comedy which is constantly being enacted around us. Going, Nicky? I thought we could drive to Frederico's and have a delightful dinner together. No, no, don't say it, or I might decide to dine alone.'

CHAPTER 16

Gareth eased his way through the throng at the bar and headed for the small table where Harry was sitting, utterly relaxed, watching the dancers on the floor.

'Can I join you?' Gareth didn't wait for a reply, but pulled out the third chair at the table and sat down, putting his spritzer on the table in front of him.

Harry's eyebrows rose, giving his face a quizzical expression.

'I'm Gareth Mowbray. Neighbour of yours, I live at Heartwell House.'

Harry held out his hand to shake Gareth's, which rattled Gareth and put him at a disadvantage.

'Of course. We've never met, but I know who you are.' Harry sat back in his seat again, leaving Gareth to do the talking.

'I'm not trying to pick you up.'

'I'm sure you're not,' said Harry politely. 'Even if you were, you wouldn't succeed. Not my type.'

Gareth followed Harry's eyes. 'Is he your friend?' he asked, gesturing towards Guy. 'Incredible looker.'

'He is a friend, but not exactly *my* friend, no. And yes, he is a looker, as you put it.'

'Who is he?'

'Interested? I don't think you'd be his type either.'

Gareth was watching Guy intently. 'I'm not gay,' he remarked. 'Good face, he'd be great on camera.'

'Don't tell me you're a film director, out looking for talent? Rather an old line, don't you think?'

Gareth took no notice of the contempt in Harry's voice. 'TV

producer,' he said. 'Not film. Do you know what that young man does?'

'For a living? He works for us.'

'Us? You run a courier service, don't you? Or is it modems and things?'

'Both.'

Gareth seemed disappointed. 'So he's a computer kid, is he? Or is he a bike-rider?'

'Neither. When I say he works for us, I mean for my family. At the Hall.'

'Cooking? Does he cook?'

'Why the interest? Are you looking for a cook? I don't think Guy would leave the Hall for a similar position anywhere else. He's planning to run his own hotel in due course.'

'So he's trained, knows his way about the kitchen?'

'That's part of what he does, yes.'

Gaareth drained his glass and eyed the bottle of champagne longingly.

'What are you drinking?' asked Harry. 'A glass of champagne?'

'Love to,' said Gareth, 'but I can't risk it. Points on my licence already, I've got to be ultra careful. I'll stick with wine and water.'

He heaved himself up and edged his way to the bar to get a refill.

'Busy here tonight,' he said when he came back. 'Is it usually like this on a Sunday night?'

'It's fairly brisk most nights, I believe. Haven't you been before?'

'No. Not altogether my scene, although I must say, I like the atmosphere. We're looking at a series on the provincial club scene. This won't do. Too civilized, and people are enjoying themselves. No conflict that I can see, nothing outrageous, wouldn't pull the viewers.'

'Here comes Guy.'

Guy slid into his place, looking at Gareth with a certain wariness. 'Not one of us,' he said. 'Why are you here?'

'Gareth's a TV producer,' said Harry. 'Out looking for talent.'

Gareth waited for the quickening of interest, the gleam in the eye, the flare of hope. Me? On television perhaps? The self-consciousness, the slight showing off.

Nothing.

Nothing?

'Oh,' said Guy, with no interest at all. 'What kind of programmes do you make?'

'They've just finished broadcasting my most recent one, *Animals under the Skin*. Very well received. Bestiality.'

Guy looked revolted. 'Tacky programmes,' he said.

Tacky? Nobody called his programmes tacky.

'Strong stuff,' Gareth said sulkily. 'Lot of complaints from the provinces.'

'More fool them for watching,' said Guy with a fastidious sniff. 'I wouldn't dream of turning on for that kind of rubbish.'

'I suppose you like comedy and sweet documentaries about animals in the wild?'

'I don't like programmes designed to make me feel uncomfortable and miserable about human beings. Okay?' Guy turned his attention back to the dancers.

Gareth tried another gambit. 'You may be more in tune with public taste than you think. There is some evidence that people aren't so keen now on downbeat, realistic programmes.'

'Were they ever?' asked Harry. 'Are there people who deliberately choose to be bored or disgusted?'

'We aim to inform.'

'No, you aim to make money,' said Harry breezily. 'So now it's some new angle on gay clubs, is it?'

Gareth frowned. 'That's in the pipeline, yes. But I feel – I keep a finger on the public pulse, you understand – I feel that there's a change of mood. I'm seriously considering an intellectual slot.' He leant forward confidentially, as though imparting state secrets. 'I'm looking for an historian, actually. To front a series. An academic, we need a name, but it's got to be someone who comes across on screen. Someone a bit aggressive. Viewers like some aggro, bit of venom, some spit on the lens.'

'I see,' said Harry.

'And we've got a brilliant cookery series. One of the top angry young chefs is going to front for us. Really rip the guts out of cooking programmes, none of your usual sweetness and light and I have here a dish I prepared earlier. We're going for a whole new approach.'

'Really?'

'He looks a nice boy,' said Guy, who hadn't been listening to a word Gareth was saying, but was eyeing one of the dancers. 'Good style.'

'How are you affected by the Aids threat?' Gareth asked.

Guy was affronted. 'I don't usually get personal with straight men who've just walked in and sat at my table. My sexuality and my sex life is my own business.'

'You see?' Gareth said to Harry. 'That look on the screen, it'd be a knockout. We'd have Sigismund – he's the chef – bitching away at Guy here, and Guy looking like that . . .'

'I beg your pardon?' said Guy.

'New programme. Look, pop over and see me. I think we could be on to something here. Of course I can't promise, there are a lot of other people involved, and of course, dozens of people in the chef business dying to get on to the series. But I think you might be it, yes, I really do.'

Guy stared at him for a moment. 'Are you saying you might want me to be on television?'

Wait for it: disbelief; gratitude; rapture.

'On this cooking programme you've just been talking about?'

'You've got it.'

'Well, really!' Guy was extremely put out. 'That's the most vulgar thing I ever heard. What do you take me for?'

He rose from his seat.

'Where are you going?' asked Gareth, perplexed.

'To dance,' said Guy.

'Are you coming back? We need to talk some more.'

'I'll come back,' said Guy pointedly, 'after you've left.'

The shopkeeper watched Sybil walking across the green, a frown on his face. He was so busy watching her that the vicar, trying to pay for his paper, had to touch his arm.

'Sorry, I was miles away.'

'It's nice to have Sybil back, don't you think?' said the vicar, quite genuinely pleased.

'Nice is not the word I would choose to use, no, vicar,' said the shopkeeper, slamming the till drawer shut with a defiant clang.

'Dangerous is what that lady is, and it's a bad day for the village when she comes a-traipsing back. I won't say poking of her nose into other people's affairs that are best left undisturbed, because she don't do no poking, she just seems to know.'

'She does keep her ears to the ground,' the vicar admitted. 'But all the women in the village like a gossip. It's human nature.'

'There's gossip and gossip, and then there's what she knows about, which is something quite other. I'm surprised you so much as pass the time of day with her; in olden times she'd have been burnt at the stake.' And a good thing, too, he added under his breath.

'Well, well, you know as well as I do that those witches of days gone by were no more than village women who'd made themselves unpopular. We live in more enlightened times, I'm glad to say, and one has to remember that even when one watches all the appalling items on the news every day. We don't behead people, we don't hang children, and we don't burn witches.'

The shopkeeper was unconvinced; the vicar could see from his expression that he probably thought a bit of beheading and burning wouldn't come at all amiss.

Sybil went on her way, passing a group of three silly teenage girls who stopped their giggling and looked at Sybil with wary, doubtful expressions.

'Beautiful morning,' said Sybil. 'And it was a beautiful night last night, was it, Jackie?'

'It were a storm,' said the boldest of the three.

'Jackie was enjoying a different kind of storm, weren't you, Jackie? Snug away from the wind in the haystack. Naughty, though, with your Bob's dad. He must be forty if he's a day.'

Jackie had gone scarlet. 'I never . . . How do you know what I was doing, bloody peeping Tom, that's what you are.'

'No peeping, I assure you,' said Sybil. 'But what a mistake it was, Jackie, that's a roll in the hay you're going to regret. What are you going to do if you've fallen pregnant, pretend to Bob that the baby's his? Go and live with him and his dad at the farm and hop from bed to bed?'

'I hates you.'

'No, you don't, you just hate facing up to what's what. You run

172

along to Dr Cordovan at her clinic, tell her I sent you, ask for a morning-after pill.'

Jackie gave a horrified squeal. 'I'm not taking any of they pills.'

The bold girl was looking at her with contempt. 'You better, Jackie, if what the lady says is true. I don't know how you could do that, Bob's a lovely boy, and his dad's a right dirty old man.'

'It's all right for you, but Bob won't do nothing with me.'

'Knows where you've been. Come on, Jackie, it's the clinic for you.' She threw Sybil an unappreciative look and, together with the third girl, dragged Jackie off towards the bus stop.

Wilf at the Bunch of Grapes in Heartsbane saw Sybil's familiar figure come into sight along the lane. He put down the glass he was polishing and called to Madge to get out the good Italian coffee.

Madge appeared beside him at the bar, ready to switch the coffee machine on.

Wilf and Madge took Sybil as they found her. What if she did seem to know that Wilf hadn't been entirely accurate on his VAT returns? It didn't worry Wilf, and Sybil wasn't about to call round at the Customs and Excise Office, was she?

Sybil had laughed at the idea. 'None of my business, Wilf, you carry on, I've no time for bureaucrats.'

'I wouldn't like to be the taxman trying to get money out of her, either,' Wilf had observed at the time. 'Must be a mort of tax due, too. Wonder how she manages to live as high as she do, though. Don't see writing can pay so well, and she's not one of they famous crime ladies, always on the telly.'

'Phil at the shop do say that she live on blackmail. She know too much, and people pay her to keep quiet.'

'Phil got his own problems,' said Wilf cryptically. 'Maybe she do get a cut off the estate agents, because there's no denying, when she say this or that, folks do move away.'

'No matter,' said Madge comfortably. ''Tis mostly the folks we don't want. I'll be pleased to see the back of that Godfrey, him and his dirty ways.'

Wilf went to the door and loomed over Sybil as she came in. 'Good morning, and very nice to have you back again. Coffee? Inside? Or there's a nice shady spot in the garden, lovely day again.'

'I'm meeting a young friend,' said Sybil. 'Is he out there?'

'Tall, dark young man? Yes, he is, and I'll bring your coffee right away.'

Fergus was enjoying his coffee in the warm, shady garden. He leapt to his feet as Sybil approached, pulling out a chair for her. Then he resumed his own seat, folded up his paper and smiled at Sybil. He liked her, no nonsense about her and a keen wit to go with her brains.

'You've got your grandfather's nose,' observed Sybil unexpectedly. 'Striking, but you'll never make a male model.'

Wilf came out of the pub, carrying a tray laden with Sybil's coffee and some biscuits.

'This is Fergus McEttrick, Wilf,' said Sybil. 'Staying at Kingfisher Cottage.'

Wilf extended a muscular hand.

'Friend, is he?' he said.

'I was at school with his mother, but I haven't seen him since he was a baby. Last time I saw him he was standing up in his cot,' said Sybil. 'Stark naked, and peeing over his nurse.'

Fergus was astonished. 'You didn't tell me you knew my mother.'

'There's a lot I don't tell people,' said Sybil cryptically. 'You used to have tantrums,' she went on, pouring out her coffee.

'How very embarrassing,' said Fergus, reddening.

Sybil looked at him thoughtfully. 'You know, despite the nose, you're very like your mother,' she said.

'Most people think I take after my father,' Fergus ventured.

'I'm not talking about looks,' said Sybil. 'Although it's no bad thing to take after your father in looks, he was a very handsome man. No, you're like your mother in spirit. She's a woman of great spirit.'

Fergus was fond of his mother, but he wouldn't have described her in those terms. To him she seemed very conventional, busy about her duties, careful with money, a hard-working, affectionate and firm mother.

Sybil dunked a biscuit in her coffee. 'I remember when she went off to Peru because a young man she met at a dance was posted there. And then, when she got there, she decided he wasn't such a fine young man as she'd thought.'

Fergus began to look alarmed. 'Look here,' he said.

'But she found lots who were,' went on Sybil.

'My mother?' said Fergus. 'You must be thinking of someone else.'

'Doesn't she talk about those days?' said Sybil. 'Well, well, you want to ask her. Remind her of Raimondo.'

Fergus was feeling more and more bewildered.

'I know my mother was in South America when she was young,' he said stiffly. 'She went to stay with some relations on a ranch, I believe.'

'She did no such thing,' said Sybil, with what Fergus could only describe as a ribald laugh. 'And when she'd made enough whoopee in Peru, she headed off to the States. She smuggled herself in across the Mexican border; then she decided she needed more education, and went to college. She worked her way through, enormous determination she always had. Once her mind was set on anything, that was it. Nothing would stand in her way.'

'My mother?'

'The adventures she had in America! Enjoyed every minute, she told me, even when she was broke and in every kind of predicament.'

'I knew she'd been to America,' said Fergus doubtfully. 'But she went there on a normal visit, as far as I ever heard.'

'What's normal?' said Sybil with a shrug. 'You aren't drinking your coffee,' she added kindly. 'It'll get cold.'

Fergus picked up his cup of coffee and put it down again as Sybil went on.

'That was where she met your father. He was very determined, wooed her up and down five states. He'd gone to America to get away from his stuffy family for a while. Good thing he did, too, because he made a packet over there. They'd never have hung on to the estate if it hadn't been for the money your father made in the States.'

'Money? In America? My father?'

'Don't you ever talk to your parents?'

Fergus thought for a moment. 'I do, but they've never mentioned any of this. Are you sure about all this?'

'Why would I make it up?' said Sybil.

Fergus apologized for questioning what she'd said, but he was still reeling from the mass of revelations about his seemingly staid parents.

'And what about you, Fergus? You're just the age your parents were when they took off. And you're at Oxford still.'

'Postgrad work,' agreed Fergus.

'Very dull,' said Sybil. 'And what then?'

'Once I get my doctorate? Find a job in London, I suppose.'

'Don't you want to flex your muscles, Fergus? Spread your wings?'

'I'm likely to get married, quite soon,' said Fergus defensively.

'Who to?'

'A girl called Charlotte. We've been together for some time.'

'And you're wild about each other?'

Fergus looked alarmed.

'I wouldn't exactly say that. Charlotte isn't the wild type.'

Sybil burst out laughing. 'Oh, my dear young man, a touch of wildness is just what you need. I think it's definitely bonnet time for you. All we have to do is find you a windmill, what do you say?'

Fergus could think of nothing to say.

At the Hall, Zoë was arguing with Gina. 'It's ridiculous, all this cloak and dagger business, it's only Fergus. He wouldn't let you down.'

Gina was standing her ground. 'He'd disapprove. He'd look down that nose of his at me and say waugh, waugh, the way you English do. No, all I've got to do is keep out of his way while he's here. This place is big enough, surely.'

'It's certainly big,' agreed Zoë, who had had a lot of trouble sneaking in to warn Gina.

First Esme had buttonholed her, throbbing to strains of Verdi.

'Hey, who are you, mate?' she said, taking off her earphones.

Zoë decided to come clean. 'I'm looking for Gina.'

Esme was joined by Guy, who was very sniffy.

'Visitors to the family use the front door. They don't come lurking round the back.'

'I am not lurking,' said Zoë. 'And I have perfectly good reasons for wanting to see Gina privately, without anyone knowing I'm here.'

'What reasons?' said Guy, folding his arms and looking, Zoë thought, quite exquisite.

'That's my business.'

'In that case, you can take your business elsewhere.'

Zoë was beginning to lose her temper. 'Listen, whoever you are, Gina will be very annoyed when she finds you've been so obstructive.'

'I don't personally care whether Gina is annoyed or not,' said Guy. 'I am employed by this family, and part of my job is keeping undesirables out.'

Esme had been looking at Zoë in a considering way. 'Come off it, Guy. You just think this is one of Victor's sheilas.'

'Victor's sheilas! Esme, this is really too much.'

'Stow it, Guy,' said Esme. 'Whoever she is, she isn't carrying a bomb, she doesn't look like a loonie, so let her in. Come on,' she said, elbowing Guy aside in one easy movement. 'I'll take you to Gina's room.'

'What a terrifying pair,' said Zoë, collapsing on Gina's bed. 'You owe me, Gina.'

Gina agreed with that, but she wasn't budging on the Fergus issue. 'I don't care if it will make life easier for you if I come clean with Fergus. It's going to make life much more difficult for me.'

Zoë sat up and gave Gina a very direct look. 'You,' she said, 'are in the shit. If Harry mentions their cousin Gina, Fergus won't take any notice, but if the name Heartwell, however it's spelt, comes out, he's going to start thinking.'

'Harry won't,' said Gina definitely, spoiling the effect by adding, doubtfully, 'will he?'

'Depends how well they know each other,' said Zoë.

'You could have found that out,' said Gina.

'I tried. Okay? I tried. I couldn't get a word in edgewise, not with him and Sybil going on and on about everything under the sun. Turns out Sybil taught Fergus's sister, some time back in the dark ages, so that brought on another great spate. Very boring for me, I can tell you.'

Gina opened the door and peered cautiously out. 'We'd better scram,' she said. 'I hear Mrs Slubs, she'll want to do my room.'

They tiptoed along the passage, down the back stairs, heading for refuge beyond the stableyard. Three steps from the bottom, Gina tripped on a loose board, and fell heavily, landing on Fergus, who was just coming through the side door.

Fergus looked at Gina, and Gina looked at Fergus.

'Hello, Fergus,' said Gina finally, in her best party tones.

'Hello, Gina,' said Fergus grimly. 'Are you hurt?'

'I don't think so,' said Gina.

'Then you and I are going to take a turn in the gardens and have a little talk.' Gina found herself moving at speed through the door into the yard.

Fergus addressed Guy over his shoulder as he went. 'Please tell my aunt I'll be with her shortly.'

What? thought Gina, not believing her ears. 'Aunt? Who is this aunt you'll be with shortly?'

'Julia Cordovan,' said Fergus impatiently. 'My aunt Julia.'

CHAPTER 17

Gina and Fergus walked down the steps to the formal garden with its perfectly coned yew trees and immaculate lawn. The whole garden was several feet lower than its surround, and since that was then bounded by bulgy yew hedges some ten feet high, it was a private spot.

'Let's go talk to the goldfish,' said Gina.

Fergus perched himself on the stone balustrade around the pond in the centre of the garden. 'Right, Gina,' he said. 'Shoot.'

'Well, I didn't go to America, okay, Fergus? I'm here in England, I stayed. Period, end of story. And if you're going to lecture me, don't. And if you're going to haul Popplewell down here so that he can arrest me, well, go right ahead.'

Fergus was hurt. 'Why would I tell that ghastly creature you were here? What kind of a friend do you think I am?'

'A law-abiding one,' said Gina glumly.

'Am I?' Fergus was startled. 'I suppose I am, in general. I do think you're mad to try and stay on in England without a visa or a work permit. I assume you have your reasons.'

'Yes, I do,' said Gina, leaning over at a perilous angle to dribble her fingers at a passing Koi carp. She was thinking hard. How was Fergus going to react when she explained that she was here at Heartsease Hall as an impostor? Did she have to tell him? If he was related to the Cordovans, then . . .

'I can't go back to the States until I've got one or two things sorted out,' she said in a rush.

'Like?'

'Like my passport got stolen. And my air ticket, too.'

Fergus frowned. 'Stolen? When? Where from? You've told the police, of course.' He thought for a moment. 'Who would want to use your passport?'

Out with it, Gina told herself. 'Um, actually, Georgie Hartwell.'

'Georgie!' Fergus exploded. 'Georgie! Gina, you haven't had anything to do with that dreadful woman?' Light dawned. 'Georgie *took* your passport. Of course, just what Georgie would do.'

'Yes, but she did leave me hers.'

'Oh, big-hearted Georgie.'

'So, um, well, the family here think I'm Georgie.'

Fergus stared at her. 'Think you're Georgie? Why should they do that? The Hartwells are some sort of connection, aren't they? They must know perfectly well that you aren't Georgie. Apart from anything else, Georgie's English.'

'I sound English,' said Gina indignantly.

'No, you don't,' said Fergus.

'In that case, they probably think it's a Scotch accent from that island the Hartwells live on.'

'Scots,' said Fergus automatically. 'Harry must know you aren't Georgie. He knows Georgie quite well.'

'Harry invited me here,' said Gina. 'He knows who I am, but he told the family Georgie was coming to stay, and they just accepted me.'

Fergus was aghast. 'Gina, this is ridiculous. You mean you're staying here under entirely false pretences? They think you're a cousin or whatever, and in fact you're a total stranger?'

'Go on, rub it in,' said Gina. 'A stranger and a foreigner.'

'Gina, you're mad. You can't hope to get away with this.'

'I have so far. Until you came along. Charming Sybil, making me stay up in that stuffy room all day and now tipping up to see your aunt Julia!'

Fergus found that very amusing. 'It was you, was it? With Sybil? Oh, it all figures. Leaving that pool up in a wind without anything to support it is exactly the kind of thing you'd do.'

'Anybody could have done that.'

Fergus was thinking. 'What were you doing staying with Sybil, in any case? If you're being an impostor here?'

'My father was here, at the Hall.'

That was too much for Fergus.

'It's not funny,' said Gina. 'You've got a warped sense of humour if you find other people's problems a joke.'

'Gina, your problems are all of your own making.'

'No, they aren't. It's Popplewell's fault. And Georgie's.'

Fergus became more serious. 'Why didn't you tell me you'd got seriously involved with Georgie? I'd have warned you off, that girl is bad news. How did you come across her in the first place?'

'I didn't come across Georgie, as you put it. She was at Sam's party, that evening in Oxford, you remember. And it wasn't a chance meeting, she sought me out.'

'Sounds like our Georgie all right.'

Gina had some questions of her own. 'Is Julia really your aunt?'

'Yes. She's my mother's half-sister.'

Gina tried to work that one out. 'Julia was a Cordovan, wasn't she? Before she married Victor, I mean?'

'My maternal grandmother's first husband was a Cordovan. They had Julia. Then he popped off, my granny married again, my grandpa this time, and had another daughter, my mum. Okay?'

'Just as long as you aren't one of them,' said Gina. 'Are you Harry's cousin?'

'No,' said Fergus patiently. 'My Cordovan cousins are Victor and Julia's children. Julia isn't Harry's mother, so he isn't a cousin. On the other hand, we've known each other since we were little.' He reflected for a moment. 'I wonder what Harry's up to in all this? Harry never does anything without a reason.'

'I expect he's amusing himself,' said Gina quickly. No way was she going to tell Fergus the real reason she was here at Heartsease. Not about Harry.

It was none of Fergus's business, after all.

'Fergus!'

Julia's clear and commanding voice wafted over the garden. 'There you are,' she said, coming briskly down the steps. She snapped off an errant piece of foliage trailing from one of the huge stone urns as she went past, and gave Fergus an auntly hug.

'Why didn't you tell us you were coming?' she said. 'Do you know Gina?'

'We met in Oxford,' said Fergus.

'Now, come and have some coffee; I want to hear all your news.'

Gina blended into a yew tree as they walked back towards the house, and then ran swiftly in the other direction, past the orangery and round to the stableyard. Esme was still there, bobbing slightly to the Verdi beat as she poured Jeyes fluid down the drain to the accompaniment of a deafening aria.

'Is Zoë still here?' Gina bellowed at her.

Esme lifted one earphone away from her head. 'Your blonde friend? No, she scarpered. Gone back to the cottage; she asked me to tell you.'

'Thanks,' said Gina.

Gina decided to retreat to the orchard where nobody would think of looking for her and she could sit among the pigs, having a good think.

Thwarted.

Hester leant out of the scullery window. 'If you're going that way, Gina, please take this colander and bring Maria some basil. Prim's working in the vegetable garden, she'll show you where the herbs are.'

Gina took the colander with a good grace and changed direction. Thinking would have to be postponed; besides, it was too hot to think clearly. And Gina loved the huge walled vegetable garden with the peach and apricot and nectarine trees espaliered against the centuries-old wall.

Prim looked up from her determined battle against the tiniest weed as Gina shut the gate behind her.

'Basil,' said Gina. 'Maria needs some.' Prim straightened up. How does she manage to work in the sun without looking sweaty and frayed? Gina wondered.

'Sweet basil, then,' said Prim. 'That's over here.'

Gina sniffed the aromatic air as she passed: thyme and rosemary and tarragon, coriander, sage, rocket . . .

'You want to pull the leaves off like this,' said Prim helpfully.

'Bit savage,' said Gina.

'No, the leaves need plucking, it encourages the plant to grow more, be bushier.'

'What happens to all these herbs?'

'They use them fresh in the kitchen, and then we dry the rest, for the winter and for pot-pourri; Hester makes a lot of that. All the family in London take back herbs from here when they're down, and Hester sends them little packages. It all gets used.'

'Is that an olive tree?' Gina couldn't believe her eyes. 'In England?'

'This is a very warm and sheltered garden. It's quite an old tree.'

'Lovely leaves.'

'Yes,' agreed Prim, her mind wandering back to the cuttings she was planting out.

'How much should I pick?'

'A colander-full?' suggested Prim. 'You can always come back if Maria wants more.' She went back to her careful green work, and Gina set about plucking the bright, sharp-smelling leaves.

And there, as though she weren't captivated enough, in the warmth of the walled garden, with the sound of bees in her ears and the scent of herbs in her nose, Gina had one of those moments when time stands still and, for a few seconds, life touches perfection.

In the distance, a tractor started up; a dog barked; Prim called out something to her from the other side of the radishes, and the spell was broken. Not before the moment was etched on Gina's mind; I can't do without this, she thought. I can't just go away and never come here again. When I could live here, for the rest of my life. Raise children; how completely different from my own upbringing. I simply have to stay.

Fergus was rescued from Julia's rigorous questioning by Don, who put his head round the door.

'Just looking for Hester,' he said, about to go away again. And then he saw who was with Julia and came into the room to clap Fergus on the shoulder and demand some coffee.

'You're very boisterous, Don,' complained Julia, pouring him out a cup.

Don took no notice; he never took any notice of Julia, having learned from long experience that he always rubbed her up the wrong way.

He enquired after Fergus's parents and brother, and the farm and land.

Fergus laughed. 'Dad's doing very well out of the subsidies,' he said. 'So he's got nothing to do. Spends most of his time in the office. He tried staying at home more, but not being out and about in the fields, he drove my mother mad.'

'I can imagine,' said Don. 'Subsidies! I could do with a few subsidies. There aren't any for English vineyards, did you know that?'

'I didn't,' said Fergus with interest. 'How many acres have you got put down to vines?'

'About a hundred. We add a few more most years. How long are you here for?'

Julia voiced her displeasure with Fergus's arrangements. 'He's not staying here,' she said. 'He's with a friend who's taken the cottage Sybil rents out.'

'Ah, you're at Kingfisher Cottage, are you? With Charlotte?'

Fergus reddened slightly. 'No, no, I'm not staying. I just came down for the weekend to settle Zoë in; she shares my house in Oxford.'

It was quite clear from her expression that Julia didn't approve of that at all.

'Zoë?' she said coldly. 'Does your mother know about this arrangement?'

'Come off it, Julia,' said Don. 'Don't give Fergus the third degree; he's of age, and I should think his mother is well acquainted with the other people in his house.'

'Yes,' said Fergus gratefully. 'Mother and Zoë get on very well, actually, Julia. She's just a friend.'

'Why is she at Kingfisher Cottage?' said Julia in her inexorable way.

Don cast his eyes up to the ceiling in despair.

'Just taking a holiday,' said Fergus. 'She's between jobs.'

'And when are you returning to Oxford?' said Julia.

'I was planning to go back today, but I . . . well, thought I might go and collect my books and come back for a few days.'

'It's lovely weather,' said Don helpfully.

'Yes, that's it,' said Fergus gratefully. 'Because the weather's so good.'

'Then you must stay here at the Hall,' said Julia.

'Don't bully him,' said Don.

'I think Zoë would be glad of someone to share expenses,' said Fergus. He quite liked his aunt, and would normally be perfectly happy to stay at the Hall, but not with Gina floating around pretending to be someone else. Fergus had an idea it could all get very sticky, and Fergus was very keen on avoiding stickiness whenever possible. On the other hand, he wanted to keep an eye on Gina; she had managed to get herself into a real heap of trouble. Whatever else, she'd need a reliable friend. Such as me, he told himself. And he could keep a watching brief on her from the cottage without getting involved.

Little did he know.

'Do that,' said Don, 'and then you can come and see how we do things among the vines. We can crack a few bottles, show you what we're producing.'

'Excellent,' said Fergus.

'Of course I'm not going to say you can't have the room,' said Zoë. 'I just want to know why.'

'I feel like a holiday,' said Fergus.

'Charlotte won't like it,' warned Zoë.

Charlotte was of a suspicious and jealous disposition.

'Charlotte won't know, because I'm not going to tell her.'

'Charlotte will find out,' said Zoë instantly and with certainty. 'She always does.'

'Too bad,' said Fergus defiantly.

'You're worried about Gina,' said Zoë shrewdly.

'I am not,' said Fergus with unnecessary vehemence. 'I'm sure she's more than capable of getting herself out of her own messes. Doesn't seem to have any trouble getting into them. Why the hell she didn't tell me . . . Oh, never mind. I need a holiday, that's all.'

Zoë didn't press him. 'When will you be back?' she asked.

Fergus thought for a moment. 'Tomorrow afternoon,' he said. 'Between three and four.' Fergus had a precise mind.

'Bring some food,' said Zoë, her thoughts running on practical lines.

'I will,' said Fergus. 'And if you're going to be out, leave the key with Sybil.'

'Charlotte ought to know about Sybil,' said Zoë wickedly. 'I think

Sybil's the real reason you want to come back.'

'Sybil,' said Fergus, 'is a charming woman, and very good company. Charlotte would like her.'

Charlotte wouldn't, Zoë said to herself as she searched through her rumpled possessions for the swimsuit she knew she'd brought. Charlotte has no sense of humour, as you'll notice one of these days, Fergus McEttrick.

Gareth mentioned to Lori that he had met Harry. 'At a club,' he said, without being precise about which club, or what kind it was. Lori might not be convinced it was all research.

'Rather offhand,' he said. 'Wish I could get a camera into that house, fly on the wall, today's gentry; just as appalling and out of touch as they've always been.'

'When anyone sets out to *show* how awful they are, the viewers all end up thinking they're *wonderful*.'

'True,' said Gareth. 'People are so stunned by the way they live, the house, the furniture, the *objets*, that they don't notice what prats the inhabitants are.'

'They all want to win the National Lottery and *live* like that themselves.'

Gareth gave an Islington shudder and turned to the sports pages of the paper. 'Oh, I met a youngster who works at the Hall. Called Guy. Bit poncy, but I've got a feeling about him. He might just mesh with Sigi. See if you can find out anything about him.'

'Is he *keen*?' said Lori, who was packing up boxes of extra tuck for her daughters.

'Pretends not, but wave a contract under his nose, and he'll soon jump. Apparently wants to open his own hotel one of these days. In which case, he can't afford to turn an offer like this down – always supposing I do finally decide to use him. He'd become a household name, really valuable publicity, this kind of thing. Quite apart from the money.'

'What about the historian you needed?'

'Nothing yet, although I've got one or two names. The trouble is, most of these academics are dry, no pep. They don't love the camera, and it shows. Never mind, I'm sure we'll turn one up.'

'It'll make a *change* from your usual programmes,' said Lori, wondering whether to be a wonderful wife and make a cold soup and something artful for dinner, or whether to nip into Heartsbury and buy everything at Sainsbury's. A new book and the hammock in the garden beckoned; Sainsbury's won. Home cooking could wait, Lori decided.

'Got to keep up,' said Gareth. 'It's all too easy to fall behind in this game.'

'I've got one or two errands,' Lori said, dropping a kiss on Gareth's head as she went by. 'Shan't be long.'

Gareth, who secretly saw himself as a seven-foot black basketball star, was buried in the depths of the American sports reports. 'Mmm,' he said, reaching out for his beer as the front door clicked shut.

'These television people,' said Guy, holding up the glass he was polishing to make sure that not the slightest smear marred its shining surface. 'They think they can buy anyone. I tell you, Maria, that man made me feel like a tart on the streets, the way he was eyeing me over.'

'You shouldn't go to such places, then you wouldn't meet men like this. Go where there are pretty girls, have a good time, no TV men there.'

'He was surprised when I didn't fawn all over him,' said Guy. 'One could tell.'

Esme came slip-slop into the kitchen just as Maria was pouring a thick, creamy and alcoholic mixture into little pots to set.

'*Ayi!* Now see what you have made me do. I look at your face, and I can see you are in agony, what has happened?'

Esme shifted her piece of gum into her other cheek. 'What?' she said, lifting off her earphones, letting out a cacophony of scraping and tinny noises.

'I ask you, why do you have such a look of pain?'

'Oh, it's this opera. World première, on the radio. It's terrible, I don't think they'll be putting this one on again.'

'Then why do you listen?'

Esme spread a thick piece of bread with butter and balanced a thick piece of very strong cheese on top. 'With opera, you never know. You've got to listen. This jerk who wrote this, he might be the new Puccini.'

Guy moved the earphones further away. 'I don't think so,' he said.

'No, well, you're right there. I'll switch it off, put on a bit of old Richard W to take away the taste. How about Venusberg, Guy, you feeling amorous?'

Guy raised his nose in the air and went back to his glasses. Maria told Esme that her tastes in food were those of a savage and went back to her bowls.

Esme spat her gum deftly into the bin, settled the earphones back in her ears, turned the volume up and sat chomping, surrounded by blissful noise and completely oblivious of the raised shoulders and long-suffering looks being exchanged by Guy and Maria.

Victor came purposefully into the dining-room, sat himself at the head of the table, spread a thick white napkin across his knees and signalled to Guy to pour some wine into his glass.

He was in an excellent temper; he had had a promising conversation with Fräulein Voesli on the phone and felt sure that, when he saw her again, she would be in a more amenable mood than last week.

'Full of snap, crackle and pop,' Harry whispered to Gina as he passed her the rolls. 'He must have been on to his yodelling floozy, look how pleased he is with himself.'

Gina felt a stab of envy for the floozy, quickly repressed. Her life was quite complicated enough as it was.

Victor's eye fell on Nicky, gazing disconsolately into her artichoke at the further end of the table.

'Ah,' he said. 'The ball, Nicky. I have one or two extra names to give you.'

Nicky looked alarmed.

'Did you send a card to Fergus, Nicky?' put in Julia. 'If not, please do so. I have his address in Oxford.'

'I don't think he was on the list,' said Nicky, who knew quite well he hadn't been. 'There's going to be a problem about where to put everyone, we're running out of beds.'

'I assume our friends and neighbours are doing their bit,' said Victor.

'I believe Fergus has a friend he can stay with in Heartsbane,' observed Julia in a slightly disapproving tone. 'Since he was there at the weekend.'

'Will he bring that depressing girlfriend with him?' said Harry, making mischief.

Julia frowned. 'Do you mean Charlotte Abyss? A thoroughly nice girl, I understand they're informally engaged.'

'More fool Fergus,' said Harry boldly.

'That's enough,' said Victor. 'You can ridicule Fergus's taste, but I don't see you finding yourself any kind of wife, let alone anyone suitable.'

'I might surprise you all,' said Harry.

Aimée lifted her eyes from her fragrant plateful of chicken in a tarragon sauce and gave him a long and thoughtful look. 'Not if you've any sense, you won't,' she said in a low voice.

'What was that?' said Victor. 'What did you say, Aimée? Speak up, I can't stand people muttering at each other.'

'Nothing, Pa,' said Aimée with one of her sweetest smiles. 'I was just complimenting Harry on his shirt. Armani, did you notice?'

Victor's expression grew darker. 'Armani. Designer rubbish, time you grew up, Harry, stopped wasting your money on showy trash, started behaving like an adult instead of a feckless teenager.'

That rankled. 'I don't think feckless teenagers run successful businesses,' he said hotly.

Victor snorted. 'Mere fashion, tastes change, you'll be left high and dry.'

'That's where you're wrong. Communications are the big thing, now and for a long way into the future.'

'Nonsense,' said Victor. 'People aren't going to pay for empty space for ever, you know. Free airwaves, that's what'll happen, and then where will you be?'

'While people have to communicate, and messages have to be sent, I'll scrape a living, Pa.'

Victor glared at him, and then looked round to see who else he could have a go at. He caught Hester's eye and she shook her head very slightly at him.

'Oh, very well,' he said. 'Of course, I can't expect my family to marry and have children as other people manage to. And those pigs are as bad, you'd think by the pair of balls on him that that boar would be good for anything. Not a bit of it, no interest, no piglets.'

'Perhaps he's a gay pig,' said Harry unwisely.

The last vestiges of Victor's good mood evaporated. Gina winced as a thunderous tirade burst about Harry's head.

Prim looked up from the catalogue she was studying. 'Victor,' she said sharply. 'That's enough.'

Victor took no notice. Prim sighed, filled her glass with water, got up from the table, walked to the head of it, and tipped the contents of the crystal glass over Victor's head.

'What did you do that for?' he demanded when he had got his breath back. He mopped his face with his napkin and handed it to a disapproving Guy. 'Get me another one, will you? Prim, I'll . . .'

'No,' said Julia. 'Prim, that was extreme but, Victor, you mustn't shout like that at the table. You'll give everyone indigestion.'

'Bugger indigestion,' said Victor furiously.

'Try some of this wine,' said Don soothingly. 'Mustn't get yourself worked up, it isn't good for you at your age.'

'My age! How dare you. Let me tell you, when I was your age, I was married and had children. What have you got? A bunch of crazy women for holidays and two or three devoted followers for the rest of the week. Immoral and foolhardy.'

Nicky gave a kind of wail and shot Victor a heartfelt look from big blue eyes which were swimming with tears.

'I'm sorry, I'm sorry,' said Victor. 'I'd forgotten you were involved in this, Nicky.' He rallied. 'But I mean it, there's no future for you with this son of mine, get back to your husband and your children, you're lucky to have them, and your parents are lucky to have grandchildren.'

Nicky sniffed and took a liberal gulp of wine.

'Not like that,' said Don, scandalized.

'Oh, piss off,' said Nicky.

'Aren't family mealtimes fun?' said Harry in bright tones. 'Pass the pepper, please, Gina, it's nestling by your glass.'

Nicky had remembered something else. 'Since,' she said in a voice which, although quavering, held a note of venom, 'since Don wants that Tara from Heartwell to come to the ball, I'll send an invitation to her brother and his wife. The ones at Heartwell House, Victor, if you remember. They'll be good for a dinner party and beds for at least six guests, I would imagine.'

Victor started to rumble once more. 'That's that extraordinary woman who tried to hassle me over the state of the roads. Over my dead body does she come into my house.'

Guy gave a little clicking noise of approval as he cleared the plates away. Then the door opened with a thump and a curse, and Esme came cheerfully in bearing a tray with Maria's little pots aboard.

'Hear you lot for miles,' she commented, putting the tray down on the sideboard with a bang which set all the lids to the pots rattling. 'Pud's up, get something sweet into you, that'll quieten you down.'

Guy, scandalized, shooed her from the room and she slopped off down the passage, singing snatches of Valkyrie warwhoops as she went.

'That seems very sensible, Nicky dear,' said Julia in magisterial tones. 'We may not like them personally, but it can do no harm to be neighbourly. There will be no need to pursue the acquaintance beyond the odd formal occasion.'

'Attagirl,' said Harry. 'Freeze them out, Julia, that's the way.'

CHAPTER 18

The house in Oxford was silent and empty. Where was Jessica? thought Fergus, as he let himself in through the front door. She had said she'd be there while he was away. He bent down to collect the little pile of post from the mat, tossed half of it straight into the bin, and wandered into the kitchen. A large note in Jessica's illiterate scrawl was attached to the fridge door.

'Dear Fergus,' it said.
'Gone to Tarhitti with frend. Ive asked Mum to colect dresses and things. Wont be back for year. Sory about room, their are some people looking for house – ask at Wellinton Colege.
Lots of love, Jessica.
XXX
PS Charlote rang. She sounds cross. I didnt say where you'ld gone.'

'Bugger,' said Fergus.
He went back into the hall, paused for a moment and then headed up the stairs. It seemed even more silent and deserted up there; ridiculous, thought Fergus, who had often been alone in the house. How was this any different from a wet November day with Jessica out doing what Jessica did, Zoë at work, himself here with his computer, and Gina with Alwyn at Jude's?
He went across to Gina's room. It appeared empty, although he knew that some of her things were still here. Stowed away under the bed and in the cupboard in case the Popplewell should attempt a snoop. Fergus frowned at the thought of Popplewell. He didn't like people being hounded out of the country. Especially not a person he

knew. And was fond of, as he was of Gina. It wasn't going to be the same here without her.

He banged the door shut behind him, and went back downstairs. Where had Zoë left the telephone directory? He found it, finally, behind the bread bin, and looked up the number for Wellington College.

'Not just rooms, sir,' the porter said. 'They'd prefer a whole house. There are four of them, Americans. Here for the whole summer. Yes, sir, I'll do that. Give you an hour or two? Yes, that's quite clear, if there's no reply, try the Golden Fleece. Thank you, Mr McEttrick. Always glad to help.'

'Bet you are, you old fraud,' said Fergus as he put the phone down. Anything for a tip, probably charge the poor saps commission on top. Never mind, that was their lookout.

As Fergus was shutting the front door behind him, a man turned in through the gate. Fergus looked surprised; the porter could hardly have passed on the message already.

'Are you looking for someone?' he said.

The man looked him over with a pair of very dark eyes, made darker and more glowing by his deeply tanned and olive skin. 'Yes. I believe Gina Heartwell lives here?'

Fergus stiffened with suspicion. True, the man had an American accent, and was therefore unlikely to be an accomplice of Popplewell. Moreover, he didn't have an air of officialdom about him; Fergus would have put him down as a writer, or perhaps a musician. Still, perhaps the US immigration service took on people like this, to lull their victims.

'Can I ask why you want her?'

The man looked amused. 'Since you ask, young man,' he said, 'I'm her father.'

Serge made approving noises as Fergus led the way into the long bar inside the Golden Fleece. Tables set in little stalls ran down one wall, copper pans hung from the heavy central beam, glasses and bottles twinkled and beamed from the other side of the wide mahogany counter.

'I just love your English pubs,' said Serge. 'It's the first place I head for when I'm in England.'

'I'm going to have something to eat,' said Fergus. 'I'm on my own, I can't be bothered to cook.'

193

'Suits me,' said Serge. 'I'm staying in a hotel outside the city. It's got some kind of a fancy restaurant, so I was planning on eating out in any case.'

'The food's good here,' said Fergus, purloining a menu. 'Let's go outside. I'm sorry Gina isn't here in Oxford. She's away.'

'I guessed she might be. I had a phone call from my ex – Gina's mother – in Italy. She was worried about Gina, hadn't heard, thought she might have overrun her visa, was Gina back in the States. She's stupid, not keeping in touch with her mother. That woman always did fuss. A postcard is all it takes.'

Fergus wondered how much to tell Serge.

'Yes, Gina's visa did expire. I think she's gone to stay with friends, and then she'll go back to the States.'

'So you don't think she's gone back already? I was worried, thought she might turn up in New York, find the place shut up, have nowhere to go.'

'No, I'm sure she's with friends, although I can't tell you where. She just slipped away, not wanting to draw attention to herself, you understand.'

'I sure do,' said Serge, draining his beer. 'Your immigration officials are kind of relentless, so I hear.'

'Can I get you another one?' Fergus got to his feet. 'And have you decided what you want to eat?'

'I have,' said Serge. 'And this is on me. I want you to bring me right up to date on what Gina's been up to. Nothing personal, a girl's got her own life to lead, I don't want to pry. But I don't even know why she's in Oxford, what she's studying, anything. She never writes, and I don't either, so we've lost touch. Which is a pity, because I like her, and I have an idea that now she's older, we'd find we had a lot in common. I didn't treat her mother very well, there's no secret about that; but just because I screwed up there is no reason why Gina and I shouldn't get along fine.'

Byron had set up one room of his dilapidated cottage as a temporary workshop. While Nadia hurled herself into a frenzy of organization and cleaning, he sat up late, first drawing up plans for the new vineyard shop, and then helping Josh Slubs cut and shape the MDF.

'A bit slow, my Josh,' said Mrs Slubs complacently. 'Never did catch on to what was happening at school, but I dare say they teachers didn't try very hard.'

That was a slur on some very dedicated teachers who had driven themselves to the verge of nervous breakdowns trying to make the slightest impression on Josh's mental torpor. A world-weary head finally put them out of their misery by advising them to give him up as a hopeless case. 'Put him down for woodwork classes whenever you can, it's the only thing he's good at.'

'No point lamenting and carrying on because he haven't got no brains. He may be dim, but he's got a wonderful way with wood,' was Mrs Slubs's view.

He had, although it was Byron's opinion that Josh's total lack of familiarity with the written word would be a drawback even in carpentry. 'He can't follow the simplest instruction,' he told Gina when she stopped to peer in at the window on her way to visit Sybil.

'Maybe not, but he cuts a neat line,' said Gina, leaning on the window-sill and watching as Josh sliced through a panel as though it were butter. 'Isn't this going to look a bit tatty? Why not use proper wood?'

'Don't you start,' said Byron. 'You'll be full of admiration once I've had a go at it. This stuff's great, you can do anything you want with it. It's going to look terrific.'

'When's Nadia planning to open?'

'Almost at once. Don says it's going to take time, perhaps open for the autumn . . . Or think of next year. Nadia isn't having any of that, she's determined to prove him wrong. Get going immediately, sell what you can make, then build up a bigger selection as you go.'

'I hope it works.'

'So do I,' said Byron in heartfelt tones. 'Apart from anything, it'd be good if Nadia can earn a bit. Times are hard.'

'I know the feeling,' said Gina, pulling her bike round.

'Are you going to Sybil's, by any chance?' asked Byron.

'Yup.'

'Tell her I'll be round later. She said to drop in for one of those amazing beers, and I'm going to need to by the time I'm through with this lot.'

*

Gina found Zoë comfortably installed on Sybil's sofa, Sybil's cat curled up on her knee, a beer in her hand, and cricket on the television.

'Come in,' said Zoë. 'I can't get up, or Heracles here will run his claws into my legs. Sybil's just finishing a chapter. Get yourself a beer, it's in the fridge.'

Gina did as she was told, envying Zoë for the relaxed way she fell into things. You'd think she'd known Sybil for years, Gina thought crossly. And Fergus was as bad.

'At least he's gone back to Oxford,' said Gina, not admitting for a moment that she rather wished he hadn't.

'Talking of Fergus,' said Zoë, keeping her eyes disconcertingly fixed on the TV screen, 'he rang up from Oxford. Big news.'

'If you're going to tell me, then turn the TV off,' said Gina. 'It's very difficult to talk to someone who's watching cricket.'

Zoë pointed the remote control at the box. 'You're just jealous because you don't understand one bit of what's going on.'

'Spit it out,' said Gina.

'Right. First and foremost, Jessica's done a bunk.'

'Done a bunk?'

'Yeah, gone to what she calls "Tarhitti", apparently. Fergus reckons that unless she's with someone she'll be at Heathrow for ever, waiting for Tarhitti to come up on the board.'

'What about the house? Did she pay her rent?'

'Oh, yes. All paid up front. Jessica wouldn't abscond. That's the good news. The bad news is that she's sent all her clothes to Oxfam, so no more Jessicas for us to wear.'

Gina pulled a face. 'Damn. I was reckoning on borrowing a frock for this ball they're having at the Hall.'

'The good news is that Fergus has found some new tenants.'

'Tenants? In the plural? Zoë, there isn't room.'

'Yes, four guys from America. They want the whole house for the rest of the summer.'

'That's impossible. What about Fergus?'

'Didn't I say? Fergus is coming back here.'

'What?'

'Yes, that's also good news. But more bad news: Fergus is having to stack all his and my stuff with yours into what was your room. To leave three rooms free. Two of these men are an item, so they want to share a room anyhow. Fat rent, Fergus says.'

'What's Fergus going to do? What about his doctorate?'

'I've said he can stay at Kingfisher Cottage for the rest of the summer if he wants. He's bringing his books and his computer, no sweat.'

'Well,' said Gina. She felt that with the departure of Fergus, however temporarily, from the house in Oxford, her one link with a familiar and secure world had been severed.

'More news,' said Zoë, taking an unladylike swig of beer from the bottle. 'Your dad turned up.'

'What? Where? When?'

'Why? And How?' added Zoë flippantly. 'Find the answer to these, and the crime is solved. In Oxford, looking for you. Apparently your ma hasn't heard from you, and nor has he, so he came on a look-see mission. To check you hadn't shipped out to Buenos Aires on a white-slaver, I expect.'

'How did he know where to find me?'

'He must have your address. Presumably he has his wits about him, why shouldn't he track you down?'

'I suppose it's logical,' said Gina doubtfully. A horrid thought struck her. 'God, Fergus didn't tell him I was down here . . .'

' . . . playing impostors?' Zoë finished for her. 'No, he's not that thick. He said you were staying with friends, and when he heard from you, he'd pass the message on for you to contact your pa. He's only in Oxford for a couple of days, then he's going to be in London.'

Gina sat down abruptly on the nearest chair. 'I don't need this,' she complained. 'Months go by, and all is calm and peaceful, then, suddenly, everyone's after me.'

'Nice to be wanted,' said Zoë, flicking the set back on. 'Oh, look, a wicket's fallen and I missed it.'

Sybil put her head round the door. 'I thought I heard non-cricketing voices,' she said. 'Hello, Gina. Did Zoë get you a beer?'

'Thank you, yes,' said Gina.

Sybil vanished, and then reappeared with a beer of her own, which she tipped deftly into a tall glass. 'I've earned this,' she said, sinking into an armchair.

'Have you finished your chapter?'

Sybil nodded. 'One runs out of puff, you know. Always thinking up a new angle – literally, of course, at my end of the market. There are limits to the number of permutations possible, the vocabulary tends to be banal, and at the end of the day one is describing a fairly limited physical act. And it all has to end in gusts of orgasmic ecstasy, total satisfaction guaranteed, how unlike real life. Oh well, it pays the bills.'

Gina was fascinated. 'Do you enjoy writing it?'

Sybil laughed. 'Does it turn me on? It might have once, it certainly doesn't now. It's a knack, you know, writing books to be read with one hand.'

'How did you get into it?'

'A chum of mine who was in publishing knew I was strapped for cash after my husband died. No fun trying to raise and educate three children on a teacher's salary. This firm wanted some books with a classical theme, so I obliged. People always imagine,' she went on, 'that the Romans, for example, indulged in endless orgies and perversions. They didn't, of course. It was a very prudish society. Love-making was restricted to the hours of darkness – did you know that? Of course you didn't, they never teach you anything at these schools. Only newly-weds could have a go in the daytime, and that only the day after the wedding. And the ladies always kept their bosoms covered.'

'Really?' said Zoë.

'Fact,' said Sybil. 'Not in my books, of course. In my sort of tosh you do a roaring trade in stiff nipples. The readers expect it.'

Gina found this very funny, and so did Zoë, who had turned the sound off the better to hear.

'How do you think up your plots?' she asked, awed.

'All the same, really,' said Sybil. 'In my case, one starts with a heroine. She meets the villain, who has a huge prick, nasty habits and repeatedly has his wicked way with said heroine. Several other men here and there, final climactic scene with hero who is even better hung than villain. Lots of exotic settings, pillars, eunuchs, slaves, what-have-you. Never fails.'

'Wow,' said Gina, full of admiration. 'What a way to make a living.'

*

It had been agreeable sitting there, laughing with Zoë and Sybil, thought Gina as she leant out over her window-sill. The moon was waxing, and spreading a thin, clear light over the remote and silent countryside.

The silence was rudely broken by a series of deep hoots from the tree just across from Gina's window. She could see the owl, the size of a cat, white, with huge eyes. The owls worried Gina. Their hoots were eerie and unsettling. Then, why were there so many owls? All in one place; it didn't seem natural. She drew back from the open window, let the curtains fall back across it.

Gina lay down on the bed, on top of the covers, thinking. Of course, she should have left Sybil's cottage the minute she started the interrogation.

On what excuse?

Feeble, any excuse would have done. No rule of *politesse* obliged you to sit around in the company while someone turned you inside out.

It had started when Gina inadvertently told Sybil what she had seen on that wet and windy night.

Sybil found it funny. 'So that's why you arrived back in such a state? Why didn't you say what you'd seen?'

'I was terrified,' said Gina indignantly.

'What, of a few men creeping round in the dark and unloading boxes? It's only contraband.'

'That's what I thought,' said Gina. 'Smuggling.'

'Supplies from abroad,' said Sybil. 'They bring it ashore in one of the coves, and store it in the cottages. It's still cheaper than going across and buying it at the superstore in Boulogne, the stuff they bring in, at any rate.'

'And people buy it?'

'Good heavens, yes. It's been going on for a couple of hundred years, probably longer.'

Gina wasn't too sure about this particular English tradition. 'Those types the other night looked as though they meant business.'

'You could say that.'

'Good thing they didn't see me.'

Sybil pursed her lips. 'A very good thing. Have a beer.'

Gina took the glass of beer, and sat back in the comfortable armchair, thinking what an odd place Heartset was turning out to be. None of this was in the guidebooks.

Sybil sat in her armchair, relaxed, smiling and friendly. And began to ask questions.

Zoë was quite happy to answer Sybil's searching enquiries. And Sybil seemed quite content with her explanations about the job and the holiday, and the uncertainty of her future plans.

Why was Zoë being so open about her life? Gina wondered. Even telling her about giving Tim the push.

Sybil had approved of that. 'Quite right,' she had said. 'Best to be off with the old.' Then she turned her guns on to Gina.

'Research? Is that a living? Is it satisfying work? Can you do it all your life? Always working for someone else? Usually a man? He publishes, gets the glory, the promotion . . . How unsatisfying. Oh, you plan to have an academic career yourself? Articles in learned journals, tenure . . . Tenure? In this day and age, how improbable.'

Clink of glass as she downed her beer. A temporary respite.

How very unadventurous. Did she want to spend all her life in one university or another? Wasn't it an enclosed and stifling world? Had she read any psychology? Did she understand about searching for security in academe?

Then she had started on Alwyn. This man you work for, does he pay you well? Does he acknowledge your contribution? Are you in love with him, how very schoolgirlish. And of course he makes the most of your devotion, naturally. He's no doubt exploited a stream of eager young women over the years.

And she wasn't thinking of marriage as an alternative, was she? Surely no one of Gina's temperament could imagine that would solve her problems?

What about travel? Novelty? Didn't she want to live in other countries, try new things, have a few adventures, exciting escapades?

Little does she know, thought Gina grimly.

'One pays a high price for not living the life one should be living,' Sybil had finished warningly. 'The life unlived poisons not only your existence, but that of those around you.'

'Oh, hell,' Gina said wearily. 'This is all I need.'

'Have another beer,' said Sybil considerately. 'Or perhaps you need something a little stronger.'

'One extra for lunch,' announced Guy as he backed into the kitchen through the swing doors bearing a silver teapot carefully in both hands.

Esme was twisting round to inspect her lower back, which was in an advanced state of peeling. 'Who's coming?' she said, shifting her gum to the other side of her mouth with a strange slurp.

Guy gave her a very cool look. 'Serge Zandermann, the American painter. Victor's just been on the phone to him, about that painting he wants to buy.'

Hester appeared from the pantry. 'Is he staying the night, Guy? Or didn't Victor say?'

'No, he isn't,' Guy replied, happy to be in the know. 'Coming mid-morning, staying to lunch, then off to London. Catching a plane to New York this evening.'

'Lucky man, getting away from this country,' said Esme.

'Nothing keeping you, dear,' said Guy in unkind tones.

'I planned to be here for a year, and that's how long I'm staying,' said Esme with perfect good humour. 'Hester, do you want me to hose down the terrace and get some bleach on to it? Get rid of those slimy bits; otherwise those guests are going to be sliding around a lot livelier than they'd planned.'

'It is rather mossy,' said Hester, considering. 'Do you mind? Jarvis should do it really, but . . .'

'Naw,' said Esme, hitching her trousers back up and pulling her T-shirt down. 'He's got his knickers in a knot as it is, all those plants and flowers for the dance. Besides, I'd rather be out there putting a bit of muscle into it than standing around in here torturing veggies into funny shapes.'

Esme had her own views on Aimée's ball. 'What a to-do, this ball business; you should have a big barbi and be done with it. All this fancy stuff, who needs it?' she said, disappearing into the yard before Guy could utter the rebuke which was on his lips. Crashings and bangings indicated that she had located the big hose and was getting herself noisily ready for just the kind of physical work she liked best.

'Really,' said Guy, casting his eyes up to heaven.

Maria set to her lunch preparations with extra vim and vigour, intent on providing a meal fit for an international traveller. One, moreover, who would be condemned to an aeroplane dinner that night. Such food ranked only a notch above the local hamburger bar in Maria's book.

'He's a very important painter,' Guy informed her. 'He's in *International Who's Who*. Any number of exhibitions. Of course he's a figurative painter, which isn't so fashionable, but he must make a good living.'

Guy had attended classes in Heartsbury on art appreciation, and so spoke with authority. Maria frowned, and made Spanish chirruping noises. For such an artist, she must indeed provide something special. Had she been wearing sleeeves, she would have rolled them up; as she was wearing a white T-shirt, she merely tightened the ties on her large apron and headed for the fridge.

Esme's radio in the scullery poured forth happy tunes from Offenbach, the sun streamed in through the window and bees droned happily in the shrubs outside.

Tranquillity reigned.

CHAPTER 19

The sun was shining in Oxford with equal intensity, but Fergus was feeling far from tranquil. The tiresome work of clearing the three rooms had been completed; at least he had achieved something. He assembled all his files and papers and disks to be taken out to the car together with his computer. Maybe it was the thought of all those words which was making him depressed; a grim reminder of how he had spent the last three years.

Or was it the knowledge that he had to ring Charlotte?

Fergus didn't want to speak to Charlotte. This was strange, because Charlotte, a very handsome girl with seemingly pleasant ways, was his long-standing girlfriend. It was taken for granted that in due course they would settle down together; taken for granted by her, her family, Fergus's family and, until very recently, by Fergus himself.

Now he didn't want to speak to her, could quite cheerfully face the rest of the summer without seeing her, and could likewise look forward to a life ahead in which Charlotte played no part.

It wasn't that he was keen on anyone else, he told himself. This alarmed him. Fergus was not a promiscuous man, although he had had his share of briefer and longer-lasting relationships before settling into this long-standing partnership with Charlotte. But no Charlotte, no sex, unless he found himself another girlfriend. And he didn't mind.

Something in the water, Fergus decided gloomily as he wrote out a list of instructions about what to do if the boiler started clanking. Or maybe it was the exceptional heat. With cooler days, his libido would surely return. Meanwhile, there was Charlotte, waiting for him to ring her, fix up this and that for the summer. She would expect all the usual: Glyndebourne, a Prom or two (for Charlotte was a civilized girl and liked music), Wimbledon (for she was a good tennis player herself and genuinely enjoyed watching the matches), visits to friends around the country, two or three weeks abroad . . .

No way, Fergus said to himself. Not this summer. After all, he had his thesis to finish. She would understand, it was high time he finished it and got down to finding himself a job.

A job. In London. Something in the City, as befitted an economist. Or a position somewhere abroad. Somewhere glamorous; Charlotte had made it quite clear that she preferred the urban life. Smart urban, that is, none of your teeming third-world capitals or brash American cities.

Fergus sighed. Better to ring her and get it over with, explain the need to escape from Oxford, terrible in the summer, going to ruralize so that I can really get my head down.

Charlotte might just accept that. Fergus wasn't too sure about Zoë. Charlotte tolerated the three girls who had shared his house this last year, although she didn't like any of them, because she felt there was safety in numbers. When she discovered he was sharing a cottage with Zoë, as she inevitably would, then she might be less happy.

Oh, to hell with Charlotte, Fergus thought, giving the house a last look round before he started loading up the car. He could ring her later, he told himself as he propped the front door open with a learned tome.

The postman paused by the low brick wall at the front of the house. 'Just one for you,' he said cheerfully. 'Going on your hols?'

'Letting the house for the summer,' said Fergus, taking the letter.

'Make sure they know where to send your letters on,' said the postman.

Good point, thought Fergus, tearing open the envelope. Thick card, tasteful black copperplate . . . a ball. For Aimée. Good gracious, was Aimée only twenty-one? Some very vivid memories of Aimée came into Fergus's mind, bringing a warm and appreciative smile to his face.

'And Charlotte,' was inscribed in a wide, flowing hand.

Back to earth.

Charlotte. Well, she'd love that. Invite her down to the cottage, let her see Sybil, pretend Zoë was away a lot. It could be made to seem as respectable as it actually was. How boring, thought Fergus, pushing a pile of books into the boot of the car. But armed with this invitation, he would phone Charlotte, right now, get it over with, and then be on his way. Free and carefree.

At least until Charlotte arrived at Heartsbane.

Gina had installed herself in the hammock at the other end of the terrace, and she settled down to do some hard thinking.

Her surroundings were not conducive to hard thinking. Thin, high wisps of cloud floated in a deep blue sky. A light breeze took the edge off what would otherwise have been an excessively hot day. The air was clear and fresh, the formal gardens entrancingly green with sharp shadows to make the fretwork shapes stranger and more interesting. There was much to please the eye and all the other senses, and little to help Gina to assess her situation in a cold and logical way.

Harry was in Bath. Gina had been avoiding Harry, and particularly avoiding Harry in the swimming pool when he seemed to be at his most dangerous. Harry, Gina sensed, was becoming impatient. He liked her, they got on well together, why worry? Why ask for more than that? Look at Byron and Nadia, a strange marriage born out of necessity and a secret agenda. They were still together, it had worked, that marriage, in its own way.

Okay, maybe in ten years if she married Harry, there might be problems. If Harry was going to spend his spare time in gay clubs, there would certainly be problems. But how, on a morning like this, could you worry about what might happen in ten years' time? It's the next ten days, the next ten weeks that concern me, Gina said to herself as she swung gently to and fro.

Her peaceful, idle frame of mind was changed into a state of alarmed alertness as a familiar voice cut across her thoughts.

'Excuse me, have you seen Victor Cordovan around? They told me he was out on the terrace.'

Gina gave such a violent lurch that she hurled herself out of the hammock, landing with a bump in an undignified heap on the stones.

'Gracious, I am truly sorry, let me help . . .

' . . . Why, Gina! Whatever are you doing here?'

'Oh, hell,' said Gina, unwinding herself from the last bits of hammock. 'Hi, Dad.'

They stared at each other, dark eyes meeting dark eyes, the olive skin of one an echo of the other.

Gina came to her senses. 'Did you say Victor was out here? Quick, he mustn't see us, not until I've explained.'

'Explained what?' said Serge, who was hard put to keep up with Gina's frantic dash towards the relative security of a patch of woodland. He stopped. 'Hey, why are we running? This Victor seems okay, why are you hiding from him?'

'Sssh,' said Gina. 'Come on, and keep your voice down. This place is terrible, you never know when or where one of the family or staff is going to pop up.'

Serge gave in to the inevitable and set off again after Gina. They came to a halt beside a rustic bench, and Gina collapsed on to it, panting dramatically. Serge sat beside her, looking down at his daughter with a questioning eye.

'What's up?' he said. 'I didn't know you were staying here, your friend in Oxford said you were with friends, but not where . . . How long have you been here? I visited not long ago, and you weren't here then.'

'I was, but I snuck off so's we wouldn't meet,' said Gina.

Serge was hurt. 'Hey, what did I do to deserve that?'

Hell, thought Gina. I've been longing to lash out at him for years, and now I get the chance I can't do it.

'No, it wasn't you, Dad,' she reassured him. 'It's just that things with me are a bit complicated. You see, although I'm staying here, they don't know I'm your daughter. In fact, they think I'm someone else, a kind of cousin of theirs.'

'Cousin? Of the Cordovans?' Serge was incredulous. 'How did you hope to get away with that one? And why?'

'I have got away with it,' hissed Gina. 'And I've got to go on getting away with it. Please, Dad, it's really important.'

Serge folded his arms and sat back on the seat. 'Right, shoot, kid. I want to know just what's going on.'

'It's like this,' Gina began.

Serge, among his other attributes of a good brain, a fair degree of

206

charm and his great artistic skill, possessed a sense of humour. While hardly able to believe what Gina was telling him, and while realizing that the visa business could be serious, he found the whole story of the impostorship very funny indeed.

'I can't see why young Harry went along with this, though,' he observed. 'Is he some kind of practical joker, a trickster?'

'It must be that,' agreed Gina.

That was the one strand of the matter she wasn't letting on about: the scheme for her and Harry to get married. If it happened, then she would present it as a *fait accompli*, but, although she didn't know her father that well, she had a sneaking idea that getting married to get a passport would seem like a sick idea to him.

Serge got up from the bench and wandered over to the other side of the path. The ground fell away steeply there, so that you were on eye-level with the tops of ancient oaks. Serge looked appreciatively down into the leafy darkness.

'This place is great,' he said. 'This is the kind of place you dream about. The Cordovans must be pretty rich to keep all this going. And,' he added, his face alight with laughter, 'to buy one of my big pictures. I take it as a compliment, though, them wanting to hang one of my canvases here, when you consider the art they've already got.'

'Victor's very successful in business,' said Gina. 'Luckily, because a lot of these English families just have to sell their old houses.'

'He'd better make good provision if it's not all going to fall apart when he goes,' said Serge. 'Taxes and so on. It'd be a shame if his kids have to sell up, let all this go, see it all broken up.'

'Yes, it would,' said Gina.

Serge became practical. 'I'm flying back to the States tonight,' he said. 'Only for a quick visit, I have some business to attend to. Then I'm coming back for a few more weeks in Europe. So while I'm in New York, why don't I drop by on this person and get your passport back?'

Gina blinked.

'You're broke, I suppose, that's all right. I was going to send a cheque to the Oxford address in any case. That'll more than cover your ticket home.'

A sense of relief flooded over Gina. She could turn up at the airport, get a standby ticket, slip out of the country before Popplewell or anyone else was any the wiser.

'What about Georgie, though? She'll be stuck in the States, no passport. She'll be mad at me.'

Serge raised a cynical eyebrow. 'I think it's you who should be mad at Georgie. She sounds to me like a girl who can take good care of herself; in any case, there's no problem. Give me her British passport and I'll do a swap with her.'

'What if she doesn't want to?'

'She hasn't got much choice,' said Serge laconically. 'The way I see it, she stole your passport – that's quite a serious offence in itself. Then, she has no right, as a British citizen, without a visa or work permit, to be in the States at all. Let alone holding down a job. No, I think your Georgie will play ball.'

Once I'm back in America, Gina was thinking, I can get in touch with Alwyn, he seemed very confident about getting me a work permit. Or maybe I could come back to study some more, do a Ph.D. That would mean at least another three years in England, bliss.

'It's great here,' she told her father as they walked back to the house together. 'It's just so beautiful.'

Serge looked at her, concerned. 'Don't fall in love with all this,' he said. 'Especially at your age. It can make for a terrible tie, just when you need to be out trying all kinds of new things, going new places.'

'Don't you love England?'

'I like it, yes. But I find it small, and the people like being depressed and pessimistic. That doesn't suit me.'

Gina remembered something. 'You and Mom got married near here,' she said. 'I found the records in the parish church.'

'Why, yes, we did,' said Serge. 'Your mother came from these parts, and she had a yen to get married down here. It was a pretty little church.' He looked away, up at the Gothic façade of the Hall. 'I'm sorry things didn't work out for me and your mother. It's always hard on the kids when a marriage breaks up.'

'Did you treat Mom so badly?'

'Is that what she told you?'

'We don't talk about it much,' said Gina. 'But I remember your rows.'

'We just didn't suit. I liked New York, she didn't. I work odd hours, have my ups and downs, like most artists. Your mother wanted a more regular kind of life. And I was a struggling painter then, life was hard. Still, we had some great times together; I wouldn't have missed it. She seems happy enough now, with her Italian count.'

'Count?' said Gina. 'Is he a count? I thought he was a crook.'

Serge laughed. 'Can't you be a count and a crook? Isn't that often the way in Italy these days?' He grew momentarily more serious. 'No, he seems like a nice guy, I don't see him as a crook. Besides, that's not your mother's style, you know that.'

True, thought Gina. Surprise on surprise. This very unexpected father, whom she liked, really liked, and who was helping her out, just as though he'd always been there. And she'd perhaps misjudged her mother. Of course, her mother had always had a rigid sense of right and wrong, no halfway houses or perhapses. Fine for her, but a nuisance for me, and out of place in this non-judgemental world, Gina told herself.

'I think I'll skip lunch,' said Gina. 'If you don't mind. It'd be very difficult pretending in front of you.'

'Okay,' said Serge. 'In any case, if they saw us together, they might think it was weird how alike we look.'

Gina stopped in her tracks, looking at her father properly for the first time. 'Is that so? Do I look like you?'

''Fraid so,' said Serge. 'Didn't your mother point it out to you?'

If she had, I wouldn't have listened, thought Gina.

'Anyway, you'll still be here when I get back from the States? It'll be a little while before I'm back in Britain, I'm stopping off in Switzerland, but I'll get that passport back to you. And I'll leave that cheque for you. What name are you going under here? So's I can put it on the envelope.'

Gina told him.

'Hartwell without the E, of course. What a stroke of luck for this Georgie character. Okay, I'll leave it for you on the hall table or wherever you leave post for guests in these big houses. The air ticket won't cost so much, buy yourself something you want with the rest of the money.'

Gina kissed him, for the first time in years. 'Thanks, Dad.'

'My pleasure,' he said. 'And don't get into any more mazes between now and next time I see you.'

'Of course not,' Gina said with dignity.

*

The front door was open at Kingfisher Cottage, but there didn't seem to be anyone in. Fergus frowned at the carelessness. Country ways were all very well, but even so . . .

The mystery was solved when he looked out of the upstairs window and saw Zoë in the garden, installed on a canopied swing in what looked like a state of complete contentment. On a little table beside her was a pile of shiny books, and a bowl of apples.

Fergus felt a spur of unreasonable resentment. Why should Zoë, jobless, soon no doubt to be penniless, have the ability to enjoy idleness to that extent?

'You look cross, Fergus,' said Zoë, glancing up from her book as he approached across the grass.

'You look very pleased with life,' grumbled Fergus. 'Move up, so that I can sit here. It's far too hot.'

'A difficult journey?' said Zoë. 'And you're hungry, too, I dare say. That's why you're so grumpy.'

'I am not grumpy,' said Fergus.

'Yes, you are. And you don't like to see me lolling here. You feel that I should be up and doing. No way. I'm on holiday, and I'm not going to fret or worry or feel I should be active.'

'Quite right, too,' said Sybil, looking over the garden fence. 'If you get too hot, though, Zoë, and have the energy to slide round here, you can sample the pool for me. It seems to have warmed up to a bearable temperature, and I just read in the instructions that it needs to be swum in, to keep the water in a good state.'

'Haven't your grandchildren arrived?' asked Fergus, secretly hoping they hadn't.

Sybil saw straight through that. 'No, they've postponed, they won't be up until the end of the month, aren't you lucky? The little one has some ailment, so is better off at home. My daughter knows I would be furious if I had to stop work to look after the boy, fond as I am of him.'

Fergus was much relieved, but too polite to say so. 'I'd better go and unload the car before someone walks off with my computer,' he said.

'They won't do that here,' said Sybil.

'There's cheese, and some fresh bread and cold drinks in the fridge,' Zoë called after him.

Sybil looked at her, amused. 'Aren't you going to give him a hand with his things?'

'No,' said Zoë. 'Nor am I going to bustle about and make lunch for him. If I start off on that path, I'll be waiting on him hand and foot before I know where I am, and I'm not having it. He's a grown man, quite capable of looking after himself.'

'Ah, but does he want to?'

'I don't suppose so, but that's just tough.'

'I gather he has a wife waiting for him. Doubtless she'll provide more creature comforts.'

Zoë gave an evil chuckle. 'A wife-to-be has found him, and yes, she'll provide whatever he wants, just so long as he comes up with the dosh.'

'A not unsatisfactory state of affairs.'

'One that has lasted the test of time,' agreed Zoë. 'Not to my taste, but then I'm not a man. And not to your taste either,' she added with spirit. 'Otherwise you'd have married again. Don't tell me you don't find life very pleasing as things are.'

Sybil laughed. Nobody could take offence at Zoë, with her easy-going brand of feminism and her light-hearted cynicism.

'You're an impertinent girl,' she said.

'Have an apple,' offered Zoë. 'My idea of heaven: a good book; several good books, in fact; sun; a bowl of crisp and tangy apples . . . Nothing better.'

Fergus called out of the kitchen window. 'After I've eaten, I'm going down to look at the vineyard,' he said. 'Want to come, lazy-bones?'

'No,' replied Zoë. 'But I tell you what, buy something delicious if Nadia's got any goodies on sale. For tonight. And then we can drift along to the pub for a drink, see who's around.'

'Okay,' said Fergus, much more amicable now he had consumed a large wedge of cheese sandwiched in a hunk of thick brown bread. 'Will you join us, Sybil?'

'If I've finished my quota,' said Sybil.

'Art first, drinks after?' said Fergus.

'You wait until you have to earn a living,' said Sybil severely.

'All too imminent,' said Fergus with a dramatic sigh. 'Offices, long hours, getting and spending . . .'

Zoë adjusted the cushions and settled herself even more comfortably. 'That's another world,' she said. 'And why worry? Look how things always work out differently from the way you'd expected.'

CHAPTER 20

Don was hard at work among his vines. Pausing from his rigorous snipping for a moment, he saw a tall figure walking along the footpath towards the vineyard. He squinted, recognized the aquiline profile and waved a hand in greeting to Fergus.

'Pruning?' said Fergus with interest. 'At this time of year?'

'Just cutting back the growth, don't want too much leaf. There's a lot this year, what with a wet May and now all this sun.'

He slung the clippers into the trailer attached to the tractor which was drawn up at the end of the row. 'Want to see round?' he asked.

'Love to,' said Fergus at once. 'But not if you're working. Another time would be fine, I'm going to be at Heartsbane for a while.'

'No, now is good.' He stuffed the tractor keys in his pocket and guided Fergus between the vines. 'What acreage does your father farm now?'

'About five thousand.'

'Arable?'

'Mostly, but he has a prize herd of Limousins as well. That's his hobby, breeding. He has a good manager, and of course, these days, with set-aside . . . '

Don laughed. 'Don't mention that word to Prim. Sets her off like nobody's business, thinks it's an offence against nature not to use good land for growing something.'

'My pa's got a fine crop of poppies. Myself, I like to see meadows. They were just pictures in a book for me until now.'

'Yes, well, as I said, Prim doesn't see it like that. Cultivation, growth, harvests, that's her scene. Meadows may be pretty, but they aren't productive.'

Don led Fergus up and down the lines of vines, holding forth on varieties, cropping, blending, yields. They were an incongruous pair, Don quite short, a little plump, and tanned a golden brown; Fergus tall and rangy and dark. Fergus looked as though he'd spent his days in the library, Don looked every inch a man who spent his time in the open air. Fergus envied him.

'These lines of willows every so many rows. Wind-breaks?'

'That's right. We need them here, look at those trees over there, you can see how the wind blows this side of the hills.'

Fergus inspected the bottling plant, empty now.

'We finished the bottling in May, there won't be any more until after this year's crop is in.'

'October?'

'We pick from September through to November usually.'

'Who does it?'

'Everybody,' said Don. 'All the employees here, people from the village, a few students early on, youngsters from the agricultural college in Heartsbury after the term begins.'

'Fun,' said Fergus, thinking of where he inevitably was at that time of year; picking words, not grapes. He told Don he thought he had the better of it, here among his twisty plants.

'Don't get any romantic notions about vines,' said Don. 'Viticulture is an ancient and honourable way of life, but it's bloody hard work. And, if you live in England, the odds are stacked against you.'

'Worth it, though?'

'For me, yes. It's in the blood, you might say. And I love wine, so what better work could there be for me to do?'

They were back in the main courtyard now, and Don pushed open a door. 'Now,' he said. 'What shall we try?'

Zoë handed Fergus another glass of water. 'Gross,' she said severely. 'You're going to have a head like a beehive tomorrow.'

'Mmm,' said Fergus, in a very happy haze.

'Put him to bed,' said Sybil.

'Will he make it up the stairs?' said Zoë doubtfully.

'We'll push him up,' said Sybil after a moment's thought. 'Only thing for him, to sleep it off. And you know, I expect Don drank just as much, and all there'll be to show for it will be a slight merriness.'

'Lucky Don,' said Zoë. 'Fergus surprises me, though. I haven't seen him blotto like this before.'

'All students drink too much,' said Sybil.

'Undergraduates, yes. Fergus may have been on the toot every night of the week when he was an undergraduate; I didn't know him then. But by the time they're postgrads they've usually grown out of that, haven't they? Fergus enjoys a drink with the best of us, but not like this.'

'He seems to have a lot on his mind,' said Sybil.

Zoë thought for a moment. 'Does he? I wonder why. Steady girlfriend, shortly to get his doctorate, glittering career beckons; all very satisfactory.'

Sybil looked foxy. 'Not satisfactory to him, that's all I can say. And I speak from considerable experience, I may add.'

'You look very cheerful,' said Harry.

'Do I normally look mournful?' asked Gina.

'No, but you've looked rather down recently. Not enough of my company these last few days. Sorry about that, I've been busy.'

Work or boys? Gina was tempted to ask.

Harry's mind was running on matrimonial lines. 'I don't want to push you into anything, but . . .'

Gina was off her guard, pleased and relieved at the prospect of getting her passport back, happy about seeing her father again. So, without stopping to think or exercise caution, she told Harry about her father, and the passport plans.

Big mistake.

'You see, we can't do anything without my having a passport.'

'I didn't know you had to show a passport to get married.'

'You do as an American citizen. All kinds of formalities.'

Harry looked very put out. 'I'd never thought about that. Well, it's no problem, you can get married as Georgiana Hartwell.'

'It wouldn't be legal.'

'Who would ever know? Slight spelling mistake on the marriage certificate, who's going to notice? And you'll be Mrs C from then on; no one will remember what your maiden name was.'

This made Gina feel very uneasy, although she wasn't sure why. When you got married, you took your husband's name. Or not, as you felt best. However, if you married a Cordovan, then you became a Cordovan, that was clear.

'No point at all in keeping your own name. You aren't a writer or on the stage or any kind of a professional. What the hell does it matter?'

'I haven't agreed to marry you.'

'Not yet, but you will,' said Harry.

Gina didn't like the note of certainty in his voice.

'Did you tell your pa you were going to marry me?' went on Harry.

'I did not.'

'Better break it to him afterwards, although he's never showed much interest in you or what you do, has he?'

Gina said nothing, filled with a sudden determination that on the day she got married, both her parents were going to be there.

'When's your pa going to see Georgie?'

'I don't know, exactly,' said Gina, grateful for the turn in the conversation. 'Pretty soon, he isn't in New York for long.'

Harry looked thoughtful for a moment. 'Want to come to Bath?' he asked.

Gina did. Her father's cheque had duly appeared, and it was more than generous. The air fare would hardly make a dent in it. 'I need to get a dress for Aimée's ball.'

'I'll help you choose. I have excellent taste.'

'I'll go and get my bag,' said Gina.

Harry watched her go upstairs and out of sight, then went swiftly into the library. Nicky wasn't about. He took a black leather address book out of his pocket and looked up a name. Code for New York, he said to himself. 001 212 . . .

He dialled.

Sports Day at Guisborn Lodge was a carefully orchestrated affair. The nitty-gritty of early heats and qualifying events were all held at an unreasonably early time in the day. Only the most enthusiastic parents, or those who knew quite well that darling Polly or dear Hermione would never make it through the first rounds turned up for

216

the preliminary sort-out events. By the time the bulk of parents rolled to their parking places on Laggard's Field, boots groaning with picnic hampers, only the fleetest and strongest were on display.

This, the head felt, left a much better impression with parents. 'We are unashamedly competitive,' she was wont to claim with a steely smile pinned to her lips. 'We insist that all our girls take part, but they must learn early on that there are no prizes, in sport or in life, for those who don't make it through the early rounds.'

So the standard in the afternoon was high, and the main events were soon over, leaving plenty of time for tea in the marquee before the five o'clock drift to Founder's Hall and the annual Laggard Address. This was the high spot of the school's public year, and was given 'by those eminent in the professions, the arts or in industry, whose achievements are a beacon lighting Our Girls to success'.

Gareth and Lori, who didn't live far away, were resolute early arrivers. Melissa and Ariadne were both sporty types and keen achievers, but there was always the prospect of a humiliating fall in a heat, as had happened the previous year, thanks to that hopeless girl lumbering about the track.

Melissa had been vocal. 'That bloody Jemima, I don't know what she's doing at this school. She should go back to her horrible comprehensive, they don't do any sports there, it's such a dump. I don't think they should give these poor girls scholarships, not for grinding away at a violin like she does. Not if they can't do sports and are always getting demerits. Eleven on the board so far this term, it's too bad, and she's in my house.'

The unfortunate musician represented no kind of threat this year as she had gone off to a more musical establishment, much to her relief. But there was that cow Veronica, who ran like the wind, and wasn't averse to a spot of shoving and tripping if the opportunity arose.

Gareth and Lori were there in position, however, eagle-eyed, deputed to make a fuss if Veronica got up to any of her tricks. Besides, Gareth liked to capture every moment of his daughters' doings on his camcorder. Being in the trade, as he put it, he prided himself on his video professionalism. Unfortunate friends who were obliged to watch the results mostly wished that he had no skill at all. What a relief it would be if he forgot to load it up or pressed the wrong button or the dratted thing went mercifully out of focus.

Melissa relentlessly acquired personal and house points as the morning wore on. Ariadne, a well-built girl, tended towards the heftier events and flung javelins and discuses with muscular seriousness.

'Miss Crump says it's the pentathlon for me next year,' she announced as she thumped down beside her parents. She was not an attractive sight, with her red face and brown, damp hair, but she was winning, and, on Sports Day, that was what mattered. A cooler Melissa joined them as Gareth hauled the goodies out of the car. Ariadne pointed out various friends' 'people', as she called them, while Lori unfolded napkins and hunted for the dinky little salt and pepper containers.

'Pretty lush, this,' commented Melissa as she sampled some pâté. 'Did you get it in Heartsbury?'

'No,' said Lori, passing a bottle of chilled wine to Gareth to open. 'From the *vineyard*. Nadia's started cooking for the shop there.'

'Nadia?'

'She and her husband have moved into Oracle Cottage. I believe she's *Russian*.'

'Oh, a foreigner. This is good, though.'

'Rather exciting *news*,' Lori said, when she finally got to eat something herself. 'The Cordovans have asked us to the *ball* at the Hall, for their daughter Aimée; it's her twenty-first. We'll be hosting a dinner party that evening, and then having some people to stay.'

'Do Melissa and I get to go?' asked Ariadne.

'No, darling,' said Lori, who had had quite an argument about this with Gareth.

'No, we cannot, under any circumstances, ring up and ask if we can bring two teenage girls,' Gareth had said. 'No, no and no. It just isn't done.'

Lori had reluctantly conceded the point, especially when she realized that she would need to use the girls' rooms to put guests up. Best that they stayed at school, all things considered.

'People to stay?' said Melissa sharply. 'Not in my room, I hope.'

'Perhaps *Tara*,' said Lori.

'Has Tara been asked?' said Ariadne.

'Yes,' said Gareth with simple pride. 'She's seeing a lot of Don

Cordovan, and is going as his partner. She'll have dinner with him, but of course she'll be staying with us.'

'I don't mind if you put someone in my room,' said Ariadne helpfully. 'Just as long as it's a dishy man.'

'You're so puerile about men,' said Melissa scornfully.

Alwyn and Angela were being entertained to lunch in the headmistress's house. Alwyn, a distinguished academic, very suitable, was going to deliver the Laggard Address. He had no connection with the school, but Angela had a daughter there. The head, casting around this year for a scholarly type to enhance the school's academic reputation, had decided to ignore the fact that Angela had carelessly cast off her husband years before and had since appeared with Alwyn in tow. Morality was one thing, the well-being of her school another. Alwyn had written several well-reviewed books, had become a minor radio personality, and, as a bonus, had an easy charm which would go down very well with both girls and parents.

Alwyn liked being flattered and deferred to, and although there were better places to be on a glowing June day than a girls' school, he was enjoying himself. As he took his place on the dais in the hall, applauded by some five hundred adolescent girls and their parents, he felt pleased with life. He sat with a clever expression on his face as various more or less shapeless girls trooped up to receive cups and prizes from the Chairman of the Governors, a tall and dissipated-looking Dean from a nearby cathedral.

Alwyn observed with malicious satisfaction that neither his age nor the cloth deterred the Dean from eyeing the more attractive sixth formers in a very unclerical way. He must tell Angela to warn her daughter not to find herself in a dark passage with the good Dean.

So Alwyn was in excellent form as he rose to address the company on the subject of History: the Mirror of our Minds. He was a brilliant speaker, with a fine voice, just enough humour, a vitality which was almost entirely missing when he was off the platform, and a gift for caressing his audience into believing that they were sharing and understanding weighty and difficult ideas.

Gareth was entranced. Before the applause had reached its full volume, he had pushed his way along the line towards the exit.

'Some people!'

'Really!'

'Excuse *me*!'

'What does he think this is, a rugger match?'

'Daddy, *don't*.'

Gareth didn't ignore the protests; he was simply unaware of them. He shot along the corridors and reached the heavy oak doors which led to the important part of the hall just as the platform party were emerging.

He brushed past the Dean, flashed a quick smile in the direction of the headmistress and halted in front of Alwyn.

'Mr Aumbry, I have a proposition to put to you. How would you like your own television series? Peak time, I can promise you, and a contract that any comedian would die for.'

Gareth had found his star.

Gina was so pleased with her dress that she had to show it to someone.

'Lucky you!' said Zoë. 'Heavenly! Carmen, only well cut. It must have cost a fortune. Is this the money from your dad?'

'Yes,' said Gina. 'It was on the sale rack, but it was still a horrendous price. Never mind, this ball's going to be something special and I refuse to creep around like a poor relation.'

'Good point,' agreed Zoë. 'Especially since you're supposed to be a rich relation.'

'I hadn't thought of that,' said Gina. 'There you are then, wise move, not an extravagance after all.'

'Did Harry like it?'

'Ye-es,' said Gina.

'What did he want you to buy?'

'Black. More grown up. Slinky. Not me, really. The sort of dress you'd look good in, but I'd just look dreary. Not being possessed of your celestial fairness.'

Zoë snorted, and adjusted her position on the swinging sofa. 'You'll have to wear a Wonderbra, though. That dress demands uplift, and you haven't got much left, all this worrying isn't good for the figure.'

'Mmm,' said Gina, her mind on other matters. She sucked up the dregs of her iced coffee through a straw. 'Where's Fergus? Slaving away at his word processor? Deep in economic cycles?'

'Not a bit of it. Deep in whatever pests attack vines. Helping Don to spray,' she added helpfully, seeing Gina's puzzled expression. 'At the vineyard.'

'How strange,' said Gina. 'It seems out of character.'

'Sybil says Fergus is in a state of confusion,' went on Zoë.

Gina blinked and concentrated. 'Fergus? I've never known anyone less confused. His life is always in order. Perhaps he's had a tiff with Charlotte.' Unlikely, there never was a man more under his girlfriend's thumb, she thought.

'Could be, but I don't think he's spoken to her since he came here.'

'Run into a problem with his thesis, then.'

'I don't think he's interested in his thesis just at the moment. You know how organized he is, and how hard he works?'

'Yes.'

'Not here, not now. His papers and files and books are either still in a box or shoved under his bed. He hasn't even plugged his computer in.'

'Burnt out,' said Gina. 'He's been working too hard. And coming here, tang of the sea, green spaces, holiday atmosphere, you idling about all day . . . Good for him to have a break. Give it a week or ten days and he'll be tapping away again.'

Zoë wasn't convinced, but she felt too lazy to argue the point. 'We can see if it's anything to do with his love life when Charlotte comes next week. Personally, I think he's gone off Charlotte in a big way.'

Gina sat up. 'Fergus wouldn't. Why, he's the most loyal man I've ever met. You are nasty about him, Zoë.'

'I speak as I find,' said Zoë imperturbably.

Gina finally registered what else Zoë had said. 'Charlotte? Coming here?'

'Yes, she's coming for the ball. Don't look so appalled, Gina. Fergus has been invited because of his auntie, I suppose, and they'll have been invited as a twosome as usual.'

'She knows who I am!'

'Of course she knows who . . . Ah, I see the problem. She might let on about you not being the piggy one, but a fiendish impostor.'

'Hell,' said Gina. 'I just think I've got one knot sorted out, and whoosh! there's another one in its place.'

'We'll have to tell her. Make up some convincing reason for it all, and persuade her to keep her mouth shut.'

'When has Charlotte ever kept her mouth shut?'

'There is that. Well, Fergus will have to keep Charlotte at his side, not give her any opportunity to yak to any of the Cordovans. He can say you're there because you're a friend of the family; she doesn't have to know that you're pretending to be a cousin.'

'A big risk to take,' said Gina, worried.

'True,' said Zoë. 'But you haven't got much choice, have you?'

CHAPTER 21

'Someone rang for you,' said Guy as Gina went through the hall.
Good, thought Gina. Dad; he's got the passport.

'A Mr Popplewell. He was extremely nosy, and I'm afraid I wasn't very forthcoming.'

'Popplewell?' Gina felt winded.

'He didn't exactly ask to speak to you, but wanted to know if you were staying here. I didn't like his tone at all. Is he a friend of yours?'

Guy's own tone indicated that he would think the less of Gina for being acquainted with anyone of the Popplewell ilk.

'No, no,' said Gina. 'A friend? Not at all.'

'He was very persistent. In fact, I thought he might be some kind of weirdo.'

'A phone pest?' said Gina.

Pest of every kind. How on earth had he tracked her down here? That article in *Gossip!*, perhaps. Had he been in touch with the Hartwell grandparents in Scotland? Discovered that they believed their daughter was in Heartset? While he knew that she had been photographed in New York? And had therefore assumed that any Gina Hartwell with or without an E who might be staying at Heartsease Hall could only be his prey?

Gina had an unrealistic idea of the intelligence of the average civil servant. Mr Popplewell had merely questioned the postman in Oxford, ascertained that all post for Fergus, Zoë and Gina was to be forwarded to Heartsbane; had made some further enquiries and located one Gina H. at the Hall.

Guy was looking doubtfully at Gina. 'Are you all right? Don't worry about this man, I told him where to get off. In fact, I lied to him.'

'Lied?'

'Indeed I did. My nose must be several inches long by now. I said that Miss Hartwell, a member of the family, had been in residence here, but had left. And no, I had no information as to her present whereabouts, but I was sure that any friend or acquaintance, such as he purported to be, would know where to find her.'

'Thank goodness,' said Gina. 'Guy, I owe you. That creep's been hounding me for weeks.'

'I should tell the police,' said Guy, shocked. 'You never know what these people may do when roused. Now, come along to the kitchen, and I'll make you a cup of coffee. You look quite pale.'

The kitchen was a refuge of order and industry. Unmistakable Esme sounds of operatic radio with accompanying hums came from one of the sculleries. Pans gleamed, the floor shone, a sweet baking smell filled the air. Light streamed in from the many windows. Soothed, Gina slid along the bench set up against the long table.

'Hester is looking for you, Gina,' said Maria, who was doing some expert whisking in a large copper bowl. 'She has an express letter that came for you, from America.'

Gina's spirits rose. 'I'll be straight back for the coffee,' she promised Guy. 'Where is Hester?'

'In the garden, talking to Prim and Nicky,' said Maria. 'I can see them through the window there.'

Gina shot out into the stableyard, through the arch and along the gravel to the sunken garden. Nicky and Hester were sitting on a bench on the upper walk; Nicky with a notebook and a harassed expression on her face, Hester with a basket full of dried flowers for sorting. They were discussing with Prim the flowers for Aimée's ball. It wasn't an ideal place for a conversation, because Prim was trimming the ten-foot-high yew hedges which ran round the edges of the walks.

Prim had twisted round on the top step of her ladder the better to express her disapproval of Aimée's plans. 'It's all very well Victor giving Aimée *carte blanche*, he might know that she'd want great hothouse flowers and plants everywhere. And it's not just a question of the shocking cost, it's ecologically unsound.'

Snip, snip went her shears as she turned her energies to the hedge once more.

'Aimée's so very headstrong,' said Hester mildly. 'Oh, there you are, Gina,' she went on, laying her basket to one side. 'There's a letter for you. Express, from America. I tried to find you because I thought it might be important.'

She handed Gina a slim blue envelope. Too slim to contain a passport, but in her father's handwriting.

'Thank you,' said Gina, retreating to the next bench along to open it. Snatches of conversation reached her from the others.

Hi Gina

'The scent of Liputian lilies . . .'

I did my best, but the bird had flown.

'Swags of Bacchus ivy . . .'

Gone upstate, no idea when she's due back.

'Netted greenery . . .'

Suggest you contact Embassy for replacement passport.

'Banks of filibusters and yellow montrose . . .'

Ask for Dan McOstrich, he's an old friend of mine.

'Negus palms in the tent, and bunches of heartsgonia for the supper tables.'

See you at the ball, if you're still at Heartsease. Love, Dad.

The words jumbled together in Gina's mind before it cleared enough for her to make sense of what was written. As though in a dream, she got up, and walked away, quickly, back to the house.

Without thinking, she retraced her steps to the kitchen. What she wanted was to be alone, to think things through, come to terms with the new, extra tricky twist to the tale. What she got was cheerful people, happy in their work, full of talk. Esme, Maria, Guy, and Mrs Slubs were all there, together with Wilf, who had come up with a delivery and lingered for a coffee and company.

Guy was supervising the coffee, dispensing a rich brew to those present, accompanied by some tiny chocolate biscuits made by Maria.

'To test,' she said, putting a plateful down on the table with a flourish. 'A layer of very plain biscuit and above it, little pieces of mint, all covered with extremely dark chocolate. I want to serve these at the ball with the coffee.'

The biscuits were welcomed, sampled, discussed and appreciated.

Gina sipped her coffee, and nibbled a biscuit so as not to hurt Maria's feelings.

The talk was lively and general. Gina took no part, trying to focus her thoughts as the gossip flowed around her.

'Nicky's looking dreadful.'

'Roger's being difficult about the children.'

'The children miss her, bound to. Roger do his best, but he has a job, and little ones to manage, on his own; it's too much. He's not the organized type, he haven't got a clue.'

'No, those children go off to school with odd socks and I don't know what. Teacher say they're none too clean, neither, and she reckon they don't eat right.'

'Shame,' was the consensus.

Esme took a hearty line. 'She should stop wasting her time mooning after Don. She's had her fling, she needs to get away from there. He's not bothered one way or the other, plenty more where she came from. She ought to pull herself together.'

'Not so easy,' said Wilf wisely. 'That Don, he fair casts a spell on they women. They're all the same, all sniffing round him.'

'That Tara at Heartwell House, she's the latest.'

'She! She and her fancy London ways. Mind you, she look like one can look after herself.'

'Besotted, that's what women are with Don.'

'Too right. He say snip and they say snap.'

'What about you and the TV, Guy?' enquired Esme. 'Has Gareth been propositioning you any more, luring you away from your work with pots of loot?'

'He has not,' said Guy. 'I don't know if he's found someone to do what he wants, but it won't be me. The nerve, thinking he only had to click his fingers and I'd be there on screen.' He gave himself an extra lump of sugar in his coffee. 'I hear he's got hold of a historian now. A teacher from Oxford. He's going to have a half-hour programme, fancies himself as the next A. J. P. Taylor, I dare say. Have you heard of him, Gina? Him being from Oxford? His name is Alwyn Aumbry.'

Gina blinked. 'On television?' She was stunned. 'Television? *Alwyn?*'

'You know him, then.'

'Oh yes,' she said bleakly. 'He's doing some very good work.

Research. The Tudors, that's his field.'

'Not any more,' said Guy knowingly. 'I heard them talking it over at the club. I wish Gareth wouldn't go there. He's straight, you can tell, and the club really isn't meant for voyeurs. I don't think this Alwyn liked it much there, to tell you the truth, but it is a fairly swanky place, more than you can say for anywhere else in Heartsbury.'

'He'll still go on with his work in Oxford, of course he will,' said Gina. 'He's a scholar.'

Guy pursed his lips. 'Gareth told him there won't be time. Apparently Alwyn has research assistants and so on at Oxford, but Gareth's going to provide researchers for him, top-class experienced ones. Alwyn said he'd be happy to give up his Oxford work. He can certainly afford to, you should hear the money he's being offered.'

That prompted a discussion about outrageous rates of pay, Mrs Slubs holding out that all telly personalities were paid too much. 'They get uppity, and fancy in their ways.'

Gina was completely floored by this third blow. Doors were slamming shut on her from every quarter. She tried unsuccessfully to keep a sense of proportion. After all, in the greater scheme of things, what did they matter, Popplewells and passports and the probability of no work in Oxford? They mattered a lot, she swiftly concluded. This was panic time. This meant no help with a work permit, no backing for any applications for further study, no more Oxford.

Guy's calm voice washed over her. He pretended that gossiping about the family was wrong, but at the same time, he loved to impart his inside knowledge. Victor was his special field. 'He's had a terrible row with Marcus, terrible.'

'What's new?' said Esme, blowing bubbles in her coffee in what Guy considered a disgusting way. 'Don't look at me like that, Guy, like I was some creature out of the deep. Victor and his eldest son don't get on; it's an old story.'

'This isn't just the normal rowing,' said Guy, reverting to his theme. 'He said Marcus's attitude to Aimée was perverted.'

'And he's right,' put in Mrs Slubs. 'I've seen what no respectable woman should see, goings-on in that indecent room of hers. That's no way for brothers and sisters to carry on.'

'Victor doesn't get on with Charles either,' pointed out Esme.

'Charles,' said Maria, raising her eyes to heaven. 'Save me from this man with his furnaces and sculptures who only eats cheese. It is fortunate he is here so seldom.'

'No wonder Victor is in a quandary about who's to inherit,' went on Guy.

That silenced them.

Mrs Slubs came to first. 'That Harry, him with his tricky ways. If he give up them sodoms and finds a girl who'll do, Mr Victor'll be that relieved.'

The table agreed, one or two of the company giving Gina quick, knowing glances.

'Mind you, Victor's in a temper anyway because of the Swiss girl.'

'Why's that?' said Esme, eating her ninth chocolate biscuit.

Maria moved the plate out of reach. 'These are for everybody, and you eat them all.'

'Aw, c'mon, Maria,' protested Esme, stretching out for the plate.

'Victor was planning to go to Switzerland immediately after the ball, for two or three days, and she's not going to be there.'

'That'll learn him, chasing after they foreign women.'

'He fancies a foreign woman, there's always that Nadia,' said Mrs Slubs, taking a good slurping gulp of her coffee. She gave a coarse chuckle. 'He likes them with a bit of spirit.'

'He doesn't usually soil his own nest,' said Guy reprovingly. 'I think Nadia's too close to home. And she has a husband in tow.'

'Yes, but how long for?' said Esme. 'Always yelling at him, you should hear her down at the vineyard.'

'She wants him to take notice of her,' said Maria. She finished her coffee, and took the cup through to the dishwasher.

Esme stared after her. 'You mean you think she's not mad at him?'

Maria came back, and took a pan from its hook with a Spanish flourish. 'I think she is mad at him, all the time. Mad so that she wants to throw pots and pans at him. Like this,' she added, twirling the pan in her hand in a dangerous way. 'You don't get so angry with people unless you mind about them. This Nadia, she would just walk away if it was a nothing between them. He is the one, this husband with the poet's name, he has to pay attention. Listen to what she is really saying to him.'

'You could be right,' said Esme. 'All that trouble for a man, she'd be better off with a girlfriend.'

'A dildo may not be what she wants,' said Guy, primly.

'Loose talk,' said Mrs Slubs with relish. 'I never did.' She manoeuvred her portly frame away from the table.

Esme scooped up the remaining cups with loud rattlings and headed for the scullery.

Wilf wiped the coffee froth from his mouth with the back of his hand and sauntered off to find Jarvis.

Guy wrapped an immaculate green apron round his slim middle in his usual elegant way and disappeared in the direction of the cellars.

Gina was left sitting alone at the table, staring into her cup of coffee while she stirred the dregs with a tiny silver spoon.

Then she set the spoon down carefully in the saucer beside her cup and swung her legs over the bench. She looked calm and decided.

'Tell me, Maria,' she said, 'is Harry around?'

Zoë was cleaning the kitchen at Kingfisher Cottage. Clad in a pair of seedy jeans and an ancient T-shirt, she was enjoying a good scrub.

'And it is enjoyable, when you don't *have* to do it,' she told Gina, peeling off a pair of lobster-coloured rubber gloves. 'Although it is rather a have-to just now; Charlotte's coming.'

Gina said nothing, and Zoë looked at her properly. She was horrified. 'Goodness, have you seen a ghost? Has something happened? You look awful.'

'I'm going to get married,' said Gina.

Zoë's eyes narrowed. 'Hold on, I get the feeling that this isn't exactly break open the fizz and save for a prezzie time.' She paused and gave Gina a long and searching look. 'We aren't talking about Harry here, are we?'

'Yes,' said Gina, defiantly. 'There's nothing else for it.'

Zoë listened to Gina's tale of the Popplewell, and of Georgie's disappearance, with disbelief.

'So?' she said, when Gina had finished and had subsided into a chair with a cup of nasty instant coffee. 'Because of that you're planning to marry this Cordovan? I thought you never had any intention of marrying him; you just took the chance to get out of the way for a while. Have you fallen in love with him after all? Or slept with him and decided he's It as far as sex goes?'

'No,' said Gina. 'I'm not in love with him. I'm not in love with anyone. Yes, I've slept with him, and he hasn't got any nasty habits that I know of, and it was okay, no, good, actually. I don't want to get married, okay, I know that, but it's nothing to do with Harry personally. I just don't believe marriage works in normal circumstances.'

'There you are, then.'

'These aren't normal circumstances.'

'Come on,' said Zoë. 'Gina, you don't marry a man just to get a passport.'

'I do,' said Gina promptly. 'And it isn't only that. I've just heard that Gareth Whatnot from Heartwell House, you know, Lori's husband, has enticed Alwyn away from Oxford and his work on the Tudors to give a series of popular TV programmes.'

'No,' said Zoë, diverted. 'Truthfully? You aren't making it up?'

'No, unfortunately, I'm not. So no further need for me, no chance of a work permit.'

'He'll need researchers, these telly programmes use hundreds of them.'

'All provided by Gareth's lot. It's not my kind of research, what I do wouldn't be any use for a TV series.'

'There are other academics at Oxford who need research assistants.'

'I haven't got time to find them, and they'd shy off as soon as the little matter of a work permit came up.'

'Let me think,' said Zoë. 'There must be some way out of all this.'

'It's no good,' said Gina. 'My mind's made up. I've told Harry it's yes, and that's that.'

'You're a fool.'

'You say that because you live here, you've got a passport, you can get a job.'

'Well, so can you, in America. It's not some bizarre poverty-stricken country you come from, no work, bilharzia and the runs with every glass of water. You're American, you're a fully-paid-up citizen of God's own country.'

'I want to live in England. I haven't got family in America, or friends. I was educated here, I feel English, I want to live here.'

Zoë tried another tack. 'Look, if you get married to Harry, you're bound to fall in love with someone else in a year or two.'

'And why should I do that?'

'People do.'

'If you really want to know, there's no chance. I fell in love; the guy ditched me. Then it happened again. You get emotional and screwed up about people, and it's hell. My parents fell in love, and look where they ended up. Walking out on each other and on me. I don't need to be in love with someone to marry them. Love has nothing to do with marriage. This is going to be a working arrangement, and I'll make it work.'

'You're mad,' said Zoë with foreboding. 'What am I going to say to Fergus?'

'Fergus? It's none of his business.'

'He won't like it.'

'Tough.'

Zoë looked at her friend, exasperated.

To Gina's relief there was a brief ring on the doorbell and Sybil, not waiting to be let in, put her head round the kitchen door. 'Hello, Gina,' she said. 'Zoë, do you still want to go to Heartsbury? I need some books from the library, but I'm leaving now.'

Zoë gave her hands a perfunctory wash, kicked off the shower shoes she had been wearing for her cleaning tasks, stuffed her feet into a pair of sandals, whisked her bag off the back of the door and announced that she was ready.

'Quarrelled with Gina?' asked Sybil as she started the car.

'The idiot,' said Zoë furiously. 'Do you know what she's gone and done? Just listen to this.'

Sybil drove in silence, waiting for Zoë to finish her pithy and indignant analysis of Gina's wrongdoings. This didn't happen until they were approaching the outskirts of Heartsbury, and rather than cope with a still fuming Zoë going off pop in the library, Sybil drew into the superstore.

'There's a café here, have a cold drink or a coffee to restore you,' she said.

Zoë was glad of the offer, but she was still muttering as they found a table and sat down on the hard little chairs.

'They're always so uncomfortable, these chairs,' said Sybil. 'Of course, they don't want to encourage punters to linger. Once you've paid up at the self-service, they want you on your way as fast as possible.'

Zoë had no time for idle chit-chat. 'What am I going to do?' she demanded.

'About Gina and Harry? Nothing,' said Sybil.

'I can't stand by and watch Gina ruin her life,' said Zoë dramatically.

'One, people don't ruin their lives so easily. Two, she and Harry may get on much better than you think. Three, they're both adults, and there's nothing at all that you can do. Friends come mistakes and all, and you either accept them and their more or less unsuitable partners, or you find new friends.'

'Oh, I suppose you're right,' said Zoë. 'I know you're right. But it's such a shame. Gina doing a thing like this, just to get a passport.'

'I think Gina may be doing it for more complicated reasons than you imagine,' said Sybil. 'There's a lot at stake for her. Any other lovers in her life?'

Zoë shook her head. She plunged the spoon into her coffee and stirred it with malevolent force. 'No. I think she was really quite keen on Alwyn, the guy she worked for. Not seriously, though.'

'Alwyn Aumbry?' said Sybil briskly. 'Well, that's a waste of time. Apart from the fact that Angela has him exactly where she wants him, she'd be far better off with Harry, who's a very charming young man.'

'I haven't met him,' said Zoë.

'Then don't prejudge him. I think you and Harry would get on extremely well. No, my advice is just to sit tight, spare Gina your rantings and ravings, and wait to see how things turn out. You may be surprised.'

CHAPTER 22

Fergus drove over to Heartsbury to meet Charlotte at the station. She usually drove herself everywhere in a smart red car, but it was out of action; cows had got out from a neighbour's field and had taken a short-cut across Charlotte's parents' drive.

'Hardly what you expect in Surrey,' Charlotte had complained on the phone. 'Rampaging, I mean. It's a terrible nuisance, my car will be off the road for nearly a week, and they haven't got a spare one available at the moment. It's too bad.'

'Hire one?' suggested Fergus.

'No, that would be extravagant, and besides, I won't need it. I can easily catch the train. You can meet me, and then I'll be with you all the time in any case. We can use your car.'

What, every day and all day? thought Fergus gloomily as he wandered up and down the empty platform. He stopped by the chocolate machine, debating whether he wanted a bar or not. No, he had a sour taste in his mouth. And why couldn't Charlotte come on the branch line to Heartsease? Why did she have to go to Heartsbury?

Trapped, he prowled some more. Perhaps he would have some chocolate after all. The machine swallowed his 30p, gave a half-hearted clank and spat out a toffee bar.

Hell, said Fergus, dumping it in the bin. Although the June sun still shone, the station seemed oppressive and gloomy. A label which had come off a parcel stirred in the breeze and Fergus watched its erratic passage down the platform until it flipped over the edge and came to rest on the line.

Ten past ten. The train had been due five minutes ago. The

loudspeaker system crackled into life, giving Fergus, who was standing right underneath one of the speakers, a nasty shock. Crackle, crackle, hiss; then it cleared enough for a robotic voice with strangely refined vowels to announce that the train due at 10.05 was running approximately twenty-three, two, three minutes late. The message ended with a loud click and the station fell silent again.

Fergus sauntered into the little buffet where three tables were set out next to a counter across which tea and other beverages and sandwiches were dispensed. Fergus eyed the inky-looking coffee brewing on a hotplate and asked for a cup of tea. He took a sip, deposited it on one of the tables and cruised along the rack of magazines and papers which stood at the far end of the room.

An article caught his eye, and he began to read.

His tea grew cold, other passengers came and went, and so did the delayed ten-five. The first Fergus knew about it was when he was addressed in cross tones by two women simultaneously.

One was the woman at the counter. 'The notice says, "No browsing",' she pointed out. 'Quite clearly, and if you can read the magazine you can read those words. You'll have to pay for it, nobody else is going to want it once you've thumbed it through.'

The other was Charlotte. 'Well, here you are. I do think you could have waited for me on the platform. I went outside and saw your car, but no sign of you. I know the train was late, but you could have noticed it arriving.'

'Hello, Charlotte,' said Fergus, giving her a peck on the cheek. 'Hang on, that biddy is making me buy this magazine.'

Charlotte plucked it out of his hand. '*Country Style*? Why are you reading this, Fergus? Of course, you don't have to buy it if you don't want to. She can't make you.'

Fergus looked at the woman's baleful expression and thought she probably could. 'I want to buy it, in any case,' he said. 'There's an interesting article that I want to finish.'

Charlotte led the way to his car, and stood by while he tucked her bags into the boot. He saw her into her seat, shut her door and went round to the driver's side. Suppressing a sudden, wild urge to hurl the keys in through the window and flee to the platform to leap aboard the train for Scotland which had just drawn in, he slid instead into the car and started the engine.

Charlotte was investigating the magazine. 'Was this the article you were reading?' she asked. 'About the vineyard?'

'Yes,' said Fergus, swerving to avoid a pensioner determined to end her life then and there in the High Street. 'Or perhaps she just spotted a particularly nice piece of Battenberg cake across the road and threw caution to the winds.'

'What?' said Charlotte, startled. 'Battenberg cake? Fergus, what on earth are you talking about?'

'Nothing,' said Fergus. 'I was just thinking out loud for a moment.'

'Well, don't,' said Charlotte. 'And I can't imagine why you wanted to read this, what a dreary, exhausting life, running a vineyard. Apart from making a product which is so bad for people.'

'Bad for people?' echoed Fergus, speeding up as they left the city behind them.

'Not too fast,' said Charlotte automatically. 'And I think you should be in fourth gear. Watch out for that motorcyclist.' She returned to her subject. 'Wine is alcohol. Alcohol is bad for you.'

Fergus flashed a quick, sideways glance at Charlotte. Was this a joke?

'Definitely not,' said Charlotte, her eyes gleaming with the enthusiasm of the convert. 'Mummy's been to see this wonderful doctor. He's written a book, you must read it.'

Fergus grunted.

'You don't sound quite yourself,' said Charlotte, eyeing him intently.

Fergus pulled himself together. 'I've been working very hard,' he said. And that was true, no need for Charlotte to know that it had been at Don's vineyard rather than on his thesis.

'Of course, and you're tired, because you'll have been eating all the wrong food. This book has recipes at the end, all designed to give you a perfectly balanced diet, eliminating acids from the system, helping you to sleep, and, most important in your case, enabling the brain to work to its full potential.'

'Oh?' said Fergus, who had a suspicion that he wasn't going to like these recipes.

'Beans,' said Charlotte triumphantly. 'That's the secret. I'm going to cook all your meals for you while I'm here; you'll be amazed at how different you'll feel in no time at all.'

Fergus felt different at once, as any last vestiges of good humour vanished. I hate beans, he thought rebelliously. And if she's decided alcohol is bad for me, she'll be on at me to drink water and juice.

'Only lightly carbonated spring water, with an alkaline base,' Charlotte continued. 'Nothing else, especially not anything which is a stimulant. Such as tea or coffee,' she added, in case Fergus was in any doubt. 'You can begin on a new regime today; I'll prepare a lunch as soon as we get to Heartsbane.'

'No way,' said Zoë, barring the door. 'I'm sorry, Charlotte, but this is a small kitchen, and I'm in it.'

Zoë was always polite to Charlotte in the Oxford house, mindful of the fact that it was Fergus's house and that Charlotte was Fergus's girlfriend and likely future wife. Mostly, she contrived to keep out of her way as much as possible, because Zoë didn't like Charlotte, thought Fergus was far too good for her, and felt hugely relieved when her visits came to an end.

'Must be like going to bed with something out of the broom cupboard,' she had said to Gina.

Gina had defended Fergus. 'He's old enough to know what he wants.'

Zoë wasn't having that. 'No man is ever old enough to know what he wants,' she said firmly. 'Except mostly what he can't have. But Charlotte's got Fergus exactly where *she* wants him, and he hasn't got the guts to tell her to push off.'

'He's in love with her,' insisted Gina. 'He doesn't want her to push off.'

'He's no more in love with her than I am with the postman,' said Zoë. 'He might have felt a frisson once, but now she's wound her tendrils round him, and he has no idea of how to get away.'

'I feel sorry for Charlotte,' said Gina. 'If you're right, and he isn't really keen on her. But I don't believe it. They heave off to the bedroom quickly enough whenever she comes.'

'Yes, but it's her leading the way, haven't you noticed? And Fergus is too lazy to go and find himself another girlfriend, so sex with Charlotte is better than nothing.'

'Such cynicism,' said Gina, shocked. 'You make Fergus seem putty in her hands; Fergus isn't like that.'

'I'm absolutely right,' said Zoë. 'Just you wait and see. It's laziness, nothing more. And not facing up to how he really feels.'

'About Charlotte?'

Zoë gave Gina a quick look. 'Among others,' she said.

Now, in Kingfisher Cottage, things were different. 'You're a guest here, Charlotte,' Zoë told her. 'And I'm doing the cooking. Unless you want to go out with Fergus, of course. Just let me know, for numbers and so on.'

Charlotte was furious. 'That won't be at all convenient,' she told Zoë. 'Fergus needs special food, so I'm afraid I'll have to do the cooking for us both. And for you, too, if you like,' she added generously. 'I'm sure a cleansing diet will do you the world of good.'

'What special food?' said Zoë. 'Fergus eats everything.'

'Exactly, and that's what's so bad for him. Everything means meat and dairy products and wheat and acidic fruit and vegetables – the system simply can't cope. Ninety per cent of what he eats is actually harmful.'

'Oh, rubbish,' said Zoë.

Charlotte had spotted the empties.

'And of course, he drinks far too much. Alcohol is poison, total poison. I can see he's been having beer, and wine, too.'

Fergus was hovering in the doorway, alarmed by the raised voices. Wonderful, he thought. Charlotte comes for a ball, and issues a ban on all the food that might be served, not to mention expecting him to drink water instead of champagne.

Charlotte was well into her stride. 'He must only eat foods which restore the chemical balance of the body. Beans and pulses, cooked naturally, without salt. And tofu.'

Fergus took a deep breath and raised his voice in protest.

'Charlotte, I had tofu once, at a Japanese restaurant. It was disgusting.'

'You'll learn to like it,' said Charlotte with superb conviction.

'Beans?' said Zoë. 'Not in this house, Charlotte. You can worship the bean in your own house, or anywhere you like, but not here. Beans are banned.'

'I hardly think you're in a position to lay down the law about what Fergus eats. I'm going to be here for a week . . .'

237

Fergus blanched.

' . . . which will give me time to set Fergus off on the right path. Then, when I leave, he can use this.'

She drew out from her bag a concertina affair, which, unfolded, was about four feet long. It was covered in columns of small print.

'This is the prohibited list. There are recipes on the other side.'

Fergus grabbed it, expostulated.

'Charlotte, practically every food you can imagine is on this list. What is there left to eat?'

'Some fresh vegetables; there are a few which are all right in small quantities. A banana once a week. Plenty of water. And, the mainstay of all your meals, as I said, is beans.'

'I said, no beans in this house,' put in Zoë.

'I hardly think it's rational to take this hostile attitude to the bean,' said Charlotte.

'It isn't a matter of reason. My objections are purely physical. I am not sharing a small house with a man who eats beans.'

'And why not?'

First funny thing I've heard today, thought Fergus, the gloom lifting. 'Come on, Charlotte, don't be so slow. Beans meanz fartz.'

Zoë laughed. 'Exactly, I couldn't have put it better.'

Charlotte disliked vulgarity and crudity, and chose to ignore the laughter. 'You seem to have a warped sense of humour,' she said coldly. 'These are serious matters. The gut adjusts to beans, and . . .'

'Then it can do its adjusting elsewhere,' said Zoë firmly.

Charlotte tried to keep calm; getting worked up poured acid into the system, so the good doctor's book said. She managed a smile, which emerged as a patronizing grimace.

'So I'm sure you understand, Zoë, why, although it is kind of you to offer to cook, I must insist on preparing our food myself.'

Zoë folded her arms. 'Not here. This is my kitchen, and you're not cooking up horrid little bean messes in it.'

The grimace never faltered. 'It is Fergus's kitchen, and . . .'

'Wrong,' said Zoë. 'I rent Kingfisher Cottage. Fergus may pay his expenses, and we share food bills, but he's staying with me. And so are you. And my guests eat what's put in front of them. You want to have a bean orgy, wait until you get married. I can see your honeymoon is going to go with a bang.'

'Ouch,' said Fergus, trying not to laugh. Any urge to do so subsided very swiftly as Charlotte turned on him.

'Fergus,' was all she said.

Zoë unfolded her arms and picked up a dish towel. 'Oh, by the way, Fergus,' she said in casual tones, 'Sybil popped in. Says Harry rang up, would you meet him at the Bunch of Grapes at half past six. Ring if you can't make it, otherwise he'll expect you then.'

Charlotte's eyes narrowed. 'Who is Sybil?' she enquired in nasty tones. 'And this Harry, is he a friend? Do I know him?' She didn't wait for an answer, but swept on. 'I suppose this Bunch of Grapes is a pub. You'd better ring up right away, Fergus, and explain that you won't be there.'

Fergus's inclination to do what Charlotte wanted, this being the easiest and least effortful course, fought against a strong desire not to be told what to do by Charlotte.

For once, his lazy self lost the day.

'Would you like to join us?' he asked Zoë. And then, to Charlotte, 'I won't ask you, because I know how you feel at present about alcohol, and I'm not planning to drink water.'

Zoë longed to give a cheer for Fergus, but felt it would be unwise. 'No, thank you,' she said, with a straight face. 'I rather think Harry wants to talk to you about a private matter.'

Charlotte had got her breath back. 'Fergus! No!'

'And meanwhile,' said Fergus, feeling he might as well be hung for a sheep, 'I'm going over to Don's; I'll be back later.'

He fled.

Mild pandemonium reigned at Heartsease Hall. Preparations for the ball were intense. The weather forecasters had promised a continuation of the hot, dry weather, with a slight chance of thunder towards the end of the week, so the indoor contingency plans were shelved. The pavilion went up, Jarvis and Esme staggered to and fro with potted bays and palms and minifers. Prim worked through mounds of flowers, while schoolgirls co-opted from the village carried green buckets hither and thither and spent a happy hour or two dunking the Oasis.

Harry was in high spirits, delighted at the thought of getting married, loving having a big secret which he wasn't going to let out until the night of the ball.

'That's the time,' he said to Gina, with affection. 'Midsummer's Eve, we'll never forget it, and a ball, very romantic and appropriate.'

'It *is* Aimée's ball, though. Aren't you stealing her thunder?'

'No one will ever steal Aimée's thunder,' said Harry, stating a simple truth. 'Besides, it's very much a family affair, not a young thing's rave-up. Just the time and place. We can let them think it'll all go on in the usual way, notices in *The Times*, engagement, wedding lists, and meanwhile, we'll pop off and get done.'

Like taking a tom to the vet, thought Gina, who was still in a state of semi-shock.

'Soon?' she asked.

'Friday,' said Harry.

'When are you going to tell them I'm not who they think I am?'

'When we're married.'

'How can you explain it?'

'We can pretend we did it so that we could be together without anyone realizing what was up.'

More pretence, thought Gina. But at least I can be myself again. Only I won't be, because I'll be Mrs Harry.

'I'm going into the office for a couple of hours,' said Harry, pulling on his leather jacket. 'Then it's back here to sort out the electrics.'

'Isn't Nicky getting professionals in?'

'We are professionals,' said Harry. 'Pa's seeing to the fireworks; Hester sees the house is a haven of welcome to all the family and guests and oversees the food; Julia presides as wife and mother, although not of Aimée, which mars the picture a little; Prim sees to the floral do-dahs; Don's arranging the wine, and I see to it that we sparkle and twinkle joyously beneath an immense midsummer moon. It'll be full, you know.'

Midsummer moonshine, Gina said to herself. How very appropriate.

'And what of the man-hating Dinah?' she asked. 'What part does she play?'

'She's her twin's emissary,' said Harry. 'He's arranged the music from London, she will see to it down here.'

'Isn't he coming?'

'Of course he is. They'll all be here on the night, every last brother, sister, aunt, uncle and what-have-you. Such fun.'

'Your grandparents?'

'Er, no, actually. Relations are still a trifle cool between them and Pa, and I don't think he wants them on the prems. They might get ideas about coming back, you see, and that would never do. No, best for the old dears to stay up in the wild and woolly north; it's not good for them to get upset at their age. I have to add that they have sent a lovely present for Aimée, so I reckon that the grandchildren haven't incurred their wrath. Just as well, in the circs.'

He picked up his gloves, put his arm round Gina's shoulders and gave her a warm kiss before donning his black winged helmet and kicking his bike into action.

I don't care if Zoë thinks I'm making a big, big mistake, Gina told herself. I feel positively carefree; I haven't felt so untroubled for weeks.

The decision had been made, her immediate problems had been solved. Perhaps she was laying up problems for the future, but the future could look after itself. Anything was better than having to go on battling round and round in her present muddle.

Gina had cut the Gordian knot, in fact, and she was relishing the relief which decision-taking brings. She went off to give Nicky a hand. Lists and guests and chairs and where the band would eat were minor problems, no trouble at all, when you thought how she handled her own difficulties.

There were slight hurdles remaining, such as Charlotte . . . but why shouldn't she, in her Georgie persona, know Charlotte? And why should anyone tell Charlotte that she was at Heartsease as the hammy heiress, not as Gina Heartwell, American from Oxford?

Nicky, pale and distraught, was coping very well in trying conditions. 'I think everything's straight, and then someone rings up, and they can't come, someone else rings and says they'll be late, or they're bringing two dogs. I ask you!'

She flapped her lists dramatically under Gina's nose. 'This is the latest, those people at Heartwell House now say they have a guest of their own staying at that time, and so one room the less. I think I'll send them cousin Belinda and her fubsy-faced dogs, that'll teach them. Could you ring them for me, kind Gina? Say please to bring this whatshisname.'

'Okay,' said Gina obligingly. 'What will you do about being a room short?'

'I'll arrange for Tara to stay with Don instead of at Heartwell House, since she's at his house for dinner,' said Nicky, consulting her list. 'I expect she's sharing his bed in any case,' she said with some bitterness.

'Don't you mind?'

'I'm past minding,' said Nicky. 'My husband rang last night, my youngest has gone down with chickenpox, quite badly; Roger can't cope on his own. So after I've got this lot sorted out, I'll have to go home and see what's to be done.'

'I'll ring Heartwell House right away,' said Gina. 'Did they mention this guest's name?'

'Yes, hold on, I scribbled it down on the back of something . . . ah, here we are. Strange name, Aumbry. Alwyn Aumbry.'

CHAPTER 23

'Alwyn Aumbry?' Gina couldn't believe her ears. '*Dr* Alwyn Aumbry?'

'That's the one. She was rattling on about how he's going to become a television star, as if I cared. Do you know him?'

'I do,' said Gina.

Never mind, she thought, as familiar fears rushed back. Never mind, that's all over now, it really doesn't matter. I'll waylay him and explain that discretion and secrecy are the order of the day. The only problem is getting him to himself for a quiet word; Gareth and Lori are bound to cling to him.

Oh, well, just as long as Popplewell doesn't come to the ball and denounce me before dragging me off to the cells, I'm safe, she told herself as she headed for the phone. On Friday I become Mrs C, Georgie's British passport in hand, citizen of Europe, home and dry. Nothing can happen between now and then to change that.

Safe! Gina breathed a sigh of relief as she walked across the springy turf of the lawn. This would be where she was going to live, among the hills and woods and lawns and terraces.

She would even, with time, get to like the owls.

Nadia had been working flat out. She had been making things for the shop, and these were going extremely well. She was now looking into ordering extra goodies from outside suppliers. She had a large order from Maria for the ball. And she herself was going to the ball as a guest, and before that, to dinner at Heartwell House.

That meant finishing early this evening in order to iron a shirt for Byron and get her own dress pressed and everything looked out ready; no easy matter when you lived in a building site like Oracle Cottage and hadn't yet unpacked most of your things. Would Mrs Slubs's niece, who was on trial for a fortnight, clear up properly at the end of the day if she left early?

With all this on her mind, she was in no mood to be nice to Charlotte who came into the shop, quivering with disapproval, to enquire if Fergus was around.

'Somebody told me he was at the vineyard,' she said. 'This is the vineyard, I take it?'

'This is the shop, and the offices are here as well. If you want the vineyard itself, where the vines grow, then that is about a quarter of a mile along that track there.'

'And have you seen my friend? He's tall, with . . .'

'I know Fergus very well, thank you.' Nadia gave an expressive shrug. 'No, I haven't seen him today, I am too busy to notice who comes and goes. But I'm sure he'll be here today. Why not? He's here every other day.'

'What, Fergus is? Nonsense, how could he be? He spends his time studying; he's working very hard on his doctorate.'

'Not unless he's going to be a doctor in viticulture. He helps Don all the time. Don owns the vineyard,' she explained. 'I think also he is a family connection of Fergus's. Now, do you want to buy anything? Food, or wine?'

Charlotte gave a shudder. 'No, I don't, thank you.'

'Fergus particularly likes these venison sausages. For his breakfast? You're his girlfriend, I think. So you cook him breakfast, I expect.'

'Not sausages, I wouldn't dream of it.'

Nadia lost interest; her thoughts turned back to her work. 'Then I can't help you. I'll see you tomorrow evening, though, I think. You and Fergus are having dinner at Heartwell House; so am I and my husband.'

Charlotte didn't look overjoyed at the news. She gave Nadia a thin and distant smile, and set off at a brisk pace along the track which led to the vines.

Nadia watched her through the window of the shop as she wiped down the counter. Very English, that one, she thought. Good-looking, but no animation. And too thin. Elegant, but ungenerous looking. The kind of woman Byron should have married. One of his own, and with a heart as cold and unmelting as his was. She sighed, gave the counter a final wipe, and went back to check the mincer.

Byron would have been very surprised to hear himself described as cold. Nor had he ever been interested in tall, chilly Englishwomen. When he had come back to England with Nadia, his brother had teasingly said that he had been born to marry a Russian.

'You never cared for all the ordinary types, not even when you were at school,' he pointed out. 'And look at the girls you went out with at university. Different, every one of them. Bohemian, or foreign, or both. All with tempers and a sense of drama. Must be compensation for being a quiet and dreamy type,' he had added. 'Or are you just afraid of your own kind?'

Perhaps he should have opted for a lean, green English wife. At least he mightn't have made her as unhappy as he had Nadia. He had been lost the minute he set eyes on her; had known at once that she was the woman he was going to marry. If he had known how things were going to turn out, would he have hesitated, behaved any differently?

'No,' he said out loud as he propped the floorboard up against the wall alongside the others. He looked at his watch. Late. And he'd promised Nadia to bring down those suitcases, and he hadn't. And at any moment she would be back, and he would have to admit that, yet again, he had forgotten to do something for her.

She might look at him with those flashing eyes, full of reproach. He couldn't bear that. Or she might shout and rage and throw things about. He couldn't bear that, either. He heard her footsteps coming up the path, the door opening.

Too late, he thought sadly. Always too late.

Charlotte's encounter with Fergus among the Müller-Thurgau grapes had not been a success. She had always bent Fergus to her will, and didn't know how to handle this new, assertive Fergus.

No, he would be at the vineyard for some time yet.

Yes, he knew his computer wasn't plugged in; that was because he hadn't been using it.

No, if he went on like this, his thesis wouldn't be finished by Christmas.

Yes, he was going to have a drink with Harry.

No, even if there was a vegetarian restaurant somewhere in the neighbourhood, he wasn't going to take her there this evening. If she wanted to go, she could use his car.

It was a disconsolate Charlotte who returned to Kingfisher Cottage. However, there was her ball dress, an expensive and becoming designer creation, to be hung out, and she could wash her hair and do her nails. And when she had finished that, what about Fergus's clothes?

'Where is Fergus's dress kilt?' she demanded of Zoë.

Zoë blinked at her. 'I haven't a clue. Did he bring it with him from Oxford?'

'He must have done; he knew there was this ball.'

Zoë thought for a moment. 'I have seen a kilt hanging up in the cupboard under the stairs,' she finally admitted.

Charlotte rummaged, found the kilt, and unearthed Fergus's dress shirt – dirty and crumpled – and one sock. With satisfied, clicking noises, she returned to the bathroom, suds flying, remarking that it was lucky she had thought about it tonight, otherwise what would Fergus have done?

Worn his grubby one, or gone out and bought a new one, thought Zoë, but she said nothing.

'Are you going to the ball?' Charlotte enquired. 'No? What a pity. Of course you don't know the family, do you? Have you been to the house at all?'

'I have ventured to the back door, on an errand,' said Zoë. 'Too grand for me,' and she returned to her book.

'What are you reading?' asked Charlotte.

I hate people who ask what I'm reading, thought Zoë, as she held up the book's garish cover so that Charlotte could see the title.

'*Coming at Corinth*,' she read aloud in measured tones. Then her eyes took in the detail of the cover illustration. 'That's pornography!'

'Not at all,' said Zoë. 'Erotic fiction, quite different.'

'I thought you were an intellectual,' said Charlotte. 'You've got a university degree.'

'What's that got to do with it?' said Zoë. 'The person who wrote this has a degree from Cambridge.'

'I doubt it,' said Charlotte complacently.

'Doubt away. It's true. She's a classicist.'

'Then she should be ashamed of herself.'

Zoë wasn't fooled, she could see the underlying glint in Charlotte's eyes. 'Try one,' she said, as though offering a tasty plum. 'There are several on that shelf there. Don't take *Hadrian's Harlot*, though; I haven't read that yet.'

Charlotte was sorely tempted, resisted, then succumbed. 'I didn't bring a book with me,' she said defensively.

'There you are, then,' said Zoë. 'Start it quickly, then you can shock Fergus in bed tonight.'

'Really,' said Charlotte, going pink. But Zoë had gone back to her engrossing read, and didn't notice.

The book did Charlotte no good. Perhaps Fergus was the one who should have read it, because he found himself quite unaroused by the smooth, naked, white body beside him in bed. He tried hard, for he was always a gentleman, but it was no good. He rolled over on to his back and cursed, then got out of bed, muttering about the bathroom.

Locked in there, he opened the window, and leant out, soaking up the heavy, fragrant air. I want to live in the country, he thought with a terrible self-awareness. I don't want to live in London or Paris or New York. I want this.

Lucky Harry, a younger son, but likely to inherit at least some of these rolling acres. While he, Fergus, had an older, farm-loving brother who would take over the family farm in due course. But he didn't want to grow wheat or raise cows and sheep. No, what he wanted to do was have a vineyard.

There, the thought was out. Clear as the moonlight streaming across the grass below. That was it, that was what he was going to do.

His mind came back to Harry. Lucky Harry, marrying Gina. Did he want to be best man or chief witness or whatever it was at Harry's wedding, when the prospect of his own nuptials filled him with such distaste?

Distaste? Yes, distaste.

Revelation.

He didn't want to marry Charlotte.

He *had* to marry Charlotte. He wasn't going to let her down after all this time; he couldn't. Just think of the fuss. And he might as well marry her as not, it wasn't as though he wanted to marry anyone else. Did he?

Fergus's mind drifted to Harry. Harry just didn't know how lucky he was. He was getting married to someone he wanted to marry, and to someone who was so attractive and such good company, although she had been a bit strange recently. Harry didn't *deserve* Gina. Gina shouldn't marry someone she hardly knew. And was Harry in love with Gina? Or Gina with Harry? Were they sleeping together? Oh, hell.

He splashed his face with water, rubbed it with a towel, unbolted the door and made his way back towards his room. Back to bed. Back to Charlotte.

Charlotte had also been thinking, but not to very good effect. What demon was it that over-rode her normal good sense and drove her to point out the obvious about Fergus's non-performance? And then to go on and attribute his failure to a hopelessly wrong diet and a guilty conscience?

'Guilty conscience?' Fergus, who had been feeling a heel, sat up in bed like a jack-in-a-box, and roared at Charlotte.

Zoë, across the way, woke from her sound slumbers, lifted her head from her pillow, sent a telepathic message of sympathy to Fergus, covered her head with the sheet to shut out the noise, and went back to sleep.

'No, I don't care if I finish that bloody thesis or not. It doesn't matter. I'm not going to have a university career, nor am I going to go and stew my life out in the City.'

'What are you going to do, then?' Charlotte asked peevishly. She had dragged her nightdress on, feeling at a disadvantage when naked, and its white, ruffled prettiness annoyed Fergus intensely.

'Why can't you sleep in an old shirt or a T-shirt or something, like Zoë does?'

'How do you know what Zoë sleeps in?' demanded Charlotte.

'Oh, come on, we share a house, she potters round in her night things.'

'Well, I'm glad you like looking at her in tatty things, but I'm afraid I've always worn these, and I shall continue to do so. Now, and when we're married.'

Fergus put his feet on the floor and buried his head in his hands. Then he gave himself a shake, leant back, and took Charlotte's hand.

'Look, Charlotte, I don't want to get married. I'm not ready to get married.'

Charlotte was quite unmoved. 'No, of course not, not until you've got a job and are earning a good income.'

'I'm not going to get a job, at least, not the kind of job you mean. And I doubt if I'm going to earn much money for the foreseeable future.'

'Don't be silly, darling. You're just tired, and you're never at your best in the middle of the night. Try and get some sleep and we'll talk about it in the morning.'

'No, I want to get things straight now.'

Charlotte arranged her pillows behind her back, and then arranged herself, a helpful expression on her face.

'Go ahead, then, tell me what's worrying you.'

Fergus didn't want to tell her anything. He chiefly wanted to go to sleep, but on the other hand, perhaps it would be better to get it over with. Clear the air, he thought hopefully and mistakenly.

Another shriek rent Zoë's dreams. She stirred again, grumbled, 'Oh, shut up in there, whatever you're doing,' and drifted off into her happy sleep.

'America? Australia? France? Learn about wine-making? I've never heard anything so ridiculous. Fergus, grow up, these are adolescent fantasies. You know perfectly well that you're an economist. You've got the world at your feet, with your degree and qualifications, or you will have, once you've got your doctorate. And then, with Daddy's help . . .'

'Bugger Daddy,' said Fergus.

Wilf and Madge had spent a pleasant evening, gossiping with locals and eavesdropping on Harry and Fergus.

'That Jackie, she gone off with her young man.'

'About time.'

'He give her a good what for when he found out what she been up to with his dad.'

'She need telling how to behave.'

'Anyway, he said he'd forgive her, this once, but it weren't to happen again. And he's upped and offed with her, reckons he can make a good living somewheres else, don't want to see his dad no more.'

'I don't see Bob's dad giving up his little pleasures.'

'Won't find it so easy, now. Try it on one of Jackie's friends, he did, got slapped good and proper. Sue Bunting, her whose husband ran off five years back with a black girl from the circus, she'd have him. For the farm and a tidy roof over her head. And she's still a cosy armful, she'd keep him off the young ones.'

Wilf ran a cloth over the bar, and nodded towards the garden where Fergus and Harry were deep in talk. 'Listen to them. Harry's telling that Fergus he's going to marry that cousin of his, Gina.'

'Don't look like that Fergus is too keen on that.'

'Harry want him as best man.'

'That Fergus have got a young lady of his own. Good-looker, too, but bony. Coathanger in bed, I'll be bound.'

'I hear they don't get on so well together. Fergus aren't none too keen to be around with her.'

'So this Gina be right for Harry?' Madge pulled another pint, pleased at the thought of a wedding at the Hall; could be good for business.

'I don't reckon. I don't see no real liveliness in them.'

'Many a slip,' said Wilf. 'Pass that glass along, then, if you've finished.'

Meanwhile, Gina was sleeping the sleep of the damned. She dreamt that she was awake. The curtains were drawn back, and flapping in a wild wind. The moonlight poured into her bedroom through bars at the window, filling the room with strange shadows. She went to the window, looked out between the thick black bars on to endless lawns. There were huge figures moving about on them, casting grotesque and threatening shadows.

The figures were the Cordovan family, playing a slow-motion game of croquet. Giants, with giant mallets, Gina thought, and then she found herself outside, on the lawn, looking up at the great house bathed in moonlight. Bars were across every window, and voices whispered in her ear.

'Gina, here,' said a voice behind her, with an eerie and unpleasant laugh. Gina turned to see who was speaking, and found it was Harry, strangely elongated, and dressed in a skin-tight version of his black leather gear, silver wings glittering on his boots and helmet.

Gina began to run, round the side of the house, away from those menacing figures. Then the owls began to hoot, closer and closer. A white, feathery body flashed across her face, another buffeted her with its wings as it flew down. Huge, pale owls, all hooting with sad relish.

The pool, thought Gina. The owls won't come to the pool. In she plunged, to find that the crystal blue waters were dark and opaque. A figure beside the dolphin moved, how could it? What was it doing?

Simply drowning you, it said in a high voice, with a silly giggle, and she felt her head being pushed down, down into deep black darkness.

Gina woke with a start, drenched in sweat, and completely terrified. The room was indeed full of moonlight, but it was a pleasant, tranquil moonlight, coming in from an unbarred window, with the curtains hanging motionless on either side, where she had pulled them back before going to bed.

Her throat was dry. She made herself sit up, still shaking from her bad dream, and reached out to turn the bedside light on. The soft light banished the shadows, showed Gina a familiar, friendly room.

I must have eaten something that disagreed with me, Gina said to herself, to have such a dreadful dream. She opened the biscuit box and took out the ginger biscuits which Hester thoughtfully put in all the rooms. She couldn't go back to sleep, not after such a dream. There was a radio by her bed, and she switched it on. The soothing tones of the World Service wafted into the room, and Gina settled back on the cushions to listen to a talk on political change in Hungary.

Ten minutes later, the light still on, and the voice still speaking, Gina slipped gently down into her bed. The programme must have finished, she thought, with the last vestiges of consciousness, as the voice changed to that of her mother, imparting invaluable advice to a sullen teenager, years before.

'Always listen to your dreams, Gina, because they tell you the truth.'

'What nonsense,' thought Gina, as she fell into a deep and dreamless sleep.

*

Charlotte left first thing in the morning, in a taxi.

'I'll drive you to the station,' said Fergus. 'Please, Charlotte, it's the least I can do.'

'You've done enough,' said a steely-faced Charlotte. 'I wouldn't drive as far as the end of the road with you, thank you very much.'

'Ouf,' said Zoë, as her taxi drove away. 'Well done, Fergus.'

Fergus looked dreadful. 'Not well done at all,' he said morosely. 'I've treated her very badly, but she's much better off without me.'

'I'm sure she is,' said Zoë soothingly. 'Let me make you some coffee.'

Fergus began to laugh. 'Coffee, yes,' he said. 'I'm spared a lifetime of faddy diets, do you realize that? Goodness, how did I put up with her for so long?' He stretched and plonked himself down in the armchair.

Zoë looked at him with affection. 'Just this once, I'll wait on you,' she said. 'How about sausages for breakfast?'

'Great,' said Fergus. 'First, I must ring the Hall and tell them I'm partnerless, I expect that'll mess up the dinner arrangements. No, hang about, Zoë, why don't you come with me? I'll fix it with Aunt Julia.'

'I'd love to,' said Zoë slightly wistfully, 'but I haven't got a dress.'

'You have,' said Fergus. 'I shoved one or two Jessicas in when I packed up her things. I thought you and Gina were as much a deserving cause as Oxfam.'

'Which ones?' said Zoë.

'A grey thing, and that dark blue one you like.'

'You are clever,' said Zoë. 'I'll come; what a treat.'

'That's settled, then,' said Fergus, pleased. He picked up Zoë's book which was on the table next to his chair, and his eyebrows rose. 'This looks good,' he said, opening it and settling down to read. 'Three sausages, please; no, four. I'm suddenly feeling very hungry.'

CHAPTER 24

As dawn broke on Midsummer Eve, a fine white mist wafted over the lawns and terraces of Heartsease Hall and hung about the great trees in the valley below.

A yawning Guy was up at five, speeding about the silent house, shirtsleeves rolled up with matching precision, a grey apron round his waist.

Esme was up soon after, full of beans, dressed in a huge pair of jeans and a sweatshirt which had seen better days. 'If I've got to wear that black outfit and an apron this evening, then I'm going to be comfortable during the day,' she announced cheerfully. And off she slopped to check the pavilion, and throw back the flaps to let some air in.

By eight the mist was gone, dissolved by a sun shining in a clear blue sky. Efficient men arrived in a large van with an artificial floor to lay on the grass in the sunken garden.

'A brainwave of Nicky's, that,' said Victor, expansive and authoritative as he strolled towards the fountain. He saw her in the distance and waved to her to come over.

Not what Nicky wanted. Up all night with her itching, poorly son, and bothered this morning by signs of her daughter also throwing out a rash, she simply wanted to get on with everything before she collapsed in a heap.

'It would be pretty,' Victor said, 'if the fountain had coloured water.'

Nicky sighed. 'Yes, Victor. All seen to. And Harry's fixing up extra lights, it will all look most attractive.'

'Ah, might have known you'd have thought of it,' said Victor, slightly peeved that she had.

'Is that all?' asked Nicky. 'Because I have a lot to do.'

'Of course, of course,' said Victor benevolently. 'What would we do without you? Run along.'

Grr, thought Nicky, as she walked at a deliberately slow pace towards the house.

Hester was in a frenzy of airing and room rounds. Every bedroom in the house had been pressed into service, even the King's Chamber, which, being small, dark and lit, for historical reasons, only by candles, was rarely used.

'Who have you put in there, Hester?' asked Julia. 'It will have to be someone sober, we can't risk a fire through carelessness with candles.'

'Family,' said Hester. 'Gray and Cora. And I've put some battery-powered camping lamps in there which I found in Heartsbury last week.'

'Which bathroom will they use?' Julia asked with a frown. Gray might be family, and therefore obliged to put up with a certain amount of inconvenience. But we must remember that he is a very important and distinguished man in his own field.'

Hester sighed. Gray could be as big a cheese as he liked, but to her he was still her tiresome younger brother. 'I do, Julia,' she said. 'I do remember it. And I think if the room was fit for a king, it will do for Gray. And they will use the blue bathroom, on the floor below.'

Julia pursed her lips. 'Sharing with Aimée?'

'And several other guests,' said Hester. 'Better than Marcus sharing with Aimée, you will agree, and I can't make bathrooms when there aren't any.' Then she whisked herself away to scatter more pot-pourri and unwrap more delicious little bars of soap before Julia could start on her hobby-horse of building a new wing, which would, one gathered, consist almost entirely of bathrooms.

In the kitchen, all was organized chaos. The caterers, who would work under Maria's directions, were due to arrive at eleven. Meanwhile, Maria was preparing vast quantities of strawberries. Gina was helping. 'I must do something,' she said. 'Nicky's got everything under control, and there's not much else I'm good at.'

Tray after tray of glistening strawberries were laid out in a pantry on wide stone shelves, cleared especially for tonight. There was something blissful about the scale and the lusciousness of it all, thought Gina, as the dairy arrived with gallons of the thick cream which the county of Heartset was famous for.

Guy was supervising the wines, chosen weeks before in consultation with Victor. This was the wine for the family and thirty other guests who would sit down to dinner in the Great Hall before the ball began officially at half past nine. Drinks for the ball itself had been delivered days before; white and sparkling wines were chilling in the gloomiest and coldest of the cellars while the bottles of red wine were stored in cardboard boxes across in one of the stables.

Nicky flew into the kitchen. 'The saxophone band will be here by six,' she said without preamble. 'Twelve of them, and they'll want dinner as well as supper halfway through the dance. And there's the string quartet.'

Maria nodded calmly. 'I know this. The caterers will see to it.'

'I've put them in the old dining-room,' went on Nicky.

'Good thinking,' said Guy, as he went past with a trayful of silver. 'They can leave their cases there and use the cloakroom under the stairs to change in. The disco team can go in there as well.'

Maria poured a coffee for Nicky.

'No time,' said Nicky.

'Sit down, I insist,' said Maria, giving Nicky a firm shove. 'Also some cake, you have had no breakfast, I can see, and you will pass out if you go on like this. How are the little ones?'

'Don't ask,' said Nicky, disposing of the coffee and cake at lightning speed; she had indeed needed them, she told Maria.

'Good for her to be so busy,' observed Maria as Nicky whirled out of the kitchen to still more tasks. 'This will take her mind off Don, and then she can think about her husband and children, which is much better.'

'What a moralist you are,' said Guy.

'The only one here, in that case,' said Maria with some asperity. 'Now, take that tray from here at once, immediately, because otherwise I become angry.'

At Heartwell House, Lori was in another great bustle of activity. She had Dr Aumbry and three other couples staying, and then more guests would be coming for dinner.

'Thirteen,' she moaned. 'It's so *unlucky*. What can I do?'

'What's thirteen?' asked Gareth.

'*People*, for dinner. You'll have to *help*, Gareth, it's too much for me to do.'

'I have to work, surely you can understand that. While Alwyn's here, we've got to use every available minute. I'm sure you can manage.'

'With no Mrs Slubs, and *bedrooms* to get ready, quite apart from dinner. And we'll be *thirteen*,' she wailed, returning to her first theme.

'Put Melissa's bear on a chair, for heaven's sake,' said Gareth. 'And why no Mrs Slubs? God knows, we pay that woman enough, the least she can do is be here when she's wanted.'

'Busy at the *Hall*,' said Lori crossly. 'And no, there's no one else who can help; they're *all* busy at the Hall.'

'I'm sure you'll cope,' said Gareth, his mind on eighteenth-century royal scandals. He removed himself swiftly, leaving Lori fuming in the kitchen.

Lori felt like sitting down at the table and screaming, but that wasn't her way. First, she'd finish the bedrooms. Then she'd find a bear, that was a good idea of Gareth's, a witty touch for blasé visitors, and enough to calm those who didn't care to sit down as one of thirteen.

Cold cherry soup, already made, reposing in the fridge. Vegetables to prepare, she could do those while listening to a favourite radio programme, if she got a move on with the bedrooms. At least Mrs Slubs had managed to make the beds when she made her last appearance a few days before. A brief air, a quick dust, towels, soap and all those little touches recommended for the well-run household . . . No, it shouldn't take too long.

Good thing she had decided on noisettes of lamb rather than fish, she told herself. Much less trouble. And then apple tart from the Hungarian patisserie in Heartsbury. She had planned strawberries, but Gareth had pointed out that they were bound to be serving strawberries at the ball. He didn't particularly like them, and once in an evening would be quite enough.

*

Don was quite unconcerned about playing host to a fair-sized party. One of his devoted attendants was seeing to it all, with a clutch of fellow admirers all too willing to troop up to his house and wait on him. He knew exactly what wines they would have at dinner, had agreed a menu with the delightful blonde from Heartsbury who was always more than happy to rush out to Heartsease and cook for him, and he thought no more about it.

Fergus was struggling with an iron, under the amused eyes of Zoë and Sybil.

'Do the sleeve, now,' said Sybil helpfully.

Fergus wished he were a long way away, or that Charlotte had ironed his shirt before she flounced off.

'At least she washed it for you,' Zoë pointed out.

'Talking of washing, how about your face?' retorted Fergus, with good reason; Zoë's face was liberally smeared with Dead Sea mud.

'Dead Sea Mud?' Fergus picked up the tube. 'Sounds disgusting. Why not Heartset mud, or Cornish sludge?'

'It works,' said Zoë. 'So I don't mind where it comes from.'

'I'll drive you to the Hall this evening and then come back for Zoë,' Fergus said to Sybil. 'No point in taking two cars.'

'That's assuming we'll all come back together,' said Sybil.

Fergus looked surprised. 'Why not? Don't tell me you're planning to do a Cinders and creep away on the stroke of midnight; I don't believe it.'

Sybil was amused at the thought of playing Cinderella, 'At my age, really, Fergus!' but said that she would be glad of a lift. 'Mind the wine at dinner, though,' she warned. 'I don't want to end up in a ditch in my best dress.'

Byron was luckier than Fergus, as his shirt had been ironed by Nadia. Not that she wouldn't cheerfully have left it to him, but she knew quite well that he never managed to iron without burning himself or scorching whatever he was attacking.

'Which is extremely feeble,' she told him. 'If you can manage a power drill, you should be able to iron.'

'Well, I'll try,' he offered.

'No,' she said. 'We can't afford a new dress shirt if you burn it. But when we are straight here, I'll find some old things and you can practise until you don't burn yourself or the clothes. Because if I'm busy with the shop, then you'll have to iron for yourself or go crumpled.'

Byron knew which he'd opt for.

By mid-afternoon, Heartsease Hall was teeming. Guests were arriving, to be met and escorted to their rooms by a calm and elegant Guy, if they were lucky, or a hot and cursing Esme if they weren't. Prim was doing the rounds of the flowers with a water spray; Jarvis was in seventh heaven driving various cars to their allotted places.

Wilf had left the pub in the tender care of Madge and a gormless young man who was learning the trade and was serving tea in the drawing-room. There, Julia was enthusiastically greeting such of her guests as wished to take tea; Julia loved a gathering.

Victor was outside with his brothers, whom he more or less liked, his two eldest sons, whom he disliked intensely, and sundry hangers-on who had been rounded up to help with the final firework arrangements.

In the Great Hall, the table was already laid for dinner. The huge table had been extended to its full length, and the gleaming surface reflected the seventeenth-century silver candelabra, the eighteenth-century French glasses and the massive Victorian cutlery, which Guy had been polishing on and off for days. Prim had done the flowers, in a dozen silver vessels dating from Elizabethan times. Very classy, thought Guy, storing the idea up for his future hotel.

Harry, who could look down into the Hall from the squint in his room, thought it all looked very festive. He turned round as someone came into his room.

'Look, Aimée, all in your honour.'

Aimée looked, and approved, taking it all as her due. But she was troubled. 'Harry,' she said, 'I've heard a whisper that you're planning to marry Gina. It isn't true, is it?'

Harry's face darkened. 'Now, where did you hear that?'

'Never mind,' said Aimée. 'You mustn't do it. You'll fall in love, properly, not an infatuation for a pretty boy, and then what will happen?'

'Divorce is easy these days,' said Harry, guarded and flippant now.

'Victor wouldn't let you have the house in that case.'

Harry put his arm round Aimée's waist and gave her a brotherly kiss. 'A chaste kiss,' he mocked her. 'That must come as a surprise.'

'Be serious, Harry, for once.'

'I am,' said Harry. 'Leave me be, Aimée. I know what I'm doing.' He gestured down into the Hall. 'Do you remember that terrific dinner Pa gave for those Russians, when I put a whoopee cushion on a chair?'

Aimée smiled, but shook her head. 'I know I'm right,' she said. 'You will fall in love, just like that, and then what will you do?'

'It hasn't happened yet,' said Harry. 'And I don't suppose it ever will.'

Aimée gave a languid sigh. 'I don't have time to argue, Harry, but you are quite, quite wrong.'

Harry's mind was on other matters. 'Are you planning to spend hours in the bathroom?' he asked. 'Because, if so, let me go in first,' said Harry.

'Too late, too late,' said his sister, flitting out of the room.

Experienced Heartsease guests all knew about the shortage of bathrooms, and they went up to dress in a bulge, long before less-knowing people had even thought about it. The remaining and uninformed guests looked a bit startled, but were held captive in the drawing-room by Julia's enthralling description of a hysterectomy she had done yesterday, with interesting complications.

Others, with weaker stomachs and nervous dispositions, had slipped outside. There they found a mass of round supper tables being set up on the terrace, while Esme stood by, wired noisily into Radio 3 via her Walkman, with armfuls of thick white damask cloths.

'We won't need those pegs,' she bellowed to Guy, who winced, and carried on with his counting. 'It's been a real scorcher today, and I reckon it'll stay warm and no wind until dawn.'

Guy took the tablecloths from her, with an exasperated look. 'Please can you check the flares, make sure they are all properly fixed. We don't want any accidents.'

'Sure,' said Esme in her amiable way, and then emitted an ear-piercing yell at some guests who had wandered that way. 'Jude! And Petra! How you doing?'

Guy stood appalled as Esme clapped the unfortunates on the back. Esme saw his expression and made a placatory gesture at him. 'It's okay, Guy, calm down. These are old friends of mine, from Ozzie.'

Rich friends, thought Guy, with a swift appraisal of their clothes. He shuddered. What a mistake to have someone like Esme working for you, you never knew where you were with people like that. He made a mental note to avoid all au pairs and house helpers from the Antipodes when he had his hotel, and went on with his methodical and immaculate laying on of the white cloths.

A hired minion was summoned, instructed in how and where to place the flowers and candles which were lined up on the wall, ready to go on the tables.

'I'd have done that for you, Guy,' Esme said, having finished a top-speed flare check. 'Aren't they dinky?'

'Carry on,' Guy said to the helper. And to Esme, 'I think it's time you got into your clothes for this evening.'

'Okay, boss,' said Esme, unsubdued, as she headed off in the direction of her friend Mona's cottage.

'Where are you going?' Guy called after her, outraged. 'Your room is the other way.'

'Yeah, but I've fixed to get dressed in Mona's place,' said Esme. 'My stuff's all there, and I can use her bathroom.'

Which she did, sharing a bath and some happy moments with Mona before she emerged half an hour later, clad in a man's dinner suit. 'I'm not wearing a black dress and pinny, not for anyone. Besides, you'd have to get it specially made, and I'd look like something off a horror show.' She had wrapped a Parisian waiter's apron round her waist, and looked very dashing, except for her feet which were large and bony in a pair of her usual flip-flops.

'No,' said Guy faintly, when he saw her. 'Proper shoes, please.'

'No way,' said Esme. 'You leave me be, Guy. This lot will all be so pissed in about five minutes with all that wine you're going to give them that they wouldn't notice if I was wearing a bloody bin liner.'

Lori hadn't expected so many of her guests to know each other. Alwyn was down first, looking slightly dishevelled in a tail suit which had fitted him rather better when he had been an undergraduate than it did now. Then Fergus arrived, with Zoë looking so spectacularly lovely that Gareth drew his stomach in at least an inch, and stopped talking TV plans to Alwyn for a whole minute.

Alwyn extricated himself from Gareth and greeted Fergus and Zoë. If his eyes wandered rather over Zoë's cleavage, his conversation was polite enough, as he asked about Gina.

Hell, thought Zoë.

Lori had sharp ears. 'Gina?' she asked.

'My research assistant,' said Alwyn. 'Former research assistant, I should say,' he added, with a thin smile at Gareth. 'Of course, I have a team of them now. She shared a house with, let me see, Fergus, isn't it? Yes, and Zoë. I hope Gina got back to the States satisfactorily.'

'Yes,' said Fergus blandly.

Lori's keen look faded; a Gina in the States was of no interest.

I'll have to get hold of him and shut him up, Fergus said to himself. It might take some doing, blast the man with his academic mind and total lack of imagination or humanity.

The knocker sounded and there was a hubbub in the hall as Byron and Nadia came through the door at the same moment that Serge Zandermann and his companion came down the stairs.

Zoë greeted Byron and Nadia with enthusiasm, and wondered why Fergus was looking at the other guest with such a lack of enthusiasm. 'Do you know him?' she whispered. 'He looks very familiar, somehow.'

'Gina's father,' said Fergus under his breath. 'Now, how much does he know about all this?'

Zoë danced up to him and introduced herself, and then said a very polite how-do-you-do to the rather dazzling brunette who stood beside him. What an exotic couple for an English country house, Zoë thought. And Nadia, too. Lori and Gareth and Alwyn looked quite dull by comparison.

The brunette was clearly admiring Fergus, and Serge, too, was expressing his admiration. 'This is Scottish evening wear, I know,' he said. 'Well, don't you make the rest of us look dull.'

'Not you,' said Zoë. 'Such a lovely jacket.'

The dark steely blue velvet jacket with a thick silk bow-tie in cloudy blues might not be standard formal wear for an English dance, but Serge looked terrific, Zoë thought.

They stood talking in a little huddle, as people do.

'Another lovely day.'

'Do you work in Oxford as well?'

Sotto voce: 'Serge, Gina worked for the man in glasses, but he doesn't know she's still in England.'

Full volume: 'The trouble that girl is causing me right now.'

'Which girl?'

'Oh, my daughter. Fergus knows her a little, from when she was visiting over here.'

'What a coincidence.'

'Are you here on business, Mr Zandermann?'

'Indirectly. Mr Victor Cordovan is purchasing a painting of mine.'

'You deal in pictures?'

'No, no, I paint them.'

Whispered: 'Fergus, did you catch the woman's name? The one who's with Serge?'

'No, but it wasn't an English name. Ask her.'

'I can't.'

The other guests came into the room with a rustle of silk and taffeta. One couple were both architects who knew Byron well and they fell into immediate shop with him. The wife of the other one was an old Oxford friend of Zoë; she was a linguist who had often worked in London with Nadia.

'Such a small *world*,' said Lori with a bright smile as she led them into the dining room. 'You never know who you're going to bump into in the most *unexpected* places.'

'I have a feeling tonight is going to prove her point all too well,' Fergus muttered to Zoë as he helped her into her seat before going round to introduce himself with great aplomb to Melissa's bear, who was his partner for dinner.

CHAPTER 25

Heartsease Hall was *en fête*. A sprinkling of people were wandering over towards the sax band, which was mooching out a genteel tune or two for starters. The disco was still virtually empty; some undemanding numbers throbbed into the heavily swagged pavilion.

Smoke from the dozens of flares drifted up in the warm, still light, evening air.

Victor and Julia were greeting guests. Julia looked magnificent in a classically draped gown in thick flame-coloured silk; Victor was tremendous in tails enlivened with a wonderful brocade cummerbund. Of course, no one really noticed what Victor was wearing, you were just overwhelmed by his vital presence and striking looks.

'Wow,' said Zoë, as Fergus introduced her. Victor was all smiles and attention, Julia looked very disapproving.

'We're so very sorry that Charlotte wasn't able to come,' she said to Fergus.

'But what a charming replacement,' said Victor, looking as though he would like to gobble Zoë up. Fergus hastily moved her on.

'What a divine man,' said Zoë. 'How come Gina's been living in close proximity to that and never mentioned him?'

'Perhaps Gina didn't find him so stunning,' said Fergus repressively.

Zoë gave him a mischievous look. 'Think again, Fergus. No woman with a working set of hormones could fail to find your Victor interesting.'

'Gina's not like that,' said Fergus with dignity. He hooked

two glasses off a tray carried by a passing waiter. 'This will cool your ardent thoughts,' he said, handing one to Zoë. 'And I need it, I hardly touched a drop during dinner; why do I always end up driving?'

'You'll have to drive back from here,' Zoë reminded him.

'Not necessarily,' said Fergus. 'I can always leave the car here, a walk will do you good after what I can see is going to be an evening of excess. In any case, the night is young, plenty of time for my head to clear.'

'Let's find Gina,' said Zoë. 'She may not know that her father's here and we ought to warn her.'

'There she is,' said Fergus. 'In a red dress.'

'Doesn't it suit her?' said Zoë.

'I suppose so,' said Fergus grudgingly. 'Who's that she's talking to?'

'Let's find out,' suggested Zoë, a gleam in her eye. 'He looks rather delicious.'

'Smoothie,' said Fergus disparagingly, as they made their way down into the sunken garden, moving slowly among the throng of guests.

As daylight faded, the by-now lively scene was illuminated by the flares and by the first light from an enormous, heavy, full moon, which hung presently just above the horizon.

'Magical moon,' said Serge, greeting Gina with a kiss. 'Sorry about the passport, have you sorted it out with the embassy yet?'

'It's all in hand,' said Gina. Which was true, if not in the way that Serge meant. She should tell him she was going to get married; must tell him, before Harry announced his engagement to the world at large. This he planned to do after midnight, he had told her, when Aimée cut her cake and the moon was high and everybody was feeling a little mad.

There was plenty of time, she didn't want to get involved in explanations and exclamations and congratulations just now.

'Where's Victor?' said Serge. 'We missed him when we arrived, I want to say hello and introduce Cucki.'

'Cucki?' said Gina.

'She's over there,' said Serge, gesturing to where Cucki stood with several admirers appreciating her noticeable bosom. 'Swiss friend of mine, you'll like her.'

I won't, Gina said to herself, and she didn't.

'Fergus does, though,' Zoë whispered in her ear. 'Couldn't take his eyes off her during dinner.'

'Off one bit of her,' said Gina. 'Very obvious, displaying your charms like that.'

'She has to flaunt something,' said Zoë. 'And your father hasn't brought her along because he admires her sense of humour.'

'He didn't need to bring anyone,' said Gina crossly. 'In fact, I don't know why he's here.'

'Now, now,' said Zoë. 'Just because he's your dad doesn't mean he's signed up for a life of single-blessedness, does it?'

Gina had to admit that her father was hardly likely to live a celibate life. 'Just the same, I don't like her, and I'm surprised that Fergus does. I would have thought he would have noticed the lack of anything other than what's on show.'

'It took him a long time to realize that Charlotte had no sense of humour,' pointed out Zoë.

'Come over here,' said Gina, guiding Zoë over to a bench behind a large stone urn. 'Now, I want to hear all about Charlotte and why she isn't here. All I know is from overhearing Julia's outbreak of tut-tuttery when Fergus rang to say he was bringing you instead. Fergus is looking quite different, positively relaxed, so I want to hear every last detail.'

'Well,' began Zoë. 'It was like this . . .'

'I know Mr Victor Cordovan,' Cucki informed Serge. 'He comes often to Switzerland and then he takes me out to dinner. He wants to go to bed with me,' she added in matter-of-fact tones.

'Ah,' said Serge. This could be complicated.

'Also, he invited me to England, I think for this party, only I knew I would be with you, so I said no, thank you. I think perhaps he may not be very pleased.'

'Ah,' said Serge again, as at that very moment Victor came down the stone steps and caught sight of Miss Voesli.

He zoomed in on her, holding her hands, kissing her forcefully on both cheeks. 'My dear, what a surprise, you could come after all, why didn't you let me know?' Victor was eating Cucki up with glowing eyes. 'Where are you staying? There would be a room here at the house for you, if we'd known.'

'I think you know Serge?' said Cucki demurely. 'An old friend of mine.'

'Thank you for the invitation, Victor,' said Serge. 'The card said, "and partner", so I asked Cucki to come with me. We're being put up at Heartwell House, all arranged very kindly by your efficient Nicky.'

Victor drew his dark brows together; in an instant, the joviality and affability had vanished from his face.

Wonder what's upset Pa? thought Harry, who was passing by. He casually joined the little group, slipping himself in beside Serge.

'What's up?' he whispered in Serge's ear.

'Harry,' said Serge. 'Let me introduce you to Miss Voesli, a friend of mine from Switzerland. It seems she is also a friend of your father's.'

Harry took one look at Miss Voesli's voluptuous appearance, well emphasized by the dress she wore, and put two and two together. No wonder Pa looks thunderous, he thought with amusement. It's the Swiss number he's been so hot for.

'Shall we dance?' said Victor to Cucki with cold politeness.

'I should like that,' said Cucki, giving Serge a swift wink.

Victor bore Cucki off, and Harry shook his head at Serge. 'Unwise, letting her go like that. Victor will cut you out.'

'I don't think so, you know,' said Serge. 'Cucki has strong views on the men in her life. She's very fussy about married men.'

'My father has very strong views on women doing what he wants.'

'He'll find Cucki has strong views on doing what *she* wants.'

Harry was laughing. 'I hope so, that would be a rare treat to watch. Have you seen Gina?'

Serge looked around. 'She was over there near the – conservatory, is it? – with Zoë, the blonde girl.'

'I haven't met Zoë,' said Harry. 'I'll go and find Gina, though.'

'You do that,' said Serge with a light wave of his hand as he eased his way over towards where people were dancing. Cucki was sound, but she might need rescuing; best to keep an eye on her.

There was a buzz of conversation rising from the supper tables as old friends clustered in groups. Music from the string quartet, stationed on a corner of the terrace, wafted out over the lawns. Tongues were loosened by good wine, people relaxed in the warm evening air, gossip flowed.

'I warned him not to buy that horse, but he only has to see a crook to get out his cheque-book.'

'She still had her knickers on, nothing else.'

'He was bound to get into trouble sooner or later, you can't sleep with Reggie without everyone knowing about it two minutes later.'

'There was no question of divorce, he couldn't afford it. And he said that if she brought up the matter of the poodle, he'd mention the Russian sailors.'

'It was there, floating in the bath, for all to see.'

'No wonder she hurt her back, up against a wall in high heels.'

'Twenty thousand pounds! Just like that.'

'Bolted! Yes, quite true. No, he's not her sixth, that was Jamie Honks. This must be the seventh, and it's six children now, isn't it?'

'First you simmer it, and then the skin comes off very easily.'

'They thought she was tucked up in bed at that incredibly expensive school she goes to, but no such thing. Extraordinary the fascination these hairy men have for some girls.'

'Then he woke up. Well, you can imagine how Flora felt.'

'Nine inches? Harbottle? I don't believe it. Besides, I was at school with him, so I know for a fact it isn't true.'

'You'll never believe this, but I bought it in Boots.'

The moon was now riding brilliantly in the sky, still huge, illuminating a few wisps of cloud with its intense white light.

'Positively operatic,' commented a man as he went past.

A night for love, thought Harry, as he went to find Gina. Tonight, under this astonishing moon, he was going to announce his engagement to Gina. That was good, and he liked Gina, and he wanted to get married. But what would it feel like, he asked himself with a tinge of melancholy, to really love someone?

He saw a flash of a scarlet dress. Good, he'd found Gina. Sitting on a bench, talking to Fergus, and . . .

Who was that girl?

Zoë turned, laughing, pushing back a strand of her pale blonde hair, silver now in the moonlight. She saw Harry, and looked full at him for a moment.

Harry just stood and stared, rooted to the spot. Zoë threw him another look.

What amazing eyes.

'Gina, who's that?' said Zoë, breaking across the conversation while Fergus was still speaking.

'Who?' said Gina, surprised; Zoë was rarely rude.

'That one. There.'

'Harry,' cried Gina. 'Oh, good.' She beckoned to Harry to come over.

He walked towards them, his eyes fixed on Zoë.

Gina put her hand on his arm. 'This is my friend Zoë.'

Harry stretched out his hand to Zoë, who took it at once.

'Dance?' he asked, in a voice which Gina had never heard before.

Zoë gave a tiny shake of her head. 'No, you should dance with Gina.'

'No, go ahead,' said Gina at once. 'Please, I'm quite happy here.'

Harry tucked Zoë's arm into his, and drew her away, looking down at her and saying something which Gina and Fergus couldn't catch.

They vanished into the shadows.

Fergus and Gina looked at each other, Fergus's face giving nothing away, Gina's thoughtful.

'Oh dear,' she said fatuously.

Fergus began to say something and then stopped. 'I think . . .'

Gina shook her head. 'Thinking doesn't come into it.' She smiled, a little sadly. 'That's what Harry always wanted, you know, but had given up hoping for.'

'What, a blonde girl in a long dress giving him the eye?'

Gina protested at that. 'No, you mustn't blame Zoë. It just happened. I wouldn't believe it could, not if I hadn't seen it with my own eyes.'

'What? Tell me exactly what has just happened?'

'Oh, Fergus, you could see. A *coup de foudre*, a lightning bolt.'

'Nonsense,' said Fergus. 'A surge of sudden sexual attraction. Shattering, but it will wear off. Sit tight, Gina, it'll come right in the end.'

'Don't talk rubbish,' said Gina. 'Harry never looked at me like that. Nor did I ever feel one-tenth of that attraction or whatever magnetism it was that passed between them just now.'

'Harry is engaged to you,' said Fergus furiously. 'Now is hardly the time for him to start making sheep's eyes at your best friend; what a bastard he is.'

'It has nothing at all to do with friendship,' said Gina firmly. 'But what am I going to do now?'

Tara was dancing with Don, and talking her usual gobbledygook.

She's attractive, thought Don, feeling her pleasing shape pressed against him, but she is also very, very boring.

He told her so.

Nobody had ever said that to Tara. Many had thought it. Past lovers, when her undoubted charms in bed had lost their novelty; her agent; her publisher; any number of readers who hastily returned her books to the library or wished they hadn't wasted the money on buying her latest sad saga of depressed office workers.

The critics weren't bored by Tara or her books. They gave her books good reviews, and she, in turn, wrote two or three columns of turgid prose praising their books.

And now this man in the country had dared to say that to her. Her eyes flashed as she drew abruptly away from him.

Don laughed. 'It does improve your looks when you let yourself go and show a bit of temper,' he observed. 'The languid pose is desperately dull.'

Bugger, thought Tara. I've thrown Hadrian out of my flat, thrown over all kinds of invitations to come down here to be with this man, and now look what happens. Men! They just can't stand the competition from an intelligent woman.

'You aren't intelligent,' said Don placidly, catching hold of her and running his hand down her backbone in a teasing and aggravating way. 'You are exceptionally foolish, and very tiresome. Do something about yourself quickly, is my suggestion, or you'll find the tide has gone down, and you're up there with the empty shells and the seaweed.'

She broke away from him, and flung herself away from the dance, running angrily and blindly until she tripped over one of the pavilion ropes and ended up sprawled at Alwyn's feet.

He was feeling at a loose end, and rather fed up with the proceedings. Gareth had disappeared, he knew very few people there, and he had decided that this kind of gathering was intolerable for a man like him.

On the other hand, he thought, as he helped Tara up and dusted her down, there could be compensations.

'Gareth's sister?' he said, as he led her towards a drink. 'Of course, the novelist. How very, very interesting. Now, you must tell me all about yourself. I'm Alwyn Aumbry, by the way. I'm an historian, and I'm going to be doing some work with your brother. I expect he's mentioned it to you. You see . . .'

Tara had met her match.

Nicky watched the dust-up between Tara and Don with a strange sense of detachment. She yearned for Don, she always would, probably, but there was no point in it. He would forever be surrounded with women, delighted to have another one join the club; but did he take any of them seriously? He did not. He drove them wild and then abandoned them. Then he shamed them back into harmony with him by little acts of kindness and warmth.

You couldn't hate him, though, thought Nicky, as she watched him suavely greet a delectable girl in a green dress and escort her back into the dance. At least, she couldn't.

'May I join you?' said a very familiar voice.

Roger. Her husband. Standing there, looking down at her slightly doubtfully, two glasses in one hand, and a bottle in the other.

She didn't look at him; instead, she watched the droplets chase each other down the chilled wine.

'I wish you'd come home,' he said, as he poured her a glassful. 'I do miss you so.'

'What about the girl from Corda Episcopi that I hear about?'

Roger gave a shrug. 'I'm glad you heard, you were meant to. I thought it might make you a little jealous.' His eyes wandered to where Don and the girl in green were dancing together, very closely. 'That was a waste of time, I suppose. But if not for me, couldn't you bring yourself to come back for the children?'

Nicky felt tears prickling at the back of her eyes. Tiredness; she was very tired. She wanted to go home, to be done with this masque.

'You can't leave yet,' said Roger gently. 'You've done a wonderful job here.'

Nicky gave a rather weak smile. 'Come on,' she said. 'Let's dance.'

Victor, enraged when his Swiss armful went back to Serge's side, prowled formidably around his lawns and terraces, growling at anyone who spoke to him. Julia, spotting him in the moonshine, sharply told him to pull himself together and behave, but Victor was feeling very hurt, and very frustrated, and didn't in the least want to behave.

Lori was sitting by herself on a bench, wishing she knew more people there, and wondering why Gareth was spending so much time talking to that beautiful young man who seemed to be in charge of the food and drink. Yes, he'd said he wanted him for a television slot, but was that all? Did he need to stand so close to him, appear so extremely interested in everything he said?

'Ah,' said Victor, sitting down beside her. 'My little enemy from Heartwell.'

Lori blinked, felt she ought to move away, he was really sitting much closer to her than politeness would dictate. On the other hand . . .

'I think we ought to discuss these matters, just you and me,' said Victor. He flicked a hand at a waiter. 'Champagne, and two glasses. At once.'

'Yes, sir.'

'Champagne?' said Esme suspiciously as the waiter stammered out his request. 'Who for?'

The boy from the caterers shifted uneasily on to his other foot. 'Big gent. With a beard. Kind of powerful. Got his hand round a woman's waist.'

'Victor,' said Esme. 'Yes, a bottle of the one over there; don't open it, idiot, he'll do that himself.' Blimey, where do they get them from, she added to herself as the boy scuttled away. 'Hey,' she called after him. 'Tell him the fireworks are due to go off in one hour.'

The boy gave the message, thick with sirs, nervously backing away as he did so.

Victor pulled the cork out of the champagne with a vigorous twist. 'An hour,' he said musingly. 'Thank you, that's all.'

His hand slid back round Lori's waist and his fingers slipped down towards the top of her leg.

Lori looked down at the hand on her lamé dress, which shimmered in the moonlight. I'm going to enjoy this, she thought, as Victor fed her a sip of champagne, following it up with a sensual and very stimulating kiss.

'Perhaps out of the moonlight?' murmured Victor. 'Inside, for a moment or two?'

Sybil was sitting at a table with Gina and Fergus and Byron. They were enjoying themselves vastly, and were by now very merry.

'Fireworks soon,' said Sybil.

'I like fireworks,' said Byron.

'You'd have to, being married to Nadia,' said Gina boldly. 'Where is she, by the way?'

'She's about somewhere,' said Sybil. 'Moping. Which is rather sad.' She waved an imperious finger at Byron. 'You need a talking-to.'

Byron liked Sybil, but he didn't in the least want to be given a talking-to by her. Particularly not when she was tipsy.

'I may be tipsy, but not so tipsy that I can't see straighter than you,' said Sybil.

'Yes,' said Gina, firmly. 'Sit right down again and listen. It's time you learned a few truths.'

Byron listened, startled but unconvinced.

'It's all very well you saying this, but it's pure fantasy. How do you know what Nadia feels, for me or anyone else? And what business is it of yours, I'd like to know?' he added, with growing anger.

There was a flare on the wall behind where they were sitting, and it burst into extra life, with flames shooting upwards.

'Gina knows what she's talking about,' said Sybil. 'Nadia talks to her; Gina is half-Russian and they understand each other.'

'Don't be ridiculous,' said Byron. 'Gina is a cousin of the Cordovans and she comes from Scotland.'

'Oh, she does, does she?' said Sybil with a loud whoop of laughter. 'We'll see, we'll see.'

'Don't worry about where I come from,' said Gina, frowning at Sybil. 'Why don't you go and find Nadia, ask her?'

'I will do just that,' said Byron. He had been fairly abstemious for most of the evening, but he now poured himself out a generous measure, downed it in one go, and set off to find his wife.

'Pot valiant,' said Sybil, glad that she was past all that. 'Does Nadia really care for him so much?'

'Yes,' said Gina. 'Very much so.' Her face clouded over. 'Lucky Byron. Lucky Nadia. To be in love like that. I wish I were. Or that someone loved me as much as Byron does Nadia.'

Fergus, who had listened in silence to Byron being sorted out, looked at Gina reflectively.

Sybil looked at Gina.

Gina watched the flares.

CHAPTER 26

The guests were moving up from the dancing in the sunken garden, and pouring out of the pavilion to get a better view of the cake which was being wheeled in by Guy. Maria hadn't made it, knowing her limitations, but she had been very happy to recommend a master baker to Nicky. It was a superb confection; rather like Aimée herself, just this side of being too much.

Aimée, exquisite in sea-green chiffon which fluttered and floated as she walked, was there, laughing and making eyes at her many admirers. Champagne was being served; Victor, looking like a large cat who had lavishly partaken of the cream, was standing by to superintend the cutting and make a speech before giving the signal for the fireworks.

A hushed and expectant silence fell, and then a woman in a short, tight, tarty Versace number and very high heels bounded forward.

'Hi, there, cousin Aimée,' she shouted. 'So glad I got here in time, marvellous, happy birthday!'

She was about to fling her arms around Aimée's neck, but Victor forestalled her. 'Just who are you?' he demanded in a very loud voice, indignant at this unseemly interruption to the proceedings.

'Hi, Victor,' she said. 'Don't you remember me? Georgie. Georgie Hartwell, your little cousin from Uish. Hi, you're cousin Julia, aren't you? And there's Harry, with a delightful blonde, haven't I seen you before, sweetie, in Oxford? And where's my namesake?' she added, looking round. 'Did you rumble her? Aren't you clever! Or did you tell on her, Harry? That wasn't very sporting of you, was it?'

Julia was rigid. 'Who do you say you are?'

'I don't say. I am. I'm Georgie Hartwell. Your cousin.'

'Our cousin Gina is here already. She has been here for some time.'

Georgie gave a peal of laughter. 'Oh, that isn't your cousin. She's an American, a nobody; she thought she could pretend to be me so that she didn't have to go back to the States. She wanted to marry an Englishman, and I gather she thought Harry was very eligible.'

Gina's cheeks were burning. Georgie! She might have known. Fergus took her hand and held it very firmly. 'Chin up,' he said.

Mutters and murmurings were flying round the guests as they explained to each other what was going on.

'Don't tell me she's still here?' said Georgie, with a little frown. 'If she is, she'd best take herself off, you aren't going to be too pleased about this, I don't suppose.'

Victor's eyes had been searching among the faces which showed so visibly in the clear white light of the moon. He saw Gina.

'Gina,' he said, shouldering his way towards her. 'Gina, is this true?'

Fergus stood resolutely beside her, eye to eye with Victor. 'Leave her alone,' he said.

'No, no,' said Victor. 'We've got to get to the bottom of this. Now.'

Serge was there, and Gina was strangely pleased to see him. Then Harry, with Zoë following, swept to Gina's side.

'Let her be, Pa. I knew who she was. I'll explain later. There's no harm done.'

'No harm done? A stranger living in my house, under false pretences? An impostor, pretending to be a member of the family. Who is she, anyway?'

'She is Gina Heartwell, but not your cousin, just the same name. She is also my daughter,' said Serge.

Victor looked nonplussed. 'Your daughter?' he said, astonished. 'What is all this? And why has Georgie arrived now, to make a scene?'

He didn't wait for an answer, which was as well, since nobody was going to try to explain it to him at the moment. He turned on Harry. 'You had an announcement to make,' said Victor. 'You told me you had something you wanted to say when Aimée had cut the cake. Is it anything to do with Gina?'

'No,' said Harry. 'And I'll do it now.' He stepped forward, and lifted a hand to quieten the hubbub.

'Just a word,' he said. 'First, I'd like to propose a toast to Aimée. Happy birthday, to a delightful and beautiful sister!'

There was a tumult of applause and cheers, and Aimée smiled and waved; the smile faded as she watched Harry hold up his hand again.

'This seems an appropriate place for me to make another very happy announcement, when so many of the family and our friends are here. I'd like you all to know that I'm going to be married.'

Shouts of approval and more hums and comments rumbled round the onlookers.

'Who to?' shouted a guest. 'Who's the lucky girl, Harry? She'll have to move fast to keep up with you.'

Friendly laughter; then Harry pulled Zoë, half-protesting and laughing, forward. 'This is Zoë, who has said she will be my wife.'

Fergus looked at Gina, who was standing stock-still, biting her lip. Victor, with a loud and unprintable exclamation, rushed away to clap Harry on the back and give Zoë a more than fatherly embrace.

'Good going,' said Fergus gloomily. 'He met her all of three hours ago.'

'They'll do very well together,' said Gina. 'Fergus, can we just slip away?'

'I don't think so,' said Fergus. He watched Aimée sink a silver knife into her cake, giving a gentle shriek as she did so. Guy took over, cutting and handing out creamy, alcoholic portions at incredible speed with the assistance of two po-faced caterers' people.

'Tell me, Gina,' he said offhandedly, looking up at the monstrous moon. 'If I'd met you three hours ago, would you agree to marry me?'

'No need to rub it in, Fergus,' said Gina crossly. 'It was a silly plan and bound to end in tears.'

'Whose tears? I'm not crying. And why should you cry?'

Gina turned her head to hide the tear which was trickling slowly down her cheek.

'Because I wanted to stay in England so much. And because I've grown to like these people, and now what will they think of me? Of course, I'm glad for Zoë. It wouldn't have worked with Harry, I can see that. It's just a good thing he found out what he was really after today and not on Saturday.'

She sniffed. 'And now I'm in the same old muddle.'

'Georgie's back,' said Fergus. 'Let's go and find her, and we'll hang her upside down and pull all her toenails out until she hands over your passport. And I think a refund for your ticket, too. God knows, she can afford to pay her own air fare to America. She didn't need to steal yours.'

'Verisimilitude,' said Gina.

'You haven't had enough champagne if you can say that,' remarked Fergus. 'She could perfectly well have left you a clutch of loot for the ticket, but she didn't. That's Georgie all over, and I just hope that one day soon, she gets her come-uppance.'

'Not she,' said Gina, cheering up for no particular reason. 'The Georgies of this world never do.'

Georgie was exercising her charm on Julia and Hester. 'Just a practical joke,' she was saying glibly. 'You know what a trickster Harry is. Of course, I never thought she'd take it so seriously. Never mind, now I'm back, I'll stay for a few days and get to know you all properly. Oh, and I'm going to get married, too, how's that for news? To an American. He's gay, which means no trouble, and I get a passport just the same.'

'Then you won't need Gina's any more,' said Fergus. 'Hand it over, Georgie.'

'She gave it to me of her own free will,' said Georgie carelessly. 'In any case, she can have it back when she gives mine back. I'll need that now.'

'You stole hers,' said Fergus. 'When you broke into my house in Oxford. So you'd better find it pretty quick, and also you can pay Gina for the air ticket you removed at the same time.'

Georgie laughed. 'You're Fergus McEttrick, aren't you? God, you're all so bourgeois in your family. I slept with your brother once, hopeless.'

'I hope he wore a condom,' said Fergus.

'Fergus!' said Gina, full of admiration.

Condoms were Julia's field, and she waded in. 'Quite right, Fergus. And no, Georgie, you can't stay here. I don't think you'd be very welcome.'

Hester smiled at Gina. 'We'd very much like it if you'd stay on, though, Gina. We've all grown very fond of you.'

'But I'm not one of the family,' protested Gina. 'I came under false pretences.'

'Never mind,' said Julia with a venomous look at Georgie. 'At least you're not vulgar.'

Harry appeared, bearing a tray with champagne and glasses. 'Someone told me you two hadn't got round to the fizz,' he said to Fergus and Gina. He put the tray down and leant forward to give Gina a kiss on the cheek. 'No hard feelings?'

Gina looked past Harry to Zoë's face, glowing with happiness. 'Of course not. I'm very pleased. Really.'

Fergus put his arm round Gina's waist. 'By the way, Aunt Julia,' he said casually. 'Gina is going to be one of the family after all. She's going to marry me. And I'm not going back to Oxford, and nor is she. We're going on a world tour of vineyards, and then we're going to buy one for ourselves and go in for a spot of viticulture and vinification.'

Gina went scarlet. 'Fergus, don't be ridiculous. You don't have to do this, my father will sort things out for me with the embassy, I'll be okay.'

'Good on yer,' said Esme, who had come into the tail end of the conversation. She gave Fergus a tremendous clap on the back, which nearly sent him flying. 'Do you know anybody in the business in Oz? No? No problem, I'll fax my dad about you. You can stay as long as you like, learn a lot there. Nothing he doesn't know about Australian wines, and it isn't all Chardonnay, either.'

Zoë had taken Gina aside. 'He's not doing it out of kindness,' she was saying urgently. 'Haven't you got eyes? Can't you tell?'

'But Charlotte . . .' said Gina.

'What's Charlotte got to do with it? Except that you kept your hands off Fergus because you thought he Belonged to Another. He didn't, he's been in love with you for ages.'

'I'm not in love with him,' said Gina defiantly.

'Oh no?' said Zoë.

Gina began to laugh. 'And I can't stand bagpipes, and I wanted to marry an Englishman!'

'We Scots are better in every way,' Fergus informed her. 'And no, you can't live in this pretty and out-of-time part of the world, because we're going to be abroad. However, we can come and stay – that is if they'll have us.'

Julia gave him an affectionate kiss. 'Of course, Fergus.'

'I don't suppose you know anyone in America with a vineyard do you, Gina?' asked Fergus.

She nodded. 'It so happens I do. My ex-stepfather. Napa Valley.'

'There you are, you see, I have to marry you. We'll get married at once, and fly straight to America. Then Australia and New Zealand, then back to Europe: France, Spain, Italy. Hey, Serge,' he called, as his future father-in-law approached, deep in conversation with Victor, 'I'm going to marry Gina.'

'I haven't said I will,' Gina pointed out.

'That's because I haven't proposed,' said Fergus at once, going down dramatically on one knee. 'Gina, I love you madly. Will you succumb to midsummer madness and accept my hand, offered by the light of this radiant moon?'

Gina gave a helpless laugh, pulled a merry-eyed Fergus to his feet and fell into his arms to the accompaniment of applause and cheers.

Harry raised his glass in a salute. 'Perfect,' he said. 'Drink up, everyone. Dawn is breaking, and it's Midsummer Day.'

All Orion/Phoenix titles are available at your local bookshop or from the following address:

Littlehampton Book Services
Cash Sales Department L
14 Eldon Way, Lineside Industrial Estate
Littlehampton
West Sussex BN17 7HE

telephone 01903 721596, *facsimile* 01903 730914

Payment can either be made by credit card (Visa and Mastercard accepted) or by sending a cheque or postal order made payable to *Littlehampton Book Services*.

DO NOT SEND CASH OR CURRENCY.

Please add the following to cover postage and packing

UK and BFPO:
£1.50 for the first book, and 50p for each additional book to a maximum of £3.50

Overseas and Eire:
£2.50 for the first book plus £1.00 for the second book and 50p for each additional book ordered

---

BLOCK CAPITALS PLEASE

name of cardholder ....

address of cardholder ....

....

....

....

postcode ....

delivery address
(if different from cardholder)

....

....

....

....

postcode ....

☐ I enclose my remittance for £............................

☐ please debit my Mastercard/Visa (delete as appropriate)

card number ☐☐☐☐☐☐☐☐☐☐☐☐☐☐☐☐☐☐

expiry date ☐☐☐☐

signature ....

prices and availability are subject to change without notice